Also avai
and

Back on Top series

In Tune
In Rhythm

Also available from JN Welsh

Pining Over You
Gigolo All the Way
Before We Say Goodbye

IN HARMONY

—

JN WELSH

carina
press

**carina
press®**

Recycling programs
for this product may
not exist in your area.

ISBN-13: 978-1-335-65293-5

In Harmony

First published in 2021. This edition published in 2024.

Copyright © 2021 by Jennifer N Welsh

For questions and comments about the quality of this book,
please contact us at CustomerService@Harlequin.com.

® is a trademark of Harlequin Enterprises ULC.

Carina Press
22 Adelaide St. West, 41st Floor
Toronto, Ontario M5H 4E3, Canada
www.CarinaPress.com

Printed in U.S.A.

To all the comeback "kids,"
believe in who you are,
don't ever give up,
reinvent yourself,
keep moving forward and
don't ever stop dancing.

Chapter One

Nyah Monroe sank her weight into the horsehair bow, pulling it across the strings, and releasing the natural sound from the belly of her double bass as it poured out rich, quick, deep notes of the fourth movement in Brahms' Symphony no. 1. Brahms wasn't her favorite, but this piece, with all its power and difficulty, had her heart—even if she was more a Samuel Coleridge-Taylor Ballade for orchestra Op. 33 kind of gal. When the notes she poetically strung together collaborated with the rest of the orchestra and spread through the venue, the music made magic. Nyah glanced at her friend Gladys Yeh on timpani, just as Gladys's powerful arms beat the instrument's skin. Her friend was only one of a handful of women principal percussionists in the U.S. Like Nyah, Gladys was a unicorn making space for more brown-skinned girls.

Nyah's gaze returned to their conductor and then down to the sheet music before her. For a moment she visualized twenty-four bars of the dance music song she'd worked on last night. The steady thump of the electro house beat tried to creep its way into the current piece she played with the orchestra. She shut it out. Now wasn't the time for producing dance music. The philharmonic's Friday night performance was days away and she needed to keep her current up and down bowing in sync with her fellow musicians.

Over the past three years, she'd been able to compartmentalize her life. She kept her moonlighting gig a secret, even from Gladys, because she'd had her fair share of judgment. Judgment when she'd finished college and postponed her classical career to deejay. Judgment when she'd left the dance music scene after a disastrous festival run. Yeah, she'd reached her lifetime quota. What she could never shake, however, was her dad's disappointment when she'd shunned his profession and gone back to her classical roots. Tension gripped her shoulder and bowing arm. Her left eye squinted as she tilted her ear toward her fingering on the neck of the instrument. She relaxed her limbs and again sunk into the fast-paced movements.

When she decided to DJ, she'd thought she was ready, but the pressure of living up to the success of her iconic dance music DJ father, Pete Monroe, had been unexpected. Her fall from grace had been public and humiliating, but being forced underground had helped her find and hone her sound. Not only had she performed and grown in popularity with her unique style, but she continued to play the classical music she loved and used it to fuel her growth as a musician in two very different genres. Presently, if she wanted to keep doing the latter, then her bass had better quit squeaking and pick up the pace.

Martin Standish, their conductor, glared her way. "Stop, stop, stop." His British accent cut through the music. Silent groans, especially from her fellow bassists, took the form of a light clattering of bows and instruments resetting as they awaited instruction. All movement ceased. *Here it comes.* "Nyah."

She'd expected to hear her name.

"Your timing is off and hurting my ears. It's too early for fatigue. Fix your form and focus."

"My apologies, it won't happen again."

"I should hope not. From the beginning." Martin lifted his baton, and with flicks and swishes that rivaled any wizard's, he kept time for the orchestra.

Nyah's bow didn't slip the remainder of the practice. At the end of the three-hour rehearsal, she packed up her bass in the case her parents had gifted her for her twenty-fifth birthday when she'd scored third chair with the orchestra. Even now, the vision of the huge pink bow around the charcoal black case tugged a smile, and her parents' cheers echoed in her memory.

Gladys cornered her, and the fragrance of fresh lilacs from her perfume mixed with the woodsy notes of rosin wafting from Nyah's case. "I know you are not going to bail on drinks, again, and leave me with Evan and his date?"

"I have to, sorry. I need to get some things done."

As if on cue, Evan Young, one of the violinists, chimed in. "Maybe drinks will help those bow skills." Evan. He sported the most basic haircut, and despite his untimely chiding, still managed to be attractive in an annoying kind of way.

"Go suck an egg, Evan. Your bowing was—"

"Near perfect, as usual," Evan finished. Never short

on self-compliments. "As we musicians know, there is always room for improvement."

Gladys rolled her eyes and tilted her head. Her auburn hair was smoothed into several flat twists and tucked into a sophisticated bun. "Your self-evaluation is so skewed, I have no words. Shoo, fly." She tapped her timpani mallets together.

"Oh, come on…" he teased Gladys. "We're the best in the orchestra."

Evan's everyday talent for bugging her was not only harmless, but also nothing new. However, Nyah's fatigue had her burning a shorter fuse than usual. "You heard her, Evan."

Evan backed off, grazing Gladys on his way out. Her friend lowered her weapons and put them away.

"He's right. I was sloppy. That one fucking phrase… I can't do that at performance."

"Shh…" Gladys pressed the air down. "Don't tell him that. It'll only inflate his ego and then there won't be room for any of us to even move in here or out there."

Nyah stood, simultaneously lifting her sheathed instrument upright. Martin calling out her imperfect technique had been mortifying at best. She'd have to find time to bump up her at-home practice and improve her concentration. On the DJ stage, her musical imperfections many times led to exceptional moments, but here at the philharmonic she needed to be perfect. She had to do a better job of keeping beat mixing and effect layering out of her head as soon as she walked through the David Geffen Hall doors.

"What is it that you're constantly jetting out of here for? Or should I ask who?"

Nyah scoffed. "I wish. The only thing that's made it past these knees recently is pink, silicone, and vibrates." She delivered the joke in a relatively hushed tone. Sometimes she wished a "who" would materialize into a regular fuck buddy, but her musical lives packed her day-to-day to the point where she barely had time to scratch her own ass, much less invite a "who" into her bedroom. Her bachelorette-hood, and situation of her own making, needed work but her commitment to the new vision for her life only had slots for the occasional dicks for fun. Nyah's current focus? Finish the tracks for her Friday night performance and don't lose her chair in the process.

"My friend's sister does those parties. You know, where you get the latest in—" Gladys looked around "—self-care."

"Sign me up. Actually, let me know when it is and hopefully it works for my schedule." At best, Nyah would request an electronic catalog and pick something from Gladys's friend's sister's lineup of toys.

"You really are busy," Gladys confirmed. "I guess I just miss hanging out with you after practice. Are you sure you won't reconsider coming out with us? First round's on me." Gladys batted her lashes.

Nyah missed hanging out with Gladys too, and felt even worse for never confessing her secret, but she already worked tirelessly to keep her worlds separate, her names straight and her outfits square. She hated giving that ginormous responsibility to another friend. "I can't, G. I promise I'll come out next time."

"You said that last time."

"And I mean it every time." Nyah offered Gladys

a quick hug, grabbed her satchel, and draped it across her body. She tilted the case on its wheels as she rolled. "I gotta go."

"Okay. I'll see you Sunday."

Nyah froze and winced.

Gladys squinted and puffed her freckled cheeks. "You still have time carved out for us to do the application, right?"

Nyah had been looking forward to a full day of rest on Sunday but she'd promised Gladys they would work on their applications for the new London symphony. As a principal, Gladys's application would likely be on fast track. Nyah, though self-proclaimed awesome, would probably need to wait a bit longer for her application to be processed.

"Nyah?" Gladys reprimanded, making Nyah feel all of three years old.

"Yeah, Sunday," Nyah returned with *of course I remember* type confidence.

"You forgot, didn't you?"

"No, I did not. I just had a temporary brain fart."

"Look, if you don't have time to devote to this…"

"No, no… I got you. I'll see you at call time tomorrow." Before Gladys could interrogate her further, Nyah squeezed her in another quick embrace and split. Her other life waited.

Nyah turned the volume up in her headphones. The songs she'd been working on for Artistique were almost done. Now all she needed to do was put a bangin' set together to play over the weekend at Rebel, the underground dance club that housed her bimonthly residency where she DJ'd as Queen Roe.

She only half hung up her classical musician's cap to produce music and wanted to record some more live samples of herself. She moved to the instruments in her apartment. "Who's up for the challenge?" she posed to her keyboard, guitar, violin, and bassoon. Most had made it onto her various tracks in their pure form. This time, her eyes settled on the bassoon. "Okay, BB-Bae. Let's do it."

She'd started messing around with woodwind instruments during her last year of college. When the music department had a sale on beginner instruments, she'd lucked out and got a sweet deal on a still-very-pricey bassoon. She'd tried using only the synthetic sounds she created on her equipment, but she loved the live music feel with all its imperfections. She folded the notes in, used them as interludes to connect tracks, and when she created her songs, she layered each sound on top of the beat and bass until the track was full and vibrant.

She pressed pause on her current track and set up the mic to record the bassoon. She could hear the melding of the sounds together in her head. Sometimes in reality they didn't sound as great but other times they were straight genius and she had to humble herself. She could be confident, but not conceited, and she worked hard to remain that way. Something she'd had to do all her life being the daughter of an icon.

She picked up the rich maple wood body of the C Key bassoon Fagotto and attached the seat strap to the bottom. She laid the strap on her chair, sat on it and scooted into a comfortable posture. With the weight of her instrument supported, she tilted it to rest on her right thigh until the double reed, attached to the long, skinny, pipe-like neck of the crook, met her mouth. She moistened her lips. "M," she said on the bamboo, and she was ready to play.

She practiced tonguing the notes she wanted to play over and over until it was clean enough for her to record. The rich-bodied melodies reminded her why she loved this particular woodwind instrument. The sound oozed like a silky, thick, savory sauce on top of the heavy tone and house-shaking bass of the song. She knew it would be good, even if it took her a few tries to combine the styles. She loved creating music like this.

In the past she'd stress over her sound. Was it too much like her father's? Did it move people beyond the sixteen bars? Was she memorable? The last question still stung. When she'd dropped off the scene, no one wondered about her after the initial media exposés about the fallen daughter of dance music DJ icon Pete Monroe. She hadn't proven herself good enough for the masses to care.

She put a tight lid on the memory and poured the energy she had left into her track. On her computer, she finished her recording and then organized her music for easy accessibility before flipping screens to check her email. Follow-up messages to the snail mail invitation requests that had been sent to her Queen Roe P.O. Box scattered her desk. "What am I going to do with this?" she sighed.

Over the past several months she'd cherrypicked the engagements she said yes to and declined the others, hopeful that that would be enough to slow the demand for her to perform. The tactic had backfired. Now more rumors into why she wouldn't perform, from increased compensation, to her being an elusive rising star, had started to rumble beyond the underground.

"I need to get a hold on this quick." She'd been her own booking agent, promoter, manager, advisor, stylist, and office admin, in addition to performer, and that was only for her DJ life. Being a classical bassist, she managed orchestra practice, performances and special donor events in an unwieldy schedule. She had to keep prying eyes out of her life if she wanted to maintain both careers.

She pounded her keyboard with a few hasty replies, declining a list of invitations but ending with a few hopeful "maybe in the future" and "when the artist's schedule frees up" postscripts. Signed, Nancy Rogers, Manager. However, one unread invitation stood out from the unending inbox. Buzz about the Boiler had floated through her tight DJ circle for months. Her fingers secured her phone by the Baby Yoda PopSocket as she thumbed the club owner's number.

"Hi. I'm trying to reach Mike—"

"Yeah." The clattering of utensils on plates and someone in the background raving on about the tender veal in their osso buco came through with his short greeting.

So very New York. She puffed her chest like the boss pigeons of the city. "This is Nancy Rogers on behalf of Queen Roe."

"Great to hear from you, Nance. This girl is tough to get a hold of."

Nyah swallowed and caged the various corrections she wanted to make behind her teeth. "She's quite busy."

"Look, I want to get her on the lineup for next weekend. That gonna be possible?" he asked.

"She's actually booked next weekend but has an opening the following Friday." Nyah tapped her pen on the desk as she waited for his reply.

"I'll take it. I've been tryin' to get her to the club for a while. I give the kids what they want, you know?"

"Yes. I'll email you her rider but can you give me a few logistics of the club?" Nyah had had her share of surprises when showing up to an unfamiliar venue. One time she'd had to wait on line to get into the spot because there wasn't a private entrance for the talent. Another time a fight broke out after some drunk dude tried to jump on her stage, slobbering "I love you" over and over to her with no security for the club, just a promotions greeter. Let her not forget nearly tripping over her bag onstage because there were no lockers for her shit and the stage was so small, she'd nearly fallen off. Twice. If she had a sense of what she got herself into, then maybe she'd avoid a possible shit show.

"Sure. It's center stage so the crowd is all around her. The place gets packed. I mention this so she don't get claustrophobic. It's happened before. *Un'altra bottiglia di Barolo, per favore.*" Mike continued, "The performances are filmed and sent to our YouTube page. It's great exposure to our subscribers."

First osso buco, now a bottle of Barolo wine? She half wanted to ask him where he dined so she could check it out. "Great." Nyah did her best not to worry about being filmed, because she liked that 360-degree layout of the club.

Without prompting, Mike offered her double what she'd been prepared to demand. "Gotta tell ya. I'm curious to see what all the hype is about."

Nyah owned her Nancy persona and endorsed her artist. "She won't disappoint."

"I'll put her on the bill. Pleasure doing business with you, Nance."

"Grazie mille."

"Prego." Mike chortled in her ear. She tapped the circular red and white telephone icon to hang up. In a few weeks she'd find out if the venue would be worth sacrificing her rare Friday nights off.

Chapter Two

Tommy Mills fidgeted in his desk chair, moments from plucking one strand at a time out of his styled-to-perfection, full head of dark brown hair. Though the California sun poured into his LA office, it failed to brighten the gloomy outcome of his call. He'd scheduled this meeting with Herman Elliot and had been sure that third time would be the charm when it came to getting one of his clients booked for the Sunburst Festival.

"How long have we known each other, Herman?"

"Since before we both started making a name for ourselves in the industry." While Tommy had started to gain traction as a young and still somewhat green twenty-year-old talent agent, Herman had organized secret raves in vacant lots and in the woods in his early twenties. When the authorities shut Herman down, he'd reinvented himself. In a saturated music market, Herman had taken the less-is-more approach and downsized from the ever-growing EDM events to create the now-popular and eclectic Sunburst festival.

"So you're telling me that Clyde's got an artist at Sunburst and I don't? What the fuck?" Tommy raked his hand through his hair. Clyde Warren was Tommy's healthy, yet sometimes contentious, competition but no way did Clyde come close to being a more established agent than him. "Am I missing something here? I know you want to present new talent with innovative sounds but you're telling me that even with the fans' endorsement, none of my clients fit your criteria? That's bullshit."

Herman sighed in his ear. "Clyde and some other reps have the kind of talent the new investors want. Your artists are already way too popular, they have deals with one of the largest Entertainment firms. They don't need a leg up. I know the exposure is great but they're already too big, man."

"Even Bedazzled Beats?" Tommy offered up his DJ duo, but already knew the answer.

Herman chuckled. "Are you fucking kidding me? Dude, they played Temptation's main stage with the likes of Tres Armadas, Tekko and Troy G. Not to mention their net worth tripled in a single year. I know because I was one of the first people to congratulate you."

"You were," Tommy agreed. Herman had his back as a friend, but with Herman, business was business.

"What I need is piping hot underground artists from all genres. Remember when Chance was coming up. His fame rippled hard under the hip-hop surface and then exploded that year. Those are the artists Sunburst wants to showcase," Herman said. "I know the dance music scene is paying the bills nice for you, man, but if you're going to come to me with that kind of talent I need the underground-type acts."

None of which Tommy had or courted at present. The choices he'd made over the years had been good ones, lucrative ones. Tommy's clients were his friends, talented and driven, and together they'd built not only riches, but wealth. His artists had a presence at every major festival and club worldwide, including monthly performance residencies in Vegas, New York and Ibiza. All major festivals, that is, except Sunburst, and it had become the bane of his existence. The rejection from Sunburst left a gaping hole in his resume. He'd somehow have to find a new artist he wanted to work with and get them on the Sunburst lineup.

"Okay, man. Thanks for the time."

"Drinks on me when you're back from New York."

"Damn right they are." Tommy wrapped up the call with a few additional closing remarks before hanging up.

He cleaned his glasses and then sent a text to Abraham Wallace, CEO of Wallace Entertainment, with the news.

Three…two…one…

His office phone rang and Tommy tapped the speaker button. "I know. I thought we had what Herman and the team wanted for Sunburst, but not quite. We'll have to go back to the drawing board, Abe."

"Hi, Tommy." A familiar female voice emitted from the speaker.

"Leona?" Leona Sable had responded instead of Abe. It wasn't a surprise she was in the office, since Luke was scheduled to play in New York that weekend. As Luke's manager, Leona would no doubt work out of her office at Wallace Entertainment. However, she'd called Tommy on Abe's line. "I didn't expect to hear you."

"I called you, Tommy." Abe's voice followed. "Leona

just happened to stop by my office and I relayed the news about Sunburst. She couldn't help but insert herself."

"I have information to add about the festival," Leona sang.

"Which is?" Tommy sighed but his ears sharpened. Leona's expertise rivaled his own.

"Forget about your current clients or the type of artist you'd normally show interest in. You want an artist for Sunburst? Then look for an artist for Sunburst."

"Tell me something I don't know." Tommy's disappointment at her suggestion increased. "I'm just pissed not one of my clients fits the bill. I mean, not even one?"

"I know you've busted your ass. Organizers should be opening the door for you and rolling out the red carpet as they hand you a glass of champagne and they beg you for one of your artists." Leona's jest exposed the ego he'd already tried to check after his call with Herman.

"Hell yeah." He didn't only expect favoritism because his clients were current and popular, but he expected his reputation to offer him well-deserved professional preference because he was Tommy "Boombox" and if he knew anything, he knew music.

"But…" Leona continued, "if you want this one, you're going to have to bust it a little more."

"It would have been great to have had one of Wallace Entertainment's current clients perform but there are other festivals and milestones for our clients. I know this one is close to you, though, Tommy. So whatever we can do to help, we will," Abe said.

Tommy didn't work for Abe or Wallace Entertainment, but rather as an independent agent to his clients. His partnership with Wallace Entertainment helped manage their careers.

"Appreciate it, Abe."

"It is a bitter pill to swallow," Abe added.

"Glad we agree." Tommy choked down the rejection creeping up like acid reflex in his throat.

"You're not a cub. You're Boombox. Lick your wounds and get your ass in gear. You'll be in New York tomorrow for the week. Seems like the perfect opportunity to head to the clubs."

"Stop reading my mind, Leona, please. It's getting annoying." Tommy sighed.

"I'm just sayin'." Leona's grin transcended phone lines.

Tommy had intended to take some meetings at Wallace Entertainment, have dinner with his client, and spend a little overdue time with his family when he got to New York this time around. Those plans quickly changed the moment Herman told him that none of his artists fit the mold for Sunburst. Now, club hopping topped his agenda. He'd definitely planned on hitting up his cousin Oscar, who owned Rebel nightclub in Alphabet City. Tommy hadn't stopped by the club in a minute but on occasion, some amazing talent passed through on the weekends.

"Thanks again, guys, for the chat. I gotta get going but I'll see you tomorrow." Tommy ended the call. He massaged the tension out of the taut muscles at the base of his neck all the way up to his ears. With his mission clear, he reviewed his itinerary. "Yaz," he called for his office manager slash agent slash apprentice, Yasmin Rosa. The woman popped her head in, her dark curls hanging at her collarbone.

"Got all that?" Tommy asked.

"Some. I was in the middle of sending contracts to Patrick, but I got the gist. I'm sorry about Sunburst." She offered him a mournful smile.

"We're not giving up." He pushed his chair back, rounded the desk and leaned against the front of it.

"No, of course not." She brightened.

"I might be spending more time away and will need your help in holding things down here at the office. How do you feel about that? You ready to take on more client responsibility?"

Yasmin's eyes danced and he thought she might, too. "Absolutely."

"I'll define for you what I'll need, but I'd also like you to think about the kind of career you want to have. We'll firm things up when I come back from New York."

"Great, Tommy. I really appreciate it."

"I have all the faith in you, Yaz." He stood up and tossed his phone into the side pocket of his distressed brown leather satchel. "I'll confirm with Remi to make sure all the checks and statements went out."

"I already confirmed with accounting. We're all set. All the bank transactions and confirmation statements are on the account."

"You're brilliant. I'll take a look on the plane." He carried the satchel cross body, with the bulk resting behind him. He felt better, as he often did after doing business with his team.

"Have a good trip, Tommy."

"Here's hoping." He'd find the right person even if he had to hit every nightclub.

Tommy's car rolled up to the house in Yonkers, NY. The familiar curves of the Saw Mill Parkway and stores lining the streets led to his parents' house. Though he'd been born and raised in East Harlem, he'd spent his high school years in Yonkers when his folks finally bought a home. One spring break to LA changed his life when he'd met Herman and a couple other wannabe ballers working toward their dreams. From then on out, his trajectory had changed.

Tommy rang the bell on the front door of his childhood home. Some kids whizzed by on their bikes, bringing back memories of him and his cousins tearing up the front yard with their own two-wheelers before they rode off to the park. His mother's geraniums and gladiolas, lining the colonial-style home, had just started to bloom and he recalled crashing into them one night he and Oscar snuck out to meet some girls at a house party in the Bronx. His mother still brought that story up at every family get-together. The humble beginnings of his youth here were in contrast to the modern sophistication of his loft apartment and first-class life he lived in downtown LA.

His cousin swung the door open. Oscar stretched his arms to the ceiling, the energetic welcome pulling up his black shirt. "Eh! Why the fuck are you ringing the bell, man? This is your home." Oscar drew him into a hug. Tommy bent slightly and embraced him.

High school hadn't only been a time of awakening for

Tommy creatively, but a coming of age in the worst way when his favorite aunt, Carmen, had passed away. A single mom, she'd left behind her son Oscar, whom Tommy and his other cousins always played with at every single birthday and holiday gathering. When Tommy's parents took Oscar in, they became more than cousins.

"Hermano." Tommy embraced him.

"I'm happy you're here, but you normally stay in the city. What made you come out?"

"It's been a while. I can hear Mom cursing my name."

By the aroma of fresh cilantro, green peppers, and citrus undertones in the air, Tommy knew his mother had been blending her homemade sofrito.

"Your ears must have been ringing. She blames me when you don't show up. *Call him on your phone. Get him through the computer,*" Oscar mimicked. "Tia Judy doesn't quit!"

"Is that my long-lost son? It's about time you made it home." Yudelkis Mills rushed toward him with open arms.

"In the flesh, Mami." Tommy bowed to his mom's height and pecked her check before drawing her small figure into a hug. He and his mom chatted on the phone a few times a week, but he actually saw his family much less. He came to New York City regularly, but he didn't have time to make it up to Westchester each visit. To his calculation, he hadn't seen her since Christmas three months ago. Much too long for her.

"Look at you, so handsome." She ran her hand through the chunk of hair at the front of his head, ruining his hairstyle. She looked at him with love in her eyes and Tommy realized just how much he missed her.

"It's the style, Mami," Tommy said.

"It's a little Brendon Urie-ish." Oscar flipped imaginary hair on his buzz cut.

"From Panic at the Disco?" Tommy scoffed. "It's not that bad." He checked himself out in the hallway mirror and smoothed the hair at his temples.

"Who's that?" his mother asked.

"A singer, Mom."

Oscar laughed at him.

"You kids and your trends. How was your flight?"

"Felt longer than usual, but I got some work done." Tommy commuted from LA to New York so often that the trip barely had an effect on him anymore. This time around he'd been agitated to get to the city and initiate his artist search.

"Are you hungry? I have a nice dinner planned for you. We're just waiting for your father to come upstairs. He's fixing something or other. You know…"

His father specialized in carpentry by trade. Now retired, Gregory Mills always seemed to find something in the house to fix, even if it wasn't broken.

"Some things never change." Tommy used to help his father when he took on a project. He appreciated the lessons because he could assemble and fix most things himself.

"Greg," his Mom called. "Your son is home."

Oscar stood by him. "Not much has changed, huh?"

"Nope. They're still the same." Tommy smiled. "By the way, I'm scouting some new talent. Anyone of interest coming through Rebel tonight?" He'd sent Oscar a quick text before he left LA that he wanted to stop by the club that night.

"Hold up. The genius agent is asking *me* for help? You didn't explain all that in your text. Wait—" Oscar took out his phone and thumbed through. "Let me document this on my calendar."

"Shut up, man. I'm serious."

"I know. That's what makes this even better. Remember when you pleaded with me to quit referring people to you because you had an exclusive list? What happened to all that celebrity swag, bro?"

Tommy sighed and let Oscar get in his kid brother digs. "Don't worry about my swag. My list remains exclusive. I'm just looking for someone new."

Oscar eyed him. "Something up?"

"Nah," he lied. His problems were minuscule to Oscar, who tried to run a club in New York City.

Oscar crossed muscled arms over an even more muscled chest. "How bad is it?"

Tommy didn't get a chance to say more when his father's big energy lifted the living space. "Boombox."

"Hey, Dad." Tommy shook his hand before embracing his father.

His father had given him the name when Tommy, a youngster in East Harlem, had been obsessed with old skool hip-hop and carried a tiny boom box around like he was a '70s kid. As Tommy got older, the name stuck. When he became an agent in the music industry, he slapped that name on a business card and it became the unique introduction he needed to be memorable.

"How's my big-shot son?" Greg Mills was a minority in a house of brown people. Even Tommy had more color, and most people assumed he was white.

"Things are good." Tommy kept his responses upbeat

and uncomplicated. No need to bring his added stress to his childhood home. "Still fixing up the house, I see."

His father grabbed his hand and yanked him into a hug, slapping his back. "Someone's gotta keep this place up to date and you know I'm not paying anyone when I can—"

"Do it myself," Tommy, Oscar, and his mother mumbled in unison.

"We know, Uncle Greg," Oscar said.

Despite his father's DIY philosophy, Tommy was glad to see his father up and about after a small injury he got on the job.

"It's about time you come and stay home for a change. I know you're busy and all but your mother wants to see you." Though his father didn't say it outright, Tommy knew his dad wanted to see him, too.

"I know, I know," Tommy said.

Like socket and plug his parents fit into each other, one at the waist, and the other at the shoulder.

"Well, get cleaned up so we can eat. Oscar tells me you two are going out later. Just like old times, huh?" His mother loved to reminisce and the older Tommy got the more he appreciated her memory.

"It's business, Tia Judy," Oscar said as he ran to beat Tommy to the bathroom.

Tommy bit back the curse word on the tip of his tongue and gave Oscar the finger out of sight of his parents.

"Then I'm happy you're working together." She beamed at them both.

Tommy was breaking bread with his family for the

first time in a long time but tonight he had to get out there and get started.

"I'm going to make a few stops at some of the clubs uptown and meet you at Rebel sometime after one or so."

"I'll make sure you get the VIP treatment," Oscar teased.

The three thousand square foot club had a great vibe, but it normalized the attendees with general admission. Everyone could buy bottles, seating was complimentary, and no reservations were taken.

"You boys need to have fun tonight," his mother said.

"Thanks, Mami." *Time to go to work.*

Chapter Three

Nyah bowed with the rest of the musicians onstage under the concert hall lights overhead. Her fingers had long since built up durability from being callused many times over since the double bass chose her. Yet after a show the muscles in her shoulder, elbow, and hands still ached and the skin on her fingertips puffed and hardened. Sweat dampened the underarms of her white blouse and dripped down to pool at the small of her back, hidden by the high waist on her black trousers. The side slits on her bottoms and the strappy black sandals she wore did little to cool her. However, like a dancer leaping effortlessly across the stage, she and the rest of the orchestra presented a flawless picture for the applauding audience, at least from afar. Their conductor's wet hair and face, on the other hand, showed the effort he'd exerted to lead them through a perfect Friday night performance.

She collected her bass and stowed it away as she congratulated her fellow musicians. A formality she did every performance, including last night before she had to flee to work on her set list for Rebel.

Backstage, Nyah glanced at the clock to calculate

how much longer she'd need to stay and decided on an hour, tops. The post-performance meet and greet with their donors required her attendance. Influence and affluence swirled around her like visual aromas off cartoon pot roasts, as well as random comments and inflated, though genuine, praise for the collective of musicians who'd played exhaustively for hours. There wasn't a requirement on how long she stayed, just that she show up, interact, and be gracious to the people that helped keep the theater alive.

Gladys, who had already made her way to the celebrations with a few other musicians, locked arms with her and dragged her to the bar. "It's about time you got here," Gladys said and then addressed the handsome bartender in tuxedo. "The Veuve Clicquot Rose and a Hennessy neat, please." Gladys ordered Nyah's post-performance drink as easily as she'd ordered her own.

When the bartender laid their drinks before them Nyah picked up the cognac. "Okay, give me the low-down."

"So you know the Los Angeles Philharmonic will be playing here soon. Well, Cecelia N'backu is here."

Nyah gasped. "But she's supposed to be in London interviewing candidates for the symphony. Did you know she was going to be here?"

Gladys cocked her head. "Girl, no. That would definitely be something I couldn't keep to myself. You know I have no lock on these lips."

The exact reason why Nyah kept her moonlighting under wraps. "What's she doing here?"

"I don't know, but you and I have a date to become two large red blips on her freakin' radar." Gladys pushed more than dragged Nyah to the crowd hovering before CeCe.

She and Gladys kindly waited their turn when Ce-Ce's eyes landed on Gladys. The woman gave Gladys an arms-length embrace. "Gladys. Good to see you again. It's been a long time since Prague. I was just telling Martin how the orchestra delighted this evening."

"Yes," Martin confirmed. "She compliments me as she tries to steal my principals for her symphony." Martin teased but the truth threaded through his words.

"Oh, Martin. It's only for the summer season. At least to start," CeCe noted. Then she glanced over at Nyah, who had been taking in the conversation like inventory for sale later. "You were gorgeous tonight as well, Nyah."

"Nyah has principal potential, once she applies herself."

She almost choked on the small sip of cognac and burned up her nostrils. Martin's statement was news to her.

"I quite agree with Martin." CeCe's narrowed eyes peered into Nyah's soul, reading it like sheet music. "What are your aspirations, Nyah?"

To play Artistique and bang out boss tracks. Nyah had to admit that her current goals related to her classical career were muddled, but honesty revealed that deejaying had begun to demand a bigger portion of her career. She'd gotten to this point maintaining as best she could because she had passion for both genres. She didn't foresee herself moving both careers forward at the same pace, but rather one at a time at her will. Now

CeCe asked her, off the cuff, about where Nyah thought she was headed.

"Well, currently, I love my work with the philharmonic but planned to apply for the London Symphony's summer season." All that was true, ergo her and Gladys's Sunday session to do their applications, but Nyah couldn't deny the fact that she'd kill to also get a chance to dive into the UK dance music scene.

"I'd like to hear a solo piece while I'm visiting. How about Tuesday?"

Nyah swallowed. "Sure. We have practice in the morning but I can do a piece for you right after." Nyah sought confirmation from Martin. His orchestra meant his orchestra's time.

"I'll be there at the tail end of rehearsals. We'll continue from there. That should be fine, shouldn't it, Martin?" CeCe asked.

"Yes, of course."

"I look forward to hearing your selection." CeCe nodded and both she and Martin walked toward some of the other donors.

Gladys clapped her hands in tiny almost invisible movements. "Mission accomplished. We have to finish our applications tomorrow."

"Do you think we can use the same performance piece for the application as the one she wants to see on Tuesday? I mean, no sense doing it twice if we'll be doing it for her anyway. If we record it, we can send it as a reminder."

"Well, if she likes the piece, yes. Percussion is a little more challenging because I don't need an accompaniment."

"Excuse me, still challenging for double bass. I need to find someone and rehearse with them before Tuesday," Nyah reminded her.

"Truth…apologies. Do you have any ideas about what you're going to do?" Gladys asked.

"Vanhal or Bottesini might be safer options."

"Get Sacchi to accompany on piano."

Nyah drummed her fingers on her chin. "That's possible." She had a performance in a few quick passing hours downtown at Rebel. How had her priorities suddenly changed so drastically?

"Yup. We can ask him once he has another Old Fashioned." Gladys pointed to Sacchi who rocked a full tail tuxedo.

"I like the way you scheme." Nyah eyed her friend. "I know you don't need an accompaniment but you could have one if you wanted. If you do, I think you should get Evan to play with you."

"Fuck, no." Had the chatter in the room not ramped up with the second and third round of drinks for the attendees, everyone would have heard Gladys's violent rejection.

"He's really good and violin would sound really nice with timpani." Nyah dared to add, "Plus he likes you."

"Smother your mouth with bacitracin ointment and don't ever spew such vileness again."

Nyah laughed at her friend's emotional response, which meant that even with Evan giving himself ego boosts, Gladys already knew and perhaps even reciprocated Evan's super low-key affection. Nyah's fake yawn felt real and she needed to get some caffeine in her soon if she was going to get to the club and play for three or four hours. "Hey, I'm dragging, so I think I'm going to head out. Cover for me?"

"You got it," Gladys said. "See you tomorrow."

Nyah slipped out unnoticed.

Nyah pulled on multicolored short-shorts and a matching crop top that formed to her body like a second skin. She angled her body to double check her butt cleavage. *Just enough.* She took a bite of her thrown-together breadless turkey, tomato, and lettuce sandwich, and put *go shopping* on her list of things to do. She wiped mustard from the corners of her mouth. Her hips swiveled and she pumped her arms as she danced to test the comfortability and constraints of her outfit. She jumped high and hard, keeping her eye on her C-cups. *Not too much underboob.* "This'll do."

The wardrobe checks were something relatively new. When she'd first launched her DJ career, she'd barely bob her head to keep time to the music while she surveyed the crowd like analytics. She had mixed music to take the crowd higher, waiting for them to indicate to her, by the speed and intensity of their movements, that her sound had penetrated their humdrum two-step. She'd needed them to show her that her music had dug its way into their soul. She had wanted her audience to dance with abandon, but all they'd done was watch her handle the equipment. Nyah had been, in a word, boring onstage. Her downfall. The connection never happened and the failure was only compounded by the fact that she was Pete Monroe's daughter. She'd been foolish to think she could fill his shoes. That's when she jumped ship and found safe passage playing her bass in the philharmonic. With classical, she wasn't the only one being watched, that is, if the audience watched her at all. David Geffen Hall at Lincoln Center became a haven for her to lick her dance music wounds before she regrouped and took another chance. A different chance.

Now as she wrestled her huge fro into two Afro puffs, she commanded forth her persona like Beyoncé did Sasha Fierce. The elaborate eye makeup covered a third of her face, adding to her disguise. She glossed her lips pale pink and felt in awe at what a difference a few years had made since she'd taken control of, well, everything and stopped letting people make decisions for her. She pumped her favorite perfume into the air, twirling and dancing through the mist. Completing the transformation from double bassist Nyah Monroe to DJ Queen Roe, the fiercest underground DJ in New York City, she donned her rose-tinted, heart-shaped glasses. She posed, checking her angles for the selfies, stories, and snapshots that'd be shared of her later. After she stuffed the last of her gear into her multicolored backpack, she hauled it onto her back and grabbed the subway to Rebel.

"I think I'm ready." Trinket stopped Nyah before she even got to the back of the club to lock her shit away. "The house party went great, right?"

"You killed it, like I knew you would," Nyah encouraged her fellow DJ and friend Layla "Trinket" Jones. "Do you think you want to do more house parties before doing something a little more public?"

"Like what?" Trinket asked. She'd recently hosted and finally played her first house party after the third attempt. Trinket's spirited line of questions showed her excitement to level up.

"Maybe a spot at a less dense part of Central Park or maybe you can do something low-key, with a family vibe, like Sundae Sermon?" Nyah suggested to her.

Trinket clutched her chest and Nyah could see the fear in Trinket's features.

"Too much?" Nyah questioned. If this was her reaction to a relaxed event outdoors, then the Rebel stage might be an overshot.

Trinket's shoulder slumped. "People have been asking me where I'm playing next and I want to give them a date but…maybe I'm not ready. You and Oscar being there helps. Once I get past the first ten minutes and start really mixing and getting creative, I'm great."

"We're happy to be your training wheels, but you've got to get to the point where you can do it with or without us." Nyah had met Trinket three years ago when Nyah started frequenting clubs to reconcile the DJ life she wanted and the one she'd lost.

Trinket's cool neo soul meets grunge appeal had caught Nyah's eye when an MC announced Trinket. Trinket's approach to the stage started with the shakes, wobbly legs, and visible sheen of sweat on her forehead. Her first mistake in getting the music started had been greeted with cheers, but by her third faux pas, the groans started and Trinket ditched the stage. Watching her reminded Nyah of her own problems performing and she empathized with how Trinket must feel up there all alone.

"Crash and burn. Maybe next time, Trinket," a girl standing next to Nyah had called.

"Is this a thing?" Nyah had asked.

The girl nodded. "She tries on the regular but never manages to perform."

Trinket's stage fright had won the day and also every attempt afterward, to the point where her struggle became expected as part of Rebel's lore. Great for the club, with people attending to hedge their bets on whether or not she'd play, but horrible for Trinket. The last time that happened, Nyah had helped Trinket recover with a bottle of Jaeger.

By the time the bottle neared the bottom, the patronless club housed few bodies, and those who remained were shutting down the venue for the night. Nyah had asked Trinket to get on the dials. "Just play to me," Nyah had said. After a lot of tipsy begging on Nyah's part, Trinket agreed and her music had filled the club. Nyah couldn't believe what she was witnessing. Not only was Trinket good, she was better than Nyah or any of the DJs playing at Rebel. From that moment on, Nyah made it her mission to help Trinket get to the stage as soon as possible.

"Your skills *are* ready, Trinket. Your head got some catching up to do. That's why I think something in the park could be a natural next step. Your progress might be slow going right now but it's going to gain crazy momentum. I promise. I can't wait for everyone to hear you play. This year I want to see you right up there on that stage. Your stage fright has gotten so much better already. Play a couple more parties and do something low-key public and then maybe you graduate to the Rebel stage." Nyah locked her valuables in her locker. "How does that sound?"

"Fine, I guess." Trinket dragged it out in a "yeah mom" kind of way.

"I just don't want you to backslide. I mean, you might, but we want just a tiny step back if it happens. Plus, you can make a killing charging for your next house party."

"You really think so?"

"Yes, ma'am," Nyah said.

Trinket leaned against the row of sticker and graffiti decorated lockers. "I don't know how you do it, Queen. I mean, you play that classical shit and then you come here. Doesn't it freak you out to be onstage?"

Trinket must have asked her that a thousand times already and each time Nyah's answer was the same. "I just focus on the music and enjoy what I'm playing."

"I'm thinking of maybe going to talk to someone," Trinket blurted out.

Nyah muscles tensed as she tried to keep her elation in check.

"I said *thinking*," Trinket clarified.

Nyah managed her expectations. "It might help and that's all I'll say, because I know this is your decision."

"Cool."

Nyah didn't say much more, so as not to sway Trinket one way or the other. "So, when's the next party? I want to put it on the calendar so I can make it." Which for Nyah meant lots of caffeine, no sleep and bouncing to several places including her apartment, Rebel and the philharmonic, several times.

"I'm going to do them every week this month."

"Wait. When did you decide that?"

"Just now."

"All right. I like the dedication." Nyah beamed. "I

won't be able to come until the end of the month because I'll be playing at the concert hall and here for the next few weeks, but I'll definitely be at that one."

"Sweet." Trinket played with a bead on one of her black, auburn-dusted locks. "Hey, did you hear from Artistique?"

The question poked at a sore spot. "Not yet. I should have heard from them by now, right? Still nothing."

Trinket cheesed with her thumbs up. "I'm sure you'll hear from them soon. Don't stress."

Nyah needed Trinket's positivity, otherwise she'd be in her head, psyching herself out. "I'm trying not to, but real talk, it's like auditioning. No matter how well I think I did or what a great application I sent, I still get the nervies waiting."

"The nervies? You're a trip." Trinket giggled.

"Have I never said that to you before?"

Trinket shook her head. "We must not be real friends."

"Stop." She bumped Trinket with her hip.

"Don't let the nervies stop you from being great, baby girl," Nyah's father would say to her before her auditions. As a young musical prodigy wannabe, she'd needed his words back then. Today, they continued to provide her comfort but she'd developed a level of toughness only earned from the bitterness of failure.

"Okay, I have to get ready to go on."

"Good thing you came through the back. The papz have been prowling the club asking about you, wanting photos and interviews."

Queen Roe's popularity had grown where DJ Nyah Monroe's failed five years ago. Though this was a good problem to have, she worked even harder to keep her names straight and outfits square. Trinket and Oscar were the only ones who knew about her classical life and about who she was underneath the makeup and without the Afro puffs. "Like real paparazzi or just influencers, contributors, and tastemakers?"

Trinket twisted her mouth to one side and squinted an almond-shaped eye. "I think all of the above. I recognize some from 'the gram.'"

"Any from the big magazines, because you know that would really be catastrophic." Nyah's curiosity mounted.

"Girl, how the fuck should I know? They're not looking for me."

Nyah laughed at Trinket's animation. "Well, when you finally play, trust me, they will."

"I wish they would. I think I could handle the media, it's just the stage."

"Can you find out for me? I'll buy you a drink later."

Trinket scoffed. "Our drinks are on the house."

Nyah offered Trinket prayer hands. "Please."

"Okay. Let me find out. You'll probably be onstage by the time I get any info, but I'll give you the download later."

"Thank you." Nyah hugged her friend. "You're the best."

Nyah rested her black headphones around her neck and grabbed her computer and glow in the dark Serato vinyl. Her muscles stored explosive energy, which she couldn't wait to release onstage. She heard the mic tap and the MC give her and the crowd a five-minute warning.

"Coming to the stage, the phenomenal, the fierce... Her Majesty, Queen Roe."

Chapter Four

Tommy swirled tawny-colored liquor in his glass and felt the rattling ice cubes, even as the heavy bass vibrated the club. He wasn't a big drinker but whatever he wanted was on the house, courtesy of Oscar. Tommy always made up for it in tips.

The DJs Tommy had seen at the clubs he attended earlier had been mediocre at best. Now, as he hitched on a barstool, he committed to staying at Rebel for the remainder or the night's acts, even if this might also be a waste of his time. He considered leaving before he noticed the fairly crowded club swell with an influx of patrons. A woman with dreadlocks running down her back squeezed her way through a gang of people and leaned her stomach against the bar in front of him.

"Seltzer and lemon, Nick. I'm going to need all the hydration for when Queen Roe comes on." She ordered and adjusted her colorful Kente cloth print head wrap. She eyed him, then, as if really seeing him, did a double take. "Hey, you're that big agent. Oscar's cousin?"

"Tommy Boombox." He held out his hand. "And you are?"

"Trinket. I'm a DJ and work here as a guest attendant. Basically I go where I'm needed." She took his hand and gave him a firm shake.

"Nice to meet you, Trinket."

"Oscar speaks about you all the time. *Boombox this and Boombox that*. He must be thrilled that you're here."

"He's a supportive guy," Tommy said. "Are you playing tonight?"

The woman's face twisted. "Not tonight but hopefully soon." He didn't get a chance to decipher if her last statement was happy about that or not before she continued. "You here to see Queen Roe?"

Tommy shrugged, his curiosity kindled. "I'm here to check out the lineup for tonight. Why?"

"Because everyone is here to see her."

"Yeah? She any good?"

Trinket looked almost offended by his question. "If you're hanging out in the clubs, then you know Queen Roe."

Tommy prided himself on having his finger on the pulse. Had he lost touch with what was popping on the scene? "Then I guess I came on a good night."

"The best night," Trinket said. "I'm trying to get a read on who's here for her, because she's getting too popular."

Was there such a thing as too popular? "That's a thing?" Tommy asked.

"For Ny—the Queen, it is."

The MC announced Queen Roe and the first thing Tommy saw were two large puffs of hair. The shimmer of the club lights reflected off her glasses and traces of gold glittered on her light brown skin. The rumbling of her first song grew in volume and intensity, and the club goers cheered as they aimed their phones at the stage. The fairly dark club made it hard to make out her figure, but Tommy could tell by the ratio of her exposed torso to the top of the DJ table that she had height. She clapped her hands above her head and pointed out to the audience, her body swaying to the music. He could feel the energy building and his skin prickled.

Queen Roe picked up the mic. "How's the kingdom tonight?"

The people roared in response as the music continued to build. Her small side-to-side bounces to the beat grew wider and higher as she tapped the knobs on the dials as if her fingers touched hot iron. Tommy sat up straighter on his stool. The music rumbled and an explosion of sound came through the speakers. The beat dropped and the fans busted loose, dancing and jumping as if freed from the excruciating buildup. The already thudding venue shook from the impact of agitated bodies heating up fast and feet rattling the foundation.

The rhythms swirling through the heated air were unexpected and the sounds were unique. Were those string instruments he heard enveloped in harmony with a Tribe Called Quest sample? The sound reminded him of dubstep but had a more epic feel to it. But those instruments... They came through so clear, as if they were played live onstage with her. Tommy's mind worked to make the connections and as his head bobbed, he wanted to hear more. All the while his gaze transfixed on the colorful figure expending max energy. The light shined on her now, and the air she caught vaulting upward showed she enjoyed her own music. Each time she jumped, it provided him a full view of the sequined orange and purple pum pum shorts that matched her bra top.

No way can she keep that energy up for an entire set.

Wrong. By the last song, this woman continued giving everything she had to the audience and they were wild with fever. Through the sporadic LED lights and the flashes from professional cameras and smartphones, she continued her focus on the dials. He thought the festivals deafened, but in the enclosed space of Rebel, bass pierced his eardrum and the vibrations of the melody fluttered over the hair on his arm. He wondered if he'd ever get 100 percent of his hearing back.

Nonetheless a smile crept on his face. He saw this woman in the open field of the Sunburst Festival with her beats and unique sound rippling over the crowd. He couldn't believe the type of performer she was and wondered why she was still locked up in Rebel. Could he really be this lucky? To go to his cousin's club and end up with an artist that would help him gain access to Sunburst?

Queen Roe tried to get off the stage, but the fans hollered her back on for two additional songs, one of which had the fans crawling the walls, which Tommy assumed had to be an old favorite. She finally closed out her set and descended from the throne where her kingdom had crowned her queen, and her followers gathered to greet her. She posed for some pictures and signed whatever they wanted. Club security did their best to manage the mayhem but the normal handlers were nowhere in sight. She was as exposed as an artist could be. He watched her pull out her phone and take selfies with her fans like they were the ones who'd been up onstage. She hugged them and complimented their style while handing out small postcards and told them to DM her so they could exchange makeup tips and music tastes. After listening and normalizing herself with her fans, she maneuvered her way to the bar through a sea of people, chatting and high-fiving anyone who engaged with her. He had to meet her.

She shrugged into a snug black hoodie, draped the hood just behind her Afro puffs, and moseyed over to the bar where the bartender had two highballs ready for her, one filled with lightly iced water and the other the color of blood oranges. He placed a clear shot glass before her and filled it to the brim with vodka.

"Thanks, Nicky." The hoarse melody of her voice made him want to hear more. Devices and electronics of all kinds continued to snap photos. With no VIP area to escape to, she kept her back to the crowd as she downed the shot and then focused on her cold beverages. Her fans hovered but left her alone. Tommy had never seen anything like it. Either she had some magical superpower or she'd trained her fans to leave her be once she'd given them every ounce of her energy.

Unfortunately, Tommy had no time to lose, so he scooted his stool closer to her, penetrating her Zen bubble. The perfume and sweat coming off her intensified the closer he got, and he had to drag his eyes away from the spread of her ass against the hard wood of her seat.

She offered him a huge helping of side eye in response to his presence as she sucked on a white straw, draining her water glass.

"What're you drinking?" He could have slapped himself for that question.

"Uh, water?" She turned her head fully to him.

He cleared his throat. "You were great up there."

"Thanks."

"You really had the crowd eating out of your hands tonight."

"It's mutual." She stirred her red drink.

"Paloma?" he asked, pointing to her glass.

She followed his point of reference. "Blood orange mojito."

They were at a stalemate. He'd run out of aimless questions and she wasn't offering much by way of conversation.

"Allow me to introduce myself. I'm—"

"I know who you are, Tommy Boombox. You're Oscar's cousin. I also know that the only reason you're probably here, since you don't come through often, is that you're looking for new talent. Tell me which part is incorrect."

He choked on what to say next for several reasons. One, she was right. He'd always been proud of his cousin and his club but he'd come into New York often and had only been to the club maybe once in two years. Two, yes, he was searching for new talent. However, what surprised him most was that her voice rang familiar and the visceral reaction of his body made him certain. He knew this girl.

"All true, but it's not the only reason. I wanted to see the improvements Oscar made to the club." Before shit blew up with Herman, Tommy had been determined to share a little family time with his parents and cousin. Oscar had carved out a little piece of downtown Manhattan for himself and kept Rebel open and profitable for the past six years. Not bad for Tommy's investment.

"Rebel is one of the best underground clubs in the metro area," she responded, her tongue finding the short brown stirrer and sucking. She placed the glass on the bar and mixed her drink with the same plastic stick.

"No doubt because you're here. Your performance should be on main stages worldwide."

She bristled, faced him fully, and when her full lips smirked at him, he wanted to know all the thoughts that went through her head. Sweat dripped down her neck and the already curly hair at her temples coiled further. Despite the business he conducted, he wanted to know what the skin there felt like.

"The main stage? You mean the likes of Bon Bon, Immortal, and Temptation?" she asked.

"Exactly."

"Not interested." She hadn't yet removed her heart-shaped sunglasses and he wished she'd take them off so he could see the confidence in her eyes when she rebuffed him.

"Not interested?" That was bullshit if he ever heard it. What popular artist playing the clubs didn't want a bigger career?

Her glasses were now well fogged over from her body heat and she slid them off her face. That's when he saw the resemblance. Her narrow, upturned eyes, the continuation of her strong nose up to the bridge, and subtly dimpled cheeks was a combination that he'd only seen on one other face. Pete Monroe.

The last time he'd seen her, she'd jutted a prideful chin out like she had something to prove and snubbed him when her father had suggested he agent her, as two young people starting out. Nyah, on the other hand, had wanted to go with her dad's agent/manager and Tommy hadn't wanted a spoiled brat who thought she was owed something because of her famous father. Now that chin seemed softer, humbled, and he wondered what had happened.

Music flooded their surroundings and though no one would have heard him even if he yelled, he adjusted his tone to her ears alone. "You're Pete's daughter?"

She gave him one of those nods that didn't quite say yes but, rather, acknowledged his sleuth skills. "It took you long enough."

He eased back on his seat before settling upright again. "I haven't seen you since Pete's birthday party years ago. Do people know who you are?"

She rested an elbow on the edge of the bar, her shoulders moving with her breath. "A trusted few but mostly, no. I'd like to keep it that way."

"So you're incognito?" He may not have meant it but he delivered his question more like a know-it-all statement.

"Yes."

"Why? Your father is a DJ icon. Surely, it would make all this, I don't know, easier? Better? More?" She obviously wanted something from playing music. If not fame and money, then what?

"That's exactly why no one needs to know." She patted the sweat on her neck. "That fact didn't get me very far the last time."

He'd heard some rumblings about her leaving the scene after a couple of bad performances, but it was obvious from the brilliance she'd just delivered on the stage that she'd reinvented herself. Yet he tasted the unmistakable bitterness in her words.

Photographers and guests of the club had snapped photos of her as she performed and smothered her when she descended the stage. He would bet money that if he searched her name on the internet that her celebrity would rival the likes of those already headlining global stages. "How long do you think you'll be able to keep your identity unknown?"

"Why is that your concern?"

"Because I think this club is too small for you. I think you can reach more people with your music."

"Land your plane, Tommy." Her tone was exasperated and abrupt.

"Come again?" he asked.

"What do you want?" She twisted her elegant and slim upper body toward him. "Spit it out already?"

He thought about laying on more compliments but he saw her future—their future—clearly. He'd deliver her as an artist with a new and fresh sound to Sunburst and the media frenzy would erupt when he eventually revealed her as a descendant of Monroe, clawing her way the top on her own. "I want you as my client. We can do great things together and—"

"No." She played with the straw on her drink.

"You didn't even hear the rest of my pitch."

"We don't want the same things." Nyah shook her head. "You want an artist you can build and I want to stay in this—what was it you called it?—a fishbowl?"

"Touché."

"You want something bigger." Even after hours of performing, she still commanded his full attention.

"And what do you want?" He wanted an answer to what felt like the million-dollar question.

"To manage the expectation, stay underground, and not be on the cover of every magazine or on every stage, nationally or worldwide," she answered without hesitation. "So how much?"

"How much?" He frowned. Their conversation had taken a dark turn.

"Yeah. How much to buy your silence and act like you never saw me?" She sipped her mojito like she'd asked him to pass her a napkin.

He reset before responding. "Is that what you think I want?"

"Well, you won't take no for an answer, so…" As if her insult wasn't enough, she spooned on a healthy dose of sarcasm.

"I don't want money. I have plenty. I don't want anything other than to work with you."

"Then we're done, right?" She turned back to fully face the bar.

"You're kidding. You really don't want to take your career to the next level?"

"No, but…"

"But?" He tamped down the hope in his voice. No need for her to sense his desperation.

"If you are looking for an artist then you should take Trinket on as a client."

Tommy raised a brow. "The girl with the dreads?"

She nodded. "Not only is she cool as shit, but she's probably…no…she *is* the best DJ in this place."

"Really?" Tommy had met Trinket earlier and though the woman chatted with him she didn't come across as interested in having an agent when she acknowledged who he was. He still had his target set on signing Queen Roe but he'd entertain her suggestion. Maybe he'd missed something when he'd met Trinket. "I'll take a listen. When does she come on?"

"Oh, Trinket doesn't play in public, but take my word for it."

His jaw didn't quite drop but his tongue cooled from his mouth resting slightly ajar. "You're fucking with me."

"No, really. She's great. She…um…has a bit of stage fright, but she really has the talent to be a star. We're working on it."

He waited for the punch line to her joke but it never came. Instead she stood up and prepared to leave.

"Okay, I see where this is going. Look." He pulled out his wallet. "Here's my card." He handed it to her.

She stared long and hard at the card before taking it and tucking it into her bag. She swirled the liquid left in her glass.

"Call me when you want to talk seriously or when you grow up, whichever comes first."

Her mouth hovered over the straw. "Grow up?"

"Not a lot, just a little." Had she tossed the rest of her cocktail in his face he would have deserved it.

She drained the rest of her drink and gave him a mock salute. "It's been real."

And with that, she was gone.

Chapter Five

Zombified and trashed from her night at the club, Nyah dragged herself out of bed. The brewing aroma of Jamaican Blue Mountain Peaberry roast, from the coffee machine she'd timed the night before, filled her apartment. She'd probably need to follow it up with a 5-hour Energy drink and a power nap in between the hours of practice she'd do in her apartment. For her performance tonight, she had to be present, alert, and perfect for the stage. Fucking up in rehearsal under Martin's watchful eye earlier that week had been one thing. Fucking up during her performance was just completely unacceptable.

Just one more performance.

She prepared her instrument and organized her sheet music. After she'd showered and put on her robe, she prepared a cup of coffee with a splash of coconut caramel creamer, the scented steam as welcoming as a warm tropical breeze. She peeled open a Korean sheet face mask to refresh her skin and prepare it for the full face of makeup she'd plaster on later, so as not to look like she'd had a wild night.

A wild night indeed. Tommy and his offer trundled

through her head like a vehicle in need of an alternator. The part where she told him to stuff that offer stuck on replay. He hadn't been the first agent or manger coming through, painting a picture of stardom for her to revel in. He did, however, know her from before she'd finished college, and also knew her father. *Talk to me when you grow up.* "Pshh…grow up yourself." If his big dick energy hadn't disarmed her, she wouldn't have given him the time of day.

She checked the mail on her way out, bypassing the bills that generally came around this time of the month, and found a letter from the organizers at Artistique. She wished they'd just emailed her the information but they still did official business via the snail mail route. Nyah offered a silent prayer and then tore open the envelope. She scanned the letter from the creative director.

> *Our office really liked your package. However, as our guidelines stated, we are currently seeking only agented talent at this time. If you would like to resubmit before the deadline through a reputable agent or agency we'd be happy to add you to our lineup of featured talent at Artistique.*

The letter topped with the Artistique logo crinkled as she fisted the stationery. She resisted the urge to throw the letter into the nearby garbage receptacle because she hadn't yet tortured herself by rereading the rejection multiple times. Instead, she stuffed it inside one of the compartments on her bass's jacket.

"This is bulls," she mumbled. With all that she had done for both her careers, *she* was a reputable agent and manager. She had no official evidence to support her claim, though, and that would never fly with Artistique. The event, with its lineup from artists in both art and music of all genres, had been on the top of her list to attend this year. This new glitch in her application infuriated her to her core. She didn't want to need anyone, least of all an agent. Her bad experiences when she first started out in music had taught her that just because she had an agent didn't mean that person had her best interest in mind. Even if the scoundrel in question was Carlo Hutton, her famous father's right-hand man for over two decades, and Nyah's first and only agent. When she failed, Carlo wasn't there with tried-and-true advice about changing direction, much less around to help her pick up the pieces.

She wanted this. Artistique got her out of the club and showcased her among what she believed were her ideal fans. Most of all, it kept her low-key famous, a position she'd do whatever possible to protect. The agents who came sniffing around only wanted her to do more so that they could get more. Like Tommy. She shuddered.

"What am I going to do?" She sighed and checked the time. She'd cut her period of moping short because she needed to get to the concert hall, which irritated her just as much as the offer Tommy had made to her last night. "Fuck!" She hauled her shit and headed for the subway.

Backstage, it had taken her an hour to calm her mind from problem-solving her Artistique dilemma. As she played in unison with the other strings, she lost herself in the pieces and her bow didn't fail her. The orchestra created magic for the attendees, and for that slice of time the music soothed her.

After the Saturday performance, Nyah had gone out for one drink with her fellow musicians but when she didn't stay out late, Gladys didn't give her shit about it. "I have to get some sleep to be ready to do the application with you," Nyah said, and Gladys was all business.

"I should get going soon, too. We have a lot to prepare for."

Back at home, Nyah showered her achy limbs and slipped into her pajamas. She plopped in a rolling desk chair, clicked on her computer and the track she'd been working on displayed on the screen. The hour crept to midnight so she eased the black, cushioned headphones over her ears. She pressed play, and the bassoon and bass, a steady stream under the track, sounded in her ears. She was known for the way her tracks built and then exploded. This one was no different. The music burst in her ears like a warm grape exploding in her mouth, delicious, sweet and tart. She bobbed her head and could almost see the crowd at Artistique living in her song.

She shoved the headphones off her head, the screechy frequencies haunting her quiet apartment. Frustration about the current situation didn't lessen with her creativity this time around like it had in the past. The problem wasn't that she couldn't locate an agent. She knew plenty. Her particular conundrum required finesse and she didn't know what it would cost her to say yes to being their client. One agent's head, in particular, popped up like the Whac-A-Mole carnival game, and she needed a cushioned bat to smash it down. Her shoulders hardened like knots with the impending decision she had to make.

Later that night, when she dug into her jacket pocket to retrieve Tommy's card, she calculated just how much humble pie she'd have to choke down before he agreed to help her.

Nyah's phone rang like clockwork on Sunday morning. She untangled her limbs from the soft warm cotton haven and silky smooth eight hundred thread count sheets.

"Good morning, baby girl." Pete Monroe's soft bass-filled voice made her sink her head back onto the fluffy pillows. In the background she heard the Miami waves that no doubt floated in from the patio doors of her parents' Florida estate.

"Hey, Dad," she croaked, her dry, scratchy throat a direct result from screaming at Rebel the other night. Fatigue, caffeine, and way too many drinks had dehydrated her. Even her eyeballs were dry.

"You must have had a night. Did you just wake up?"

She sat up and cleared her throat. "You know how tired I get after performances."

"Right, right. So how was your week? Tell me what you can before your mom grabs the phone from me like she always does."

"Things are good. CeCe from the London Symphony is in town and wants me to do a solo for her during practice on Tuesday."

"What's that, an audition?" he asked.

"Kind of but not really. I think since she's here it's probably a good idea for us to get on her radar." Nyah quoted Gladys, though right now the thought and added pressure of performing for CeCe elevated her stress levels.

"Have you submitted your application, yet?" Her father gulped, and from living with him most of her life, she knew he sipped his morning tea.

"Gladys and I will be working on it today. Anyway, enough about me. How are things with you guys?"

"Well, it looks like some people want to honor me as one of dance music's icons. I don't know about that title, but I guess since I'm an old man now that makes me one." Her father had had her late in life but he'd been no less active with her. Her parents made sure to put her in activities that helped their only child learn that the world didn't revolve around her.

"That's great, Dad. Who's honoring you?"

"Apparently the new organizers for the Sunburst Festival. They support the up-and-coming artists. I like being a part of that." He hummed into the phone.

"Wow, Dad. Look at you influencing the youngins," she teased.

He hemmed and hawed like he sometimes did before bringing up a touchy subject. "It would be nice if you dusted off your DJ equipment and we did a spot together. What do you think?"

The pulse in her neck pounded all the way up to her eardrum. "I don't think so, Dad. All people will do is compare us again." Guilt strained the muscles in her throat. She'd kept her DJ life a secret to get out of her father's shadow, because when she'd bombed those years back, the criticism and insults had attacked her like a nest of agitated hornets. She thought she had tougher skin until the media had portrayed her as an entitled celebrity's kid who thought she could get by without talent. Carlo had made the whole thing worse when he refused to speak to the media on her behalf. In his words, she wasn't big enough, and wasting time on fighting with the media was pointless. She did what she could on social media but her bland performances had only fueled the fire. No one knew her and what kind of artist she wanted to be—including her.

Undercover, she'd found her sound, built her brand, and when it came to music, she took risks with extreme confidence she hadn't even known she had. Getting onstage with her father would undo everything she'd worked for.

"I know you had a bad run of it those years back. I'm as proud of you then as I am now. Your feet are firmly rooted in the classical scene, but, well, think about it. I'd love to have you up there with me, Nyah. It's a few months away. You can always change your mind."

Nyah gave a complimentary "yeah," but she heard the disappointment in her father's voice. Knowing that she played clubs and had a following as DJ Queen Roe made her feel like the worst kid ever pushed out of the womb. Her only saving grace? Saying no to her father meant saying yes to life as a dynamic artist, doing things her way. That small acknowledgment would have to help her sleep at night.

"Everything else good?" Nyah asked.

"Yeah. You know, the normal aches and pains but I'm still groovin'," he said.

"Is that Nyah?" She heard her mother in the background.

"That's more time than she gave me the last time,"

her father mumbled. "Let me pass you to your mom. Love you."

Nyah was in the middle of reciprocating her father's love when Eva Monroe's voice boomed in her ear. "Hi, baby, how are you?"

"I'm good, Mom. I was just telling Papa Monroe about the London Symphony." Nyah repeated most of the same information that she had just relayed to her father.

"You all recovered from that really bad cold you had a few weeks ago? That awful cough sounds like it's all gone."

"It was a bee-otch to get rid of. The ginger, garlic and turmeric home remedy you gave me worked wonders."

"Remember, if you feel like you're coming down with something, a little oil of oregano in some water or juice will knock that baby right out. And don't forget to take your elderberry every day."

"I am, Mom." Nyah had been running around for months playing the orchestra and deejaying. Sure, she'd survived on tons of caffeine, but her nutrition and sleep suffered. Eventually her body had taken her out like a light and she had a severe cold for over a week. She'd medicated enough to do one performance but then she had to be replaced for the next day's performance and miss two rehearsals. Enter Mrs. Eva, the reigning queen of home remedies, to the rescue. Her mother wasn't averse to medical science but spending her summers with family in Jamaica and Ghana, she always used homeopathic first and traditional medicine second.

"Are you excited about Dad's news? It really is a great honor for him," Nyah said.

"Of course." Her mother all but squealed it. "He's done so much in the community and he's the first person people mention when they talk about their influencers. I'm thrilled for him."

"Me too."

"He wants me to perform with him, but… I can't, Mom," she blurted.

"Hmm. I know you still have some feelings about what happened a few years back, Nyah, but you are the daughter of a DJ, you have professional skills and you've been on various stages. It would be a nice moment for you to share with your dad."

"No need to ply on more guilt. I already feel it, having said no."

"Well, then maybe you need to say yes," she suggested.

"Mom?"

"You're going to have to put all that behind you for good one day, baby. The sooner you do, the better decisions you'll make."

Her mother's words put another layer of salve on old wounds, yet still the injury ached. Nyah didn't know what it would take to heal the deeper damage. "I hear you."

"Regardless, this is an honor for your father and he really wants you to be there. Please make every effort to attend."

"I will, Mom. No matter what, I'll be there." Nyah not only made the promise to her mother but to herself.

"That's my girl."

"Well, I have to get ready. Gladys will be here soon."

"It would be wonderful if you got that assignment. It

will give your father and me a reason to spend a month in London."

"A month? Oh, that's right. I forgot you two are ballers."

"Retired ballers," her mother reminded her. Nyah could see her mother going to her charity calling people *retired ballers* just to make them laugh. A true comedian and lover of people, her mother never missed an opportunity to make people feel good.

"Even worse." The thought of her parents staying in London for a month should make her cringe but she'd likely invite them to stay with her even if they'd probably decline.

"We claim our blessings." Her mother's laughter spread mirth through Nyah. "Enjoy the rest of your Sunday, honey."

"You too. Hugs to both you and Dad." Her mother returned the sentiment before hanging up.

Nyah's father's invitation lodged itself in the back of her head. She knew it would keep popping up, but she was determined to keep the promise she made to herself. No one would connect Queen Roe and Peter Monroe if she could help it.

A few hours later Gladys marched into her apartment with her bag and a bundle of energy. Nyah followed Gladys's perky movements with lethargic steps. "Hey, girl."

"Did you just get up?" Gladys asked with the speed of someone who'd ingested way too many double espressos.

"No. I've been up for a bit. I had a rough couple of

days, so I slept in some." It had at least been an hour since she got up.

"Well, let's put on a pot of coffee and get going." Gladys clapped her hands together, a *chop-chop* the only thing missing from her statement.

"Uh…you need more coffee?" Nyah asked.

"Yes!" Gladys exploded.

"This is my off-coffee day. I have way too much caffeine during our performance days so I try to catch myself."

"Tea, then. Or a cold shower. I just need you to meet some of my energy, boo."

As someone who was about to apply to the Black and Minority Ethnicity classical symphony, Nyah should be busting out of her skin and simultaneously dancing on every surface in her apartment, including the ceiling. In addition to her BME application, she'd been granted a special audition with the maestro, the creator herself, CeCe Hines. The stars had aligned to give her a great opportunity to excel as a musician, yet Artistique had drained the problem-solving part of her brain.

Nyah summoned vitality and vigor, then grabbed some cold seltzer and various cheeses from her fridge. "We need some snacks for this," she said, swinging the cabinets open and pulling out a box of rosemary and garlic herbed crackers as well as some wasabi chips. "I'm here. Get set up and help yourself to anything else you want in the kitchen. I'm just going to grab my laptop."

Nyah unplugged her silver laptop from a host of other wires she used to transfer the music she created to the set list she performed. She always covered her DJ equip-

ment whenever Gladys or anyone came by. Having a
controller and scratch pad wouldn't be completely out of
the ordinary. After all, Gladys had met her father when
her parents attended performances. However, Gladys's
simple questions might have Nyah fumbling with ex-
planations and she hated lying. So she avoided any in-
quiries with a quilted black nylon cover.

"Did you decide on what you're going to play for
CeCe on Tuesday?" Gladys asked when she returned.

"I think I'll do a Taylor-Coleridge for the application but Bottesini for her on Tuesday. But if she really
likes the piece I do on Tuesday, I think I'll just use that
for the application with whatever notes she may have
for me. How about you?"

Gladys flattened her palm on the countertop. "Well,
I was thinking of doing the four mallet Bach *Air* for
marimba solo with my own arrangement, and then the
Emmanuel Séjourné *Concerto for Marimba and String
Orchestra* for my application, as planned, with you on
double bass, of course."

"Of course."

"Both are lively enough, uplifting and dynamic. I
thought about doing a timpani solo etude but I think
marimba is better. I mean, who doesn't love marimba?
Since she'll be sitting in on rehearsal, she'll see me with
various instruments, but I can really shine on marimba,
especially during the latter phrases."

"Just rock out on the drums."

"Nyah…"

"Kidding. Your choices are perfect." Nyah thought
about it for a minute. "So…no Evan accompaniment,
huh?"

The glare of death said it all.

"O—kay." Nyah bravely suggested something else. "This might be unconventional, but what about doing one of your own compositions?"

Nyah had never seen Gladys choke on a frog in real life, but with all the sputtering and rubbernecking her friend did, Nyah would bet money that it looked similar. Trinket and her stage fright popped into her head. "Never mind." She waved her hand frantically as if to erase the thought and cast her eyes down at her computer screen. "The application mentioned that submissions with an original piece were welcomed."

"I guess I can think about it. I'm just not sure it's ready."

Nyah fake-typed. "I've told you how awesome I think your compositions are but if you don't believe me, then why not ask one of your trusted fellow percussionists, or Martin?"

"Maybe."

"Whatever works." Nyah glanced up to find Gladys staring off into the distance. "Let's get back to the application pieces and make sure all our ducks are in a row." Nyah shrugged in an attempt to make it no big deal. Gladys had been composing music since her teens for other people but never once attempted to play one of her own pieces. The only way Nyah had found out about it had been when she stumbled on her sheet music. She'd love to see her play one of her creations one day.

They worked on their application and essays until the late afternoon when Gladys had to head home to get in her mandatory three hours of practice. Nyah also needed to do the same.

"Thanks for today, I think we are in really good shape," Gladys said.

"I should be thanking you, I don't know if I would have gotten all this done without you." Nyah hugged Gladys.

"You still want this, right?"

The question took Nyah by surprise. "Yeah." As soon as the words were out Nyah felt the uncertainty vine its way to her lungs, and she breathed in deep. She blamed it on the organizers of Artistique. She wanted to be a part of history and work with CeCe and BME London Symphony. "I think I'm just a little nervous about the audition slash 'I'd like to hear you play' bit that's happening on Tuesday."

"You're going to do great."

"We're going to do great," Nyah corrected.

"Exactly."

"See you at rehearsal."

After Gladys left, Nyah made a pot of tortellini soup with Italian sausage and kale. When it was ready, she fixed herself a bowl, garnishing with a little Parmigiano-Reggiano. The weather offered a few glimpses of spring, but the temperature remained on the colder side. Regardless of the temperature, a chill ran through her. She curled up on her couch and drank a spoonful of the hearty soup to warm her up. What if she did all this for London and her desire for it waned? If she didn't really want London, then what did she want? She wasn't sure anymore and that did not sit well with her at all.

Chapter Six

Tommy's fork paused mid-air when an unknown number illuminated on his cell phone. The aroma of spices from his mother's roast pork, stewed vegetables, and rice and beans flaunted its flavors from the utensil, resting only inches from his mouth. He gobbled the bite before picking up the phone. His cell phone number was unlisted, so if someone called him, he'd likely given the person his number, and it was certainly about business.

"Boombox," he stated.

"Hello, Tommy? It's Nyah. Nyah Monroe."

He cleared his throat free of the grain of rice lodged there, because if he thought of the last person on earth he'd expected to hear from, Nyah Monroe would be it. "Well, hello. I didn't expect to hear from you."

"I didn't expect to call you." The distinctive rasp on her melodic voice was less snarky than the night they'd reacquainted at Rebel, but not by much.

Silence.

"Okay." *This is how we're going to play this?* "What can I do for you?" he finally asked.

"There's this thing." Her sigh weighed heavier than his mother's biggest cast-iron pot. "I...need some help."

"Thing?" He set the fork down, surprised that her conversation had become more important than his mom's cooking. Nyah didn't give off the "I need help" kind of vibe. If she asked for it, then he was interested.

"An agent thing," she confessed.

His curiosity bubbled. "I thought you didn't want an agent."

"I don't," she stated. She seemed not to know how asking for help worked.

He leaned on the backrest of his chair. "And you're calling me, why?"

"Because I need an agent. There's a gig I'm trying to get, but they won't let in unagented talent." She sounded in a bind but he'd be a fool not to enjoy this.

"So you need me," he returned.

She gave him that bottom-of-the-pot exasperation again. "I need an agent."

The last time he'd seen her, she rebuffed him so hard the black and blue bruises on his ego remained. What had changed? He half thought to ask her if she'd grown up yet, but no sense in poking the bear. "Well, how about we discuss this over lunch. I'm in the middle of dinner, and I actually have a couple of meetings in the city tomorrow that I need to prepare for."

"Lunch is tough."

"Breakfast?"

She hissed. "I'm working.

"Wanna help me out here?"

"How about coffee tomorrow afternoon?"

"I'm booked."

They went back and forth several more times, consulting calendars to the point where he questioned whether they'd find a time that worked for them both.

"How about Tuesday at two p.m.?" Nyah offered.

He double-and tripled-checked his schedule. "That works. Where do you want to meet?" He waited several seconds too long for her response. "That wasn't supposed to be a trick question."

"David Geffen Hall," she said at last. "There's a cafe. I'll meet you there."

"At Lincoln Center?" *That's an unexpected location.*

"Yeah, well, now that you know you're going to a fancier place, get your etiquette credentials in order."

"You're funny."

"I'll see you on Tuesday." She hung up before he could offer any departing words. Her request for him as an agent had a story attached and his anticipation in getting the details was almost as potent as his desire to see her again.

Tommy passed the iconic Revson Fountain at Lincoln Center. Curiosity as to why Nyah had picked this location piqued. It was sentimental to him, like it was for many New Yorkers, as a cultural hub for the arts. Ballet, opera, and orchestra could all be found here. The location housed various events, including Midsummer Night's Swing and Jazz at Lincoln Center. He'd taken a date here once to show her his dance moves but the woman had been versed in all the Latin dances and spun circles around him, putting his roots to shame.

He showed up, with almost an hour to spare, in an attempt to beat the school bus traffic. With ample time on his hands, he decided to entertain himself in the hall before heading to the cafe to perhaps check his emails, make a call or two, and close a few deals. He heard music coming from the concert hall and the tune of instruments merging together into a piece drew him. An usher dressed in black stood just outside.

"Is there a performance?" Tommy asked as he approached.

"Practice for the philharmonic performance tonight," the usher explained.

"Mind if I go in? I'm waiting for someone and it would be a nice way to pass the time."

"You need a ticket. You might be able to get one at the box office if you like. It would still be valid until practice is over."

"Can I do it online? Here?" Tommy pulled out his phone, fingers at the ready.

"'Fraid not. This session is no longer available on the website, but the box office is just outside to left."

Tommy thought it over.

"It's worth it," the usher said. "Someone from the London Symphony is visiting and there are a few solo performances being done at the end. It's a real treat."

"Yeah? Do you know who?" Not that Tommy would know anyone, but he might.

"Principal percussionist Gladys Yeh and double bassist Nyah Monroe."

She still performed as a classical musician? And deejayed? *The plot fucking thickens.*

"I'll be right back." He'd seen Queen Roe in action at Rebel. To get the full picture of who he wanted to represent, he wanted to see her on this stage, too.

He trotted to the box office to get a ticket, which

was no small feat since the attendant expressed major qualms about selling him a ticket for a practice that had less than an hour left. With some convincing and his sales pitch about how the arts deserved every dollar, along with prayer hands and a plea, she sold him the ticket.

He hurried back to the concert hall and the usher let him in when the music paused. An almost full house greeted him. *This is a rehearsal session?* A few people exited, and because it was general admission, he found a middle seat on the right-hand side where he could see the bassists. The performers dressed casually and he half expected to see Nyah in Afro puffs and pum pum shorts. Instead her charcoal dress hit her knee with a bright red shirt layered underneath. The sleeves were rolled up to accent the dress but she pushed them up above her elbows. A black obi belt, wrapped twice around her narrow waist, made her outfit and slim body even more elegant. She wasn't hiding behind heart-shaped sunglasses. The stage lights made her, and all its occupants, visible. If he hadn't admitted it to himself before, there was no denying it now. No matter what arena she played, Nyah's beauty and stage presence couldn't be ignored.

The conductor commanded the musicians' attention and offered suggestions, which they all listened to with reverence, taking notes and repeating phrases. The exquisite pieces soothed him and he hadn't even known he needed to be soothed.

Soon activity broke out on the stage and a pianist sat at her instrument and Nyah came forward with her bass. A videographer stood poised to capture the performance and a photographer snapped photos. Tommy thought it apropos that both Queen Roe and Nyah Monroe attracted celebrity treatment.

The pianist played an introduction before Nyah began. Her bow glided over the stings, producing a key so pleasant it hurt. To watch and hear her awakened all his senses. He inhaled as if he'd stepped out into a fine fresh day. Rosin, maple and steel mixed with the age of seat cushions and carpet in the hall. The people who remained breathed less and slower as if to experience every note and nuance played. *Magnificent.* She was a female version of Orpheus, charming him effortlessly. He wished his aunt could hear this. Tia Carmen hadn't loved classical music specifically but she loved any music that sounded beautiful and Nyah's playing was exactly that. His vision blurred, then a heavy droplet fell to his cheek and he tapped the spot to be sure it was real. He swallowed and blinked his eyes dry. Half of him wanted to leave the concert hall to give his brain a moment to catch up, but the other part was riveted.

When she finished the audience broke into applause. A woman stood up in the front row and spoke.

"A very nice version of the piece, Nyah. I'd like to see you take a bit more risk on the middle phrase—" the woman sang the notes "—and instead of a steady bow, work with varying tension." The woman again sang the demonstration, but lost him when she went on to chat about perfect fifths and diminished notes. This time Nyah's bow stroked softly, and then the sound grew louder, taking the phrase from wow to perfection. Watching this was better than binge watching a series on Netflix.

"Lovely." The woman clapped. Whoever this woman was, she knew her shit, and Nyah, though professional, nodded like a nervous performer wanting to please. "Wonderful. Thank you, Nyah. I look forward to your London symphony application." The woman turned to someone behind the scenes. "I'm ready for Gladys."

Tommy felt like he'd just witnessed a mic drop moment, not for Nyah but for him. Did she plan on trading in her New York citizenship for London? He'd seen what he wanted to see and so he used the pause in performances to head out.

"Did you enjoy the performances?" the usher asked.

"More than you know. Thank you for the recommendation." Tommy headed for the cafe and settled down from the magical moment he'd just witnessed, readying for his lunch date with Nyah. He sat at a table in view of the iconic fountain and waited.

Twenty minutes later, Nyah approached him with confidence that increased with each step, as if she recaptured it on her way from her critique experience in her hall. That she slipped so easily back into the command she showed onstage as Queen Roe roused him at his core. She waved to someone before her eyes found him. "Hello, Tommy."

"Hello." He rose to his feet and shook her hand. "How are you?"

"I'm good." She sat down and crossed her long legs, then wrapped her ankle around her calf and tucked the whole thing to the side. He checked his fantasies from imagining what other ways she could demonstrate such flexibility.

"Can I get you something?" she asked. He might

have taken her formal greeting personally had he not just witnessed her give what appeared to be a high-stress audition.

"Shouldn't I be asking you that?" He sat on the edge of his seat.

"I invited you. It only seems fair." She folded her hands over her lap, her fingers hanging over the hem of her dress.

"How about you let me get you a coffee?"

She shrugged. "I'm capable of ordering."

"I don't doubt that. Would you like anything else?"

She leaned slightly against her backrest. "Chicken salad on a lightly toasted croissant with lettuce and tomato. It's my Tuesday usual. Do you need to write that down?"

He pinched the material of his slacks at the thighs and tugged them down to smooth his look. "I think I can handle it."

"And instead of a regular coffee, I'll take a cappuccino. I'm back on caffeine today."

He adjusted his glasses, which had slid down slightly. "Were you off it before?"

"Only on Sundays, but I extended it to Monday. I'm kind of feenin'."

He arched a brow. "Any other adjustments I need to make?"

She shook her head and grinned. "That will be all."

He placed his orders with the barista and waited for their coffees. In the distance he saw Nyah focused on her hands. She pressed her fingertips together like they were puppets talking to each other. In his opinion, she'd played a masterpiece on that bass. Surely her hands paid the price. He returned with their drink orders, a cappuccino for her and an espresso for him. "Someone will bring over our food."

"Great. Thanks." She brought the cream-colored mug to her lips and blew before taking a quick sip.

He set the demitasse and saucer on the table. "So... classical bassist, huh?"

She gave him a quizzical look.

"I was inside during rehearsals and saw your solo."

"You did what?" Her light skin crimsoned over and she'd leaned so far forward he thought she'd either spill her coffee or fall off the chair.

"Wow. You're all kinds of red." He sunk his teeth into his lower lip to tamp down his amusement.

"How long have you been here? I didn't expect you to come here in time for rehearsals. You had to be really early."

"Forty minutes, to be exact. You were outstanding."

"I did okay."

"I'll make a note that *okay* equals amazing in Nyahnics." That drew a smile, and he monitored the little jump his heart made in his chest.

"Whatever." She waved a hand. "Can we talk business now?"

"Sure."

"Have you ever heard of Artistique?" she asked.

"Yeah, it's an art installation festival and features a few music genres. I've never been but I hear it's pretty cool." His client list played a few other eclectic festivals but Artistique's smaller scale wasn't up their alley. His artists wanted big spots.

"I really want to play there and the creative director

really liked my submission. However, they don't take unagented talent anymore. See where I'm going with this?" Her sleeves had slipped down to three-quarters and she pushed them above her elbows again.

"So you need an agent." He sweetened his espresso with half of a sugar stick and stirred.

"I don't need an agent, per se. I just need someone who is an agent to submit for me."

"So you need an agent. More specifically you need me to be your agent. The only way that can happen is if you're my client. My real client."

"Yeah, but like I said…"

"Let me stop you there." He didn't bother to hold up a hand. She wanted to talk business and that's what he'd give her. "My profession is agenting. I don't take what I do, or my reputation, lightly. So when people hear that Boombox is representing an artist, they expect a level of excellence."

"You've seen me perform. It's not like if you represent me on this that I'm going to be a trash performer. I just want you for this one thing." She tapped the fuller part of her bottom lip. "Like a la carte."

"No. That's not how this works? I have a short list. If you qualify—"

She gasped. "Qualify? At the club you were all like *I want you to be my client* and shit."

He did but he needed to keep the upper hand, because Nyah had no idea how many cards she held. He didn't want to wait until she found out. "That was then. This is now. You need me. So the next thing we need to do is identify our terms."

She scoffed, huffed, and blew air out her nose all at the same time. "This kind of sucks."

"I can bet that coffee and probably something like Red Bull are staples in your diet just so you can get through your gigs."

"How?"

"I know you're tired and I think you might need more than a planner at this point. I didn't realize that you were managing a whole other career in addition to deejaying."

"Well…"

"According to the usher there is a Friday night performance and then you perform at Rebel afterward, only to practice on Saturday for a Saturday night performance?"

She gulped her coffee. "When you put it like that it sounds pretty bad but I love both careers."

"Then get some help managing them, so that you can do them well. I can help and I know an entertainment company that can help you."

"You mean Wallace Entertainment, don't you?" She mentioned the company like a curse word.

"Why not? I've worked with them in the past and—"

"Not interested."

"You haven't even given me a chance to give you any details about working with them." He wanted to huff and puff, too. "Despite what you may have heard, or your preconceived notions about the company, I can assure you that they have some great people who can really help you."

"I don't doubt it, Tommy. I just… I really don't want

a team like that. I want to keep my contacts to a few people who can organize my two worlds."

"So you do need help?" He needed her to admit it in order to be of any use to her.

"I guess," she mumbled.

He squinted through his lenses to try to identify her resistance. "Why don't you want to admit you need help?"

She seemed at a loss and he wasn't about to push now, when she at least seemed pliable to the idea of having him agent her. He didn't get the chance to think more about it when a pretty woman who looked mixed walked by with a very white-looking man trailing her. The woman almost looked like she tried to shoo him away before she spotted Nyah. Her face brightened and her mouth crept into mischief.

"Hey, Nyah," the woman said. Her tone spoke volumes that only a true friend could decipher.

Nyah jumped out of her seat. "Hey." Her breathlessness made his lungs ache. "I stayed for your session with CeCe. You were on it. How'd *you* think you did?"

"It went well, I think, but you? You made me cry," her friend said.

He could relate.

"Well, she had critiques so…" Nyah's humility was admirable but quite unnecessary.

"That's why she had corrections. She can make you greater than you thought you could ever be. I really want to work with her." The woman's wide-set eyes gave away her Japanese descent, but her skin was closer to Nyah's.

Tommy cleared his throat.

"Oh, sorry. Tommy, this is my friend Gladys, principal percussionist." Nyah frowned over Gladys's shoulder. "And this is Evan, a violinist."

Tommy stood and shook Gladys's hand. "Nice to meet you." He turned to Evan and did the same.

Gladys's eyes rinsed him like an overhead rain shower. "Is this the guy you've been jetting out after practice for?"

Nyah's cheeks flared and she scrolled through the number of choice reasons to offer her friend that would explain Tommy's presence. When Nyah chuckled he assumed that she was either hiding something or needed to allow her friends to think they were dating. No matter the cause, he was up for the game and rolled with it.

"I keep her busy." Tommy thought his answer was ambiguous enough to elicit creativity, yet not give up the jig. He could almost hear Nyah gulp over the innuendo.

"Okay…" Gladys fluttered her brows. Pretty dark freckles speckled along her nose and cheeks. Her tenderness toward Nyah made him pleased that she had a close friend who seemed to be invested in her happiness.

"We thought you were a figment of Nyah's imagination," Evan said. Tommy had almost forgotten about him. Maybe it was a good thing, because Evan's condescending tone toward Nyah made Tommy step closer toward her.

"You can rest assured I'm real," Tommy said. The strength in his delivery had Evan looking down at his shoes.

Tommy hadn't noticed how much Nyah's shoulders had tensed until that moment, but when they sank back down from her ears, he thought that perhaps he'd done a good thing by putting that Evan kid in his place.

"We're just having a coffee before Tommy has to leave."

A server approached them. "Chicken salad on lightly toasted croissant?"

Nyah raised a finger, and redness again splotched her face.

"And chicken, avocado rice bowl?" the server asked Tommy.

"Yes, thank you." He pretended to adjust his glasses in an attempt to stifle the laughter puffing his cheeks.

"Looks like you guys are having lunch or else you could have come with us." Gladys's shoulders sagged.

"You guys… Where are you guys going?" Nyah tilted her head and asked.

"They asked for a few musicians to head over to Alice Tully Hall for a kids' concert happening there. I guess they want some additional musicians onstage to help with instruments, so we offered."

"You volunteered, Evan? That's a first." Nyah seemed to be getting back to normal.

"Well, it's for the kids…" Evan's eyes slid to Gladys.

Gladys shrugged. "We should get going. It was nice to meet you, Tommy. I hope we see a lot more of you." She gave a hard wink at Nyah and he couldn't help but let his humor rip.

"It was a pleasure, Gladys," he said. "Evan?"

"Yeah, you too," the man said.

When the two musicians were out of earshot, he nestled back into his seat. "So…"

Nyah dived into her sandwich and chewed slower

than a panda with a bamboo stick. He didn't repeat himself and ate his warm avocado bowl.

She enjoyed two more bites and wiped her mouth with a napkin before she spoke. "Thanks for not saying anything. No one needs to know what I do at the club. They've been hounding me about bouncing after practice. That's when I produce music for my Rebel set. Gladys is always covering for me after performances when I leave, too, but she thinks it's because I have a…you."

"A me?" he asked, intrigued.

"You know? A sexy dude that I'm running home for."

He fisted a hand over his mouth and spoke between chews. "I wasn't expecting that compliment."

"I didn't mean…" The stain on her cheeks intensified and he languished in her discomfort. "It's just that none of them know that I'm a DJ…like at all."

"It's okay. I followed your lead. Any reason why you don't want them to know?"

"I have my reasons but mainly, I think it would be frowned upon, especially because it will give people like Evan more opportunities to point out that my DJ life is why I fuck up here."

"Is it? I mean, how have you been able to manage all of this so far?"

She scoffed. "I'm organized. Sometimes I'm a little tired, but I try to rest as much as I can or get an energy drink and caffeine when I need it."

"Drugs?" He worried that if she straddled these two words with such intensity that it was only a matter of time before things got out of hand, especially if she was the only one handling the business aspects of her career.

"No. It's not my thing, honestly, but… I can see the pull."

"You're doing a lot to maintain these two worlds, Nyah. Yet you're so adamant about not having an agent or a manager. What do you think will happen after Artistique?"

"I can handle it." Her mouth twisted, wrinkling with doubt.

"Even I know you don't believe that shit."

She sighed.

He offered her an option that might serve them both. "How about this? You become my client. I help you get into Artistique and manage some of your engagements. If you want, I can even introduce you to some new ones and we see how it goes?"

Her doubt wrinkled and pulled her face. "But you're not a manager."

"No, but I can do it for a little while to get a feel for what you actually need. At that time I will suggest you take a meeting with Wallace Entertainment. If not there, then we can try to find a manager elsewhere who will fit your needs, or you can keep managing it yourself."

She studied the ceiling and he hoped she at least evaluated the options he presented. "I don't know."

He knocked the table twice with his knuckles and leaned back. "You need some time to think about it. I don't expect you to take this lightly, but I do suggest you don't wait too long. I'm sure there's a deadline. When is it?"

"Two weeks."

"I'm heading back to LA on Sunday but you have

my card. You can get me anytime. Will that work for you?" he asked.

She swallowed hard. "I guess."

He touched her hand. "Nyah. This is your choice. It's obvious to me that you want to stay in the driver's seat, but a copilot or a backseat driver can come in handy sometimes. Think about it and let me know?"

Her shoulders thawed a bit and he took in her toned arms. He didn't want to take his eyes off her. A dangerous thing, considering he courted her as his client. If she hired him they were already going to be arguing enough over her career choices and work/life balance without adding sex or emotions into the mix.

"You okay?" She waved at him.

"Yeah, why?"

"You're staring at me weird."

It was his turn to blush. "I'm good."

"Well, thanks for meeting me today. I appreciate it."

"My pleasure." He stood up and straightened his clothes. "Take care, Nyah."

He hated leaving her so undecided, because she needed him, but he wanted her as a client. She definitely made things interesting every time they met. Though she hadn't jumped at a chance to sign with him, he had a strong feeling he'd hear from her very soon.

Chapter Seven

Nyah downed the last bits of her energy drink as she prepared to blow Rebel's Saturday night crowd away. She jammed her belongings in her locker and slammed the door.

"Whoa! What did that locker ever do to you to treat it so very badly?" Trinket emerged from the bathroom.

A chill ran up Nyah's spine and her muscles seized when Trinket materialized out of thin air. "Were you hiding in there?"

"Girl, no. I had to do my lady business. Though I must admit we have to stop meeting this way." Bangles jingled and beads clinked with Trinket's every move and the scent of woodsy patchouli and jasmine mixed with white musk grew stronger as she neared. The heavy fragrance should have brought Nyah down to a cushion for relaxation, but her stress level was beyond its pull. "What's got your Afro puffs all tangled?" Trinket asked.

"I'm just having a day." Nyah didn't know what irritated her more. The fact that she needed Tommy or that images of his warm brown eyes smiling at her made her feel more trust than she'd ever had in Carlo.

"Obviously."

Nyah had submitted her application for the London Symphony and celebrated with Gladys. After their Tuesday session with CeCe, even Martin had raved about the integrity of his musicians and their ability to rise to the opportunities. Her problem wasn't with her day job. Since her meeting with Tommy, she'd been stewing about needing someone like him so she could DJ at Artistique.

"Arghh! You know, I don't get why an agent needs to vouch for me. What good have they ever done for me?" Nyah complained. Trinket's question unleashed a reservoir of Nyah's damned emotions. "How the fuck do they think I delivered that package? I did that shit on my own. I'm a professional classical artist playing with the fucking New York Philharmonic. I don't need a vouch," she fumed, delivering the last bit in hushed tones.

"But no one is supposed to know that really, right?" Trinket offered.

Nyah's back flattened against her locker and she banged the back of her head with a loud clack. "No."

"You really want this, so maybe this time you suck it up and let an agent get you in and then bounce. I'm sure if you explain it to them, they can help you out."

"It's not that easy." Nyah stood the length of her five-foot-eight-inch height. "Getting an agent is only going to bring more attention to me, especially if they're someone who knows what they're doing."

"You mean like Boombox?"

"I mean exactly like Boombox. Don't you think that being a client of his will bring unwanted attention to me? His reputation in the industry comes with some expectation, you know?"

"Yeah, but that also gives him some insight into how to avoid some of the problems you're having in trying to balance your lives. I know you have me to talk to but you're living this covert life and that only makes it harder for you to navigate through all this."

"I've put my career and success in the hands of people before. People who either underestimated me or thought they knew what was best for me without listening to the vision I had for myself." The truth was, Nyah was petrified of going through what she went through with Carlo again after working so hard to cultivate her near-model career.

"I get it and you know I'm here for whatever you need."

"What would I do without you, Trinket? You've been solid. For real."

"That's me. At least in most things." Trinket nibbled on her lower burgundy covered lip. "You're still coming next week, right? The party's gonna be hot."

"Yeah. I play Boiler on Friday. So, I'll be there after the concert." Every few weeks the philharmonic was off on Fridays. With no classical performances or residency at Rebel, the freedom gave Nyah time to either have a life without performances or add on another gig. This week she'd be playing Boiler.

"Cool." Trinket lingered. "Are you going to make the call to Boombox or what?"

Nyah had a half hour before she went on. "I guess I'll bite this bullet. But if he thinks he's running my career, he's got another thing coming."

"Das it!" Trinket exaggerated.

Nyah laughed as she pulled out her phone. "Can you stay for moral support or whatever?"

"Of course." Trinket leaned against the lockers.

Nyah dialed Tommy's number, each digit bringing her closer to surrendering a piece of what she'd worked hard for. Independence. Though she did it for Artistique, she had a strong feeling that nothing would ever be the same.

"Boombox."

"Hi, it's Nyah."

"Hello. I wasn't expecting to hear from you so soon." His silky greeting almost made it worth calling.

"Well, the clock is ticking so…"

"Yes, it is," he confirmed.

"I'm calling to accept your offer, but I have a few things that I need to make clear." She looked at Trinket, who pounded her fist in her palms and mouthed, "That's right."

"Shoot."

She switched the phone to her other ear to adjust her headphones around her neck. She paced the small back room. "My two identities don't overlap. Like I mentioned, not even my father knows. Secrecy is paramount. First sign of a leak and I'm out."

"Your secret is safe with me and I'll make sure it stays that way."

We'll see. "Also, I don't mind you seeking out opportunities, but they get run by me first."

"Sure thing," Tommy said.

"And I don't want to play the big festivals."

"No big festivals? Not even one?" The drop in his intonation voiced doubt.

"None." Lengthy silence followed on his part.

"But I can present any opportunity to you?"

"Yes."

"Like a festival?" She could almost hear him grinning.

She rolled her eyes and Trinket mouthed, "What?" with an elaborate hand gesture.

"If that's the way you want to waste both our energies so that I can say no, then yes." Nyah couldn't restrain her snark. Hadn't she just said no to festivals?

"Okay." He paused for long moment.

His voice deepens when challenged. Noted.

"I can email a contract to you before I leave the office today," he continued. "When I get it back signed, sealed and delivered, I'll work on Artistique. Like you said, the clock is ticking."

She hoped she wasn't making the worst mistake of her life.

No. She was sure she'd already done that with Carlo. "I'll get it back to you tomorrow."

"Send me your complete schedule for the next few months so I can review it and we can chat on the phone, or in person when I'm in New York next week." She liked that he didn't jump right into big ideas but rather wanted to get a sense of what she actually did.

"Okay, but I'll warn you. It's a lot."

"I'm sure it is." His silky laugh made her blush. *Why the fuck am I blushing?*

Trinket gave her the thumbs up and Nyah couldn't

meet her eye. It's not like she and Tommy were kissing, or touching or… "Well thanks."

"Nyah?"

"Yes?" she croaked. She really needed to stop thinking about Tommy kissing her.

"Welcome to the team."

Gladys was so close to her that she could feel her breath on her ear. "Stop hovering."

"Hit *send* already," Gladys whispered.

Gladys's teasing did nothing to lighten the weight of the moment. Nyah virtually signed her summer release from the orchestra so that she could go to Artistique and London. Her plans were moving forward, even though she'd only gotten a confirmation from Artistique that they'd received her resubmission via her agent.

Once she'd signed Tommy's contract, he'd moved pretty quickly to get her application in for reconsideration to Artistique well before the deadline. Now she waited, hoping that the festival's creative director hadn't given away her time slot. She pressed send. Either way she was free from the philharmonic from June through August.

"Done."

"London, here we come."

"*If* I get it." Nyah logged out from the library system and grabbed her stuff. They had a Wednesday performance that only happened every few weeks. With no performances and her set for Boiler the coming Friday, she used the time to catch up on her regular life duties, including her way-past-deadline paperwork.

"You'll get it." Gladys patted her shoulder. "I have a good feeling. I can't be in London without you."

"You were in LA without me and Chicago before that. No me." Nyah batted her lashes.

Gladys pressed her palms over her wounded breast and with her best British accent delivered her line. "Now I cannot possibly live without you."

Nyah laughed and draped her arm around her friend. "Come on. Let's steal some chocolates off Martin's desk before showtime. It's our civic duty."

A chocolate filled mason jar sat on Martin's desk, proof of his addiction. Their conductor tossed back handfuls of the stuff, especially on stressful days. On occasions, such as these, Nyah and Gladys snuck by his office to help him ingest less sugar and sample the international varieties.

"Yes…let's."

Later that night, when Nyah arrived home, she settled with a rare cup of tea. She streamed a few episodes of *Schitt's Creek* and Tyler Perry's *First Wives Club* as she tidied her apartment. Nights like these allowed her a moment to catch up on the steps forward she'd made. Her unconventional approach to success had its lonely periods, and doubts about her approach surfaced as they always did. She lost count of how many times she'd heard "If Pete Monroe was my father…" or "If I had your connections…" growing up. She had always been grateful for what she had and the family she'd been born into, but her parents had also taught her that they worked for the lifestyle they had and she wanted to do that, too. To do things her way and not just take, but create, buffed her bill with glimmering pride. Every time she got on either stage, she etched deeper grooves into her path and lined it with trees she had nourished to root. Now those trees flourished and shaded her journey from those who might knock her off course.

She liked Tommy and hoped that he'd honor her wishes and privacy, and wouldn't turn out to be the latter, but she gambled with the chips of what she'd built. Only time would tell if she cashed in or went bust.

Chapter Eight

The Boiler displayed overhead in neon, devil red, blazed against the dark building. Graffiti, random pop culture stickers, old stamps, and photographs decorated the depressed entryway, and the crowd wrapped around the triangular block. Camouflaged in a hooded long trench coat, she followed Mike's instructions and headed to the back entrance.

Someone exited, squeezing through the entrance. "It's packed in there, I don't know if they're letting anyone else in."

"They gotta let us in. Queen Roe will be on soon," another person complained.

Her eyes widened and she walked a little faster. They were talking about seeing her and the line looked like it was getting longer. If the club was packed, all those people would get the shaft. She buzzed the ringer on the black-painted steel door and it cracked open. A sliver of a man in black attire was barely visible.

"Queen Roe. I'm performing tonight."

"You alone?" The interrogation in his tone was all business.

Her face must have shown smug with a side of duh. "Yeah."

"Password," he demanded.

She recited the password.

The door swung open, revealing a bouncer three times her size in bulk. "You're lucky they didn't maul you. You see that crowd?"

"I didn't realize that it would be this packed. This isn't my regular spot."

"Lady, either you're bullshittin' me or you have no idea how popular you are." The bouncer's head tilted up at her and she slid past his muscled torso. She may have been taller than him, but she was a waif compared to his size. He locked the door behind her. "Follow me. I'll take you to Mike."

They did a little dance to switch positions in the narrow corridor.

A leaner but still fit man in a dark blue shirt, jeans and brown leather shoes barked a few orders at a few people. He was way too casual, in a polished kind of way, for a club owner. This had to be the man whose restaurant life she coveted. This had to be Mike.

"Eh, Queen Roe," he said when he saw her with the bouncer. "See? I knew getting you here would be a good thing. We can't even fit them all in here."

"You must be Mike." She stretched out her hand for him to shake.

"That's me." He grasped her hand in his but looked around her. "Where's Nance?"

"Nance?" Nyah asked.

"Yeah, your manager. She was nice. I wanted to meet her and thank her for finally booking you for my club."

"Oh." Confusion clarified. "She's not here." *Yet another alter ego to keep track of.*

"Sweetheart," Mike cooed. "You have to have people. Who am I going to talk business with when you're on-stage?"

She hated doing this but if she didn't do it now, this man would never respect her. "Mike, right?"

"Yeah."

"Here's the thing, Mike. I'm not a big fan of the term *sweetheart*. My friends and business colleagues call me Queen Roe or Queen. You may use either. And if you want to talk business, we can do that now or when I get offstage."

"I don't mean anything by it, sweet—"

"Well, I just wanted to clarify for you. Where can I get ready?" She purposely steamrolled him so he'd get the picture.

The buzzer to the backdoor sounded again. "Take care of that, Tiny. I'll get our guest set up." Mike nodded to the bouncer.

"You got it, boss." Tiny left to tend to the door.

Mike escorted her to a small but comfortable lounge with a couch and mini bar. Like in many of the underground clubs, she had a locker to secure her personal items. She shrugged off her coat and stuffed it into the tall rectangular compartment. Instead of her shorts she wore the matching leggings to her bustier top, and she took a moment to double-check her clothing.

"Don't take this the wrong way, you look spectacular, but this is why you need people. Do you know the things that are running through my mind, right now?" he asked. "You gotta protect yourself, hon—"

Mike cut himself off and she, at best, tried to appreciate that. She'd spent a lot of time exploring the city and the clubs, and she also did some other gigs in the boroughs. She'd mostly felt okay being at her gigs alone, until now.

The rumbling of male voices sounded outside the door and Tiny came in. "Boss?"

Tommy entered the room and his eyes ping-ponged between her and Mike. Tommy's normally warm brown eyes darkened and he moved closer to her.

"Boombox." Mike cheered. "Long time, my guy."

"Mike." Tommy's eyes connected with hers. Nyah's brain still tried to figure out what the hell Tommy was doing at her Boiler gig. "You okay?" he asked.

"W-what are you doing here?" A sigh of relief escaped her lips. She didn't sense danger but Mike's constant mention of "people and protection" had started to penetrate her New York City tough shield.

"You're my client, remember?" He half smiled.

"How'd you even know...?" She remembered when she had sent him her signed contract that she'd also provided him with her comprehensive calendar. "Right. I sent it to you."

"I figured it would be a good idea for me to just make sure everything met your needs." Tommy's gaze panned the lounge before returning to Mike.

"We're taking good care of her," Mike announced. Tommy's eyes warmed up again, thawing her shoulders like a cozy fireplace.

"What happened to Nance? You replaced her with this guy?" Mike asked.

"Yeah, Mike. I did," Nyah responded as she put the

rest of her things in her locker except for her computer and headphones. There was something charming about Mike—not that she wanted to be friends with him or anything, because she could almost guarantee that *"sweetheart"* only scratched the surface of his chauvinism.

"That's a shame. We had a connection, you know?" Mike said.

"Yeah." Nyah choked back her humor over Mike's obsession with nonexistent Nancy.

"Who's Nancy?" Tommy asked.

Nyah shook her head. "I'll explain later."

"I got a club to run, so here's the short stack. You can get ready here and chill out. Drinks are on the house. Anything you want. The stage is set up to the specifications in your rider. You're on in thirty. I'm looking forward to the show." Mike gave her bare skin and tight clothes a good twice over, and Nyah rolled her eyes.

"Do you often go to your gigs alone?" Tommy asked once Mike closed the door.

"Yeah, I guess." She did.

He sighed. "I'm sure you can take care of yourself, but it doesn't hurt to have someone with you."

"At Rebel, I know everyone there. I've done other engagements, but it wasn't until I got here and saw the crowd…and Mike pointing it out that I needed people." She pointed at the door. "Whatever. I gotta get ready."

"You want me to go?" Tommy stepped toward the door.

"No!" The words rushed out before she could formulate a less animated response. "No." She tempered her tone. She'd been fine for three years. Part of her hated the vulnerability that surfaced. She was tougher than that.

"I just want to know you're safe." His tender delivery defused the charge running through her. "You're my client now," he added.

"You kind of busted in here like someone set the house on fire."

"Yeah, well, I know Mike, and he speaks his mind without much of a filter." Tommy scratched his brow with his thumb then rested his hands on his hips.

"That the only reason you came?" She didn't even regret the question but couldn't deny that she wasn't usually this direct without a little liquid courage.

"Yes."

She barely heard him. *Liar.*

She stepped closer to him, her boldness, she only assumed, coming from her need to get back in control after feeling like a woman in distress. Tommy felt safe. Even those years ago when he'd snubbed her as talent he wanted to work with. No matter how he came to be here, he was here for her. She lowered her gaze a hair to meet his eyes. She had less than thirty minutes, more than enough to drown in their toasty depths.

His aftershave tickled her nose, supplying another level of familiarity and security. He withdrew. "I see you're all set. Have a good show and I'll check in with you afterward."

"Right." She might not have room in her life for a relationship but she sure as hell knew if someone liked her, and Tommy liked her.

Tommy slung back his vodka and water with a splash of bitters and undid the top button on his shirt. He wanted to kiss Nyah and that was both the first and last thing he should do. First came attraction, then wild sex, then him wanting more. That's how it had gone with Isabelle. He'd been a smitten fool for her. He hadn't even ventured to touch Nyah, yet his obvious desire to do so frustrated the shit out of him. He had a lot riding on Queen Roe and though dating clients wasn't off limits, he didn't generally do it. Somehow, the loophole grew more appealing by the second. He hadn't even broached the subject of her possibly playing Sunburst and he had a long way to go before earning her trust, especially since she was anti-festival.

"Coming to the stage…the one, the only…you know her, you love her and we're glad to finally have her at The Boiler tonight. Show your love tonight, party people, for QUEEN… ROE!"

The crowd's cheers did nothing to wipe away the image of Nyah's lips only inches away from his. He had to get a hold of himself and stop leading with his dick because his heart often followed. His aunt Carmen had taught him how to treat women, how to be a gentleman and how to be tender. *You have to pay attention, pa. No matter how hard or how soft she may be, she will always appreciate it if you pay attention.* His father taught him how to be a responsible man, to persevere and keep his word. The combination, he thought, would eventually lead him to the love of his life when he was ready. So far, he'd struck out, and the most recent fail had left a lasting mark.

He'd been attracted to Nyah since that first contentious conversation at Rebel. He no more fooled her with his professionalism than she fooled him with her tough exterior. Smart, talented, overachiever. He thought he'd seen it all with his clients and how hard they worked, but Nyah? Two demanding careers? She was in high demand and bound to crash eventually without assistance. He'd seen it many times, but he refused to let that happen to Nyah. Her kingdom surrounded her, cheered for her, reached for her and she exploded onstage, dancing, singing and doing what she did best, working the dials to perfection. Despite his own warning, he wondered if she gave that kind of energy in bed.

"She's fucking amazing." Thankfully, Mike interrupted the wild jaunt Tommy's thoughts were about to take.

"Yeah, she is," Tommy said.

"So, let me talk to you about a residency. I know Oscar's got her locked in for one at Rebel but I'd like to have her here." Mike began his pitch.

The semi chub that pulled Tommy's pants taut simmered down and he agented up. "I can pose it to her. She wants to stay in the underground. What frequency are we talking about?" Tommy negotiated effortlessly as he quelled his desire.

"Twice a month."

"She's in high demand and is very selective about the gigs she takes."

"But you can talk her into it, no?" Mike asked.

"No one gets Queen Roe to do anything she doesn't want to do, but you're welcome to try."

"I'll add a little sweetener."

"I'm listening." Tommy doubted Nyah wanted a residency at a club so close to Rebel, but he didn't know for sure. He envisioned her taking a more upscale residency, but it would take time for her to see the benefit of expanding her vision.

"A little signing bonus. Maybe a couple grand."

The sweetener paled in comparison to what he usually negotiated, which made him feel like a novice haggling his first deal. "We'll discuss it and get back to you."

Probably not the answer Mike wanted. Bodies packed the standing-room-only club like anchovies in a jar of oil, in addition to a line out the door. Tommy understood the lure.

"Yeah, all right." Mike dawdled. "And here I thought I couldn't keep my eyes off her. What she must be like? You two bangin'?"

"What?"

"She's a beautiful woman, man." Mike kissed his fingertips. "My dick doesn't discriminate, but I'm a professional."

Before Tommy could stop himself, his palm whacked against Mike's chest and he grabbed his shirt and probably a few chest hairs.

Mike pushed at him. "Get the fuck off me, man."

Security in black materialized from the shadows, yanking the two men apart, but Tommy's unyielding grip continued to punish Mike for his filthy fucking mouth.

"Not about her," Tommy shouted, his temperature rising. "You understand?"

"What the fuck is wrong with you, man?" Mike's face splotched red.

Tommy let Mike go, shrugged off the bouncers and settled back in his seat at the corner of the bar. "She's

my client. Have some respect when you talk about her."
Heart and lungs pumping, he drained the rest of his
vodka and ordered another. He blinked away his spotty
vision.

Mike smoothed his shirt and nodded to his security
team. The men backed up but stayed engaged with his
and Mike's interactions. Mike ordered a shot of rum.
"I didn't know you two were a thing."

"Like I said, she's my client." Tommy prided himself
on being too polished for violence, but he'd gone after
Mike without even thinking. What claim did he have
on Nyah? Tommy had heard men say worse things and
he had no problem checking them, verbally. He didn't
like being a match easily lit by a few vulgar statements.

"That what we're callin' it nowadays?" Mike chuckled. "If that's the reaction you have then you might want
to check yourself. Luckily for you, I'm a forgiving man.
We can still do business but don't ever fucking put your
hands on me again or I'll throw you out on your ass so
fast you'll forget your own fucking name. Capeesh?"

"Fair enough." Tommy's eyes went to Queen Roe
onstage as if she'd called him, and through her rose-
tinted glasses, he felt her eyes on him. He wondered
just how much she'd seen.

Chapter Nine

The Lyft neared Nyah's apartment on West 94th Street. She had been biting her tongue the whole time as she listened to Tommy drone on and on about a residency at The Boiler, and the sweetener Mike wanted to add. But she had other questions. He and Mike had seemed to be fine when she descended the stage at the club. Both men had congratulated her, but she wanted to know what all went down with the shoving match.

"You didn't have to come with me all the way home." Her lies were piling up.

"What kind of gentleman would I be? It's late. You know what they say about the freaks."

She smiled at the Houdini reference. "They come out at night."

He shifted in his seat and groaned.

"What's wrong?"

"I should have pissed before I left the club."

"Oh." She didn't need a reference to his dick to peek between his legs, but since he'd given her one, she gave a gratuitous glance downward. "We did flee the scene kind of quick."

At the club, they'd wrapped things up with Mike at

record speed. She wasn't complaining. Her limbs ached, and her top and leggings were sweat soaked several times over. Had it not been for her coat, the car would have reeked. However, their departure hadn't given her or Tommy time to do much more than share a couple words with Mike, get her stuff, and leave.

"Mind if I come up?" he asked.

She gulped. He wanted to enter her secret lair, her private nest and the place where she transformed. She now knew exactly how all the superheroes with day jobs felt. Not only was he asking to slip behind the veil, but their flirty discourse earlier had only added to the fact that fucking him steadily climbed to the top of her wish list.

"No, I mean…"

"If it's a problem, I can always just go in the bushes or behind a building."

She puffed her cheeks. "It's cool. Come up," she blurted.

They took the elevator to her apartment on the twenty-fourth floor. She flicked on the switch and the soft white light overhead illuminated the room, touching every corner of her living space.

"This is nice," he said of the lavender walls and the mostly black and white photography on the walls. Her dark wood shelves were made feminine with the fluffy rainbow of pillows and modern accents.

"Thanks." She bent over and unzipped her boots. "No shoes."

"No problem." He slipped out of his dark tan leather dress shoes and paired them neatly by the door. He closed the space between them, the open flap of his suit jacket inches from her exposed belly. The Hemsworth suit he wore was also an item in her father's closet and her palms itched to smooth his shoulders. She wanted to run her fingers over the lapel, open the suit jacket, and slide inside of it with him.

"Nyah?"

"Mmm-hmm?"

"The bathroom?" he asked, as if not for the first time.

She jolted back from her fantasies and the heat on her face had to be visible. "Oh, right. First corridor, make a right and it's the first door on the left. If you open the closet, you've gone too far."

He inched past her, his body grazing hers. Once he disappeared, she jetted into her bedroom. She took a glimpse of herself in the mirror and groaned. Her hair had curled so tightly it'd be a nightmare to detangle, and though her makeup was still on her face, her blue eyeliner had smudged down to the tops of her cheeks, competing with her blush. "Wow." She peeled out of her frowsy clothes and slipped on an oversized, gray, off the shoulder tee shirt and pink velour sweatpants. She needed a shower but right now she needed to not look so damn messy.

"Nyah?" Two knocks on her bedroom door followed.

"Coming." She snapped a few Kleenex from the box on her dresser, dabbed it on her tongue and wiped to at least clear the mess under her eyes.

"I can let myself out if you're busy."

No way did she want his last image of her tonight to be her post-performance dishevelment. "I'll be right there." She finished up and opened the door. She peeked down the corridor but didn't see him.

"I'm right here." His lowered tone prickled the hairs at the back of her neck and she near jumped out of her pants. "You scared me." She clutched her chest.

"How?" he scoffed. "I just called you."

She got a good look at him and dampness rimmed his open collar and his hairline. "Never mind that. Why are you all wet?" she asked.

"I needed to cool down. Cold water helped."

Nyah felt her forehead crinkle. "I try to keep it at seventy in here because of the instruments. I can open a window to cool it down a bit—"

"The temperature's fine in here."

Her mind felt like it had just been pretzeled. If it was fine in her apartment, then why—*oh!* His eyes lingered on her with desire she couldn't mistake, and her throat parched to the point where she croaked her words. "Let me get you a hand towel."

"I used the one in there. Hope that was okay."

"Of course. You all good?"

"Yeah, thanks." He hesitated and looked up and down the corridor they were in.

There wasn't any real reason for him to stay any longer. Given that she'd been hesitant to let him up in the first place, she should just let him be on his way, but she didn't want him to leave. "Want the penny tour?"

He smiled with his eyes more than his mouth and that made him even more adorable than she could take at the moment. "Sure."

"You saw the bathroom. This is my bedroom." She widened the door and he peered in. Beside the bed, a few small watercolor canvases decorated the walls. She leaned against the doorframe and crossed her arms. "It's not a portal to another dimension. You can step inside."

"I'm good." He adjusted his glasses by the rim as he scanned the room. The pale pink tufted headboard leaned against the cream-colored walls. Her bedroom always offered her a secondary sanctuary in her apartment. Perhaps Tommy would toss her against the gang of pillows on her white duvet any minute.

"It's cute."

You're cute. "Thanks."

"These are spectacular," he said.

Photographs of her with her family and friends, as well as other stills her mother had taken, many of Nyah, surrounded her with love. Another of her and Gladys after they'd performed and a selfie of her and Trinket at Rebel when they'd first met.

"My mother took many of them. Some I took. The pictures in color are professional ones from my classical performances. I like having photos of the people I love around. The rest sort of document my life. Why have them on a gallery on a website when I can reminisce while I have breakfast or create music."

"And your Queen Roe images?" he asked.

"I keep those on my computer or on her website."

"Too bad you can't display them with all the rest. I bet some of them are phenomenal."

"They are. I project them on the TV on flip mode when I'm alone or Trinket comes through. They get seen." She might hide her DJ life from others but she gave it the respect it was due.

"I vaguely remember your mom talking about photography at Pete's party, all those years ago." He continued evaluating her space. "I had a different focus."

"Same focus if you ask me." His ambition had always been a staple of his personality. All these years later, with all his success, she only saw his ambitions had grown.

"You gonna take this moment to bust my balls?"

"Not ball busting." She held up her hands in surrender. "Just stating the obvious. Follow me, sir." She took two whole steps behind a small partition. "Here's where mama makes her magic."

He stepped before her, zeroing in on her instruments. "You play all these?"

"Some better than others, but yeah."

He touched the end of the keyboard before his hand floated reverently to the bocal of the bassoon. He craned his neck to look at her. "Bassoon, right?"

"You are correct."

His body followed his head and he faced her. "Interesting instrument."

"Woodwinds have their own technique but BB-Bae here—"

"BB-Bae?"

He might think her naming convention ridiculous but these were her babies. "I name them all based on the first letter.

"KK-Bae for the keyboard?"

"Yes. Exactly." His response delighted her more than it should.

He squinted toward the ceiling. "Well if BB-Bae is for the bassoon then what do you call your bass?"

Excitement puffed her chest. "I'm so glad you asked. My bass is my first love. She chose me. I call her Big D."

His laughter resonated in her extremities and she hugged herself. "Big D, huh?" He licked his lower lip and his thumb swept over it.

She must have been horny as all get out because his level of sexy increased with every move he made. "Like I was saying about woodwinds, a lot of the work is from the breathing and…" She pulled out the reed and "M'd" it into position. She blew puffs of air between the double strips of bamboo, and a loud, high-pitched noise sounded. "As well as blowing and tonguing." She regretted the words as soon as they fully left her mouth.

His humor ceased and his eyes dropped to her mouth. The ventilation from her off the shoulder shirt did little to cool her blazing body. Her last romp had been with a barista from her neighborhood coffee shop that she'd dated for two whole weeks, eight months ago. They'd parted ways when she could barely grab a cup of coffee with her schedule. Shortly after she invested in high-end mechanics to satisfy her urges. She did, however, miss a warm body in her bed.

Tommy's warm brown eyes shined. "You're exceptional."

She felt naked—not in a someone-just-pulled-the-shower-curtain-back kind of way, but free and holistically authentic. The way his gaze landed on her made her feel both valued and seen by him in a way that completely freaked her out and exalted her at the same time. Her heart pounded so hard and fast in her chest, he had to hear it or feel its vibration. Her neck muscles strained when she swallowed and no response came.

How was she supposed to respond? She tried to clear her throat and it sounded like she had a sputtering pipe that needed work. "I try."

He glided toward her in what felt like slow motion and lightly touched her chin. "You are, Nyah."

"Thank you." She couldn't release her eyes from his. She thought they were his best feature, in addition to his lips, his hair, his style, his... He had a military bed type ass she longed to bounce a coin off of. She craved his lips for one kiss, maybe more, but when he dropped his hand and broke their connection, her hopes were obliterated.

"I should get going." He walked toward the door before she had a chance to catch her breath.

"Hey, hold up." She shook out of her trance. "Before you go, can I ask you something about tonight?"

"Shoot."

"Did something happen with you and Mike tonight? It looked like you two were, well...had a disagreement."

His tongue rested on his top lip for a few seconds as if mocking her. "We did."

She waited. "Would you like me to write you a letter and wait for a reply or..."

He scratched his eyebrow with his thumb. "We had a conversation about respect."

"Not cryptic at all." She frowned. "Was it something to do with me?"

His silence affirmed her suspicion. "I just needed to clarify for Mike what is and isn't appropriate. It's squashed. No hard feelings."

"Oh. Okay," she whispered.

He opened the door and spoke to her from the other side of the threshold. "Think about his offer."

She shifted her weight. A plea for him to stay sat in the center of her chest.

"We should hear from Artistique soon."

Right. Her reason for living. "Great."

"I, uh, I'd like to put some things on your calendar. Like when I'm out of the country and when I'm back in New York."

"Why?"

"Sometimes it's good for you to know so we can be in sync and if you need me what the time zone difference is or when we can meet up."

"Oh." She thought about it. "I guess it's cool. Just don't fuck up my shit." She smiled.

"I'll keep that in mind." He walked to the door. "We'll be in touch. Goodnight."

"Goodnight." She closed the door and leaned her back against it, wondering which of them would cave first.

Tommy gave his reservation to the hostess at Up Thai on the Upper East Side to meet Luke and Leona for dinner. It had been a week since he'd been in New York and a few weeks since he'd seen his friends. At that time he'd been sulking over his Sunburst rejection.

He felt someone squeeze his traps from behind and then slap his back, and immediately recognized Luke's signature greeting. Tommy turned to his client and friend. "It's about time your ass got here. I've been waiting for almost half an hour." Tommy slapped hands with Luke and gave him a pat.

Luke frowned. "Really?"

"Nah, I'm messing with you. I just got here," Tommy jested.

Luke twisted the dark patch of hair just below his lower lip. "I see the type of night we're going to have."

"You're looking oh so fresh. I like those kicks." Tommy pointed to Luke's light gray sneakers with white soles.

"My lady likes it." Luke popped the collar on his jean jacket and pulled the dark gray hoodie off his head.

"Speaking of… Where's Leo?" Tommy searched the distance behind his friend.

Luke jutted his thumb behind him. "She's finishing up a call, she'll be right in."

What a difference a year made. Back then, Tommy had been the one keeping the lines of communication open because Luke and Leona had a tumultuous start to their manager-client relationship. Now Luke and Leona were as solid a couple as they came. Luke had moved to New York to be closer to her, even though he kept his San Francisco home, and they spent time touring for his performances. As his manager, Leona still did the best for Luke's career.

"I heard this place is supposed to be pretty decent. How're your folks? You stayed with them the last time you were in New York, right?" Luke asked.

"Yeah, they're doing great. I'm going to try to make it a habit to stop up there when I come into town. Sometimes it's hard to do but it's worth the effort."

"Cool."

The doors to the restaurant opened and Leona Sable walked in.

"Hey, Tommy." Leona embraced him. The side ponytail, a departure from her normal tight and high bun, rested on her shoulder and cushioned his chin when they hugged. She held him at arm's length and gave him a once-over as if she checked his health. Satisfied, she let him go.

"You look lovely, Leo."

"Thank you." She grinned.

Luke reached for his girlfriend's hand, drew her into his arm, and kissed her temple. "Everything okay?"

"Yeah," Leona said. "I just had to confirm your call time for the spotlight you're doing for Maxim because I heard three different times, so I went up the chain to get a solid confirmation. It's all good."

Tommy fanned his nose. "Where are you guys coming from? You smell like booze."

"We just came from having drinks with Izzy. She would have totally come, but she has a work dinner. She says hi."

The mention of Isabelle Fisher caused a less visceral reaction than Tommy expected and a mental image of Nyah staring at him with those lustful eyes the night before might have had something to do with his tempered response. "How's she doing?"

"She's good. You guys should meet up while you're in town. I know you're busy, but try. Okay?" Leona urged.

His and Izzy's passing fling started out as casual as all his other interludes. It had long been over but that hadn't stopped Leona from trying to cultivate a more substantial friendship between them. Tommy wasn't sure that was what he wanted. He'd seen little of Izzy since their tussle between the sheets. He wasn't mad about the way things ended between them. He'd had an inkling that he was short-term fun for Izzy, but the rejection when he suggested he wanted something more still stung, no matter how dull the point had been waxed over.

He informed the hostess that their party had all arrived. They were seated immediately at a corner table. "I'm hungry as hell, so let's just get all the curries," Tommy said.

"Your eyes are bigger than your stomach," Leona chided. "Let's share some dumplings before you and Luke devour the actual menu."

"Me?" Luke shrugged. "I didn't even say anything."

"You nodded." Leo knew them both well, which is why Tommy didn't complain about her accusation.

"She gets me beyond words," Luke teased as he shook out of his jean jacket.

"What's been going on, Tommy?" Leona asked. "You've been here more often."

"I have a new client," Tommy announced.

"Oooh. Tell us more." Leona leaned in, her eyes gleaming with interest.

"She has a lot of potential but she's convinced that she doesn't need or want an agent or manager." Tommy continued, "I did convince her that she should at least have one. I'm going to do both for her because she has a lot on her plate."

"Like what?" Luke twisted to hang his jacket on his chair.

"She's managing too many projects and needs a better strategy to keep things low-key." Tommy wasn't sure

how much he should say because Nyah didn't want anyone to know that she was Pete Monroe's daughter and
Queen Roe the DJ. He could trust Leona and Luke but
for now he'd hold on to that information.

"Keeping things low-key?" Luke crooked an eyebrow.

"Yeah, she wants to DJ but she's too good to do the
run of the mill wedding, prom or anniversary. She's
from the underground," Tommy added.

"Hmm…" Leona eyed him like she gathered evidence.

"So, I'll be representing her and managing her as
best as I can until I can get her to even agree to a meeting with Wallace Entertainment."

Luke and Leona exchanged glances at his last statement.

"Let me get this straight." Leo tapped her chin. "You
found a super-talented artist you want to develop but she
wants to stay, well, fairly unknown but known enough
to have a career as a dance music DJ. She doesn't want
to be represented by an agent or a manager but you convinced her you'd do both."

"When you say it like that it sounds unwise but it's
not." Tommy tried to defend himself but among his
two friends he didn't stand a chance. He'd taken on a
situation that in the past he'd have sprinted from. He'd
worked his ass off to cruise in his wheelhouse, now
he'd have to roll up his sleeves to have any chance of
getting Nyah to Sunburst.

Leona and Luke again shared voiceless thoughts.

"Have you asked her why she doesn't want stardom?"
Luke asked at length.

From Nyah's father's notoriety, to her wanting enough time for her classical career, Tommy had his assumptions about why she shied away from stardom, but that's all they were. "No."

"Maybe you should." Leona straightened her already straight flatware that was rolled in a napkin on the right side of her place setting. "So what's her name?"

"What?" Tommy asked.

"The girl that's got you doing all these things that are totally not you."

"What do you mean?" Tommy pretended he didn't know what his friends were talking about and feigned confusion.

A waiter interrupted them briefly to pour water into their water glasses.

"Boombox. You couldn't wait to hand over managerial responsibilities to Leona when she came on," Luke said, reminding him about his shortcomings as a manager.

"Also, you're a star-maker. You see talent and you can't help yourself. You have to develop it. When you see the artist's potential, you're really good at charting a path for them. You've got a golden touch. You, talking yourself into one, managing and two, downplaying someone's talent are just not you. You'd only do that for someone you had feelings for. Someone special." Leo gave him her best dazzling smile. "We just want to know who she is. Right, babe?" She deferred to Luke.

"What she said." Luke pointed at Leona.

"Smartass." Tommy shook his head. He longed to share more with his friends but even without Nyah here, he needed to earn her trust.

The hostess came by and Luke ordered a bottle of red for the table. Given that Luke owned a vineyard in California with his sister, the wine selections naturally reverted to him, even though Tommy had a set of wine skills, too. They each ordered a specialty drink for their pork and vegetable dumplings.

"What are you drinking, baby?" Luke asked Leo.

"I'll have the lychee martini, please," Leona ordered. "Tommy?"

"Thai Old Fashioned," he said.

"And the lemongrass, lime, and Thai basil mojito, for me. You can bring the wine with our dinner," Luke instructed.

"Got it." The waitress scribbled on her notepad. "I'll bring that right out."

"You know, the short ribs are supposed be really good here. I've also read in the reviews that their specials are phenomenal." Tommy rattled on in the hopes that his friends would forget about their previous line of questioning.

"Nice try." Luke guzzled his water.

"It's okay if you don't want to talk about it, Tommy," Leona comforted him.

"No it's not," Luke complained. "I want to know who has you so whipped that you're making all these exceptions for."

"First of all, she doesn't have me whipped." Tommy stopped abruptly when the waitress returned with their drinks and appetizers. He dove into the row of dumplings and Luke smacked his hand.

"Fuck, Luke." Tommy chuckled in spite of himself. "Did you just whack me?"

Leona giggled.

"What are you doing, man? Ladies fucking first." Luke served Leona.

"My bad, Leo. I'm about to eat my hand off," Tommy apologized.

"It's cool. Eat," Leo said, reaching for the black coffee-colored sauce and pouring a little on the small dumpling on her plate.

Tommy plucked two dumplings off the plate and stuffed one in his mouth. The savory onion, sautéed pork and Thai spices exploded in his mouth. The first flavors for the *hangry* tasted divine.

Leona pointed her fork at him as she chewed. She wasn't about to let up. "You were saying?"

"I'm not whipped," Tommy repeated once he swallowed the bite. "I like her as a client and think she's really special."

"Special, huh?" Luke asked, dipping his steamed dumpling into a small bowl of sauce.

Tommy sipped his drink. The Mekhong rum and orange and chocolate bitters refreshed his palate like the clean start he wished this conversation would take. "You know what I mean."

"Not really. Help me understand." Luke was a smart man and Tommy knew his friend liked seeing him squirm under their third degree. Why shouldn't he? Tommy had grilled Luke countless times about Leona before they got together. Payback time.

"I like her. I think she's talented and as interesting as she is frustrating and challenging. She has two careers that she's trying to pursue and she wants to keep them separate. She's been doing it alone this whole time and it's wearing her down. She has a vision. I guess I'm trying to help her expand that vision, even if only a little," Tommy said at last.

"But you like her?" Leona asked, peering up from her menu.

"If you want to know if she's smart, beautiful, and sexy, the answer is yes, but she's more than that. Her mind. The way she puts music together and how she functions in two very different musical spaces is fascinating." Tommy rubbed his lips remembering how much he'd wanted to kiss Nyah last night. How she took his breath away. He did like her, and more than a little. He looked at his friends. The great relationship they had was the envy of anyone who met them. Perhaps that's why he'd jumped the gun with Izzy.

Leona squealed. "You like her more than a little, especially since you've kissed her. You have kissed her, haven't you?"

"I haven't kissed her yet." Tommy stuttered, "I mean, I haven't kissed her."

"You said *yet*, that means you really want to." Leona wiggled in her chair.

"He really wants to," Luke added.

"Guys," Tommy tried to interject, but Leona reached for his hand and held it for a few seconds before she spoke.

"It's okay to want something special with someone, Tommy. You're great and she sounds great. I know she's your client but look at how things turned out with me and Luke."

Tommy swallowed emotion that hijacked his throat.

Leona read him like tea leaves. He stuttered before relaxing into the moment.

"I hoped things with you and Izzy would—" she paused "—be something more. I liked the idea of us double dating and vacationing together and stuff. I wanted you both to be happy. Like us."

The truth nearly knocked him out of his seat. He did want what Luke and Leona had.

"Jeez, Leo. I wasn't ready for a therapy session," Tommy said.

"She's incredible like that." Luke massaged her shoulders.

"I want to meet her." Leona let his hand go and asked, "Can we come see her play?"

He hmmed and hawed. He wanted nothing more than to introduce Luke and Leo to Nyah, but a performance might not be the right time. "I don't know if that's a good idea. Luke brings a lot of attention and…"

"We could have drinks, lunch, or dinner." Luke checked in with Leona.

"Yeah, like a double date," Leona said.

Luke cheesed at Tommy from across the table. "Exactly, like a double date."

Leona almost fell out of her seat. "Yes."

Tommy rubbed his forehead. "Oh boy. I just signed her, guys. Let that settle before you get ahead of yourselves."

"But you can't deny that you're thinking about kissing her." Leona couldn't stop the smile from spreading up to her ears.

Tommy shook his head. "You guys are full-a shit, you know that?"

They placed their dinner order with their waitress.

"Well, the good news about all this is that we'll be seeing more of you since she's based here. You'll be doing a lot of work and traveling with her so it's only a matter of time before..." Leona made a kissy face.

"Mature." Tommy groaned. "Yeah. Someone's gotta keep an eye on you two."

They chatted some more and enjoyed dinner with laughter and lively banter as friends did. After they finished up at the restaurant, they headed to Luke's residency at Aurora Nightclub. On their way, Tommy got a text from Oscar.

OZ: Forgot to mention Trinket's playing her house party 2nite. Come thru.

The address followed.

Nyah and Trinket were friends and she would likely attend. Tommy's motivation to stop by immediately multiplied.

Boombox: I'll try

Chapter Ten

Nyah squeezed her way into Trinket's Harlem apartment through gyrating sweaty bodies. The scent of African musk and burning herb hung heavy in the air. The mosaic cloth and urban artwork by Frank Morrison decorated the walls. The darkness of night and city lights created a classic backdrop behind Trinket. Familiar faces from local Harlem hot spots and Rebel regulars made up the motley guest list that came out to support. As usual, Nyah came through with her heavy makeup and sunglasses. Many greeted her Queen Roe persona and she flashed back to catching reruns of *Jem and the Holograms* on a pop culture streaming channel. She definitely lived a Jerrica Benton life.

"Whattup, Queen," Oscar greeted her when she made her way closer to the turntables where Trinket stood. Oscar's swoon-worthy support of her friend always made Nyah believe in happily-ever-afters. Her parents, too, had their ups and downs, but their loyalty to each other and ability to fall in love again and again was impressive.

"Hey, Oz. Are you ready to hear your girl blow up

the spot?" Nyah eyed Trinket, whose eyes were focused on the equipment below her. "How's she holding up?"

"Hands are still shaking a bit but she's looking strong."

"That's great. She's doing Popup Sounds in the Park. If that goes well, you should totally put her on the Rebel stage in the coming weekend and keep her there. She can't lose momentum."

"No doubt." Oscar agreed. "I'd hate to see her lose any more opportunities because of her stage fright."

"Word," Nyah said. "Are you going to head back to Rebel after this?"

"Nah. Dane's closing for me tonight."

"Cool. Hey, let me go talk to her," Nyah shouted over the music.

"You want anything?" Oscar made a drinking motion. "Tony's tending bar."

"Oh, in that case, a Sidecar, please."

"Something with cognac? What a surprise." Oscar rolled his eyes.

She put her finger over her mouth and shushed him.

"I'll be back." Oscar slid through the crowd to the bar.

Nyah slid behind the DJ table and tapped Trinket on the shoulder. Trinket had been so focused that she hadn't even see her come in. "Hey, sis!" Trinket pulled her into her arms. "I'm glad you're finally here."

"Me too. You are doing so great. I love this," Nyah said, referencing the "I Feel Love" by Donna Summer and Kaskade's "Nobody Else" mix. "This is so sexy and silky and you have everybody grooving to it."

Trinket nodded to the beat and smiled. The air from

the cracked window behind her cooled in gentle wisps to unsuccessfully tamp Trinket's sizzling performance. Lots of people had talked about Queen Roe's talent but they had no idea what they were missing with Trinket. She had more creativity in one of her long dreadlocks than most of the DJs at Rebel or on the scene had in their whole body. Nyah was so glad that Trinket had finally gotten to this point.

"It's your time to shine, babe! Kill 'em with it!"

Trinket clapped her hands overhead and Nyah slid out from behind the table, giving Trinket the much-deserved spotlight.

Oscar found her and gave her a martini glass filled with cognac, lemon juice and Cointreau. "Tony hooked you up with that VSOP shit." Oscar referred to the cognac in her drink.

"Nice. It does make a difference." She took a sip and then gave him the thumbs up.

They watched Trinket for a bit and then when they finished their drinks got their dance on.

Bodies moved to Trinket's groove and since she'd been playing for well over two hours, she looked comfortable and energetic as she connected with the crowd. Trinket delivered mixes that filled the room with what Nyah could only describe as both emotional and physical joy. At least that's how the music wove its way through Nyah, puppeting one of her arms up into the air and pumping it to the beat. Her thighs burned as she bent her knees and shook her hips. Her orange and gold-layered spaghetti straps top clung to the perspiration rising on her skin.

Nyah pulled out her phone and captured Trinket on

video so that Trinket could see just how awesome she moved the crowd. Nyah didn't make a big deal of it. She didn't want to let anything take Trinket out of her groove, and she wasn't the only one who captured the magic that happened right in front of them.

"Enough of that," Nyah muttered, and then she fully committed to jiving to the music and letting go. Trinket's BPM sped up and the party, now in full swing, shook the place. Thank God Trinket lived on the bottom floor because even though she had an agreement with her neighbors, the building rocked.

Turning, spinning and enjoying the music, Nyah danced to song after song by herself and with those around her. A familiar fragrance wafted around her and she peered over the top of her glasses.

"Tommy?" Her body heat soared and perspiration pimpled everywhere. "I thought you were back in LA?" Her buoyant groove on the dance floor turned into a modest two-step.

"Oscar reminded me that Trinket had a house party tonight. So here I am?"

"Aww, shame." Nyah's shoulders slumped. "You missed the best part of her set."

"I know. Apparently everyone I saw on the way out shared a similar sentiment."

"I'm telling you. She's really good. You should take everyone's word for it and just sign her."

Tommy danced to the music and she wished he'd stayed still because he only got sexier. "You know I can't do that."

"Why?" She put her hands on her hips. "Because you don't trust my talent scouting skills?"

"No, because I'm a professional. I can't blindly sign her, even if I trust the person recommending her."

"So, you trust me now?" Nyah asked, strangely flattered.

"You haven't given me any reason not to, yet."

"Ditto, sir."

Trinket and Oscar came up to them.

"Hi, Tommy." Trinket, high on her performance, hugged him. "I'm surprised to see you here."

"Oz texted me a reminder earlier to come through," Tommy explained.

"Did you get a chance to hear her set, man?" Oscar asked.

"Unfortunately, my client performed tonight, as well, and I needed to stay longer than expected. I came in at the tail end."

Trinket's features fell and Nyah knew her friend's disappointment ran deep. Trinket tried really hard to put herself out there despite her fear and the ridicule she'd experienced. On nights when they boozed out, Trinket would dream about playing big stages and having an agent, even though she'd heard Nyah's horror stories. Trinket was so brave and Nyah wanted her to finally win.

"What I did hear sounded great, though," Tommy politely encouraged Trinket but Nyah wished he could have been there to see her friend shine.

"I've been letting some songs play for the past half hour so I could mingle. You kind of missed the whole thing." Trinket's lips disappeared in her mouth.

"I'm sorry, Trinket. My schedule gets hectic. I'll try

to make one of your sessions while I'm in New York."
Tommy's weak promise irritated Nyah.

"Yeah." Trinket put on a hopeful mask.

"How do you do this with your neighbors? I'm surprised no one's called the cops."

"We're a community here. Most of them were here at the party and I always let them know in advance. We agree on a turn down or end time, and we respect what we decide. It works. As gentrification continues it gets harder but for now we're good."

"Nice." Oscar was giving his cousin the stink eye and Nyah shared Oscar's sentiment.

"Well, we're going to talk to some people before they bounce." Trinket excused herself and Oscar followed.

"I guess they're kind of disappointed."

"Maybe a little." If he'd played dumb to Trinket's hurt feelings, he would have lost a little of her respect.

Tommy shifted in his stance. "I didn't realize it was that important to either of them. I really thought Oz just invited me to hang." His weariness about the whole thing softened his features.

"They'll forgive you," she offered and started to walk away. Tommy touched her arm. "Hey, can I talk to you for minute?"

"We normally help Trinket clean up her spot after the party. If you're willing to help, then it would be nice and quicker, and we can chat," she smiled.

"I'm in."

"Cool. We can start with the trash." Nyah winked at Oscar, who had been stifling a smile ever since she asked Tommy to help. Surely no one usually asked the super-agent to lift one of his stardust fingers to do manual labor. Rather, people likely plied Tommy with drinks, VIP, and free shit to get him to sign them so that he could make them famous.

That she wasn't that thirsty gave her the upper hand, but she did need him for Artistique and that would at least cost her sole control—and what else, she wasn't yet certain.

Tommy pulled the recycle bag from an open black trash bin. By the extra air leaving him as he lifted and the multiple clanking bottles, the bag must have weighed quite a few pounds. "This one's done."

Nyah peeled open a new recycle bag and handed it to him as she walked around and grabbed any stray cups, bottles or cans that never made it to the bin.

"So what did you want to talk to me about?" Nyah asked.

"I heard from Artistique."

All her movements halted and she faced him. "You did? How come they didn't contact me? What did you hear? Did I get in? I mean, they sounded hopeful. They just needed you to rep me. So what is it? What'd they say?"

He put a hand on her shoulder. "Take it easy."

"This means a lot to me." Her chest inflated and she huffed audibly.

"I know it does." He sounded unaffected and maybe even amused by the avalanche of thoughts that made it past her lips. "Because I rep you now, they contact me with the decision. It's standard."

"Oh." She waited and when he didn't respond with the urgency she obviously felt the moment deserved she prompted, "What's the verdict?"

"You're in," he said simply.

"I am?"

"Yes."

She jumped up to wrap her arms around his neck and hugged him. Her lips mushed against his before she could stop herself or remember that they weren't alone.

"Um. I'm sorry, I don't know why I did that and—"

"I…it's okay." He cleared his throat. "I would have loved to keep some suspense going but I wasn't sure you could withstand a moment longer of not knowing."

What am I doing? Besides their temporary professional relationship, Tommy lived in LA, had crazy ambition that would ultimately clash with her philosophy. Not to mention that he was too damn attractive and even though she might want to flirt with the idea of having a bone buddy, she was just too damn busy. Bonus, if she got accepted to the London program, she be a country away. *It's a wrap!* "And that's only half my list." She shifted from foot to foot like she should leave or something.

"You have a list for me?" Tommy asked.

"Huh?"

"You said something about a list."

"Oh. I think I was just…never mind." She hadn't realized the effect of being so close to him. On those nights when her Satisfyer Pro 2 vibrator had worked overtime between her legs, she pictured him there because it was safe and problem free. Damn her thoughts. Her scorching cheeks must have shown fire-engine red, because Tommy's lids lowered as if she'd voiced her fantasy out loud. Luckily the place had cleared out and only she and Tommy were left with Trinket and Oscar, who were cleaning up.

Tommy licked his lips and she didn't know if he did that because his lips were dry or because he wanted to taste her again the way she wanted to taste him. He couldn't have read her that easily. She was failing at keeping him in his place as agent for hire.

Act your age, Queen. "Thank you." She dared not touch her cheeks and draw more attention to the fact that being close to Tommy set her skin on fire. She pivoted and picked up a few lingering cups and bottles.

"You're welcome." He tended to his clean-up duties. "Which leads me to something else I wanted to propose to you. One of the gigs on the list of places that want you to play is Oh Ship. I thought it might be a good spot for you because it's fairly contained and even though it exposes you to a new audience, I think the response can still stay manageable for you."

Her temperature chilled. "Are you talking about the cruise ship?" She didn't even need to add more commentary. Her question reeked of judgment. "We agreed that I didn't want to play any large events."

"We agreed that I could present a gig to you that in my professional experience might be a good opportunity. Oh Ship is not a large event, per se."

She gave him a quick up and down. "That's where we disagree."

"You can only hold so many people on a ship and it's not a festival-sized event by any means, even if it has a festival feel."

"Throw in some more glow sticks at Rebel and we got ourselves a festival feel," she said with hands on hips.

"It's a great appearance that pays very well. You'll also have some networking opportunities."

"With people who will want me to do bigger events. I'm not a novice, Tommy."

"So what's the problem, here?" he asked.

She threw out a random response. "I have to play the philharmonic."

"We'll have you back in plenty of time for your performances. My research on that has already been done."

She scowled at him.

"I assumed you'd have questions," he said.

She liked having things in their neat compartments and Oh Ship sounded like it wanted to test those boundaries. Wasn't this what she needed Tommy for, in addition to Artistique? "I don't know, Tommy. That's not really my thing."

"Nyah, if you wanted to just play music you can easily do that behind closed doors or do house parties. No offense, Trinket, you're a special case."

Trinket deadpanned, no doubt wondering how she even became part of their conversation. "Uh…none taken?"

Tommy continued, "You could be a hobbyist but you want to perform…need to perform to an audience. It doesn't have to be a main stage at a gigantic festival, which is why I'm proposing something like this."

She tossed a few more cups into the trash. She must be an open book, because his words were true. Whether she performed with the orchestra or on the Rebel stage she needed an audience. Just because she didn't want the big stages didn't mean that she couldn't say yes to some of the other invitations. There had been a time when she'd wanted all that and to be challenged to new levels in her DJ career. Now she worried that one wrong move could catapult her career into the vortex of viral sensations, and the next big dance music DJ, gracing all the magazines. She wanted success, loved to be successful, but if things got out of hand and her identity found out, then people could show up to her orchestra performances and ruin things for her. She didn't want that. She wanted both and would do whatever she needed to have both and keep each of her identities safe. "I'll think about it. No promises, though. It's my choice."

"And your choice alone. I appreciate you taking the time to consider it." A slight bite nipped on the heel of his words. Surely she wasn't the only one who challenged him to think a bit more outside the box. She still had control over where and when she played, no matter what Tommy's title was, per their signed agreement, or how charming he was. This was her career and she'd fight tooth and nail to keep control. She needed to get her head out of her pussy and remember that.

"I'm into the teamwork you guys got going on," Oscar sang like a kid who'd opened the door on his friends during *Seven Seconds in Heaven* as he moved furniture back into place.

"Fuck off, Oz," Tommy threw at his cousin.

"You kiss Tia Judy with that mouth?" Oscar returned.

Tommy fanned him off and they finished cleaning up for Trinket.

Trinket's doorbell rang. "Pizza's here!" She rushed over to open the door and grabbed two pie boxes from the delivery woman.

"Allow me." Tommy pulled out his wallet and a few bills.

"You don't have to do that," Trinket said as she put the boxes on the table. The scent of hot pizza in cardboard flaunted through the living area.

"It's the least I can do." Tommy gave the bills to the delivery woman. "Thank you," they both said at the same time before he closed the door.

"I appreciate it, Tommy." Trinket smiled.

"I was wondering if you were going to feed us this time," Nyah said. "I would have been fine with it if you didn't, but you know."

"Pizza is always a crowd pleaser at this time of night," Trinket said, organizing the pizza boxes close by. "Dig in, guys."

They plopped on the couch and chairs in her dance floor returned to living room and shared late-night pizza and beer.

"Mmm." Nyah's mouth found the tip of the slice and she took a bite that was more appropriate for private consumption. With a mouthful of hot melted cheese, and herby sauce that nearly burnt the shit out her tongue, she said, "So good."

Oscar and Trinket both went silent as they devoured their own slices.

"Have some, Tommy," Trinket encouraged.

"I'd rather not."

"Pizza too good for your refined palate or what?" Nyah teased.

"No, I'm lactose intolerant."

"Whaaaaahhht?" Nyah said mid-chew.

"It's true," Oscar chimed in. "Growing up being lactose intolerant was brutal on him because it didn't stop him from having mad dairy."

The color splotched the tops of Tommy's cheeks and he avoided her eyes. "I think you can spare the ladies the details, cuz."

"Was it a…shit show?" Nyah winked at him. Both Oscar and Trinket snickered.

"You're funny," Tommy tossed at her.

"Oh man. I'm sorry, Tommy. Had I known I would have ordered something without cheese," Trinket said.

"And punish us all? Nah, he's all right," Oscar said.

Tommy threw a used cup at Oscar. "It's okay. You didn't even know I was coming."

"I can make you something. I'm sure Trinket has some ingredients you can have," Nyah offered.

"I'm okay. Really. I had dinner with a client earlier. I'll take a beer, though."

Nyah tossed him a cold beer from a cooler that still had a few bottles inside. Tommy grabbed it midair. "Thanks."

"You're welcome." Nyah made space on the couch next to her. She wanted him to feel welcomed. "Wanna sit?"

"You guys want to hear anything special?" Trinket asked. With pizza-filled cheeks, Nyah and Oscar held down the cricket crew.

"'Queen Tings'," Tommy requested, his eyes never leaving Nyah.

Nyah's head whipped to Tommy and she caught the pizza slipping from her hands just in time.

"The Masego track?" Trinket asked.

"The very one." Tommy smiled.

"Smooth," Nyah heard Oscar say under his breath.

"You got it." Trinket beamed and Nyah worried her friend's face might fossilize with that brimming smile.

As the groovy track oozed through the speakers, Nyah swayed to the music. The sound and lyrics penetrated and inspired her to her core. She sang the words of the song Tommy had chosen for her through constricted lungs. His musical request shifted something in her. He kept her guessing about who he was and her ideas about what he really wanted.

Chapter Eleven

Tommy wanted to solidify Nyah's attendance at Oh Ship! On top of that he had to somehow keep Herman engaged on a Sunburst spot without confirming anything. No small feat when he had to travel and work on closing deals for his other clients. His talent was in high demand and booked out through the next year. That didn't stop them from getting endorsement deals and collaborating with their publicists on magazine spreads and interviews.

The white space with deep orange posts brightened the office even with the setting sun. He wished he could be thankful for the little time he had to twiddle his thumbs, but the memory of Nyah against him scorched his body like the tattoo on his upper back and arms. His tank of willpower ran extremely low. Had he even another day in New York, he'd have found any excuse, a lost cufflink he didn't wear, the watch he'd left in her bathroom, anything to find his way back to her apartment. He'd be back in New York next week with Yaz and already counted the days.

His team gathered casually around a circular conference table that shared a space with Tommy's glass desk. The nutty aroma of MCO roasted coffee and the yeasty fragrance of baked bread and butter-rich pastries welcomed him back.

"Nice." Tommy pointed to the matcha latte, his favorite, placed in front of the empty seat at the table.

Patrick Beckham, his lawyer, pointed to Yasmin.

"You're coming to the meeting, hot off the plane. I thought this would be a treat for you." Yasmin tucked her large dark curls behind her ear.

"Thanks, Yaz," Tommy said as he shook Patrick's hand. "Patty, still formal as usual."

"Someone has to be." His friend smiled and gave Tommy's jacket-less, tucked in white shirt and his charcoal and gray slacks a thorough appraisal. "You're slipping. You could have at least worn a vest. Get it together, man."

"You wish." Tommy chuckled and looked over the dark rim of his glasses at Patrick's full vintage Glasgow brown tweed suit.

"Break it up, kids." Remy Keyes stood up and hugged him. His accountant's low-cut curly hair was a few shades darker than her skin, and the ends were copper-dusted. "It's good to see you, Tommy."

"You too, Remy. How's Cam?"

"She's doing well, thank you." Remy spoke of her wife of five years. Tommy had been friends with Remy since high school and when his business as an agent grew, he'd only trusted one person to work with him. Since then, Remy had been a trusted member on his growing team.

"I hope you've got all good news for me." He released her.

They all looked at each other.

Tommy froze and wondered what turn he expected his day to take once Yaz caught him up.

"I told you he hasn't seen it," Remy said.

"Seen what?" he asked.

"Clyde has another artist at Sunburst," Yaz said through a sour face.

"Another one?" Tommy's voice boomed. "I can't fucking believe this."

"Well, the good news is our clients are doing great. Clyde is in his wheelhouse with scouting talent. You haven't scouted like that in while," Patrick offered.

"Why the hell do you think I'm traveling to New York so often?" he snapped.

The room went quiet and Yaz chewed her lip.

"Shit. Sorry. I'm just…a bit frustrated." He huffed out a force of air. How the fuck did Clyde keep beating him in this area? Tommy rubbed his face. He was working on getting Queen Roe to perform but maybe he wasn't aggressive enough. Instead of spending time requesting songs for her, he should focus on doing his fucking job.

"How can we help?" Remy asked.

"I'm working on it but keep your ear to the ground. Thanks for telling me."

Yaz arched a brow.

"No, really. I know I'm…passionate about the news, but shit like this just reminds me to stay focused. What else is going on?" Tommy wasn't sure he wanted to know.

"Last note on Sunburst, some invitations came for

you, more specifically from Herman for their honoree ceremony."

"Cool. I'll check it out eventually. But if it fits my schedule go ahead and RSVP. You can even be my plus one."

"Sure thing, boss."

"Thanks, Yaz."

Tommy settled into his seat and Patrick slid a few papers his way. "This is just an update on where all the contracts are in the process and what's coming down the line. Yaz has been on top of it even with her new client." Patrick, an audience of one, applauded in Yaz's direction.

"You really have been able to find a nice balance between your job here, holding down the fort while I'm traveling, and handling your first client. Great work," he said to Yaz, who beamed.

"It hasn't all been crisp pickles. I knew there'd be stumbling blocks along the way, but I'm getting to know my client. I think we've found some unique opportunities. I can't wait to go to New York next week."

"It'll be our first meeting at Wallace Entertainment." Tommy sipped on his iced latte and the leafy vegetal flavoring, the creaminess of oat milk, and a slight sweetness brightened his taste buds.

"So while I'm here I'll be in LA and Vegas, I'm also scaling back on the international travel until later in the summer unless I'm on the Oh Ship cruise with Queen Roe."

"How's it going with Queen Roe, anyway?"

"Slow," Tommy said. The statement was loaded in

all sorts of ways, but the news about Clyde bugged the shit out of him.

"Are you sure she is who you should be pursuing? You're a talent hound dog, Tommy, but it kinda sounds like you might be putting all your eggs into one basket," Remy said.

He hated to admit that Remy had a point. "My gut tells me she's worth it."

"Then we have your back," Patrick said.

Tommy half smiled but his mood had shifted. "Let's cover the rest of the agenda and call it."

They adjourned and Tommy slipped behind his desk to start tackling his inbox. His confidence in his skill wavered. Maybe he'd overshot with this goal to get Queen Roe to Sunburst. He sat up in his chair. "You gonna let one artist denounce a career of success?" Fuck that. He had the skills to court any artist and Queen Roe was not different. He had to devise a new strategy.

As he scrolled through his emails, his eyes stopped on an email from Izzy. "Are you fucking kidding me?" he sighed. Isabelle Fisher was the last person he needed to hear from and made another ding in a dud of a day. The message contained a brief sentence, asking him how he'd been doing. She then cut to the chase and inquired about garnering an audience with Candy and Velvet from Bedazzled Beats before ending her message with a closing full of Xs and Os.

That's how they'd started out. Working on booking together. At that time it was to get Luke for her magazine. Their attraction shot off the charts, and their banter was lively and flirtatious. He had wanted to pursue something long-term with her until she made it clear that she was a Boy Toy Huntress and enjoyed her life just as it was. Even as the thought crossed his mind, he recalled that Nyah also had no desire for commitment.

They had history, however brief, but the signs were there. His pulse racing when he was next to her, his interest in learning about endless layers. He'd love to take Leona's advice because despite the warnings, he was falling for Nyah and fast. Problem was they didn't want the same things. Most of the women he'd casually dated hadn't been shy about what they wanted from him. Sex, access, and advancement. Over time, he'd actually been able to spot them from a mile away and they had indulged themselves for the short ride. After Izzy, he decided that he was tired of tether-less romps, and ready to find something real.

Nyah gave him a glimpse of a future together and he wanted to chase that vision all the way home. He wanted what his Aunt Carmen had groomed him for and what he longed to be to someone. If he let his feelings for Nyah get away from him…

He cut the thought off. When his aunt had died, the loss was devastating. He hoped he'd never lose someone he loved again, but life didn't work that way. He leaned back in his chair and stretched his arms behind his head. Confusion over what he wanted and respecting her boundaries had him both clearing everything in his path to chase her and throwing up walls against her powerful allure. He was hot and cold, and sending a mixed tape of messages.

Nyah.

That evening, Tommy's empty loft-like apartment greeted him with the blue evening skyline of downtown LA. He didn't need artwork for half his apartment, given the aerial views offered by the floor to ceiling windows. Thankfully, his cleaning service came twice a month or his green palms would be brown and dying of thirst. He rolled his luggage and left it by the couch. On his way to his bedroom, he rounded the island into the kitchen to fill a kettle with some water.

He took a quick shower to wash off his travel. Tomorrow he'd head to Vegas. He liked to show up regularly at his clients' performances, even with their manager present, to witness firsthand how things were going. Reminding organizers and handlers who represented his artists had its benefits. Despite his travel to New York, he had other clients who needed him and he wanted to make sure he continued to do his best for them.

Exhausted from the fight, his flight, and a day of work, he called to his home pod. "Play Giovanni Bottesini Double Bass Concerto no. 2 in B Minor." The voice confirmed his selection and the music began to play. As the deep sound of the double bass filled his loft, the image of Nyah onstage almost materialized before him. He inhaled his lungs to capacity as if it was the first time he'd breathed since leaving New York. She would have finished her philharmonic performance by now and might be out with her friends or at home making music. He imagined her in the queen-sized bed he'd seen that night in her apartment and him in it with her. His erection poked against his boxers and, without waiting for him, grew through the front slit, exposed and shiny with precum. "Nyah," he sighed. "Look what you do to me."

Stroking his girth and length until he jerked himself to satisfaction, he envisioned her small breasts in his palms, his mouth kissing the soft skin of her inner thigh, her long legs wrapped around him as he filled her. His imagination couldn't settle on a position, because she'd be lovely in any one. His mind's eye zoomed in on the beads of sweat on her neck, he heard her pant his name in Dolby surround sound and he exploded in his hand at that thought. Could he have her and, if yes, at what cost?

He needed to hear her voice and called New York. She played the hall tonight and should be home. Perhaps if she relaxed enough she'd see the Oh Ship was a great opportunity.

"I can't talk right now," Nyah said.

He sat up from his ejaculation fog. "Everything okay?"

"I fucked up." She sounded shaken.

"Can I help?" He smacked himself upside the head. What the hell was he going to do from LA?

"No. I have to go."

"I'm back in NY on Monday. I guess we'll catch up then."

Click.

He didn't know what had happened but whatever it was didn't sound good.

Nyah had no time to talk to Tommy. She threw off her clothes while simultaneously scrubbing makeup off her face. She swiped through the clothes in her closet for a performance outfit, which would normally be placed out on her bed. Not today. "How the fuck did I let this happen?"

Here's how…

It had started out when she received a call from Trinidad, a well-known classical musician that she'd played with over the years, who coincidentally had a spot at Artistique and wanted to collaborate with her at one of the art installations. She had accepted, which prompted her to reevaluate whether or not she'd actually needed to become Tommy's client. She then justified that going into the festival as Nyah Monroe with a well-known, agented, classical musician was different from going in on her own as Queen Roe.

One of the bartenders at Rebel texted her to do a quick spot at the park that evening. Floating off the high of her luck, she was in. She'd played Rebel the night before and slept in on her day off. She had finished practicing, and with no other plans, was down to spend it with the crew from Rebel for a little fun. Excited to play an impromptu set outdoors in the park with Trinket, she had quickly donned her Queen Roe attire and headed for a long overdue day on the grass and under the spring sun. There were hours of drinks, a little smoke, and a lot of irresponsibility on her part once her guard had fallen. She had been too spontaneous and hadn't double-checked her calendar in two days. All hell broke loose when she got a call from Gladys around seven.

"Where the fuck are you? You missed call time and Martin is freaking out. You better be hospitalized or dead. If neither one of those things applies, then your ass better be limping, bloody or both when you arrive."

"I'm supposed to be at the concert hall?" Nyah had been too fucked up to look at her calendar to see just exactly how she'd gotten her weeks mixed up. Drunk or stoned, she had always got it right—except that one time when she'd gotten halfway to the elevator, and dragging her bass behind her, before she realized she had on psychedelic booty shorts and platform Dr. Martens.

She had always made it, had always caught herself before disaster struck. She had never dropped a fucking ball.

"I gotta go," she announced vapidly to Frisbee tossers in the distance.

"Where're you going, Queen?" Oscar had asked her.

"I gotta be somewhere."

Trinket had hurried over.

"You good?"

Nyah shook her head. "I'm supposed to be at the concert hall. Fuck! This is the worst possible fuckup of all fuckups."

"No!" Trinket had said, sloppily, still drunk and high.

"I can't go like this. I gotta get home, change, sober up, and—"

"Yeah, go. Call if you need anything."

Nyah had grabbed a Lyft back to her apartment and now, as she tried to get herself together to get to the concert hall before intermission, her stomach flipped and her heart raced. This was bad. Really, really bad.

She packed her bass and clamped it shut, throwing random plucks of Kleenex and candy into the side pocket. When she realized that made no sense she started on her hair. With each comb through her strands, her shoulders sagged lower to the ground with the time-consuming activity. Her phone chimed.

Gladys: Martin is piiiiiiiiiiissssed

Though Gladys had been giving her the play by play, the expletive text was way less than helpful.

Nyah: Heading over now

The lie made her feel better but she still smelled like the park, her hair was a mess and she had that alert type of buzz that made her nauseous.

Gladys: Intermission is over

Nyah's shoulders slumped. Any chance of redemption for tonight had passed. How was she going to explain this? She paced until she tired herself out and plopped into a chair, where she stayed for what felt like an hour but had likely been ten minutes.

She jumped up to get her phone so she could check her calendar. Her performance wasn't in its normal place. "What the fuck?" She clicked into today's box and saw an entry from Tommy. *Back in LA and on to Vegas—Back in NY on Monday.* The location of the entry was lengthy enough to hide her philharmonic event because of the other standing appointments in the box.

She threw her phone, hard, into the couch. Her hands flew to her mouth and she blew into her hands. The heat on her face burned so much that she went to the bathroom to rinse her skin and cursed Tommy the whole way.

This was his fault.

Chapter Twelve

Tommy met Nyah at the café across from her apartment. Her no-frills text response to his request to connect had felt dry, but he reminded himself that this was about business and he needed to stay focused on what he wanted. A coffee and a little persuasion to steer her toward Oh Ship rested at the top of his agenda. Right under it was Sunburst.

His breath hitched in his chest when he saw her. She wore a matching pair of off-white sweats, black-and-white-striped shower slides, and white socks. Her hair was a full-blown Afro with no accoutrements like her usual headbands or scarves and she looked like she hadn't slept well. She stopped before him with arms crossed.

"Uh…hey," he tentatively greeted her.

She dropped into the chair across from him at the round wood table. "Hello."

Given her formality, he knew something was up. "How's it going?"

Her sigh was like a light whistle right before a kettle screamed for attention. "I've been better."

He wasn't meeting her for a game of riddles, but he'd play. "What's up?"

"Besides the fact that I missed my philharmonic performance, nothing at all."

His body hit the backrest as if the news had traveled on the physical plane. "Oh shit. What happened?" He rushed to pull up her calendar on his phone.

She flattened her palms on the table and leaned in. "Your entry on my calendar fucked me up."

He stopped scrolling and his eyes lifted to the accusation on her face. "Me? What? How?" If he had anything to do with ruining her schedule and her performances, he'd lose her—not to mention feel absolutely horrible.

"I'm sure you think it's great, letting me know your comings and goings, but your entry blocked my performance event."

He squinted, trying to figure out exactly what she meant. Being a detail-oriented kind of guy, he wanted to undo whatever he'd done and prevent it from happening again. He needed her to know he'd never do anything to hurt either of her careers. "I don't understand. Did I delete your philharmonic entry?"

She tilted her head and her Afro followed. "Well, no, but moved it down."

"Moved it down?" he parroted.

She nodded.

"Okay, so did you check your calendar?" he asked.

She frowned and chewed her lip. "I know my schedule but I got my weeks confused."

"So you're the one who didn't look at your calendar."

"I did. Well, I glanced at it, and my performance wasn't visible but your travel plans were."

"You glanced at it. Did you have an alert?"

"No." She sputtered. "Why are you cross-examining me? I told you what happened."

"I'm gathering the facts." He knew he sounded detached but right now he didn't need to add the gas of his own emotions to the fire.

"I told you the facts."

"Okay, so explain to me again how this is my fault?"

"The entries you put on my calendar moved my events below the content box, so I couldn't see it." She huffed.

"But you know how to scroll, right? You have two careers and have even created a fake employee named Nancy. You're telling me that you don't know how to check your schedule beyond what's there."

"Of course I do." Her agitation grew with every move, which wasn't his goal, but he also didn't want to claim fault unless fault was due.

"Nyah, help me out here. I put entries on your calendar with your permission. So far, it's been fine."

"Yeah, but your entry screwed things up." She rubbed her reddening eyes.

"How? I'm sorry if the entry confused you but your performance is right here." He showed her the calendar.

"It doesn't even matter. I missed my performance and I don't know what that means because I've never screwed up like this. I always have things separate and organized, so I can manage them. I meet with Martin tomorrow and I don't know what to tell him. He…" She choked.

She guzzled down some water.

He knew how much classical music meant to her, so the prospect of losing her place in the philharmonic couldn't be easy. He was meant to focus on their business relationship, but how could he when she was clearly upset. "I'm sorry. This must be stressful. How can I help?"

"You can't. No one can. I'm the one who'll have to sit across from Martin and explain myself." He didn't think it was possible for her to sink lower into her chair but she somehow managed to do it.

He scooted his chair over to her and took her hand and warmed it between his. "It'll be okay."

"How can you say that? Are you a fly on Martin's unruly hair now, too?" She tilted her head.

Though in despair, a bit of the firecracker he knew shined through. "Because you're talented and amazing and they'd be fools to let you go."

She stared at him for a few seconds and looked down at his hands wrapped around hers.

He released her hand but stayed by her side. "Let's get you something warm to drink," he said and called over the waitress.

Nyah ordered a ginger mint tea with lemon.

"Be right back," their waitress said.

"So," he ventured. "What were you doing that day?" He doubted she'd forget her performance for just any random thing.

"I met up with the Rebel crew. Played a small set in the park with Trinket. I was having fun and enjoying my *day off*." She air-quoted.

The idea that she'd lost herself in her DJ life confirmed what he already knew even if she didn't. Though she may enjoy her classical career, she lost herself in her DJ life. Her tea arrived and she dunked the tea bag a few times before taking quiet sips as the steam rose up to her forehead.

"Maybe it's what you needed. I know that doesn't help your situation, but you're human," he said.

"You mean I'm not a super badass bitch who has all her shit together. No!" She poured drama over every word.

"You're a badass bitch that is fallible. Welcome to the club."

She smiled for the first time since they'd met up and the joy it gave him was also troublesome.

"Hey, I have to head to Brooklyn in a bit, but I wanted to touch base with you about Oh Ship. Have you given it any more thought?"

She shook her head "This weekend really threw me and, honestly, Tommy, I won't be able to think straight until I meet with Martin."

Her answer wasn't a straight no. "I understand," he said, but wished he could close this deal sooner rather than later. He'd just have to hold off any confirmation until she gave him a firm answer.

"I'll let you know," she said.

"Do you feel a little better?"

She pinched her fingers together.

"A little is better than nothing," he returned. "Also, do you want me to clear your calendar of any of my events? I'd hate for this to cause a problem in the future."

Her cheeks reddened. "For now it's okay. I just need to double-check the days."

"You're sure?" he persisted.

"It's fine, Tommy," she said. "Thanks for the tea."

"Anytime."

He left for his meeting more stressed than before he'd met with her. He didn't know how her meeting with her conductor would pan out but he prayed that whatever happened steered her toward a festive cruise.

Nyah's mouth hung open for about five seconds before she spoke. "I'm what?"

"You're suspended," Martin repeated.

"I...but... No, I mean..." She sighed and swallowed the thick saliva in her mouth. Suspensions were things that happened to other musicians. Not her. "For how long?"

"Two weeks."

She blinked in disbelief and to clear her tear-blurred vision. She'd expected to be reprimanded but a full suspension sounded horrible. Had she ever been suspended? For anything?

Martin had expressed his disappointment, especially when she told him the truth that she'd just forgotten. What else was she going to tell him? That she'd been in the park deejaying, drunk, and faded?

"Use your time to reevaluate your commitment to the philharmonic. The only reason why you won't be replaced is because I believe in your talent. Until recently, you've always been a reliable musician with untapped potential. It's your choice as to how you want to move forward, but should this ever happen again, Nyah, you will lose your chair."

Her inner gasp was louder than the ones heard upon a mystery reveal. "Yes, sir."

She left Martin's office and headed home. On her way she texted the headline to Gladys, who responded with many sad face emojis.

Gladys: On my way to practice. Talk later?

Nyah gave her a thumbs-up. On low battery mode, she walked to her apartment with the agony of defeat. What she wouldn't give to undo all of this.

"What the hell am I going to do for two weeks?" she asked her living room.

She opened her computer in an attempt to be productive, but she scrolled and clicked on autopilot because her mind remained overstimulated from her conversation with Martin. Maybe her chaotic mind needed more chaos to calm down. She typed into a search box and clicked on the official website for Oh Ship.

Nyah's thumb glided back and forth gently against her bottom lip. Her thoughts drifted as she clicked through videos and images of the cruise. "I can't believe I'm actually considering this."

Sure, the event was on a cruise ship, but when they docked, masses of fans crawled the beaches. Tommy said she wouldn't be headlining and could safely avoid super large crowds if she did a ship performance and maybe a day party on the beach. If she agreed, which she hadn't decided, she'd make that part crystal clear.

She went over Tommy's email, which listed the terms, as well as encouraging her to request what she needed to give her best performance. That is, if she agreed to perform. She stretched her arms and back. With nothing but her thoughts and her suspension to pine over, she fooled herself into believing that a cruise out of New York to overdose on sun wasn't a good idea. "More like a stars-fucking-aligned type of idea," she muttered.

Her phone rang and when she saw Gladys's number, she put it on speaker.

"Whatcha doing?" Gladys cooed.

"Wallowing in self-pity, how about you?" Nyah asked and waited for Gladys to present an alternative.

"You and I are getting some dinner at seven," Gladys said. "I mean, unless you and Tommy are hooking up."

Nyah smothered her face with her hand. "He's out of town, so an opportunity to get out of the house for food sounds perfect?" All true, but eventually, Nyah would have to give up the jig.

"Good, because you need some cheering up and some comradery—my specialty—especially after what happened today," Gladys said.

Nyah groaned. "Don't remind me."

"Meet up with you in a few."

After they hung up, Nyah went back to her evaluation of Oh Ship. She had to admit that the depression from being suspended might be influencing her decision but so what if it was? Should she stay home and take her punishment, agonize over not being at the concert hall and replay her fun day with the Rebel crew as some sort of penance, or just wild out? Even now she still had to weigh the pros and cons of going for her DJ career. She'd been subsisting on guilt and needed a real meal.

A few hours later, Nyah met Gladys at Miss Lily's

in Soho for some Jamaican fusion. Gladys squeezed her like she hadn't seen her in months. "I'm sorry this is happening."

Contrary to Nyah's mood, the familiar reggae and dancehall music livened up the red and yellow diner. The place offered a pleasant departure from the classical music they played and also from the dance music of Queen Roe.

"I'm so glad you agreed to come out," Gladys said, as she munched on her jerk chicken and rice and peas.

"I needed this. For real." Nyah rolled her shoulders. "I just can't believe this is happening."

"Do you know if you have to let CeCe know for London?" Gladys asked.

"Shit! I didn't even think about that." Nyah dropped her fork. "I'm going to go with no."

"I feel like I'm stressing you out more. I'm normally better at this."

"I know you mean well." Nyah knew Gladys worried about her career as much as she did, so it was no surprise that Gladys gave the situation a 360-degree perspective.

"Let's just enjoy ourselves and fuck the philharmonic," Gladys said.

That made Nyah laugh. "Yeh, mon! Fuck the philharmonic. For now, anyway." Nyah sucked on a piece of her curried shrimp, and the bright flavor of peppers and jasmine rice exploded in her mouth. "Okay, here's your second shot at taking my mind off today. Tell me what else is going on."

"Oh, Evan asked me out." Gladys dropped it as casually as she lifted her fork to her mouth.

Nyah choked on her food. She reached for her glass of rum punch and took a gulp to clear her throat. "What?"

"Yes, ma'am."

Nyah wiped her mouth with her napkin. "I knew he liked you. So when are you two going out?"

"We're not. I turned him down." Gladys rolled her tongue in her cheek.

"Stop. Why?" Nyah asked.

"Because he's Evan and I just can't right now." Gladys mixed her rice around on her plate.

"Gladys?" Nyah had to agree that Evan's personality had some rough edges and wasn't one she appreciated half of the time, but beneath it all he wasn't a bad guy. He just found it impossible to hide his feelings when it came to Gladys.

"If he really likes me, he can wait a little bit." Gladys smirked.

Nyah pointed her slender pinky at Gladys. "I see you. You're playing hard to get."

"I gave him some goal posts to hit. If he does well, we'll go out."

"Oh my goodness. Like what?" Nyah moved closer to Gladys.

"Checking his ego for one. Being nicer."

"Gladys. You can't change him. It's either you like him or you don't."

"I think he has potential, but he needs improvement." Gladys may have been nonchalant but the way she bit her lip and suppressed her smile showed she really liked Evan.

Nyah giggled. "I cannot wait to see how this pans out. What if you get London?"

"He can visit." Gladys scoffed. "I mean, we haven't even gone on one date yet."

"But you like him. Admit it, you like him."

Gladys chewed her lip. "I guess."

Nyah grabbed at the air in front of her. "I'll take it."

"How are things with you and Tommy?" Gladys asked.

Nyah hadn't found the courage to clarify Tommy's role, which would mean outing her dual life to Gladys, and things were getting more complicated. Nyah's mouth hadn't been the same since it had met Tommy's. However, her desires were only contained by distance and the fact that Tommy's very existence and profession reminded her of Carlo and his cavalier handling of the DJ career she held dear.

"We were thinking of going away for a few days together." Internally Nyah smothered her face, like the emoji. She really needed to fess up, and soon. "I don't know, that's why I'm bringing it up." Nyah left out a lot of details about this trip, but still, having a friend to talk to who was part of her other life had its benefits.

"That sounds like a great idea.

"I think it's too soon and I should be here suffering." Even with the rollercoaster events of the past few days, she found herself replaying their kiss, and how powerful he'd felt between her legs when she'd jumped on him in excitement over Artistique.

"Oh, come on. It's not too soon. You're right on schedule. This is where you find out if he puts the seat down and brings you a cup of coffee after a disagreement and if you can even stand each other after twenty-four hours together," Gladys rambled.

"You know how hard it is for me to date. Maybe I don't really want someone like Tommy muddling my life."

"Maybe he can muddle it into a lovely mojito or caipirinha?"

Gladys offered this with the innocence of someone who only knew half the life of her close friend. After what Nyah had been through with Carlo, she'd dissected her life into decisive parts. When she'd first met Tommy, she'd stressed her need to stay incognito. Her need to hide her identities in order to be successful was likely part of the reason she was single. Tommy's knowledge of both sides of her life made her feel defenseless, scared and alive all at the same time, professionally but especially personally.

If you only knew, my friend. "Well—"

"Bah-bah-bah. Why can't he enhance it? You know how I feel about you and your love life. I'm thrilled that you found Tommy, even though you've told me this much." Gladys pinched her index finger and thumb together. "Are you hiding some odd kink of his or something?"

"No." Nyah chuckled. "It's just new still. I don't want to make him a bigger part of my life in case things don't work out." *Wow! Best bullshit I've come up with in weeks.* Funny thing was that the bullshit rang true.

"I hear you. Do you trust him? Because you know that's a big deal breaker."

"I don't not trust him," Nyah said.

"We need to go out. When you feel comfortable, we'll all go out for drinks or something."

"Yeah, with Evan," Nyah threw back at her.

"Uh…okay." Gladys was no closer to a commitment with Evan than she had been when she'd dropped her bomb earlier.

"Uh-huh."

"Back to you. I think you should go on this trip with Tommy. YOLO." Gladys raised her hands in the air like the fans at Queen Roe's shows.

"That came out of nowhere."

"I want you to give this a chance. We have to be able to find a balance with our demanding musician life. Just make sure to carry your bass and practice for when you come back. The last thing you want to do is show up sloppy on the fundys. Martin already has you on his shit list."

Nyah threw a napkin at Gladys. "Thanks."

"I'm just looking out for you, girl." Gladys raised her glass and encouraged Nyah to do the same. "Cheers to you, girl. May all your ups and downs be between the sheets."

"Cheers," Nyah said through laughter that busted from her gut. They clinked glasses and Nyah drained the rest of her drink and ordered another.

Her evening out with Gladys had not only cheered her up but given her some insight. She had two careers and though she had fears of doing something to tilt the balance she tried to maintain, during the suspension she had free range to focus on her DJ career. She could stay in New York and stick to what she knew or she could venture out and take advantage of the time she had been given, no matter how much she wished she could turn back the time and make her philharmonic call time. It was only when she and Gladys were walking to the 4-train subway station that she realized she'd made her decision. She'd play Oh Ship, but Tommy was off limits.

Holy shit.

Chapter Thirteen

Nyah glided her rotational luggage by her side with her portable double bass strapped to her back. The massive cruise ship nestled in the ocean at Port Canaveral awaited her. *Time to walk the plank.* She climbed up the ramp. The fans were already wild with booze or substances and the music blared from the deck with the sounds of the hottest hit from the summer. "Love Me Love You" by Bedazzled Beats featuring Tekko, Rob Ready and Zazzle. The song by Tommy's most recent successful clients only proved to remind her of Tommy's influence, ambition, and success. She had swapped the hectic city vibe for an even more wild and self-contained one.

She shouldn't have agreed to this. Once she set foot on the ship she'd be trapped. Between the drones whirring overhead to capture the live action and the cameras and film crews lurking around and adding to the media kit for post cruise highlights, this was more exposure than Nyah had had in a very long time. Still, the excitement of performing to a new demographic of fans energized her steps enough to keep moving forward. She and Tommy would only be on the cruise for three days together before they docked in the Bahamas and returned home. The ship would then sail on to Punta Cana.

Tommy waited for her at the entrance in casual shirt and slacks, and she didn't miss her city or her apartment as much as she had a few seconds ago. He wore a dark pair of gold-rimmed shades that only showed off the brown in his hair. He handed over his luggage to the attendant and the daylight highlighted his defined arm through his ivory-colored linen shirt. She wanted to be in his arms again and experience a longer hug than the one he'd given her the last time. The reasons she'd bulleted as to why she and Tommy were a bad idea seemed to cross themselves off the list every time his behavior contradicted whatever she thought of him, like the fact that he actually cared about his artists, even though the jury was still out on whether or not he cared about her as a person.

"Hi," Tommy greeted her. "How was your flight?"

"Early." Nyah groaned, remembering the early flight she'd opted to take rather than spend the night at a hotel close by the port.

"You had a choice." His not so subtle "I told you so" lacked any negativity.

"True." She agreed. "Don't let me choose that poorly ever again."

"Noted." He took her rolling luggage from her. "Glad to see you ditched your coat."

Along with carrying her luggage, he draped her coat over his arm. "The weather's much nicer here." She stated the obvious, folded her coat, and stuffed it into the attached carryon bag. She felt comfortable in her white sleeveless fitted midriff tank top and high-waisted jeans but with the rising sun she'd be ready for less clothes in an hour.

"Need anything in here for the next few hours?" Tommy asked as he handed her luggage over to the attendant to be taken to their rooms.

"No, I'm all set."

"Your artist pass and key." Tommy handed her a black lanyard badge and envelope. His friendly greeting carried a detachment that she'd noted in their last meeting at the café. That was, until she'd had a meltdown about her suspension. Wasn't that what she'd wanted? Everything in its place and behaving as expected? "Let's get familiar with our home for the next few days," he added.

Bodies ready to discard their clothes, soak up the sun, get trashed, and absorb a marathon of musical performances trotted through the corridors, pulling her from her thoughts. As artists and agents, she and Tommy had been let on the ship via a separate entrance, but so were VIP guests and fans that looked no different from general ship population. Tommy accompanied her and they were quickly led through security and directed on board.

She liked being close to Tommy and reminded herself that she'd come to work. She'd already made the hard choice of crossing fucking him off of her checklist, but the way he somehow continued to make her heart patter didn't give her much of a shield to protect against that sweet smile, smooth eyebrows, and great hair. She'd often seen him as this driven-at-all-costs kind of guy but when she'd seen him interact with his clients, he reminded her of a dad looking out for his kids on the circuit. It was endearing. Endearing and dangerous.

After Artistique would she be so pliable to his suggestions? She'd already done what she didn't think she'd do for him. She was on Oh Ship, for fuck's sake. It wasn't a festival, per se, but everyone knew Oh Ship and many big names had sailed the seas, blaring EDM to the marine life under the sea. Would she be able to keep her celebrity contained? Without the philharmonic performances hovering, she didn't have that to use as an excuse for anything. What that freedom did was bring up some of the cacophonous concerns she'd muted. For a millisecond she thought about giving a shitty performance, but her early performances, that had been criticized and compared to her father's, replayed in her mind. Back then, disappointment of being left out on a limb to either balance or plummet to the ground knotted her stomach. She'd never put herself or the fans through that again, intentional or not. The Oh Ship fans had paid money for a cruise devoted to EDM and Nyah neither had the heart, nor the lack of integrity or professionalism, to fuck it up. She vowed once and for all to give these people her best.

"Wanna drink?" Tommy slowed by one of the attendants holding a tray of blue, pink and yellow liquid in bowl-like glasses.

Hands free, and already overstimulated by the surrounding color, sights, and sounds on an already fatigued brain, she struggled to decide. "I don't know if that's such a good idea. I've been up since three to make all this magic happen." She circled a spread hand around herself. "Coffee might be better."

"Coffee," Tommy ordered from the bartender.

"With a splash of cognac, please," she added.

"Ah," he said to her. "A carajillo. My aunt drank hers

with Ron Barcelo rum. She'd have it with her dessert." His smile faltered and he struggled to get it back.

She couldn't shake the feeling that what he had shared was important in some way. And though sunglasses shielded his eyes, something in his voice rang of sadness. Her heart raced at the thought of him hurting in any way and she pivoted. "Smart woman. Might as well be awake and somewhat twisted. I don't perform until tomorrow afternoon on the pool deck. Most I'll do is catch some sun and some Zs."

He recovered effortlessly. "You're bullshittin' me. You're on a cruise. Go see a DJ or a show. Jump into the pool or go dancing. Make some friends."

"Thanks, Dad. I appreciate the suggestions, but I don't know."

"Why? You have the VIP pass. Have a meal, mountain climb, do that surfing shit. Maybe go to the spa, get a massage, and a happy ending if your masseuse is willing."

"Tommy!" She blushed so hard she could have been a tomato.

"Just making sure you're listening." He gave her that smile that left her defenseless against his magnetism.

"I'm listening." With any luck her face wasn't as colorful as her tinted sunglasses.

"All I'm saying is to have a little fun while you're here. It can't hurt to enjoy yourself. Can it?"

"I guess not."

"I have to make a few calls before we do the safety check. You okay here on your own?"

She smirked. "I'm not five, man. I'm good."

He smiled. "I'll be back in a few."

Nyah enjoyed the banter between them, and commanded herself to chill and yes, have a little bit of fun. She eased onto a stool, sipping her coffee, the heated cognac clearing her sinuses like a menthol vapor rub. She was glad that Tommy's spirits had leveled up again. Now that her initial curiosity about what caused the downturn in his mood was growing, she wanted to know more. The deck buzzed with pre-sail-away excitement. No sooner did Tommy leave than the bees swarmed. She'd often met men who used her as arm candy, until she started to talk about things they didn't have the levels or the interest to verbally spar with her. She blamed her height, made higher with her three-inch wedge sneakers that only lengthened her legs more. With those, along with her huge Afro puffs, she couldn't be missed. Most dudes taunted, blew kisses, and kept it moving, with the exception of one bee that plopped down in the seat right next to her.

"Hey, beautiful, you're going to stick to that old lady drink or can I get you something stronger? I mean, I'm not saying that coffee's not a good choice to stay amped, but thought I'd ask."

"I'll stick with this for the time being." She kept her hand over her coffee as she held it and sipped.

"I'll have what she's having," he said to the bartender.

Her chuckle was lighter than the steam warming her palm. "Sure you can handle a little cup of coffee?"

"I can handle it." His attempt at flirting, though cute, didn't quite move her, but he seemed harmless enough.

Play at your own risk, sir.

The bartender set a short cup of coffee in front of her gentleman caller and when he brought it to his lips, his eyes blinked several times. "You turned up your caffeine. I'm down with that." He took a sip and immediately started sneezing. "I underestimated your alcohol game."

"Facts. You're not the first." She pinched a napkin from the holder and flagged it to him. "You okay?"

"Getting there." He coughed into the napkin. "I'm Irwin."

"Nice to meet you, Irwin." When she didn't immediately serve up information, he asked, "So what's your name?"

"My friends call me Queen but you can call me Roe."

His jaw dropped. "Oh shit, you're Queen Roe. I heard you play at The Boiler a few weeks ago. Everyone says Rebel is your home but that set was tight."

"Thanks."

"Sorry I didn't recognize you."

She waved him off. "It's cool. Glad I blend."

"You'll be performing here, right?" Irwin's excitement enlivened his entire body.

"Yeah, tomorrow. I hope you'll come through."

"Hell yeah! I'm pumped. You're the real deal." He watched her for a few seconds and she was hip to this pick-up game to sense the courage he summoned to shoot his shot. "You'll probably be partying with the bigwigs, but maybe you want to hang out by the pool. I could buy you a drink or something," Irwin said.

He was not blessed with game, but Nyah appreciated the effort. She was about to tell him so when Tommy returned. Her agent's movements stiffened as he approached.

"I see you took one of my suggestions." Tommy's body blocked the sun like a sequoia and Nyah could have sworn that he'd also grown to the size of one, by the way he towered over both her and Irwin.

"Friend of yours?" Irwin asked.

"My agen—" Nyah was about to explain.

"I'm a friend of hers." Tommy pointed to the stool under Irwin's ass. "That's my seat."

"Oh, my bad." Irwin made little attempt to rise to his feet.

"Boombox? Irwin? Meet each other." She made the introductions.

"For real? You're Tommy "Boombox?" Irwin scrambled out of the chair and Nyah respected Irwin's investment as a fan. He probably knew more industry people on the cruise than she did.

"You sure know a lot about everyone here, Irwin," Nyah noted.

"Are you with the press?" Tommy asked as he claimed his seat next to her.

"Nah, I live for EDM so I make it a point to know, like, everything. I used my whole winter savings to do a VIP ticket so I could meet the artists and stuff. My friends, too."

"I love the dedication." Nyah had memorized and catalogued the musicians whose techniques she loved and mimicked as a young girl. As an adult, her voracious musical consumption continued. Irwin grew on her the longer he lingered, and whether he knew it or not, he'd been friend zoned. Great for her, maybe not so great for him. "That's cool."

"Yeah." Tommy added, "Make sure you check out Queen Roe when she plays tomorrow."

"I will." Irwin's eyes smiled at her. "I also owe you a drink. I hope I see you...like this again."

Tommy's smug expression was only visible to her as Irwin gave her all his attention before turning quickly to Tommy. "Oh and you, too, Boombox. It's an honor."

Even Tommy couldn't deny Irwin's charm.

"Thanks."

"Well, I'll see you guys around. Bon voyage." Irwin shot the rest of his coffee and then waved his last round of goodbyes.

"You're like a honeybun in the middle of an ant farm."

"Because one guy chatted with me? It's not that deep." She was a queen with an empty throne that Irwin wanted to fill. For all his sweet flirtations and attention, Irwin wasn't who she wanted. "I think I'm going to take a look around the ship."

Tommy stood. "Mind if I come with you? I'd like to see the ship, too. Get my bearings. Plus, I can save you from another Irwin."

She side-eyed him. "Did I look like I needed saving?"

"I guess not," Tommy said. "I'd like to come with you if you'd like the company."

"I'd like *your* company," she emphasized.

Tommy leaned toward her and she smelled the light fragrance of his cologne as the wind whipped gently at his shirt. He reached for her hand. "Nyah, I—"

The announcement requesting them to meet below deck for the cruise safety check came across the speakers.

Tommy drew back and let her hand go. "You should finish your drink and we'll head down."

Damnit. He could have told her anything. He could have explained his quick mood shift earlier, recapped his business call, or told her that he couldn't stop himself from kissing her any longer. Now she'd never know, and maybe that was for the best. "Yeah, okay." She drank the remnants of her coffee and hoisted to her feet. "Ready."

She and Tommy were corralled with everyone else on the ship according to their section to go over boat safety. Crewmembers handed them life jackets and gave their spiel, a combination of welcomes, warnings, and hazards. Nyah hadn't been on a ship since her first spring break with her friends, but she was no stranger to boat safety. Before that it had been private yachts with her father in high school, either for his gigs that she'd been allowed to attend or with her family.

She fixed her life vest before the announcer gave instruction.

"You're a pro at this." Tommy fumbled with the latches and strings. "I always have trouble fixing this thing."

"You've probably been on more boats than I have, being in this industry. I'm surprised this is where you struggle," she teased. "Need some help?"

Tommy nodded. "It shouldn't be this complicated."

"No, it shouldn't. One of your latches is a little worn."

"Great. I get the defective life jacket." His sarcasm vibrated though the thick, light flotation material around his neck.

"It'll still work, but we should probably let them know." She secured his life vest with a few tugs and pulls. "Now I get to keep you safe." She returned her attention to listen to the safety instructions.

She felt his warm strong hand envelop hers and all her body functions ceased.

"Thanks," he whispered into her ear, his breath bringing her back to life.

Nyah had never been so disappointed when the cruise safety check ended than when this one did because it wasn't until their safety lecture ended that Tommy released her hand.

"We should check out our rooms," Tommy suggested. "We'll take the scenic route so we can see the ship."

"Okay." When they were on deck, Nyah saw Port Canaveral in the distance. "We're moving? I didn't even feel it."

"Wow, you noticed earlier than most people do when they're at the bar."

Nyah hadn't even bothered to look where they were and followed Tommy, her mind hazy from holding his hand a short while ago. However, when they took the corridor to the staterooms, she paid attention.

She rushed to unlock the door with her key and skipped inside. She'd been in fancy places before because of her father, from great parties on yachts, and in hotel suites, to private planes and islands, but she'd never stayed in such accommodations on a cruise before. When she'd gone with her friends, they barely spent time in their room so they'd gotten whatever was available to house their stuff while they partied. Now as she beelined for the large sliding glass doors with the balcony and the surrounding views of the ocean, she thought this was something she could get used to. She continued to survey the cabin with Tommy hanging at the doorway. He finally followed her in.

"Wow." She was awed. "This is phenomenal."

"You're one of the performers and my client." He

didn't boast but Tommy had shown her his provider side before. He'd made sure she received the royal treatment. The ship still sailed close enough to see land but soon the expanse of the ocean would be her only view.

"I can't believe I have a stateroom!"

"*We* have staterooms."

"Wait, what? Where's your room?" she asked.

Tommy pointed to an open door with a connecting suite. "Right through there. We have adjoining suites."

"Well isn't that something." She blindly felt for something to lean against until she found a chair. She tried to appear casual but her stomach flipped at the intimacy and closeness of having Tommy this close for three days.

"Yeah. We can share our living space so if we want to debrief or do work, we can connect, but we each have full privacy, also."

"This is great, Tommy. I really appreciate the hookup." Nyah was still wrapping her head around the close proximity she now found herself in with Tommy.

"My pleasure." He offered her a slight bow. "Get used to it. There's a dinner tonight at Bistro at seven. We can go together if you want."

"I'd like that," she said.

"Then I'll knock at six thirty."

When he left to enter into his suite, she stared at the partition that separated them. With Tommy this close to her would the barrier be enough to keep them apart?

Chapter Fourteen

Tommy sharpened the hairlines on his cheek, chin, and neck. He liked to look good, but he'd be a fool if he didn't admit that he wanted to impress Nyah. He rinsed the razor and sighed. Had he made a good choice with the adjoining suites? Was that too close for comfort for her? For him? She seemed to be okay. He'd gotten to know her over that past months and was confident that if the arrangements weren't to her liking, he'd have heard otherwise via her witty sarcasm that he'd come to appreciate.

He smoothed his hair with a light mousse to give it some finger-raking friendly hold. He traded his dark, black-rimmed glasses for brown ones. He'd hoped to have his contact lenses by the time he took this trip but because of the customization for his astigmatism they took longer to make. He preferred glasses mostly, because it gave him something to do when boredom struck or to make a point. He understood how Nyah felt to some degree with her dual identity, because when he wore contacts no one recognized him. He splashed on his aftershave and misted his cologne. The woodsy, sweet scent of oud oil and bergamot filled the bedroom.

He dressed quickly in his white shirt and slowed his pace. The countdown to Artistique ticked away, which also meant that Sunburst drew closer. If he didn't lock in an artist soon, he could kiss the potential spot that Herman was trying to hold for him goodbye. His jaw tensed. He couldn't rush Nyah. Her unshakable philosophy on performing at festivals presented a major obstacle, though the success of her performances here at Oh Ship might open her up to the possibility of expanding her view. Most of all he wished she'd have a little fun and open up. He never had to tell his clients this, but Nyah managed her duality with such precision that he thought letting her Afro puffs loose might do her good. During their last chat, she'd confessed her suspension, a situation that created an opportunity for him, but had also hurt her. If he could at all aid in making her feel better, he would. Visible or not, each passing minute changed something between them without much help from either of them.

He struck his knuckles on the partition door between their suites.

"Come in. It's open," Nyah called. He entered but didn't see her. She'd left the entryway on her side unlocked to allow him access to her suite. His heart fluttered when she emerged from her bedroom, a vision in a clingy, white, sleeveless dress. Like an artist, she had stroked creative designs over her eyes and cheeks with liner and colored powders. The neckline plummeted to her navel and his stomach dropped with it as if he were on a wild rollercoaster ride. Her breasts were kept covered by hope in the form of double-sided fashion tape that she pressed on occasionally. He wanted to gently peel the material to the side to expose what lay beneath. The deep cuts on the sides of her garment revealed the calligraphy tattoo on her ribcage. He longed for a close-up of the words.

Tommy vaguely heard her. "What?"

"I guess we got the memo. We match," she said. When he didn't respond, she pressed. "Tommy?" She waved at him. "Hi. You okay?"

He sucked in air. "Yeah." He blinked a few times, his face ablaze. "You look lovely."

She slid her tinted glasses over the rich, deep war paint as if embodying her dual identity holistically. "Thanks. You're stopping NYC traffic, too, I see." Her face grimaced like someone had shoved a quarter-cup of slugs in her mouth. She rushed, tossing her suite card and phone into her clutch. "I mean, you look handsome." She flattened her palm against a nearby wall to steady herself as she slipped on one strappy sandal at a time. The moderate heel made her slightly taller than him even though her hair always gave her a bit of a height advantage.

"Thanks," he said. "Ready to go?"

"I am."

He opened the door for her, resisting the impulse to reach for her hand as they strolled through the connecting corridors. They passed a viewpoint by their private elevators. The secluded and serene location resembled a wallpaper of sea and horizon. If he meditated it would be a good spot. The corner tucked behind one of the mid deck promenade areas and away from the loud roaring of the engine on the other end of the ship.

"This is a great place to truly chill," she said.

He could see why she liked the location. It was as quiet as the concert hall before the tap of a baton on a music stand, awaiting the first notes to be played. "No doubt." He noted the location but continued to advance toward the restaurant.

They arrived at Bistro and were welcomed to the restaurant along with other artist and industry folks. The moderate volume in the restaurant offered them, and the other guests, a reception space to network. "Boombox" and "Hey, Tommy" zipped around him as soon as they entered. He shook hands, waved, and acknowledged his colleagues by name.

"Queen." A shout for Nyah's attention carried over the hum in the room. Obviously, he wasn't the only one who had contacts here.

"That's Rize. We met at one of my gigs last year. I didn't expect to see him here."

Rize waved and started to make his way toward her.

"I'm going to go say hi," she announced. "I'll be back."

Tommy's gaze lingered after her to the point where he didn't see Clyde, another agent and Tommy's competition, coming toward him.

"Boombox." Clyde extended his hand and Tommy shook it. "How's it going, man?"

"Good. I'm surprised to see you here. I thought you'd be in Scotland."

"No, I'll be there in August for Summer Sessions and decided that a cruise with some of my upcoming artists might be time better spent. Plus, everyone's a captive on the ship. They can't hide if you want to talk business." Clyde nudged him.

"True." Tommy liked Clyde. They had always been friendly competitors but Tommy couldn't help the fact that he enjoyed having a significant edge ahead of the other agent. "Congratulations. I heard you got another artist for Sunburst."

"Yeah. They're really happy about it. I'm trying to be like you, though, with all these big-ass acts, man. Are you ever going to give me your secret?" Clyde often finessed a rub with a compliment.

"We can swap cards on that and you can school me on your secret to finding talent that Sunburst wants." Tommy would gladly divulge his trade secrets if Clyde could guarantee the end result Tommy wanted.

"I thought for sure when you signed Bedazzled Beats that they were going to be it, but they got *caliente* quick." Clyde had used random Spanish words ever since learning about Tommy's Dominican roots. "I hear you're looking for new blood. Any luck?"

One time Tommy had walked in on Clyde bragging about how he'd one-upped another agent and snagged her client. Tommy didn't believe, for one moment, that Clyde didn't enjoy having pulled off something that Tommy hadn't been able to do. Why shouldn't he? Clyde held company with a small club of super agents, himself included. Tommy had recommended Clyde as an agent to hopeful clients, given that Tommy curated such a short list. Now with grooming Yaz, his protégé got first dibs on any recommendation. However, the sting of not having that last notch on his championship belt started to fester. Tommy wanted Sunburst and he was going to get it. The vow melded to him like an unbreakable bond. He just hoped that Nyah would get on board with the future he saw for her, including his plans to showcase her as Queen Roe at Sunburst.

The fragrance of seafood and rosemary in melted butter made his mouth water and his stomach rumble.

"Well, I see you're on board with Queen Roe. Word about her is starting to spread and it's probably going to spin out after she performs here. I've heard good things, so I'm psyched to see her play." Clyde's words forced Tommy's focus from his belly.

Tommy didn't get a chance to respond as Nyah finished up the conversation she had with Rize and a few other artists who'd joined their conversation and returned to his side.

"It smells amazing in here. I mean, let's eat already, right?" Nyah announced.

Tommy refrained from telling her how adorable he found her and kicked his professionalism into high gear. "Queen, I'd like to introduce you to Clyde Harris. Super agent, friend, and rival."

"All those things, huh?" Nyah asked.

"What can I say? I'm multifaceted." Clyde offered her a slanted smile that Tommy had seen work on many ladies in his day. "Nice to finally meet you. I'm hearing all good things and looking forward to seeing your set tomorrow."

"Thanks. I'm looking forward to entertaining the fans. Meeting other artists and people like you are a bonus," she said. "How long have you two been…what was that? Friends and rivals?"

"Oh, about six years, right?" Clyde checked in with Tommy.

"About that, I guess. Feels longer," Tommy confirmed and monitored the exchanges between Nyah and Clyde closely.

Servers came through with various appetizers and drinks and Nyah chose a shrimp cocktail shooter and Tommy plucked a Bellini off a tray and handed one to her and took another for him.

"So, Queen," Clyde continued. "Have you been introduced to everyone?"

She covered her mouth with the back of her hand as she finished chewing. "I've been making the rounds."

"Tommy probably has some people he'd like to introduce you to, but if he's unavailable and you need company, I'll be around. Feel free to use me." Clyde's octave deepened and Tommy frowned, well aware of Clyde's poaching tricks.

Tommy's back went rigid. He hadn't claimed Nyah or Queen Roe publicly. "You trying to steal my client or what?" The question came out firmer than he intended.

Clyde cocked his head at him and smirked, his eyes bouncing back between Tommy and Nyah. "Boombox gets a little nervous 'cause I've done it before."

"Ah." Nyah sipped her drink from the condensation-frosted champagne glass. "I'm not that easy. Tommy knows this firsthand."

Tommy's body flamed hot at her loaded statement. His attraction for her slowly chipped away at his professionalism and his mind flashed to taking her in his arms and kissing her right in front of Clyde.

"I can be quite convincing." Clyde took a step toward her and Tommy didn't know his hand had fisted until his nails dug into his palm.

"Too bad I'm not the convincible type." She leaned

over to Tommy. "Don't worry. He won't steal me." Her soft yet resolute statement hardened everything hanging and soft. Then she turned to Clyde and smiled.

"I see what's up," Clyde said. Before Tommy could demand an explanation from Clyde, dinner service began, and they all shuffled to their tables.

He and Nyah were seated at a table for two by the window with an ocean view and even if he didn't want to, he had to admit that it was quite romantic.

"I thought we'd be seated with some other artists," Nyah said as she slid into the banquette-style booth.

"Is that what you prefer? I thought you might like this better. I figured we could debrief your first day and that maybe the meet and greet at the beginning would be enough. I can request a change." He remained standing as he blurted the information at her. *Gather yourself, man.*

"You did this?" She looked up at him from her seated position.

He hoped he hadn't fucked up as much as he thought. "Yeah," he responded.

"I like it." She beamed and patted the space next to her. "Sit."

"Good." He relaxed and finally sat down, knowing that he'd done the right thing for her. Their glasses were filled with water and a server came by with wine. They both selected red varietals.

"Clyde seems like a character," Nyah said at last.

He brought his bowl-shaped wineglass to his lips and pulled a healthy sip. "That's one way to describe him."

"It's pretty cool that you can chop it up with your rival-friend-agent." She raised a brow.

He offered her a modest smile while his competition with Clyde, his desire for her and his business goals had a shoving match for priority within him. "It's easy to shoot the shit. It's festival season. When we talk about where our clients are playing throughout the year, we're basically flexing our muscles on our closed deals from the previous year. Then we talk about next year, which is stating our goals. Sometimes we purposely misguide the other to distract from deals we want. It's like a chess game."

She plucked her napkin off the plate and placed it across her lap. "Are your goals met for this year?"

"No. I'm still trying to get my recently signed artist to play at a festival this year," he admitted, yet omitted the details.

"You mean me?" She pointed a thumb at herself.

"Yes."

She blew raspberries. "Don't hold your breath."

Additional servers circled the place offering various entrees and sides that they could either accept on their plates or pass. Nyah, an obvious fan of seafood, nodded excitedly when a medley came her way.

"Tell me something. Why don't you want the fame that you could get playing the big festivals? Most of these cats would be thrilled to have a father with strings he could easily pull for them. And an icon no less?" Tommy asked. Leona would have been proud of him for finally asking instead of assuming he knew Nyah's intentions.

"I know they would. I'm the poster child for 'the grass is greener on the other side' campaign."

"So what's the story?"

She slipped her glasses off and placed them on top of her clutch. She stared at him like he'd asked her to elope.

"No one has ever really asked me that." She stared up at the enchanted ceiling with crystal chandeliers.

What kind of shitty agent doesn't ask their client why they don't want to perform at the big festivals, especially since that's exactly what he needed Queen Roe to do? Imaginary fingers pointed at him from all sides.

"When I bombed, it sucked." She forked a grilled shrimp into her mouth.

"That can't be all," he stated.

"Allow me to define suck." She placed her knife and fork on the white porcelain plate. "You can't imagine what it's like to be the daughter of an icon. It's a lot to live up to. Before I even got up on that stage, I'd been compared countless times to Dad. Everyone wanted to see if I would be as good or better. I'm not allowed to be worse. When I bombed as a performer, the critiques destroyed me for not even meeting the minimum. Do you know how much pressure that is? I get no slack. I wasn't prepared for it and so I let it go."

"And your agent? Didn't he help you through it?"

"Carlo." Saying his name left a sour taste in her mouth.

"I thought going with him would have made the difference, but Carlo had already made his icon. I was a pet project for him, not a client. He took me on to appease my father. Damage control for my career had been nonexistent."

When Pete had asked Tommy to agent Nyah back then, Tommy had declined. Perhaps Pete had seen something in the match between two young and hungry kids. Tommy hadn't seen it that way. Neither had Nyah, when she rejected the suggestion, as well. Could their business union have always been fated to land here?

"I love seeing the crowd get it. You know? When they break free of themselves and whatever is going on in their lives or their head and just let the music take over." She fidgeted in her seat before reaching for her wine and gulping it. "I couldn't make them do that because they needed me to help them get there. I was the fucking boring-est performer. I mean…" She spat a disgusted laugh as if she relived the moment. "I barely moved. I failed them and my father on a really big stage with all eyes watching and I couldn't find the courage to put myself out there again." A mournful chuckle escaped her. "I take responsibility for that, but Carlo was my agent and also managed my career. He'd been a family friend for decades. He didn't help me through it, encourage me to try again, or offer constructive criticism. He was my agent/manager in name only. We didn't even strategize a different approach. Our work relationship disintegrated and by the end I guess something inside me got broken." Her voice cracked.

I'm so fucked. This version of Nyah opened up to him, sucking him into her vortex, and he went freely. He reached for her hand under the table, and out of view, his thumb stroked, attempting to soothe. "I'm sorry that happened to you. You should always feel supported by those you work with, especially in this industry."

She cleared her throat. "Thank you."

"Did your father know about what happened with you and Carlo?" he asked.

She shook her head. "Not really. When I dated, a lot of people, especially guys I dated, tried to get at my father through me. I thought complaining to him would make me be like one of them. I was an adult, so I handled it my way. Plus Carlo was a great agent for my dad. I didn't want to ruin that."

Tommy had learned from watching the greats and Carlo had been one of them, but he hated what happened with Nyah because it was clear Carlo hadn't done his best for her. He'd only heard her side of the story but that was enough for him to choose her side. "What did you do then?" he asked.

"I wimped out and the concert hall became my safe house. No one wanted to report that Pete Monroe's daughter played with the philharmonic. If it wasn't for classical, I don't know if I would have been allowed the time to recover, heal, and try again. It took a lot for me to remember that I'm a good musician."

"You're an awesome musician," he corrected. "How long have you been playing instruments?"

"I started playing at four." She went for another sip of wine and returned it to its spot. "I need something stronger for this sad tale."

"I'm sorry," he said, again. What the fuck was he doing here with her? He felt his Adam's apple bob in his throat.

"Why? You didn't fuck up back then."

"For not asking you about this sooner."

The memory of her ordeal still shone in her eyes. She shrugged. "When I decided to DJ again, I didn't want prying eyes or judgment or comparison. Dance music is in my blood, I have to do it. I *wanted* to do it, but my way. I busted my ass building up stamina to dance my whole set. I poured my all into creating interesting music and a heart-pounding sound and promised myself I'd be the entertainer I knew I was in my heart."

"You're exhausting to watch." That made her smile. "I think that experience helped you to be the artist you are now."

"I guess you're right."

"No." He stopped himself from using her real name in earnest. "You're incredible and growing in demand from your performances alone. Your father has to be proud."

"He doesn't know I'm Queen Roe and doing the music that he plays, fulfilling his legacy. He just knows that back then, I gave it a shot and had some skills. Do you know they're honoring him at Sunburst this year?"

Holy fuck. He struggled to contain his composure. "I heard he's being honored but I didn't know all the details."

"He wants me to be onstage with him when he plays at this honorary ceremony but I can't. I just can't do it." Her body caved and her head hung. "It was the shittiest thing for me tell him no. He'd never tell me it hurt him, but I heard it in his voice." She pressed on her chest as if also wounded. "But when do I stop doing things for my parents instead of what's best for me and my well-being?"

"Is it that you don't want to do it or are you scared to do it?" He challenged her by using the s-word, but whether she liked it or not, she'd made a full recovery and become an artist in demand.

Her chest heaved and she exhaled what felt like the weight of her world. "Maybe a bit of both. I don't know how revealing Queen Roe will impact my classical career and that is still very important to me. I also don't know if I can manage both if I got too big. I'd lose control over, well, everything." Her chest moved quicker and he continued to caress her hand. He pushed a little further.

"You can't know unless you put yourself out there, Queen."

"Maybe you're right, but I'm not ready to find out." With her free hand she called over a server and asked for a cognac.

He left it at that and focused on his meal. "Let's eat." He'd learned a lot. He was glad that she trusted him to tell him what happened. He'd have to change his strategy if he wanted to see her on the Sunburst stage. Maybe she just needed to know she could get up on a big stage again. The pool deck was a bigger stage than Rebel, even though it looked deceivingly smaller. It wasn't a festival stage, per se, but it did have a festival feel. He'd survey the scene carefully. Nyah might just be ready to take that next step in time to help them both meet a milestone.

"Hey, Tommy?"

"Mmm," he responded with a mouthful of food.

"I, uh, I'm sorry I blamed you for missing my call time. My suspension from the philharmonic was on me."

He hurried to finish his food. "I didn't expect that."

"Trust me. It's not easy but it's the truth. I messed up and I guess I wasn't willing to admit that to myself," she said.

"I understand. I appreciate the apology," he said. He felt lighter, as if the yard between them had chipped away to a mere foot. "I didn't want to bring it up in case it was still a sore spot, but how are you doing with that? The suspension, I mean."

She rolled her tongue in her cheek. "I'm here. Living it up instead of flogging myself in repentance."

He laughed. Something she drew out of him so easily. "Good. Like I've said a thousand times, you should try to have some fun."

"Yeah, yeah."

They finished dinner and before they were even out of their seats the mood in the restaurant changed. The artists were excited to party, especially now that they'd been fed and plied with complimentary drinks.

"I see people are trying to wild out but it's been a long day with travel. I'm going to catch Rize's set and then maybe take the long way back to the room and check out that spot we saw on our way here," Nyah said as they headed toward the exit.

"Cool. I have a little business left to conduct. I'll probably call it an early night, as well. That is, if one can call one in the morning an early night. In our business, it's literally the equivalent to five p.m."

They shared a laugh, one of many that night.

"I'll catch up with you." He angled toward the opposite direction.

She stopped him. "Thanks for listening, Tommy. I think I might have been wrong about you. You really do care."

"You're welcome." He placed a hand on his chest. "It was my honor to listen." He *did* feel honored to hear her story, yet he grappled with the reasons why he felt gutted and guilty in the same breath. He did care for her, despite his work affirmations, and wanted the best for her, but the fact that he'd kept a key component from her started to gnaw at his core. They both could win, but if he fucked this up, he'd lose exponentially more than he'd bargained for.

Chapter Fifteen

The packed crowd on the main promenade cheered for Rize, their arms reaching for the sky as they jumped. Nyah wondered if anyone had lost their life on previous cruises. The fans teetered so close to the rails as the ship drove full steam ahead toward the next port. Sweat dripped from Rize's dark skin and his blond, natural curls tightened further from perspiration. His energy had everyone dancing, including her. She could see the appeal of the cruise immediately. All attendees had to do was get wild, enjoy themselves, and then stumble to their rooms. No drunk drivers, 4:00 am streets to walk alone, or buddies to text that you got home safe.

Nyah watched Rize with a few other artists but with the loud music—and as those around her turned up their party with a pill, a spliff, or some snow—conversation was a challenge. She accepted a shot someone offered her and danced it off before Rize finished his set.

"You heading down?" he asked, after she'd hugged and congratulated him on his set.

"Yeah, I'm performing on the pool deck tomorrow and I want to go over my set. I'll see you there, right?" she asked.

"I'll try. We're going to keep this party going. No doubt it'll be a late one. If you change your mind, text me and you can come to my suite," he suggested.

"Cool." Nyah had no intentions of going to anyone's suite when she had a banging stateroom of her own. Plus, she was well aware that as the hour grew later, so did the debauchery. Tempting as it may be, Tommy popped into her head, and going to a suite party didn't entice her as much as it should.

She took the long way to her room with the intention of finding the spot she and Tommy had seen on their way to dinner. They had talked about her failings when she first started out. She hadn't meant to share so much with him, but those fucking brown eyes of his had often made her divulge more than she intended. They were eyes to the soul of a man she trusted more and more with each passing day. On her way, moans echoed from crevices and corners, and she caught glimpses of couples and thrupples who'd also sought semi-seclusion for kissing, canoodling, and copulating. She hoped no one occupied her spot. When she found it empty, she clapped excitedly as she gripped the rail and watched the white caps forming at the side of the ship. This was way better than being in her apartment sulking over her two-week hiatus from the philharmonic.

Earlier when she'd heard Tommy moving around in the other suite, his nearness influenced her movements, the outfit she chose to wear, her heel height, the fragrance she misted, and the lotion she moisturized with. Tommy's touch from when they held hands at the safety check and at dinner haunted her palm and fingers.

Her phone buzzed and she checked her text.

Boombox: Still partying?

Nyah: It was wild. I left it to the fans. Hanging by that spot we saw earlier.

Boombox: On my way.

Nyah's tummy flipped. How had three little words gained so much power? *On my way.* She leaned against the balcony and stared into the endless horizon and the starlit sky. The whoosh of the ship, gliding through the inky waters, soothed and invigorated at the same time. The music from the partying all over the ship thudded but added to the serene moment rather than destroying it. She couldn't remember the last time she'd stood still for this long.

"Hey." She heard Tommy's soft greeting and her eyes followed the sound. He stood finer than the best packed cigars in his fitted khaki suit and crisp white shirt. His lean muscled thighs and his just-round-enough ass weren't playing around, and Nyah was at their mercy.

"Everything okay?" she asked.

"Yeah." He breathed out and moved to stand by her at the railing. "Just talked business and new opportunities. Plugged your performance."

"You can't turn it off, can you?" She shook her head.

He nudged her arms with his. "I can turn it off."

"Then do it." She half expected to see beads of sweat on his forehead.

"Now? I can't do that. I'm literally on a business trip."

Nyah's heart pinched a bit. So far, things felt like

more than just business between them. Perhaps she, too, should stay realistic about the current situation. Tommy was a more than adequate bowl of spaghetti, and she'd love to twirl her fork into him on the regular. Not only was he charming but he wasn't trying to slide into a relationship either. What was wrong with a little no-string sex to break her fast? This wasn't a lovers' getaway. She needed to remember that they'd both come on this cruise to work.

"True, but I think you can take some of your own advice and relax." She moseyed over to a raised large block covered in white paint, topped with a small rectangular tan cushion. She hopped to sit and Tommy joined her.

"How's this? I'm relaxing," he said.

"Yeah, yeah…we'll see how long that lasts."

They sat in a few moments of silence, which was just as nice and chill as their conversation.

"I heard you practicing earlier." He stared down at his feet, then at her. "You sounded beautiful but made me want to hurl at the same time."

Laughter busted from her gut. "Vomit exercises. A classic technique."

"The way you were sliding those notes together." He placed a palm on his stomach.

"There are so many different versions but the hurly feel would be correct."

"Did you get in the hours you needed?" he asked. The gentle swinging of his feet knocked the seat.

"Sort of. I didn't do my breathing exercises for the bassoon. It's not my primary instrument, but I try to stay consistent with everything so that I get better."

"Can you do them here?"

"Why didn't I think of that? I can, actually. Do you mind?"

"Uh…why would I mind?" He smirked.

She shrugged. "I normally do it with a balloon or the actual instrument. Obviously, the bassoon is not here and the balloons are in the pocket of my bass in the room. I can manipulate my hand to do it. It's all about the diaphragm. The more air you can accommodate the better and—" She cut herself off. She driveled details and information that likely didn't interest him. "This is probably boring for you."

"Not at all. I find most things that you do to be quite entertaining."

She didn't know how to respond. Did he see her as weird…interesting…sexy? She brushed it off and focused on her exercises. She flattened her palm against her stomach and placed the opening created by her fisted hand over her mouth. She inhaled and blew, adjusting the tension of her fist. Her cheeks puffed as she continued to blow. She slid her eyes to Tommy to find him riveted by her process.

After a few minutes, she changed her fisted palm to a thumbs-up hand shape and "M'd" her thumb between her lips to practice her tonguing technique. Tommy's hair came into view before his eyes were literally leveled with her mouth.

She frowned and laughed at the same time, stopping her process. "What are you doing?"

"I didn't mean to interrupt you. It's fascinating. I guess I wanted to see what your mouth was doing?"

Perhaps it was the wine and cognac at dinner, or the

fact that instruments and playing them were so second nature to her. Maybe she just needed to connect with Tommy again physically by any means necessary. "Do you want to feel it?" she asked.

He didn't hesitate to stand before her and offer her an outstretched palm.

She took his right hand and placed it on her stomach. He shuffled closer and the front of his leg touched the outside of her knee. She repeated her breathing exercise, taking in a deep diaphragm breath. Tommy's eyes widened and hers mimicked his.

They both erupted with laughter.

"Don't make me laugh or else I can't do it right," she said through giggles.

"That feels crazy," he said with his hand still on her belly.

"I know, but we haven't even gotten to the fun part yet." She flubbed her lips to get the laughter out.

"I'll try not to do anything ridiculous," he promised.

She reset. "Okay. Here we go." She blew again and then expelled air in rapid staccato spurts, her cheeks following. When she refilled her air to begin again, he inhaled in unison with her, though not as quick or as deep.

Tommy shook his head as his eyes went back and forth between her cheeks and her stomach.

She stopped after she expelled her last breath of air.

"That's amazing." Tommy withdrew his hand and she gripped his wrist, sliding her fingers to curl around his thumb, bringing it to her mouth. She "M'd" the tip and tongued the pad with similar movements to her breathing, moments before. He inched even closer to her and his free hand stroked up her arm to her neck and caressed her there.

"Nyah." He whispered her name and it covered her like a satin sheet.

She leaned into his touch and took his thumb deeper into her mouth. She sucked gently and slid it out slow and steady. Tommy's chest inflated and fell, each time quicker than the last. She manipulated his hand to slip his index and middle fingers into her mouth, wetting and laving from base to tip. A moan escaped her.

Tommy pressed his head against the side of hers as she sucked. "I'm going to kiss you, Nyah. I have to kiss you now. Is that okay?"

She nodded her permission, rubbing her head against his, and released his fingers from her mouth. "I'm going to put your fingers between my legs. Is *that* okay?" she asked.

"Fuck yeah," he huffed out and his caresses on her skin crept up the back of her head until his hand cupped her neck. He pulled her to him and his mouth covered her.

She widened her legs and guided his hand to her center. As Tommy devoured her mouth, she shifted her panties to give him direct access to her hot folds. She'd wet his fingers but she felt the cool air hit the slick readiness seeping from her slit. Tommy rubbed her, and the pleasure he bequeathed her liquefied her like a puddle of hot caramel.

He separated from her long enough to yank off his glasses and fumbled to pocket them while his hand still worked between her legs.

"Can you see me without those?" she panted.

He removed his hand from her pussy and brought his fingers close to his nose. "I can smell you." He licked his fingers. "I can taste you." He rejoined their mouths and tongues, sharing what he savored. "I've had you seared in my head since the moment you played Bottesini in your audition. I see you, Nyah. I always see you."

"Tommy." He kissed her deeply and his hands slipped back to her craving pussy. This time she reached down to rip the barrier obstructing their contact. His fingers sunk inside her and his thumb rubbed her clit. Her hips circled and she inched closer to the edge of the seating. Tommy's legs straddled her thigh and she raised her leg slightly to gently knee his package. She wanted to see his hard and heavy cock, to feel it, and release it from the constraining material of his pants. With free hands she unbuckled his belt, worked the button free, and unzipped.

"You're so hard, Tommy," she whined, as his fingers continued to build a storm within her. She plucked his rigid muscle from his underwear. Fearless, she squeezed and rubbed him. Slippery liquid oozed from him and she circled her thumb against the sculpted tip. Her hand wrapped around him and up and down she stroked, desiring to pleasure him the way he did with her.

"I want to feel you, Tommy."

His breath hitched in his throat. "Condoms are in the room."

"I don't care." She'd been patient and waited. Now horny as fuck and out of her mind, she crumpled the rules and functioned on pure need.

"You will tomorrow." His sexy humor rumbled in his chest.

She groaned in disappointment, yet moaned in pleasure as he worked her middle. Her body shook, clinging on to the edge of something extraordinary.

"We're not done, angel," he hissed against her ear. "I have to hear you, and feel you come on my hand."

She pumped his cock harder. "I will if you will." Her tongue lapped at his mouth and he gave her his tongue. They crashed together in a bubble of passion, his fingers the bow strumming her stings. Neither of them caring if anyone spied or heard their passionate exchange or concerned as to where they were, as long as her hands were on him and his hands were on her. The way he kissed her freed her of all inhibitions and made her feel like she'd never had lips on hers before. A surge rose up from her core and rhythmic contractions quaked every muscle in her body. "Tommy." She cried his name into his mouth. Her insides clenched for more of his hand and her hips bucked. "Harder. Oh God. Deeper." She jerked on his stiff cock, needing him to feel what she did.

"Fuck, Nyah. I'm—" Tommy hunched and pressed his head against her shoulder. With his free hand he pushed her hands and his cock down to the floor, emptying his load.

Breathless, they stayed like that, both of them raw and satiated, at least for that moment. Minutes of recovery passed. But how could she recover from that?

"You okay?" he asked at length. He stuffed himself back inside his underwear and tended to his pants, the belt buckle clinking into place.

"Yeah. You?" Her underwear was still attached on one side and she pulled her dress back down.

"Yeah." He pulled his glasses out of his pocket and wiped sweat off his brow before putting them back on.

Silence hung between them. She'd experienced raw and intense moments before but never like this. She wanted, no, needed more. Tommy had to know that he'd opened the floodgates.

"So…we're on this big ol' boat together for the next forty-eight hours." She let her statement breathe.

"Yes, we are." He stared at her, his forehead wrinkling.

She hopped to her feet and smoothed her clothes. "That all you got?" she teased.

He intertwined his fingers with hers and kissed the back of her hand. "Not even close."

Thank God.

Chapter Sixteen

Second thoughts threatened to taint the moment. Nyah's scent lingered under his nose and he savored her taste. He wanted to show her what more he had to offer and to please her in a way that would buckle her knees and have her cry out his name in complete and utter surrender. She touched his face and all the thoughts that ran through his mind blurred to the background as he focused on her eyes. He wanted to see her undisguised by layers of face paint. His thumb smeared at the makeup to remove it but it stayed put.

"Let me take this off." She caressed his hand and pulled away, but he held her to him.

"I won't be able to wait that long." He pulled her to him and pressed his lips against her.

"Don't you need something?" she asked, her upper body concaving to his fingers as they slid down the silky material of her plunging neckline.

"*Carajo*," he cursed in Spanish. "I'll be back." Her alluring giggle only provoked his already hard dick.

He tore himself away from her gravity and sped to his suite. He dug through his luggage to find the condom box in one of the inside pockets of his luggage. He hadn't planned on using them even if he'd hoped that things would escalate between him and Nyah. Being with her wasn't a guarantee, but damn if he wasn't glad he'd come prepared. He longed to touch her again. *And then what?*

His mind leapt into the future. Vignettes of wild and breathless moments were followed by "thanks for a great night," or the "it's been great" statements that ended things. The chill of being in an empty bed swept over him and his heart cramped at the thought of that vacant spot ever having belonged to Nyah. He shoved the condom box in his pant pocket and traipsed back to her.

He found her, makeup-less and drying her face with a towel. She took one look at him and asked, "Having second thoughts?"

He raked a hand through his hair. "I'm your agent. If we do this the waters could get muddy."

"I'm not gonna lie. You're not the only one. But…" She sauntered toward him and pressed her modest curves against him. "Some of the best things come from muddy water." She nuzzled his neck with her nose and he drew breath. "Sunscreen for elephants." Her lips grazed his jawline. "Lotus flowers." She followed the line of his chin all the way to his other cheek, kissing along the way. "And—"

He silenced her with his lips, his ravenous tongue grateful for the welcome reception her mouth offered. He couldn't believe how much he needed to taste her again until the sweetness of her tongue folded with his. He wanted to know what she liked and memorize every inch of her. He delighted in learning what he could do to make her feel good. She moaned in a note that her bass had created the day he'd first seen her play, and he logged the positive reaction for the future. The memory of her, lovely and bowing her instrument, crossed his vision. He clasped her face on either side and studied her low lids and desire-stained cheeks. He didn't need to imagine her or visualize her to jerk off in his loft. She stood here beautiful and open before him, and he filed the images with the others he'd collected of her so far.

She used the inches of space between them to seize the opportunity and slink out of her dress from the top, revealing small breasts that he craved to touch. When she slid the material down over her waist, he flattened his palm over her and she felt amazing in his hand. Her tits could be any size and she'd still be perfect to him. His hand appeared massive as he rubbed and massaged her.

He pinched the dark, protruding nipples and her mouth opened to release a throaty sigh. His hand crept down to her hip as her legs marched out of the dress, and his head dropped to capture one sensitive bud in his teeth. The intoxicating scent of the sea on her skin blended with the musky fragrance of tuberose in her perfume. He lost himself in this moment with her. His tongue mimicked the technique she'd tortured his finger with earlier and he thought it only fair that he return the favor.

"Tommy." Her hands clasped him by the neck and she pressed him to her. She took his glasses off and placed them on a nearby table. He applied pressure with each nibble before releasing the taut bud, only to lave the sensitive area with his tongue, and then suckle with intensity.

She squealed and he relished in the sound. He replaced the intensity with gentler licks and Nyah bowed over him.

"Who the fuck are you?" she gasped.

He laughed wickedly. His deep humor sounded altered even to him. He straightened, releasing her hard, swollen areola that he'd refrained from marking, and she groaned in protest.

"You're about to find out." His fingers already unbuckled his belt and he undid his pants button while Nyah untucked and unbuttoned his shirt. She petted the layer of short curly hair on his chest and slid her hands up over his trapezius and shoulder caps. "I didn't know you were inked here." She slipped the shirt off him, following the expanse of the angel wings that crept slightly up his neck and spanned his upper back and arms. She circled him, her fingers tracing the feathered wings he had tattooed into his skin over a decade ago. Her fingers stopped at the spot where the shaded name in calligraphy tatted him. Long seconds passed as she continued her evaluation.

"This is beautiful, Tommy." She said it softly and reverently, like she somehow understood how much the tattoo meant to him. He released a lungful of air and goosebumps raised on his arm as Nyah's lips touched his shoulder. She looked up at him as she traced kisses from his triceps all the way down to his elbow. The combination of shyness and hunger sparkled in her eyes. She ducked under his arm, her mouth torturing his side and arcing toward his stomach until she squatted before him and yanked down his pants. The linen settled around his ankles.

She planted a kiss on his stomach, sending shocks through his abs, and the muscles contracted when her tongue flitted around his belly button. "That's not where I want your mouth." He hauled her back to her feet and devoured her, moaning as he licked, sucked and nibbled with frightening hunger.

"What do you want, Tommy?" she choked out as if she rationed air.

He was suddenly a novice at all his languages. She raked her fingers through his hair and toyed with his ears. "Tell me. Please, tell me."

He'd been asked what he wanted countless times but he'd never been with someone who looked at him with such attentiveness and caring as if her pleasure depended on his. How could he not divulge his desires to her.

"I want your mouth. Give me your mouth, angel." He lurched to reclaim her lips and she evaded him.

"Where?"

He stepped back to get a less blurry visual of the mischievousness dancing on her face.

"Here." He pointed to his chest. She kissed his pectoral muscle and sucked his nipple lovingly before delivering her own bite. He hissed as the sensation spread through him.

"And?" she asked.

He pointed to his abs and Nyah obliged. In the low light, the pink of her tongue wet his skin, leaving a light sheen on the hair there. Her soft lips haunted every spot they touched. "I like this game."

"I thought you might." She grinned up at him from her location. "Where else, love?"

He gripped his cock, which had reached a new level of rigidity, and stroked. "Here. Kiss me here," he told her, his voice shaky and eager.

She dropped to her knees, her eyes following him as he stroked himself. She stayed his hand and took over. "Just a kiss?" she asked, then pecked the shiny tip of his dick and licked her lips, tasting him.

At that moment he'd literally jump off a cliff to have her do that again. "Again, angel."

"That all?" She teased him with tortuous skill.

"Fuck, Nyah. Suck me. Take me into your mouth and suck me."

His dick disappeared as she covered him in a scorching hot cocoon. Her hands and mouth blew him with unmatched expertise. He rocked his hips, withdrawing and then once again feeding her inch by inch. She made a small gurgling sound around his dick and he pulled out completely, staring down at her watery eyes. The air in the room cooled his shiny member. He berated himself for not being attuned to how much of him she could handle.

"What?" She shook her head as if clearing her haze and sat on her heels, confusion on her face.

He wiped the teardrop that escaped. "Shit! I'm sorry, angel. I should have been gentler with you." He always tried to be a good partner, but it felt even more important to treat Nyah with the utmost care.

"I don't understand. I thought you were enjoying it." She folded her hands on the tops of her thighs.

"I was. I mean, I am. It's…you gagged. I didn't mean to do that to you."

"Oh." She smiled and he noticed her shoulders relax away from her ears. "It's okay. Sometimes, in the moment, I like it." She held him by the hips. "Trust me to know what I like and to tell you what I need." She guided him back to her open mouth and he drowned in her caress.

"Woman, you are going to destroy me, aren't you?"

She nodded as the muscles in her mouth worked him. Fire and ice blazed in every area she covered and the sensations growing at the lowest part of his pelvis mounted quickly. Her eyes burned with seduction as her head bobbed. Her enchanting scent and the heat of her mouth on him was more than he could endure. She fumbled for his hand and moved it to her head. As he tangled her fingers in her soft curls, he trembled at the thought of her wanting this from him. Trusting him. His heart pounded and he held her head to encourage her speed, which accelerated. "Nyah," he called, tension gripping his limbs. He tried to extract himself from her jaws, but she sucked him harder and received him deeper. She felt so good around him that he lost all control.

"Shhhhhh…fuck!"

He gently touched her cheek. The intense tingling in his groin maxed out and he erupted, shaking and shivering. He emptied his load, and her throat contracted around him as she swallowed. He buckled, his legs and arms numb, and reached for the table near them to keep him from face planting on the carpet. She reigned supreme over him and he bowed to his queen.

* * *

Nyah palmed Tommy's ass as the last droplet of his satisfaction dripped down her throat. The taste of his thick salty release left a slightly sweet finish on her tongue and she wanted to savor him again. She put the thought to bed. He'd likely want to sleep until his prolactin levels recovered. She'd taken a human sexuality class in college to understand her own body and learned loads. He needed to recover and though she was disappointed, she couldn't be mad at him, even if her pussy salivated like Tommy's dick was a meal at a Michelin starred restaurant.

"Nyah." He caressed her hairline down to her jaw, where he tilted her chin up to look at him. He grinned down at her and the unmistakable heat she'd seen when she sucked him still flamed in his brown eyes. He helped her to her feet and hooked his arm around her waist, pressing her against him. "Take me to your bed."

"I thought you'd be..."

"What, angel?" Confusion crinkled his face.

"I'd understand if you—" She guided his gaze down with her own. "—if you're done for the night."

"Oh." His chest rumbled with laughter and the vibration stimulated her already sparked nipples. He wrapped both arms around her and squeezed her in a hug until they were fully pressed against one another. "We're not done yet, Queen," he whispered in her ear, and his teeth captured her lobe and tugged. "Now, take me to your bed."

Relief and excitement buzzed through her and her pussy applauded, standing ovation style. They left their clothes in individual piles and she led him by the hand to her room. Still in her panties, she crawled up onto the bed, giving Tommy a full view of her ass through the lace of her burgundy underwear. He clearly had other plans when he caught her by both ankles and dragged her down to the edge of the bed. She flopped to her stomach and yelped at his strength. Giggles poured out of her and she craned her neck to see him grab the top of her panties and peel them over her ass, down her legs and off with zero protest from her. He tossed them aside and kneeled between her opened legs. He caressed the back of her legs and she sunk into the mattress.

"My turn to be on my knees." He tickled kisses over the areas his hands traveled. "Are you comfortable?"

"Yes." Her answer rushed out of her.

"Good, 'cause we're going to be here a while." His hands massaged over the crack of her ass and down to her center. "Open wider for me, angel." She did as he instructed before he finished his sentence, exposing herself to him. Tommy caressed around her opening and slipped a finger inside. "You're beautiful here, Nyah. So shiny and wet. I have to drink you. Tell me I can have my fill." He spoke so close to her pussy she could feel his breath. She bit hard on her lower lip.

"Yes. Please, Tommy. I want to feel you." She squirmed as he toyed with her and poked in and out of her slit. She arched her back to raise her ass higher. He kissed her butt cheeks and as his teeth grazed and bit, she moaned. She felt him slide another finger inside, loving the way he stretched her. He retracted his fingers and the heat from his mouth replaced them. "Oh, Tommy. Yes, baby." Her hands clenched the comforter. She sunk into the pleasure he served her and when he spread her ass and his tongue glided up to her hole, she cried out.

She'd heard her friends talk about "eating shorty from the back" or "eating the booty like groceries" but she'd never experienced it firsthand, until now. Tommy, clearly a consummate expert in the art of ass eating, tortured her hole. She felt his hand on the flesh of her ass and then one of his thumbs pushed slowly inside, deeper and deeper, while his tongue continued to flicker around and down to her pussy and up again to where the pressure of his thumb drove her wild. He pulled his thumb out and covered her hole with his mouth, sucking and playing.

"Do you like it when I kiss you here, Nyah?" he asked, his warm breath against her.

"Fuck yeah. Oh fuck, Tommy," she moaned.

"Does it feel good, baby?" he questioned, teasing her asshole.

"Uh-huh…f-f-feel s-s-so f-fucking good." She shivered and hissed, and though she squirmed, his mouth followed her. He hummed with a combination of humor and hunger as if enjoying giving pleasure as much as she did receiving. That knowledge shot her arousal through the roof. His lips, tongue, and teeth pleasured her in a way that she was thoroughly unprepared for. She couldn't control the noises she made, nor did she want to. Her feet tried to wrap around him but in her position, she needed to keep her feet on the ground. She reached around and when her hands found his hair, she rubbed his head in gratitude. Her body shook from head to toe and she soared fast.

Tommy halted his assault on her ass and turned her

over. "Sit up, love. I want you to see everything I'm going to do to you." She sat on the edge of the bed, her body hot with tiny spasms that promised larger ones. She braced herself on the bed with one arm slightly behind her. She caressed his messed hair. Moisture from her decorated him from his nose to his chin. The image of him sloppy from eating her out delighted her and her chest rose and fell from what they'd shared.

"You okay?" he asked.

She swallowed against dry mouth. "Yes," she croaked. "Please don't stop, Tommy."

He put both her legs over his shoulder and his head dipped between her legs. He'd positioned her to see every lash of his tongue, nibble of his teeth and dig of his fingers. Her slick insides glistened on his fingers and he offered her a taste. She sucked on his fingers as he assaulted her clit. She held his wrist and when she'd licked his fingers clean, slid his hand over her breast and flung her head back. She barely hung on and the ball of energy building inside her threatened to explode and take out the whole fucking ship.

"I-I'm gonna come. Tommy, I—" she gasped.

He lifted to his feet and she saw his sheathed cock. He fell onto her, into her, and she wrapped him in her arms and legs as he filled her. He wasted little time sliding in and out, pumping her to the finish line. She held on a little longer because his rigid member delivered delirious fulfillment. "Oh my God, Tommy!" He fucked her into the mattress, and she exploded, hollering with unfiltered power.

"Fuck, angel. You're so special. My dick is fucking smiling inside you right now."

He made her laugh and aroused her further, both of which she thought impossible. He gobbled her mouth and his tongue stabbed uncontrollably. She slobbered back with terrifying desire. After this would she ever be satisfied by another again? He'd cracked her open and she doubted that there was little she wouldn't do for this man if he asked. Her body tingled and jerked with each spasm that rocked through her. His forceful thrusts came in short, quick bursts that thrilled her and he huffed against her ear, groaning until he gave one pounding plunge into her.

"Nyah," he whined, then roared in indecipherable ecstasy.

"Yes, Tommy. Come hard for me." She stroked him as his cock vibrated inside her and micro shocks fluttered through her.

They both collapsed on the bed, drained, melded together and motionless, their breathing heavy and louder than the hum of the ship. Tommy propped up on his hands and gazed down at her. "Still okay?" he asked.

She nodded and smiled up at him, working overtime to put what had just happened between them into some kind of perspective.

He tilted his head at her. "Did I fuck you speechless, angel? Say something. You're freaking me out."

"How do you do that? Make me laugh and turn me on at the same time?"

"You make it easy. Plus, I like being the reason you smile."

"I gotta tell you, Boombox, you didn't oversell your bedroom skills. That was pretty fucking amazing." The confession was a novice move but his cum must have been laced with some sort of truth agent because all she wanted to do was confess.

"This was a dual effort." He chuckled. "And this mouth...well worth the wait." The tender lip action he laid on her made her pelvis inch to him again, even though he softened inside her she still loved how he felt. He gently slid out of her, his hand gripping the latex. He removed the glossy rubber to reveal a glossier coat on his skin. Even at rest his cock impressed. He knotted the condom and trashed it. Her eyes gobbled up every inch of the creamy skin covering his slightly muscled chest, strong legs and slightly round ass. "Come on."

"I don't mind being sex messy with you." She reached for him.

"Let me clean you up." He gently pulled out of her grip and she watched him as he wet a washcloth. Steam rose from the faucet into the bowl underneath. He eased her legs open and he gently wiped her from front to back. "Mmm." She lay back against the bedding, enjoying the spa effect of the heat from the washcloth and his meticulous strokes. When he left her, she opened the bed, dragging the comforter and sheet down and sliding underneath. From her position, she saw Tommy cleaning his dick off. She wouldn't consider him super fit, but he was toned and healthy, and she liked his body. *And damn could he wear a suit.*

He returned and jumped back into his boxer-briefs and gathered his clothes. "I should probably get going. You've had a busy day of travel, plus it's late and—"

"You're leaving?"

Something in her voice must have resonated because he stopped all movement and finally looked at her. "You have a performance tomorrow and need to be fresh for that. I assumed you'd want some space."

Her inner voice barked about keeping things casual and turning off her emotions that threatened to complicate things. She should listen but instead turned down the volume because the last thing she wanted was space from Tommy.

"Relax, Tommy. I got this. Come here." She cuffed both his wrists and dragged him down on the bed with her. "Stay with me. Just be here with me."

"What, Queen Roe has time in her schedule for post-sex cuddling?" He sat on the bed and faced her.

"After what just happened? No. I'd like you to stay." She pressed her palm to his sternum and pet the hair there. She hadn't thought she was a chest hair-loving woman until now. "If you want to."

He slipped under the cover with her. "Yes. I want to."

Tommy wrapped her in his arms, and she nestled against him. His chest and the hair upon it were the perfect pillow. His breathing steadied and slowed against her ear and though his fragrance still wafted under her nose, it had dulled since their sex sessions. Sleep started to weigh on her lids. The intimacy between them replayed in her dreamlike state and she moaned. Tommy had been a generous and extraordinary lover, but why had he thought she'd wanted him to leave? She saw clearly the image of the angel tattoo on his back behind closed eyes and one other burning question remained.

Who was Carmen?

Chapter Seventeen

For the first time since they'd been on the ship, he and
Nyah were on different schedules. He'd gotten up this
morning and pounded weights at the gym. Only one other
person used the place, given that most cruisers at that hour
were just going to bed. He'd had a late night himself. He
increased the weights to burn out the arousal for her that
still flowed through him, as well as the doubt that seeped
in, attempting to poison his thoughts.

She'd needed him for Artistique and to help get her
dual careers under better management. The hypocrisy
of his own intentions burned his muscles as he bench-
pressed. He needed Queen Roe for Sunburst and his
lies by omission had started to gnaw at him. He'd struggled with her dueling personalities but the truth was he
desired all of her. In the end he and Nyah would hurt
each other. Why couldn't he just stick to the boundaries they'd set? She'd been generous in bed with him to
the point where his feelings had a mind of their own
and he'd refrained from admitting to himself how easy
it would be to love her. She admitted how intense their
connection was but did that mean she wanted more, too?

He returned to their stateroom to find it empty, yet

her scent, their scents, lingered in the room. He hoped she would explore the ship and socialize or eat at one of the many restaurants. Perhaps she'd decided to get a spa treatment. She was young, lovely, and way too serious at times. Even though he'd tried to work those feeling out in the gym, he admitted to himself that he missed her.

He had a few meetings before her set that afternoon and would have to skip the Champagne Brunch, which meant possibly not seeing Nyah before her set. These questions never posed a problem for him before. All he needed to do was conduct business as usual. Regardless of the warnings raging through him, he sought her out.

After about half an hour of searching the faces, he found Nyah in a bikini top, a towel wrapped around her waist, and her skin considerably darker. She flip-flopped across the deck in her tinted shades, her skin glossy from either sunscreen or tanning lotion. Rize jogged up to her and handed her a blue bottle.

"Thanks again for hanging out with us for a bit, Queen." He kissed her cheek and when they went their separate ways, Tommy witnessed Rize turn back and give Nyah's backside a detailed read. Tommy's jaw tensed as did every muscle in his neck and shoulder down his back, but he got a hold of himself, given the fact that he'd done the same thing countless times. The difference was that his emotional investment in Nyah continued to grow in equity.

Feeling stalker-ish, he bolted to catch up with her before he lost her in the crowd. She greeted a few fans briefly and from his distance he heard her encourage them to attend her set that afternoon. His chest swelled with agent-pride. Nyah's impressive self-promotional skill had gotten her to her current level as much as her talent had. His only wish? That she'd let him expand her brand and popularity so she received the accolades she deserved.

He'd finally caught up to her when she stopped again near a few fans doing some wild waterslide thing that had to be about four stories high. Had he not been dressed for his meetings he might have done it himself—with her.

He stopped behind her and leaned in to announce himself close to her ear. "It's okay to join in."

She whipped around. "How did you—where did you…?"

He straightened at her protective stance. "I spotted you on my way to my meetings," he responded. She smelled like tropical fruits and warmed coconut oil, and he would have loved to bury his face in her neck and fill his lungs with her mellow fragrance instead of air.

"Boy, you are so lucky. You know I live in New York, right? You can't roll up on me like that."

He frowned. "You're on a ship. I don't think you have to watch your back that hard." He eyed her mosaic pink bikini top so closely he saw the square outline of what he believed was her key card tucked inside.

"Tell that to my *Spidey Sense*." Her shoulders thawed. "I didn't see you this morning."

"I went to the gym for a bit. I didn't want to wake you and thought you'd sleep in 'til you got ready for the Champagne Brunch. Did you sleep well?" he asked.

"Yeah. I did. I always sleep well at sea. Not to mention, someone wiped me out last night." She arched her body toward him before taking a step back. "I'm a pretty early riser because of rehearsals, so I got up and practiced, got a fucking phenomenal massage, then decided to get some sun," she said. She didn't mention hangin' out with Rize.

He slid her glasses down to the tip of her nose. "Without your makeup?"

"I didn't stress. I did, however, keep my glasses on. When the masseuse wanted to do my face, I replaced the glasses with cucumbers. They worked with me."

"They? How many massages did you get?"

"I had a nonbinary masseuse. They worked out all the kinks. I was pretty sore when I got out of bed." She rolled her shoulders and he saw that the label on the bottle in her hand read sunscreen.

"In a good way?" He had to know.

"Definitely." She winked at him.

His throat tightened and his mouth watered for her lips. "I see you got a little...a lot of color, actually." Her skin had tanned to the color of rich brown and he'd lick every inch of her if she'd let him.

"Really? I've only been out there for about an hour."

Tommy pointed up. "Not a cloud in the sky. You've been in full sun, angel."

A hue of pink on her cheeks came through her tan and spread just under her glasses. He'd only started to call her angel last night when it had rolled off his tongue as a nickname. Perhaps that blush meant she didn't like it, or felt embarrassed by it. But when her lips turned up in a lazy smile, he wondered what memory from their bedroom games she'd recalled.

"I need a shower. It's already after noon. If I don't hurry, I'll miss my chance, and I could definitely eat, especially after being in the sun drinking with Rize and his crew."

He felt like a dumbass. "Did you have fun?"

She nodded. "They're cool people. We talked shop. You would have been proud."

"I already am." They shared a brief but intense stare.

"I guess I'll meet you at the brunch since you have your meetings."

"I have to skip it." He hated saying the words, but he had business to tend to.

"Seriously?"

"Unfortunately, I have some important meetings I have to take before your set this afternoon. I also want to check to make sure that everything is set up for you. You'll be cool to go without me, right?" he asked.

The disappointment on her face came through the tinted shades and she played with the sunscreen in her hands. "It would be nice to go with you but, yeah, no worries. It's cool. Do what you gotta do."

They'd shared intense closeness last night, but the distance and the morning exercise still offered little clarity for him to know how to proceed with her. He almost wished he'd kept his dick out of her mouth.

"I have to start packing, too, since we fly back when we dock at Cape May," she rattled off. "Maybe I can get in another hour or two of practice later, since I feel really good about my set this afternoon. When I get back to New York I'll have to jump right into rehearsals. I want to play well for Martin."

He didn't know whether or not the last bit of information had been for him or part of a list she needed to remind herself about. "Take it one performance at a time. You're far away from New York and the demands on you there. You practiced already. Go eat and enjoy the brunch. Put classical you to bed for a few hours."

She sniffed in air and blew it all out. "I know. I'm good."

"If it's any consolation, you look nothing like Nyah," he teased.

That inspired the same laugh from her that he needed to tempt from her more and more often.

"Let me walk you to the elevator."

"Don't you have to get to your meetings?"

"It's on my way," he lied.

"You act like I don't know the layout of the ship, sir." She nudged his arm with hers as they walked, causing him to sidestep.

The guests were active and already filling up the various pools and buffet lines, and music came from everywhere. "Are we going to talk about last night or keep pretending that that shit didn't go down?" She shot straight to the point, and though he liked it, he didn't know what to say about last night.

He encouraged his feet to keep moving forward. "It definitely went down." He licked the corner of his mouth, remembering every detail of how she made him feel. "You have the brunch and then you have your show at three. Talk later?" They arrived at the elevator and he pressed the down arrow on the panel. Part of him thanked all the gods when the doors opened immediately, the other part wanted to slip inside the steel box with her and make her "sex messy" again.

"Sure." Her simple response as she stepped inside the elevator gutted him. If she thought he was avoiding the conversation, she was right. The dynamic conflict of emotions within him wasn't helping him open up about their incredible night and what that meant for their future, professionally or otherwise.

He kept the door pressed open with his body and tapped her chin. "I'll meet you at the pool deck. I'll be there, checking to make sure that everything is set up for you and that there aren't any problems. Even if you don't see me, I'm there, okay?" He needed his words to make her feel protected and cared for, because his actions were failing. "I have to go."

"Yeah, get outta here," she said as nonchalantly as possible.

"Good luck, Queen." He held her by the shoulders, the simple touch magnetizing them where they connected. She offered her lips, but he kissed her on the forehead instead and she stiffened before easing out of his hold.

"Thanks."

He focused on why they were here. To get her to perform and build up her muscle for performing to larger audiences that would hopefully end with her in the lineup for Sunburst. Anything else would lead to inevitable pain for him when she'd decide their bedroom fun was over. He needed her more than she needed him.

He hurried away while she stayed planted where she stood. "See you in a few," he said just as the doors closed. Tommy left to go have his meeting with Herman.

Tommy shook Herman's hand. "Still avoiding me?" Herman tapped his watch to reveal the time. "You're late."

"I wasn't avoiding you. I didn't know you were on the ship or I would have scheduled something with you." Tommy settled in a seat across from Herman. "I had to check things out for my artist before showtime."

"I'll buy it. I'll come back around to that," Herman said. "It's good to see you, man."

"You too. I see you cut some off the top," Tommy teased his balding friend, and Herman gave him the finger.

A waitress came by with a beer and set it down in front of Herman.

"I'll take one of those and water, please," Tommy said to the waitress, then returned his attention to Herman. "What are you doing on the ship anyway? You're a festival organizer and your event is ramping up."

"I came to check out some of the talent in Rize's crew. So far, I'm not terribly impressed but there's still some potential among them. Rize is definitely in. His set was savage. Did you catch any of it?" Herman asked and then took a long swig of his beer.

"A little bit." Tommy had been with some industry folks when he'd heard the last half hour of Rize's set the night before. He'd found Nyah afterward, and the rest unfolded in the most amazing dream he'd ever had in real life.

"Tommy?" Herman called.

"Yeah?"

Herman scoffed. "I asked what you thought of it."

"Rize was clutch." Tommy swallowed cottonmouth and wished for that beer. "You're right to be interested in him for Sunburst."

"The new organizers are really pushing into the creative aspect with a heavy hand. I'm going to need you to get an artist there this year. I don't know what the festival will look like next year."

"I can't believe you're giving it up."

"It's an eight-figure payday, my friend. Plus, it's time. I'm trying to get my hand in something else that I can build from the ground up." Herman wiped the moisture from his beer glass on his blue and white checkered shorts.

Tommy leaned back against the seat rest and evaluated Herman's features. His friend's color was a few shades lighter than Nyah's after a bout in the sun. *There she goes again.* Tommy knew how fucked he was when Nyah came up as he looked at Herman's mug. "I'm interested. Tell me more."

"Cool your speedos, dude. It's in incubation, but I'm trying to create a new experience. These festivals have everything now. I'm trying to get it back to the music but in new ways. I'll keep you in the loop."

Knowing Herman, he already had a good idea about what that looked like and Tommy wanted in. "You better. I'm down to see what genius you create this time."

"No doubt." Herman nodded. "From what I've heard you're here with a new client."

"Queen Roe."

Herman's hand palmed over his low-cut fade. "She's got a small following here on the ship and you've been setting the grapevine on fire."

"It's my job." Tommy's beer arrived and not a second too soon. He took a healthy drink of the cool fizzing drink, the slight hint of orange coming through the vibrant hops.

"You're talking to me, Tommy." Herman sipped his beer, the slight foam sticking to his mustache before he wiped it clean. "This Queen Roe any good?"

"Haven't you checked her out online? You used to be more thorough, man."

Herman returned a *Fuck you. I'm still the shit* glare. "I don't have time for this YouTube shit. That's why I hire the talented to do that part. I can't get a real sense of someone from watching them online. It's decent, but I want to be there and feel the vibe. We've been burnt when that excitement didn't translate in person. Another small fact, I didn't know you were going to be here. You normally make a bigger splash when you announce a new client. What gives?"

"She's different. I'm managing her, too. We're just putting some feelers out." Tommy had spent most of his time on the ship campaigning for Queen Roe to get an interested showing at her performance. He knew he walked a spider-web-thin line between his ambition for her and what she wanted.

Herman slapped his knee. "You? Not possible. How long are you going do that for? You're too hungry for this snail's pace shit. Tell me the real story."

"What? I work for my client, not the other way around." A chunk of Tommy's ego liked having Herman out of 'the know'. That's how his friend made him feel every time he rejected his clients for his festival.

"Boombox. Cut the shit."

Herman had him pegged from the moment he'd sat down with him, but Tommy had already decided that he'd let Queen Roe's performance do the rest. As the clock neared time for her to perform, his nerves for her grew.

"No shit to cut, man. She's talented and has a lot of potential. Bottom line."

"So what? There are a lot of talented people with potential. If you're vouching for her, I want to know her superpower. Reveal."

"Her set is getting ready to start. I've got to go." Tommy dodged Herman's inquiry like it was a right hook to his face.

"If you think you're leaving me here, you're kiddin' yourself, dude. I want to see her in action."

Hooked. Line and sinker. "Sure, man, let's go."

"Does she know who I am?" Herman asked.

"I'm not sure."

"Well, don't tell her. The last thing I need is some newbie slobbering all over me for a spot at the festival."

Tommy scoffed at Herman's ego, even though Tommy had witnessed the slobber fest firsthand. "Not a problem."

As Tommy walked to the pool deck with Herman, their party grew as both he and Herman were well-known and used their strides to catch up and jot notes and dates on a calendar. Even with a whole day on a ship, networking never ceased.

Tommy made his way to the stage to find Nyah handing her laptop over to the techie. The light hood connected to her tee shirt draped over her Afro puffs and her makeup was bright yet fierce for the occasion. She followed the techie up onstage and hovered over him like a helicopter mom. At first, he thought their interaction might be on the hostile side of things as she communicated with the nodding young man. She tested her equipment and then gave him the thumbs up. They slapped high fives and Tommy immediately felt left out. He should have been here already, encouraging her and being the go-between for her and any possible problems. He'd been doing great agenting for her, but a piss poor job managing at the moment.

She ran down the steps and Tommy hurried toward her.

"Hey, everything all right?" he asked.

"Yeah. Why?" Her shoulder dripped with icicles as she surveyed everyone around them. If her response was any more dismissive, he'd have been communicating with the back of her head.

"I saw you with the tech guy and wondered if something—"

"I got it. I'm used to handling my performance details." Her statement stung the shit out of him. One thing he knew from his upbringing and from the women he'd been with was that whatever bugged her, he'd caused it. He should have wrapped things up with Herman sooner and been here for her.

Their entourage chatted with other popular DJs scheduled to play on the ship and gathered in the VIP area. Herman had caught up to him. "You must be Queen Roe." He introduced himself.

Nyah eyes slid from Tommy to the man and back again. "Queen, this is Herman Elliot."

She shook Herman's hand, and smiled. "Nice to meet you."

"You're a tall drink of water, aren't you?" Herman stated more than asked.

"Why? Are you thirsty?" she teased back.

"Gorgeous *and* witty."

"Excuse me?" She glared down at Herman.

Nyah was already tight. The last thing Tommy wanted was for her to take it out on friendly and unsuspecting Herman.

"Forgive me. It's just that online I didn't realize you had so much height. This your first Oh Ship?" Herman asked.

"Yeah."

"Nervous?"

She pinched her thumb and index finger together. "I think a few nerves are good."

"I like that," Herman said just as someone called him over. "Knock 'em dead, Queen."

"Thanks."

In a few minutes, Herman had done everything that Tommy himself should have done for Nyah.

"Have a good sh—" was all he got a chance to offer before the MC interrupted him. If Tommy pushed in to wish her luck, he'd likely annoy her further and she needed to focus on her performance. He did the only thing he could do, yelled the loudest when the MC announced Queen Roe, to make sure she heard every cheer.

Chapter Eighteen

I'm about to body this set. Nyah drew her energy from the crowd who looked to her to dazzle them. They whistled in anticipation of her first sounds. Her nerves tingled with excitement of what she hoped would be a great show.

She moved her fader and when static and feedback blared from the speakers, Nyah froze. The audience closest to her got it the worst and their hands flew to their ears accompanied by massive growls. She hastily started to fiddle with the wire, making it worse. "Fuck!" She'd just gone over this with the techie. She cut the beat and the crowd groaned. She closed her eyes for a moment and breathed. In the past, this would be the moment where she'd fall into herself and focus on the mechanics of deejaying and then fail. She clapped her hands overhead and encouraged the fans to do the same. When they joined in she held tight to the fact that they hadn't yet completely given up on her. She unplugged all the wires and redid the hookup herself and tested it.

She had something to prove every time she got up onstage. She wanted to demonstrate to the shamed version of the Nyah living inside her, hugging her knees and rocking back and forth in humiliation, that Queen

Roe had her back, front, sides, tops and bottoms. Nyah's alter ego put her arms around her and promised to never let either of them get booed away from the stage ever again.

She sweated under the sun and adjusted the tee shirt that hung loosely where her butt cheeks and thighs met. The fishnet stockings she wore added more edge to her outfit while keeping her cool, and her knee-high black and white Converse sneakers would provide the comfort she needed. She stretched for the two-hour workout ahead. Tommy had exhausted her last night but the anticipation of her current performance filled her up again on another level. She felt good, and despite not being in the familiar club setting, she had this. Her intention, however dangerous, was to draw everyone on this ship within listening distance to her.

She began her work on the dials and the full-bodied sound of her bass hugged her and everyone on the pool deck. The sound rippled over the open air. *That got their attention. Let's see how they like this.* She pressed one of the sound buttons on the dials, and her fingers flicked the fader. The slightly higher note of the bassoon fluttered over the bass. Memories of Tommy mimicking the tonguing technique on her finger, her nipple, and her clit rushed back, even though she was pissed at him. The thoughts blazed hotter than the overhead sun and infused her with intoxicating energy she had to release and share.

She listened in her headphones and turned the knobs to speed up the fluttering instrument, teasing the listeners in an attempt to bring them to the bursting point. The crowd cheered and their hands lifted to the sky.

She had them right where she wanted. She let loose the melody and the crowd exploded. The bikini and trunks-clad cruisers splashed in the pool and tossed balloons around. She danced onstage like she performed high-impact aerobics. *That's right...come with me. We have places to go.* Her hands mimicked the same welcoming gesture as she jumped up and down and bounced from side to side. She smiled and as she looked into the faces for as far as she could see, they smiled back. Her eyes landed on a familiar face. "Irwin," she called and blew him a kiss. *That should make you the envy of your crew.*

On and on she went, mixing in the songs she'd prepared for her set. Tommy had inspired her in many ways. He'd been fucking up all day. Just because they were boning buddies didn't give him license to stop doing his job. She'd jabbed him enough times for him to recognize her particular varietal of saltiness. She didn't see him or know where he hid, but she intended to draw him out. She mixed "Queen Tings" by Masego into her track—the song Tommy had requested Trinket play at her friend's house party—and turned the song into a souped-up club-banger. Her energy multiplied as her long legs alternated high knee-kicks around the stage. She touched the hot keys on the controller to enhance the song with effects and sang to the songs she played. She exhausted her body, giving everything she had to her performance. These music lovers deserved her best and in that moment with them, she didn't think of disguises or consequences, of media or the drones flying overhead. She'd move the crowd at all costs.

The crowd that had gathered for her had swollen to concerning numbers and the immense pool deck now felt too small. At the end of her set, she saluted Bedazzled Beats's hot summer collaboration "Love Me Love You" and slapped a brand spanking new and unexpected drop. The crowd went wild, their dancing feet vibrating the ship. Nyah worried that the massive vessel may have lost people overboard. Perspiration drenched her shirt but her Afro puffs were still tight. Her *edges*, on the other hand, might be less *snatched* and more a hot mess of curly, drenched baby hairs. Her makeup normally withstood her performances but the smudge stains on her light shirt revealed that she'd sweat some of it off. Her saving grace? Breathless, she peered through her tinted shades at the jubilant crowd who mirrored the magic of the moment. *Yes!*

"Thanks for having me, Oh Ship! You guys have been great!" She closed out her set and the MC voice boomed through the speakers.

"GIVE IT UP FOR QUEEN ROE, SLAUGHTERING THE BEATS FOR YOU MUSIC MONSTERS OUT HERE ON THE SIZZLING POOL DECK!"

Nyah's eyes stung from the perspiration and makeup seeping into her eyes; still, she waved to the new additions to her kingdom. They roared and clapped back, happy and spent.

You did well, Queen.

She skipped down and off the stage, and followed her post performance routine, posing for pictures, shaking hands, and speaking to bloggers and vloggers. She put her hood attached to her tee shirt over her hair, but when she tried to squeeze to the bar, she was bombarded. Industry people congratulated her and questioned her about where she'd play next. Several people asked her to connect with her, shoving cards in her face. Her glasses got knocked and she adjusted their crooked feel. She wanted out of the claustrophobia the smothering crowd created around her. She plastered a shaky smile on her face and pushed through with more aggression.

Someone reached for her and she recognized Tommy's beautiful and strong hand. After all, it had been all over and inside her body 'til the early hours of the morning.

"Ease up, guys. Let her through. You want a piece of her? You gotta go through me first." He made space for her and pulled her through the last aisle of people and fans. "I got you," he said, and draped a protective arm around her waist. He took her to a corner of the deck.

"You okay?" he asked.

"That was eventful." Still winded from her performance and the adrenaline pumping through her with the onslaught of bodies she'd just made her way through, she gasped to catch her breath.

"A bit understated but I'll take it." He rubbed her shoulders. "That set, though… I've seen you at Rebel, but this? It'll go down as one of the most savage performances of the cruise, if not in Oh Ship history."

"That good, huh?" She'd slayed the stage but kept the praise in perspective. "The pool deck definitely felt like the turn up spot."

"Woman, you brought the house…ship down, and had everyone eating out of your hands." He shook his head at her.

"Thanks."

"How do you feel?" he asked.

"I feel good. Plugged in." Thirsty and dehydrated,

she licked her lips. "I could use a drink, though. I think I splashed my water on the crowd."

He stared at her mouth long enough for her to notice. "I, uh, fuck, I want to kiss you."

"I know." She briefly inspected the laces on her sneakers. "You do this thing with your tongue just before you kiss me."

"What thing?" he asked, and she ran her tongue along the middle of her upper lip and his focus on her mouth intensified. He straightened as if returning to the present moment. She wanted to learn every dirty thought that ran through his head. She blamed her lustful state on post-performance adrenaline but then again...last night and this morning.

"I had to get you out of that crowd. I didn't expect backstage to get at you like that. Even professionals can be fans." He changed the subject without any transition, and she wondered if he pulled back because he was on the job or maybe the realization of what happened between them came with some regret. She could relate. She gave her emotions a quick smack down and did her best to keep their interaction business casual.

"It's cool." She shrugged but deep down the reality started to break through. In the heat of the moment she'd wowed the crowd and set her demand on fire. Maybe things would cool off. After all, she'd played the day party on the pool deck. With all the other big names on the ship, she'd likely be a passing blip on the ship's echo sounder.

"Well, Queen. Allow me to serve you with all the libations you require." He placed his hand over his heart as if pledging to provide her with a plethora of liquids to hydrate with. He followed his verbal promise with an offered arm. "May I?"

"You may." She hooked her arm with his. A calmer flow of interested enthusiasts approached them, and Tommy expertly handled the mayhem, which was gold. She didn't bring up last night again, but given that they shared a stateroom, there would soon be no place for either of them to hide.

Chapter Nineteen

After Nyah's performance Tommy kept her busy with introductions and conversations about her next engagements. He'd single-handedly advertised for Artistique, sure-ing up the likelihood of seeing familiar faces at the small festival.

He could easily conduct the additional meetings when he got back to LA, but he wanted to strike while the iron seared white hot. He choreographed it all to avoid being alone with Nyah for fear he'd consume her whole. However, there remained a cold front coming from her. He'd address it as soon as they were alone.

"I hear Pete Monroe's daughter is going to be playing there," someone said and Tommy's senses dinged like a warning button.

"Oh, word?" Tommy raised his brows so high with feigned curiosity that his muscles twitched. He glanced at Nyah, who went rigid and via their voiceless communication questioned if they knew who she was.

"Yeah. Some classical shit. That's a hard pass for me," a spiky-haired DJ announced. "Yo, did you guys hear they are honoring Pete at Sunburst this year? Sucks that he didn't have a kid to pass down all that genius to. I'd gladly apprentice."

Tommy gaped at the guy who didn't even realize he'd been listening to classical instruments the whole time Queen Roe played. The corner of her lip twitched and even if she'd never admit it, that lame ass's comment had to prick her, even if only a little.

"Yeah, I heard that, too." Nyah joined in the conversation. "That's going to be epic."

Tommy bit his tongue when it got all twisted with what to say to her statement. Nyah's amusement with this muted version of him didn't help.

"For sure. I can't wait. Tommy, any of your people up for Sunburst?" someone asked.

Fuck! "Nah, man. Not this year. My clients are either too big or not interested but I'll be there."

"Cool."

Tommy had at least managed to inhibit further investigation.

"Well, guys, I think I'm going to call it." Nyah finally tapped out.

"No way. Come on, Queen?" a blond-headed DJ begged, her ponytail swinging as she spoke. "Don't leave me with these bums."

"We have to book it to the airport when the ship docks in the morning and I have quite a bit to pack," she said. "Not to mention you guys have been plying me with drinks."

"Don't you want dinner?" Rize asked.

"I'm going to order a shit ton of room service is what I'm going to do and devour that shit in private." She rose to her feet.

Everyone laughed. Her personality and ability to win over, well, everyone so far, made him even prouder to know her.

"I have to stop by reception, maybe I'll meet up with you guys later. If not, I'll see you at the next one." Tommy rose with her. "I'll come with you."

Once they were well out of view, he heard Nyah breathe for the first time. "That was fucking close."

"They had no idea," he assured her.

"You sure about that?" she asked with raised brow in her tone.

"Pretty sure. You would have been grilled much longer if they had."

She seemed okay with his explanation, yet fixed a frown on her face.

"Nyah, about earlier—"

"What about earlier?" she snapped.

His meeting running over and checking things out earlier were all truthful reasons he'd loaded in the chamber to shoot at her but that she didn't even look at him meant he had little room for error. "I should have been at your set with enough time to take care of you. I fucked up."

"Yeah, you fucked up." She pursed her lips.

He reached for her hand and slowed down to a stop. He faced her. "It's my job to be there for you, at all costs. I'm sorry."

She kept a hard façade.

"Forgiven?" he asked, giving her arm a shake.

"This time. Don't let it happen again." She poked his chest.

Glad to be forgiven, he continued to walk with her.

They passed reception and Nyah stopped. "Okay,
I'll see you later."

"Huh?"

She pointed. "Reception's that way."

"Oh. That was bullshit. I'm ready to be shipwrecked.
I'll head back with you."

"Cool." She shrugged.

When they arrived at their stateroom, Nyah opened
the door to her suite's side and he hung in the entryway.
She didn't speak to his awkward move and parked her
rear on the arm of the couch, giving him a thorough
low-lid study.

He finally spoke. "You're giving me that look again."

"What look?" she responded coyly.

"The kind that makes it hard for me to walk away,"
he said. She knew exactly how to make him hornier
than an ungelded stallion sniffing out a mare in heat.

She sauntered toward his figure by the door. "Then
why don't you come in, take your clothes off and show
me why they really call you Boombox."

He sucked in a sharp breath. His dick jumped at her
words, making his slacks two sizes too small as he hardened behind the material.

"I've never met anyone like you." The words drib-
bled out.

Her fingers curved around his tie and she slipped the
length through her hand. His mind flashbacked to her
performing the same motion around his cock. "What
do you mean?" she asked, tugging on his tie.

"You know what you want, and you go for it, un-
apologetically, unfiltered. But more importantly you

know what you don't want. You're not afraid to say no, or rock the boat. That makes you—"

"Annoying?" she asked.

"Powerful. More powerful than you realize."

She folded her arms over her chest and studied them before returning her gaze to his. "I don't think most people would agree."

"If you haven't already noticed, I'm not most people. Don't make yourself small because someone can't match up. Make them rise to you."

"Including you?" She tugged on his tie.

"Especially me."

She tugged again on his tie and lifted to her toes.

He stared into her passionate and trusting brown eyes and his earlier words about Sunburst echoed in his head. *My clients are either too big or not interested but I'll be there.* Without her knowledge, he groomed Nyah specifically for that purpose, and the closeness they shared made him feel guilty enough to pull away. Even as his cells, down to the atom, screamed for her embrace, he slipped his tie from her fingers and her seduction-infused features were wiped clean.

"I should go. You need a good night's rest for tomorrow. I'll see you in the morning."

"Hey." He heard her gulp. "Did I say something wrong? I was teasing… You know, flirting. I thought we were on the same page."

He mustered a smile. "You neither said nor did anything wrong. It's been a long day and I think I'm gonna crash. I'll see you tomorrow."

"No… I mean, of course." She tried to appear unaffected but he disappointed her. Again. His dick slapped him around for denying it her pussy, but he had more to protect than his urges.

He ducked into his suite's entrance as quickly as his fingers would let him. Once inside he breathed a hefty sigh and ran his fingers through his hair, pacing the gold trellis designed navy blue carpet. He froze when Nyah's figure stood in the frame of the open door that led into her suite. Her eyes clouded with confusion and dismay. Her head hung as she gently closed the door, and the sound of the lock followed.

Fuck.

Nyah rinsed the disappointment down the drain along with the soap and conditioner. The activity on the cruise had been nonstop with music, socializing and networking, and her only desire was to snuggle into bed and be with her feelings. She toweled off, tended to her wet hair and slipped on a night shirt that she could easily smoosh into her luggage in the morning along with her toiletry bag.

Damn Sexy, the front of her red nightshirt read. "Damn right," she affirmed. She needed the boost and who better to give it to her than herself?

Her body, however, needed Tommy more than she wanted to document. After witnessing him in his suite, she felt like a toy he'd gotten tired of playing with. She'd deliberately avoided crowding him. Hell, she hadn't even asked him to talk again, even though it had been on the tip of her tongue most of the day. She silently thanked her classical training for discipline.

They'd been building up to this since she sat with him at Rebel. On rare occasions she misread a sexual invitation. Certain she hadn't misinterpreted Tommy's desire for her, she racked her brain. *What went wrong? What did I say? What didn't I say?*

"Stop!" she shouted. "Check your fucking ego, bitch. Not everything is about you. It's not your fault."

She and Tommy had spent some time together since reconnecting at Rebel, but Tommy proved to be more of a mystery than she'd originally understood. She went through the list of potential reasons. Maybe he was worried she was getting the wrong idea about their time together and thought she wanted something long term. Maybe he didn't date clients, or maybe there was another woman? Maybe *she* was the other woman.

None of them hit red on the truth meter. They'd chatted and he neither alluded to nor had a slip of the tongue regarding any of those things. Surely, Oscar would have clued her in when they'd chatted. Back when she met Tommy at her father's party, she couldn't retrieve anything from that time either.

Her self-confidence deflated like a punctured bicycle tire. She sighed. "Maybe he just doesn't want me." *That's bullshit.* Tommy wanted her as much as she wanted him. "So, what's the fucking problem?" She didn't know but if her pussy could talk it would urge her to make haste and figure it out, because it was open and ready to welcome Tommy.

A knock on the door adjoining their suites sounded.

"Yeah?" Nyah asked.

"Can I come in?"

"No." She regretted the decision as soon as it left her tongue.

He sighed and something hit the door. She hoped

it was his head hanging in disgrace. "That was a dick move, angel."

"Glad we agree." She crossed her arms.

He tried the door again. "Will you let me in so I can apologize to you?"

"You don't need to see me to apologize. Think of it as *The Voice* for jerks. I'll hear if you're genuine or not."

"You're a tough lady."

"If you're just figuring that out, then you're not the crunchiest chip in the bag. That's disappointing."

"Nyah."

"Tommy," she mimicked.

His sigh echoed against the wood door.

"I had a great time with you last night. All day, I wanted to touch you and taste you again and feel you come under me. But I'd be irresponsible if I didn't consider how this could affect our working relationship. It's not the best idea and I think you know that," he said.

She leaned her head back on the wall next to the door and stared at the ceiling. Her thoughts were filled with Tommy and how good he made her feel for the early part of the day. Later on, with him doing his agent-y shit, she'd started to question whether or not they'd made a wrong move giving into their attraction. She didn't believe that Tommy would screw her like Carlo or else she had no business having him as her agent, but if he did, would she be able to let him go? If he realized that she wasn't the kind of artist he wanted to continue to work with, how would she feel? Even though their situation was supposed to be temporary, what if she wanted a long-term work relationship with him? Tommy had more than grown on her and she wanted more. Of what, she wasn't yet sure.

"Talk to me, angel."

She wanted to make him wait it out a bit more, but his statement resonated with what she'd been feeling. His chilly response to her invitation, however, had done little to cool her down and she still craved for whatever closeness she could get. Her fingers turned the knob and opened the partition between them. She leaned against the door as it clattered against the wall, the sound of wood meeting wood reverberated against her back.

"You have a point, Tommy, but what happened between us last night is not something that can be easily put back into a box."

"I released the kraken," he teased.

"Literally." She homed in on his dick, surprised to see a larger bump than before. "You don't actually call it that to people in real life, do you?"

"No." He snorted.

"Good choice."

"It's not easy to walk away from you. This has been…different from what I thought it would be. I'm not used to being in this position." His admission hit the soft spot in her chest.

"What do you mean by that?" she asked. When his cheeks rouged all the way to his hairline, her eyes widened. She grabbed his hand when she feared he'd flee. "Tell me what you mean, Tommy."

"This was supposed to be casual, right?"

"Boat boning buddies," she said.

"Is that what you call me?" He half frowned, half smiled.

"Uhh." She pursed her lips and forced herself not to joke her way out of this conversation. She cared about what he felt and what he thought and she didn't want to miss an opportunity to know how he saw her. How he saw this. "Never mind that. Finish what you were saying."

He sighed. "I'm hard pressed to think that boat boning buddies won't be enough," he mumbled. "Are you surprised?"

"What makes you say that?" she asked, her defenses up.

"Because those gorgeous eyes are about ready to pop out of your head."

"Oh." She closed her eyes for a second and tried to soften her features. "It's just that dudes are normally the ones with commitment issues. I mean, am I even your type? What's your type?"

"Independent, knows what she wants and goes after it, powerful…women I find to be sexy as fuck." He appraised her up and down as he spoke.

"I'm your type."

"Clearly," he responded, but she couldn't help but get the sense that he held back additional attributes. The bad ones.

"What else?" she asked.

He took off his glasses to clean them, which he did when he was either bored or avoiding something.

"It's okay, Tommy. You can be honest."

"Unavailable or uninterested in a relationship."

She twisted her mouth thinking about their interactions and how well they matched. They verbally sparred with ease and their attraction didn't fizzle but rather grew with each encounter. That alone had been unlike anything she'd experienced in her previous relationships. Something different existed between them. Tommy saw her, and not just one part of her, but all of her parts. Was that why she'd allowed the lines to blur when she was so used to keeping everything in its clearly plotted garden? How could she declare any of this to him with so much at stake for the careers she managed. Was she unavailable? Could she make space for him? Would they be able to work and love together without convoluting their relationship roles?

She swallowed and her heart rate doubled.

"What wrong? You look like you're being hovered over the edge of Big Sur."

"Do I?" She licked her lips. *Love* rolled around through her head like a pinball in the machine, ringing as it hit "hell no" side rails and "what the fuck" bumper caps.

"I'd say you were absolutely petrified." He stroked her arms. "I didn't tell you this to freak you out. I just wanted to be honest."

"Maybe we didn't think this through all the way." She stepped closer to him and rested her arms on his waist. His hands glided up over her shoulders to form along the sides of her neck where he continued his divine caress.

"But like you said, all of this is hard to repackage." His face inched toward hers and she nuzzled her nose against his.

"Maybe—" Her lips grazed his. "We can try to pack it up after..." She didn't wait for him to pull her to him before she joined their mouths, her tongue licking into the welcoming warmth of his.

"After what, Nyah?" He bit her lower lip.

"While we're here on this ship, let's pretend that we want the same things. That this won't change anything and let's promise to be honest with each other and re-alistic about what might or might not be when we get back to our 'real' lives."

"And now…" His hand teased down the front of nightshirt.

"Now you can take me to *your* bed," she whispered.

"I thought you were hungry and were going to order a shit ton of room service."

"I am. It'll be just the sustenance I need after you fuck me. Don't you think?"

He licked his lip in that divine way that let her know he wanted to kiss her and she opened to him, for him. He pressed his mouth against hers and released her just as quick. He gave her ass a firm but lingering smack. "Go to my bed, Nyah."

She did so with him close behind her.

He picked up the cordless room phone and the menu binder and pushed them both toward her. As she ordered room service, he nuzzled her neck and undressed her.

Chapter Twenty

Tommy's labored breath swirled with Nyah's as they chased the addictive rise to ecstasy.

"Don't come yet," Nyah instructed. "You have to earn that."

Tommy's dick felt like a boiling kettle whose steam was about to whistle right through the condom. "Fuck, Nyah."

"You want to earn it, right?" she cooed. Her limits had been pushed just as much as his as he braced her hips for his movements, grinding his hips with hers and thrusting deep and hard, like she requested.

"Yes. Fuck yes." He'd do whatever she wanted, including eating dairy and running around the ship naked. Anything to explode in pleasure with her.

"Harder, Tommy. Don't stop. Don't you dare fucking stop." Sweat glistened over her collar bone and a misty pattern covered her chest down to the well between her small breasts. "Yes.

He captured her mouth, mushing his lips into hers, his tongue darting and licking into her heat. "Did I earn it?" he asked.

"Yes." She huffed.

"Can I come now?"

"Y-y-yes. Tommy, please," she squealed. "I'm com—" Nyah swallowed her words and twisted and flailed on the bed but he grabbed her and wrapped her arms around his neck, then again locked her hips in his hand as he piston-pumped her pussy. The pressure in him had nowhere to go but out and he released with a shout that vibrated the walls like the bass in Queen Roe's set earlier.

He gave her everything he had left, pushing into her and holding her, even as the strength left his arms. He held her close to him. She shivered against, shaking out the last spasms of her orgasm.

"Mmm," she moaned, hugging him.

"How didn't I know you were a low-key freak?"

"Not so low-key. You forgot about last night already?" she teased. "Plus, where's the fun in that?" Her nipples hardened against his chest from the air-conditioned room that was too hot not less than a minute ago.

"Hang on," he said as he lifted her on wobbly legs and brought her up to the top of the bed. His dick softened inside her but he wasn't ready to separate from her delectable insides. He opened the bed and placed her inside, lying on top of her.

"I don't want to leave." He peered down between them even though his body sealed to hers. His statement got a giggle from her and he wanted to capture the sound like she'd blown him a kiss and place it right on his heart.

Nyah stroked his hair with lazy fingers and he flattened one side of his face against her chest. He knew he had to pull out, or what use would the condom be, but *fuck* if she didn't feel like home.

He slid out of her with a firm grip on the latex, protecting them, and he couldn't remember a time when he'd filled the bag so much. "I'll be back," he said to her and her outstretched arms. His bare feet thudded toward the bathroom and he handled the condom with care before tossing into a trash bin. He cleaned himself quickly so he could prepare a warm washcloth for her and returned to his comfort spot between her legs, then wiped her pussy and inner thighs with delicate strokes."

"Thank you," she said, her voice hoarse and thick with gratitude.

"My pleasure, angel." She deserved to be cherished from beginning to end. He kissed her inner thigh before rising again and taking care of the washcloth. When he returned, he slipped on his boxer briefs and sat on the edge of the bed, his back to her. He needed a minute to come back down to reality, which got harder and harder every minute more he spent with Nyah, in or out of bed.

She stroked his back and from the movements of her hand he knew she traced the angel wings spanning his back and arms. "Who's Carmen?" Her soft question punched him in the stomach and air left him as if she physically had.

"My aunt."

"The same one you mentioned before? The one who drinks her carajillo with Dominican rum?" she asked.

"Yes. Oscar's mom," he answered. "She loved seafood, too. I remember our family went to City Island for my high school graduation. There was a ladybug in my mother's salad and the service was so slow, I could have gone in the kitchen and cooked my family dinner myself. The manager felt bad so we ended up getting a lot of complimentary wine and seafood. Tia Carmen must have eaten a sea of shrimp that night."

They laughed together at the memory. "She sounds like a lot of fun."

"She was." He swallowed hard. "She, uh, passed away that following year."

Her hands outlined his skin from his neck down to his triceps She kissed one of his shoulders. "I'm sorry, Tommy."

"Most kids have a best friend their age. Tia Carmen was mine," he confessed.

She ran her hand over his tattoo, and then turned her body into his lap and wrapped her arms around his neck.

"She taught me so much about life. I mean…nothing was off limits. She never judged me for the questions I asked about work, relationships, sex, and politics. I learned about the kind of man I wanted to be because of her. The kind of man I wanted to be to the women in my life. She listened. I mean really listened to me and the lessons I learned from her, I keep with me. Here." He touched his heart. "And here." He pointed to his back. "She's my guardian angel."

"That's really sweet. I'm sure she's very proud of you from where she is."

He loved that she spoke of Tia Carmen in the present because that's how he felt, like his aunt was always with him. "I can see how important and special she is to you."

"Tell me about yours." He asked more than stated it

as he ran his hand over her left rib. This morning, as she slept, he'd freely ogled her body and the tattoo on her rib in beautiful calligraphy he'd memorized. *Failure will never overtake me if my determination to succeed is strong enough. Tell me the reality is better than the dream.*

"When I came back and decided to DJ again, I got this." She stretched her naked body before him. "It was important that I reminded myself in a bigger way than just a mantra or promise. I wanted the words etched into me. I needed to commit to it with more than words."

"Do you feel like you've stuck to your commitment?" he asked with genuine curiosity.

"I do. Don't get me wrong, I still avoid some venues and festivals that I worry will only result in failure. I'm determined to attack it my way, instead of letting others lead me too far away from the path I want to walk."

"But you did great today. Isn't that a step in the right direction?"

He justified the guilt that once again bubbled in his chest.

"What direction is that?" she asked.

He foresaw their conversation quickly derailing. "You tell me." He threw it back to her.

"Whatever direction *I* want to go," she stated.

He slowed his breathing. "I'm willing to help you with that. You don't have to tackle it all on your own," he said.

"On my terms," she reminded him.

He chuckled. "On your terms." He nuzzled her neck, ready for another round with her, but a low knock on the door interrupted his plans.

"Room service," a muffled voice called through the door.

He didn't want to let her go and though her stomach growled several times during their lovemaking, she made no move to get up either. He eased her off him, feeling the reluctance in her arms. "You need to eat."

She backed up onto the bed and slid her naked body under a sheet while he left to answer the door. He returned with a tray filled with food. He wheeled it into the bedroom and her eyes lit up. She stretched back into her night shirt and skipped to the tray, opening each cover to reveal a different appetizer and entree.

"Dessert's on the bottom."

She plucked a mozzarella stick off the appetizer tray and dipped it in marinara sauce before gobbling half the stick in one bite. He took a wing as she took a salad plate and put a few of the different appetizers on it, grabbed a fork and sat cross-legged on the bed. She nestled the plate between her legs.

He uncovered a plate of fried calamari and hovered the plate in front of her. She popped one in her mouth and forked a few more onto her plate.

He sat across from her and ate with her. When she finally came up for air, she gave a deep exhale. "I'm so hungry."

"Hence why you wanted privacy," he noted.

"Exactly." She smiled. "But I don't care. Mama's gotta eat."

He slurped on Clams Casino, the salty goodness of the clam enhanced with the addition of pancetta to the breadcrumbs and tomatoes.

He loved that she ate without reservation. Women in

his culture knew how to throw down some food. Nyah also shared a culture where food and family were front and center. Pete hailed from the South and her mother from Ghana and Jamaica, if he remembered correctly.

"You worked up quite an appetite today with that performance. I should have fed you right after, instead of letting those guys buy you all those drinks." He frowned.

"I was too amped to eat. The drinks were a good choice." She pointed to the tray. "Can you pass me the salmon eggs Benedict, please?"

He did as she asked and she switched out her greens for the velvety beautiful plate of eggs, salmon and hollandaise sauce on two toasted slices of English muffins. A side of fragrant home fries with onions and peppers rested on the side.

"I got you a burger without cheese and French fries. Also salad. Besides the mozzarella sticks and three cheese mini mac and cheese bites you should be able to eat everything else.

He wanted to wrap this woman in his arms and never let her go. "Thank you."

"Anytime." Her features changed from humor to something more intense. "Thank *you* for sharing Tia Carmen with me."

"Thank you for listening." He near choked on the calamari he'd been devouring. *Esta mujer es asombrosa.* "You were really amazing tonight, Nyah. I've seen a lot of performers but you were incredible. Hypnotic."

"Keep it comin'," she egged him on.

"No, really. It was an absolute smasher. I bet the fans would agree.

"Every day I'm with you, I see just how amazing you really are."

She wiped her mouth with a napkin. "Took you long enough." She winked at him.

"*Que modestia.*" He laughed. "What modesty," he translated for her.

"I have my moments." She covered her mouth as she chomped on savory eggs.

He stared at her for a long time. Adorable and happy, she ate and sucked on her fingers with a half-eaten mini brioche lobster roll on the edge of her plate. For the first time, he thought even though she was his type, maybe she didn't have to be part of his pattern.

Chapter Twenty-One

Nyah suffocated from Gladys's hug at practice. "I missed you. I know it wasn't that long but you're my philharmonic sweetheart."

Nyah needed the embrace. Since leaving the ship her skin felt foreign without Tommy against it. Not to mention three more days of not having a club gig or practice and performance for the philharmonic. Being in the familiar setting of the old hall and seeing the other musicians and the stage almost made her weep. "I missed you, too. I'm so glad to be back. Anything gossip-worthy since I been gone?"

"Not really. We're just wrapping up the season and getting ready for the summer series in the park." Nyah knew all too well the scramble that the musicians who didn't have anything lined up for the summer underwent to find gigs to keep their skills sharp and supplement their income. "Oh and word on the street is that CeCe is making her decision about the symphony within the next two weeks. We should probably hear a yay or nay soon."

Nyah crossed her fingers at Gladys. "I hope you get it."

"I hope you do too," They touched crossed fingers. "Hey, I saw you're playing at Artistique. Why didn't you tell me?"

Nyah stared and blinked, then blinked and stared. "What?"

"What the fuck is wrong with you? Artistique, with Trinidad? You okay?"

Nyah's relief had to be visible. "Yeah, I'm great. It's no big deal."

"It's not a big deal that you are doing a classical fusion set with an eclectic Californian artist? Nyah?"

"I wasn't sure they'd let me in." Nyah had been so focused on getting in to DJ as Queen Roe that she almost forgot Trinidad had asked her to do a classical improv piece with him. The brain fart was highly unlike her, but she recovered. "I only found out right before the cruise."

"Oh. How was the cruise?" Gladys winked so hard her eyelashes tangled. "You know you have to give me every detail. Okay, maybe not every detail. Keep it high level with a dash of dirty."

"Gladys!" Nyah laughed. "We had fun."

Her friend put her hand on her narrow hips. "That's all you're going to give me? Stop it."

"We got to know each other better, we dined, met some really interesting people and that's all." This might be the best time for Nyah to break the news to Gladys that Tommy was just a friend, but the word didn't feel right anymore. During the cruise, he'd become much more. As much as the thought unsettled her, it comforted her as well.

"Liar. Your pants are smokin,' bitch. Come on. Just a crumb?"

"He was great." Nyah fluttered her eyebrows.

Gladys clenched her chest. "He rocked your world, didn't he?"

Nyah neither confirmed nor denied.

"He looks like he has porno swag, you know? Freaky deaky?" Gladys laughed.

"Okay, that's all. Let's not talk about this again." Nyah pressed the back of her hand to her hot face.

"Wow. He really worked you over. Look at you." Now doubled in laughter, Gladys's body swayed when Nyah pushed at her shoulder.

"You can stop now." Nyah looked around. "For real. Before people start looking at us weird."

"Congratulations," Gladys said. "Now I can tell you that Evan and I made out last Saturday."

"What?" Nyah exclaimed.

"Let's get started," Martin's voice interrupted at a key point in their conversation. One that Nyah would never forgive. "Welcome back, Nyah."

"Thank you, Martin. It's good to be back." Nyah's eyes threw flames at her friend's back as she moved to percussions. Gladys even had the nerve to smirk at her.

"I got you," Nyah mouthed.

"Let's start with Tchaikovsky, Symphony no. 6, 'Pathétique'."

One of the symphonies that changed the world. Nyah organized her sheet music and followed along with Martin's notes on the piece. Movement after movement they played and she settled into the piece like her favorite cozy chair. At that moment she vowed never to fuck up with Martin again. She loved being here, playing her bass with other musicians in this collaborative way, but she had a second equally important love, deejaying at Rebel. With Nyah's performances Friday through Sunday, she wouldn't play at the underground club until the next week.

After practice Nyah headed home but not before getting the details from Gladys about her little romp with Evan. Nyah smiled and shook her head, recalling Gladys's sarcasm at every stage of her and Evan's fast-growing relationship. Gladys had always been honest with her even if it sometimes came with a sharp edge, and Nyah loved her friend, nonetheless. She decided that no matter what, she'd tell Gladys the truth about Queen Roe after Artistique. She didn't want to deal with the possible fallout before an event she had looked forward to for months, but the decision weighed on her. Was she being selfish? *Why am I doing this to myself?* Again she prayed her friend would understand why she kept the secret. They'd known each other for the last two years, since Gladys came to the philharmonic. Nyah's DJ career had not yet started to encroach on her classical life the way it had now. *After Artistique. I promise, Gladys.*

The layout of Nyah's apartment felt foreign without a partition to connect her to Tommy. In the short time they were on the ship, she'd gotten used to his cologne lingering where he'd been, seeing him most of the day, and dining with him. Nothing, however, prepared her for missing the closeness they shared in bed.

"We'll touch base when I'm back in New York" were Tommy's last words to her at the airport before they separated—him to LA, and her to the city. They'd slept together in his bed, and the morning of their departure, when she had gotten up to get ready to leave, the distance divided them like a ravine. She figured that he dealt with all his clients this way and that she should welcome his professionalism but she wanted more and that scared her enough to keep her mouth shut about it, nod, and wish him a safe flight.

She took comfort in the photos on her wall of her friends and family to cope with his absence. She'd captured a few snapshots on the ship, including a selfie with Tommy and one of him looking out at sea. The wind flattened his shirt against his chest and stomach and blew through the back of his shirt like a balloon. Her neck still hurt from hanging her head, most of her flight back, to pine over the photo. The images she'd taken were categorized as before and after they'd sexed.

Over the next week she settled back into her normal routine. Trinket had texted her a few times and though they had a quick chat they promised to reconnect at Rebel for Queen Roe's set on Friday night. Her grind didn't let up, but she looked forward to seeing her friends and the regulars. "I hope it's a good night."

Little did she know the absolute shit storm that awaited her.

As soon as Tommy had gotten back to LA he had festivals and club circuits for his clients to attend. The hot months were here and his clients were everywhere. He'd devoted a lot to time to Queen Roe, but he had to keep his other clients progressing, growing, and happy. He'd gotten a few texts and messages from people wanting to book Nyah once Oh Ship had concluded and docked at port. On the ship, service to land had pretty much been nonexistent, or spotty at best. He hadn't read many of his messages since he'd bypassed the names in search of one. *Nyah*.

She hadn't reached out to him since they'd separated at the airport but that didn't stop her from filling his every waking thought. Now, finally back in his office, he tried to get back to business.

"Tommy," Yaz called to him.

"Yeah." He blinked back to the present.

"Okay, that's the third time you've gone off to Wonderland. One time, I can understand, but three times in fifteen minutes?" Yaz raised a brow in her something-is-up kind of way.

"Sorry about that. I guess I'm a little distracted this morning." He'd been more than distracted. Last night he tossed and turned most of the night and even after rubbing one out, he still longed to have Nyah in his arms again, talking to him, comforting him, fucking him. He missed her penetrating eyes and humor, the way she drew him to her without a word. His favorite breakfast tasted bland and lifeless and his coffee like muddy water.

"You okay?"

"I'm all right." He wasn't. He was homesick and sleeping between Nyah's legs, caressing her body, listening to her laughter vibrate against his face and feeling her fingers glide through his hair was the home he longed to be again. In so little time she became what he wanted to eat, breathe, and sleep 24-7.

"Then can you focus long enough for me to get through this status. You'll be in New York next week and then you have your crazy ten days in Austin for Be-dazzled Beats, Ibiza with Luke, London for Magstripe, and then Artistique in Michigan with Queen Roe."

He hadn't been home that long since the cruise and already he was ready to get on a plane and head back to New York to see Nyah. "Sorry. I promise you have my full attention," he said.

Yaz eyed him for a long time with one squinted eye.

"What?" Tommy said between knitted brows.

"Something happened on that cruise with you and Queen Roe, didn't it?"

The forward question was a Yaz special. "What do you mean?"

Yaz tapped her chin. "You're distracted and you have a goofy smile on your face when you drift off. Plus you keep doing this thing with your mouth." He'd seen Yaz blush a few times but she turned full-on red this time.

"I didn't realize…never mind."

"You like her. A lot, obviously."

"Let's get back to your status report."

"Tommy…"

He raked his hand through his hair. "I like her."

Yaz's triumphant grin had him hanging his head. "I knew you did. I bet she likes you, too. Oh, the things that must have happened on that Love Boat." She laughed.

"Yaz." He shook his head to stop her from going any further.

"I'm impressed that you can admit it. Now that that's out of the way, can you please focus for thirty minutes? Please."

"I'm all yours." Tommy did his best to focus but

didn't worry if he didn't since Yaz's detailed reports would give him anything he missed.

"So Herman called."

That got his attention.

"He called here, too?" Tommy asked. Ever since Nyah's performance, his phone blew up with requests for her. He'd been too busy bedding her to attend to any of them. "He sent me a few messages."

"Maybe you should call him back." Having let Herman sweat it out a bit, Tommy agreed. "I will after we're done."

Yaz gave him a few more updates before they separated to tend to their own work. He wondered what Nyah was up to. He read the time, and by now she would have finished practice with the philharmonic. He pictured her in her apartment, looking at her picture wall and then practicing with one of her many instruments. He could smell the bamboo of the reed on her bassoon and the rosin from her double bass. She'd walked in her socks the night he'd first been there after her performance at Boiler, and on the ship her slender feet padded on the carpet in his suite. Which one did she do now? Was she home or out with friends, chatting about her trip? Did she talk about him?

Tommy settled his racing mind and slipped behind his desk. He dialed Herman who picked up immediately.

"It's about time you got back to me," Herman barked into the phone.

"Sorry about that, man. It's been nonstop since getting back from cruise." Tommy offered little by way of excuse.

"Yeah, yeah. I would have taken a text," Herman grumbled.

"I thought that perhaps a conversation would be better."

"Preferred, but still…"

Tommy half smiled. "You gonna keep bustin' my balls or are we going to talk about what you want?"

"I'm about to give you what you've wanted for years. I want Queen Roe to play at Sunburst."

Yes! Tommy punched the air. "Finally, one of my clients cleared your strict standards?"

"She more than cleared it. She blew them right out the water. Her performance was the best of Oh Ship. Have you not seen the write-ups?"

He hadn't because he'd been too busy replaying the moments he'd brought Nyah to ecstasy multiple times over the course of their time on the cruise. He'd also had a hard time saying goodbye to her at the airport, no matter how diplomatic he'd behaved. He didn't want to admit to Herman that he was behind the eight ball. "I've been traveling and catching up on business. What's up?"

"Queen Roe's performance has been trending since the ship got into port. Apparently, the organizers put it up as part of a 'wish you were here' teaser but it's killin' it out there. Dude? How do you not know this?"

As Herman said the words, Tommy clicked to an Internet page and typed in Queen Roe and the video came up immediately. Tommy should have known this and should have alerted his client. A trending video could go viral and she should be prepared for the possible storm that came afterward.

"I need to go, Herman." Tommy needed to reach out to Nyah as soon as possible.

"Wait. What about Sunburst? Can I add Queen Roe to the lineup?" Herman asked.

"I need to present it to my client before I agree."

"You're kidding, right? I thought she'd be an automatic yes."

"Look on the bright side. At least I'm not saying no."

"Ha ha. Do me a favor and give me an answer. I'd love to have her but I'll only hold the spot to the end of the week."

"I'm not back on the east coast until next week and this isn't something I can pose to her over the phone."

"Why?"

"You want her to say yes, right? Give me two weeks?"

Herman sighed. "I got the bigwigs breathing down my neck for my confirmed spots. I'll try but I can't promise you that when you get back to me, I'll still have a spot for her."

"Do your best, man, and I'll try to give me an answer as soon as I can." *Fuck!* Tommy hadn't planned to head back to the east coast until next week. With all the information he'd received from his one phone conversation with Herman, going back to New York sooner was vital, as was seeing Nyah. He needed to see that woman more than he wanted food or drink.

"Talk then," Herman said. "And Tommy. Don't let me down. With the new organizers, this might be your last shot."

Like I need motivation... Tommy hated the low-key threat, but Herman had clued him into this months ago. "I hear you." They hung up.

Why send a text or call when he and Yaz could deliver the information in person? He sent Nyah a text
that he'd be back in New York sooner than expected
and had news to share.

"Yaz?"

"Yeah, boss?"

"Change of plans."

Chapter Twenty-Two

Nyah's phone wouldn't quit buzzing when she climbed out of the subway. "Who the fuck is blowing me up like this?" She pulled her phone from the side pocket on her cargo jeans.

Trinket: Don't come here!

A car screeched to a halt. The driver honked and practically blared her Afro puffs right out of their pink and silver glittered hair ties. "I got it," she yelled back with her entire body. Her heart raced even more than after receiving Trinket's cryptic text. She stopped by a bodega and responded to Trinket with startled energy in her fingers.

Queen: ??

Trinket: Don't come to Rebel. It's fucking mayhem... like... BANANAS

Queen: Why?? What happened?

Trinket: YOU BEEEEEETTTTTTTCCCCCHHHH!

"What the hell is going on?" All she'd done was get her shit together, got on the subway and headed to work like she always did after her performance at the concert hall.

Queen: ME? I'm performing 2nite

Trinket: I know but...
Trinket:...

Nyah watched the ellipsis of death pulse before disappearing. "What the fuck, Trinket?" She huffed and paced in a small space, which probably looked like she spun in circles, wondering what she should do. Trinket finally responded two long minutes later.

Trinket: Oscar said come through the back. I'll be there with security to get you
Trinket: Don't say I didn't warn you

"Security? Not nerve-wracking at all." Nyah shook her head as she strode toward Rebel.

A block and half away from Rebel, the crowd swarmed like ants circling a hearty bread crumb. People waited to get inside with energy in their bones. The last time she'd seen a crowd like this was when Rob Ready had come to the spot two years ago. She gawked, speechless, as she made her way to the back of the club. She pulled her hoodie over her large puffs and dipped her head. *Not fucking suspicious at all, Nyah.* The staggering lines made it almost impossible for her to get through to the back entrance, but when she did get to the heavy steel door she banged fast and hard.

Her hoodie slid back off her head and she felt the stares on her. Photographers came out of nowhere and flashes nearly blinded her. The crowd moved in on her like slow-moving walls on slow-suffocation mode, and her pulse pounded in her ear.

"Queen." A few people on line called her name, taking selfies with her in the background and pawed at her shoulders or tugged on her multicolored backpack.

The door slammed open and Trinket reached for her with two security guards, who made room for them and separated Nyah from the crowd.

"Back off," Trinket yelled, then she yanked Nyah inside and the two of them hurried backstage to the lockers.

Nyah dropped her bag on the floor and, with hands on knees, asked, "What happened? Why are so many more people here?"

"You really don't know?" Trinket asked.

Nyah peered up at her with murderous eyes. "Trinket, if you don't tell me, I swear—"

"Okay, okay." Trinket put her hands up. "Your performance on Oh Ship has been trending. Now it's viral."

Nyah jolted upright. She remembered that performance. She had been pissed at Tommy for giving her the shaft and wanted to get his attention. His and everyone else's. She had been in a surreal zone and when she came off stage, people had been all over her; like they were outside. "Oh no." *Let this be a lesson. Trying to get revenge only hurts you.*

"Girl, that fucking set. Even on video you bullied that shit."

"I didn't know. We left the cruise when it docked in the Bahamas. Why didn't it show up then?"

"You don't get any service when you're out at sea. When the ship pulled into port and people had service again, the organizers must have posted the performance. It's everywhere." Trinket crossed her arms. "Isn't this something Tommy should have warned you about? Real talk, though, it only made its way to me tonight, but doesn't he have like some agent pipeline to tap?"

"Yeah. He should've." Why hadn't Tommy given her a heads up about this? With the exception of a text he sent her two days ago that he'd be in New York, he hadn't spoken to her since they'd disembarked from the cruise and departed to their respective coasts. Now here she stood smack dab in the middle of her newfound celebrity. "This is crazy."

"I did warn you." Trinket shrugged. "Oscar called in extra security when the crowd showed up around eight."

"Eight? But I don't even go on until after midnight." Nyah rubbed her palms on her jeans, nerves suffocating her like ivy up a brick wall, digging its roots into her. "Where's Oscar?"

"He's out there shot-callin' and collecting his money. This huge attendance might be freaking you out, but more patrons means more dollars at the end of the night. Not a bad problem for Oscar to have." Trinket smiled.

Nyah had always felt at home on Rebel's stage, but now with hundreds of unknowns swirling with the regulars at the spot, the old worries over whether or not she'd fail crept up again. On Oh Ship she'd had a decent crowd, but most of them had come after she was already in the zone, so it hadn't bothered her. Now, the audience at Rebel kept coming and wanted her to deliver a moment that had already passed. "How am I going to go out there?"

"Hey," Trinket said, and then wrapped an arm around Nyah's shoulder. "Damn, gurl! You're shaking like someone slipped ice cubes down your back."

Nyah had promised herself never to let fear consume and paralyze her like it did back when her inexperience onstage had driven her away from the music and career she wanted to pursue. However, her own performance had rocked the boat and hijacked the calm seas she'd been sailing. "I should have known. I should have been checking, but when I came back from the trip things felt quieter. I don't even think I checked Queen Roe's mailbox."

"Go easy on yourself. You're allowed to slack off sometimes. So what? You didn't check email." Trinket guided her over to one of the old dark gray—almost blue—sofas, the cushion worn and the springs less bouncy than when Nyah had first started playing at Rebel two years ago. "And what's this about not going on. You're going to let a bigger crowd intimidate you? That's not the Queen Roe I know, who has been helping me with my stage fright."

When she returned from the cruise, she had put most of her time into getting ready to reenter the philharmonic after her suspension. Her confidence in Tommy to handle her logistics had made her slack, this time with her DJ career. In the past, getting ahead of anything that registered higher than "some buzz" helped her manage her two careers without clashing. That, and cases of caffeinated energy drinks.

"You don't understand, Trinket. All I'm going to do is let them down."

Trinket rubbernecked. "I've seen you tear that stage up every time you're out there. You do all the things I wish I could do."

Nyah inhaled to interject.

"I know you're going to tell me that I'm the best DJ you know but the point is no one will know it unless I get past my stage fright. But you? When you get up there you own that shit. Tonight is no different."

Nyah shook her head. "People are going to want to experience a moment that I'll never be able to recreate."

"Aww, Nyah. All you can do is your best. I've seen you do it here week after week. So have many of the regulars and the media that have been following you all this time."

"I don't know—"

"Bitch, you are going to get your ass out there and give them a Queen Roe show. No inhibitions. No apologies. You do what you do best. Tear the roof off!" Trinket jumped up from the couch. "Right?"

"Well…"

"Don't give me that wack doubtful shit. Get your ass up and give me that energy that makes everybody here at Rebel gravitate to you." Trinket pulled her up from the couch. "Come on. The kingdom awaits you."

Nyah rose to her feet and shook her shoulders. The action didn't quite release the bundle of nerves in her stomach, the tightness in her neck. Her hands were cold, but she was a true performer; she'd do what she came to do. Honor those who attended the Rebel royal court.

"Light it up," Nyah said.

"That's what I'm talkin' about."

* * *

I'm not going to make it. Tommy glanced at his watch as he ran toward the taxi stand, carryon in hand. "Fuck." The earliest flight Yaz had found for him landed at JFK around midnight. The cool spring night in the city did little to stop the tiny droplets of perspiration on his fore-head as he ran to the car that waited for him.

He wished his notifications had been locked out in air-plane mode, because the constant buzzing did nothing but raise his anxiety while the plane caged him in air. Several media alerts with Queen Roe and Rebel in the headlines, including texts from Oscar, who was thrilled that the club was packed and Yaz, who informed him of every new update. His confined space closed in on him when all he wanted to do was get to Nyah. He'd sent her several texts once he got wind of the flood of people at Rebel, but with no response. He was too late. She'd be performing or get-ting ready to. Any message from him was too late.

Now, as the driver navigated through Midtown Tun-nel, Tommy stared at the live streamed broadcast from Rebel Nightclub, and the masses that assembled outside the venue. For all his other clients, a crowd quadrupling in size would be reason for celebration. Not for a clas-sical musician with a double identity as an electronic dance music DJ who tried to keep her career fluttering under the radar, permanently.

"Fuck." He cursed himself this time and replayed all the mistakes he'd made. Herman had told him about the video trending. He could have easily texted Nyah at that time to give her a heads-up. A call would have been even better, given how anxious he'd been to hear her voice and be close to her again. Then why hadn't he?

He'd wanted to meet up with her in person during his stay in the city, to gently introduce the possibility of her playing the Sunburst Festival. After her success on the cruise and the reasons she had confessed to staying away from bigger stages, he wanted to contribute to helping her overcome her fear, as well as to finally get one of his artists on the festival's stage. With her video blowing up to this degree, his current mode of operation? Damage control.

His car stopped in front of his hotel. "Keep the meter running," Tommy said.

"Yes, sir," the driver responded.

Tommy zipped through the vacant lobby, checked in, and left his luggage at concierge before hopping back into the yellow cab and on his way to Rebel Nightclub. He checked his watch. *Three a.m.* He called Nyah in vain, because she was still performing. Downtown traffic on a perfect spring Saturday night could give a shit about the urgency of his travel to Alphabet City.

He arrived at Rebel and the club still crawled with people exiting the club. He had completely missed the performance. He entered the club and saw Oscar standing by the crowded bar where Tommy had met Nyah a few months ago.

"Hermano," Tommy said and slapped palms with his cousin.

"What up, bro," Oscar returned. "You missed a good show. Queen did her thing. The place was packed. We couldn't fit them all in here, but from what we could, we made bank."

Great for business, bad for Nyah. "Where's my client?"

"I think she's still in back with Trinket." Oscar tilted

his head in the direction he spoke of while still evaluating the club.

"Let me hit you up later." Tommy gave Oscar a dap
and wiggled sideways through the sea of bodies grooving on the dance floor, to find Nyah.

Backstage lacked chatter and the space felt vacant
in comparison to the crowd outside its doors. Nyah was
nowhere in sight.

Trinket, however, greeted him with hands on hips
and a frown that morphed her whole face. "Oh, it's
you," she said.

He prepared for a Dutch oven-sized pot of attitude
that he deserved. "Is she here?" he asked.

"She bounced. It was crazy in here since her video on
Oh Ship dropped." Trinket swung the dreadlock tendrils
that had slipped out of her messy bun over her shoulder.
"Something her agent should have warned her about."

The shade Trinket threw his way was cooler than
lake-effect snow in winter. He didn't know if Nyah had
gone to the bar to just have a post-show drink or home
to call it a night. "Is she okay?"

"She got mobbed at the bar. The regulars let her be
but everyone else just wanted a piece of her. Even with
extra security in the club, she gave up." Trinket flapped
her arms. "Why didn't you give her a heads-up?"

He had no real answers so he gave her what he had
in the hopes that she'd drop Nyah's location. "I thought
the news would be better in person."

"How'd that work out for you?"

"I got here as soon as I could," he snapped then adjusted his tone when Trinket whipped her head at him like
his mother did when he tried to back-talk her as a child.

"Look, I know I'm on your shit list. Maybe hers too, but I really need to see her. Do you know where she went?"

"I don't think she's in the mood for visitors." Trinket's pursed lips accompanied her appraisal.

"I'll take my chances," he said. When Trinket didn't jump to give him the information he requested, he gave it one last shot. "Trinket, my flight just landed and with the exception of stopping at my hotel to check in so I had a place to sleep and drop my shit off, so that my cabbie didn't drive off with my luggage, I came right over. I really need to see her."

Trinket softened for the first time since he had arrived backstage searching.

"She went home."

He went to squeeze Trinket in a brief hug but she stopped him. "Nah-uh. My loyalty lies with the Queen. She forgives you? I forgive you," she said.

Tommy nodded and appreciated Trinket even more. "No doubt. Wish me luck?"

"Luck and all that," Trinket returned flippantly. Tommy chuckled. He needed whatever good vibes thrown his way because he had no idea what state he'd find Nyah in. He just hoped she'd let him see her.

Boombox: In NY...on my way to your apt

He texted her but got no response. Still, he took a chance and hopped in a Lyft uptown to her apartment. Her building loomed like a fortress holding Rapunzel, but this time instead of keeping her in, it kept him out. Inside, he announced himself to the doorman. He half expected the gray uniformed man to turn him away when he called Nyah.

"You can go on up," the doorman said.

Relief spread through Tommy and he sped to the elevator for fear the doorman would stop him to relay that Nyah had changed her mind. He took the longest elevator ride up to her apartment and rang the doorbell. He could see movement and light in the peephole.

Come on, angel. Open the door.

A few seconds later, she swung the barrier between them open. "Hey." She held a beer mug filled with amber liquid that looked like cognac, mixed with something fruity by the smell of it.

"Hey." He entered with tentative steps and stopped by the door, taking his shoes off and leaving them on her multicolored welcome mat.

"What are you doing here?" A plush yellow robe decorated with stars wrapped her in a cozy nest.

He followed her as she walked into the kitchen area. He'd been all over the city and washed his hands in her sink. "I wanted to see how you were."

She scoffed. "Why?"

"Because of what happened at Rebel tonight?" He heard her gulp her drink in the quiet of the apartment. Her contemptuous smile raised his caution flag. "What happened at Rebel tonight?" she inquired.

He treaded carefully like he wore eggshells instead of soles. "I saw the crowd and—"

"Oh, that." She tsked, and he braced for a blowup that was sure to come. "Apparently, there's some highlight video of my performance from Oh Ship that's trending? No. Excuse me. It's kind of viral now."

"Nyah—"

"I have an agent and I can't figure out why, for the life of me, he didn't warn me." The exaggerated way she pondered dripped with sarcasm.

"That's why I came to New York."

The intensity of her scrunched-up features looked painful. "There are several forms of communication that would have gotten here faster than you: email, a text or a phone call." She placed the mug heavily on the counter and the liquid sloshed around like a contained mini wave, suggesting that perhaps this wasn't her first glass.

"I texted, but you were performing by then and—"

"The point is to warn your client before the shit storm?"

He sighed and avoided the bait. "How was your performance tonight?"

She tightened the robe around her and he wanted to be the material holding her. "I had no idea what I walked into. My hands…" She spoke as if in a daze, fisting and releasing her fingers. "They were so cold. I couldn't stop shaking. I was so scared I barely got the headphones over my head to play." Her uneasy laugh sent chills up his spine and over his shoulder like the wings tattooed on his skin. "I needed you."

The pain in her voice elbowed him in the gut and he saw how much he'd let her down. "I found out about the video two days ago when I got back to the office. I should have said something but I figured I'd get here, we'd talk about it and some other things, and then it wouldn't be a big deal. The alerts about Rebel came through on my flight here and…" His shoulders hunched. Surrender in his muscles. "I know it's an excuse but it's the only one I got."

"Fucking Nancy! You know… I blame myself. I've been handling things, but then I got lazy. I started to depend on you. I should have known about this. Regardless of you, my job is to take care of my own shit," she explained as if an epiphany had whacked her upside the head.

That she referred to her third identity was another sign that perhaps she may have had much more than her usual post-show drink. He had worked tirelessly to earn her trust. Now she didn't think he was dependable.

He took a step toward her and she held him at bay with one movement of her palm.

"The crowd just wouldn't quit. I couldn't even have a drink in peace because they kept pawing at me." She shivered as if she felt the confinement created by the suffocating masses. "You left me out there. That's some shit Carlo would do."

The comparison hit him like an uppercut to his jaw. "Come again?" His frown gave him a headache, as did the constant dance and readjustment he did to communicate with her.

"I haven't heard from you since the cruise and now you're at my apartment? I don't need you here. I needed you when I was backstage freaking the fuck out." She yanked her drink off the counter and it splashed with a slap on the linoleum kitchen floor as she walked into the living area, circling around the glass coffee table. "Why don't you just go back to LA?"

Her rejection unbalanced him and he shifted his stance. "You really want me to go?" he asked empty space until she came into view through the large opening between the kitchen and living room. "Nyah?" He raised his voice, demanding an answer.

She didn't respond. Instead she placed her drink on the coffee table. She lay down, wrapping herself tighter in her plush yellow robe.

He already felt guilty for not communicating with her about the Oh Ship video. Maybe he'd fucked up but he was here, up front and present. He wanted to talk to her about it, to work it out and make things better, and she was pushing him away? He strode to the door, about to stuff his feet back into his shoes, when her sniffles stopped him in his tracks.

His body responded to her on a cellular level and the next few seconds were a blur until he found himself kneeling in front of her. He dared not touch her but even though she rejected his excuses, he couldn't leave her. "I'm so sorry, angel. I should have reached out to you sooner. I fucked up. You needed me to protect you and I didn't." He meant every word and hated that anything he'd done had caused her pain.

He waited as if ready to receive a slap in his face, but when she reached for him and pulled him to her, he climbed over her and nestled her against him, spooning her from behind. She made space for him, and his arm cradled her and his legs draped over hers. His need for her to feel physically secured by him mattered more than the crowd at Rebel, his fuckup, her rejection. He needed her to know that with him she'd always be safe.

"I'm not crying." She sniffled again. "I'm just slightly allergic to the white grape juice I put in my drink."

"Got it." He smiled in her hair. "It doesn't matter. I'm here. I'm here for you now."

Chapter Twenty-Three

The aroma of fresh French Roast started to fill her apartment. Nyah had set the trusty timer on her coffee machine last night when she got home from the club, knowing that, after drinking the mugs of her way-over-proof version of a Long Island Iced Tea, she'd likely need coffee in the morning. Her phone chimed and she unraveled her body from Tommy's to receive her regular Sunday morning call with her parents.

"I'm fine, Dad. I'm actually looking forward to time off from performing at the concert hall. I have some performances lined up so it'll be fun until, hopefully, I get accepted for the symphony," she responded to his question about her summer plans.

"Still no word from London, huh?"

"Not yet. The official announcement date is next week, so we should know by then."

"I know you'll get it, baby girl." Her father paused. "You're sure everything is okay? If something is up or you need anything, you can always tell me, and I'll do what I can to help. Mom, too."

Nyah hugged the phone. She'd never told her parents about her suspension because of all the questions that could pop up. It had been months since she'd seen them, and with the way last night's events had unfolded, she could sure use their loving. "I'm good, Dad. I'm planning to come see you guys after I perform with Trinidad at Artistique," she said.

"We're looking forward to seeing you, sweetheart." He switched gears. "I got the program for Sunburst. You're still going to try to make it, right?"

Her stomach flipped. She knew her father wanted her to do more than just attend the honoree event. He wanted her to play with him. "I got it on the calendar, Dad. I don't know if I'll be in London by then."

Nyah heard rustling outside her bedroom and softly entered the living room. Tommy's disheveled hair and wrinkled shirt had "Walk of Shame" written all over him.

"I thought the performances didn't start until August," her father asked.

Nyah directed Tommy to the mugs by the coffee machine. She opened the fridge, pulled out a container of oat milk, and handed it to him. She'd seen Tommy have it in his coffee on occasion and the item had somehow made it into her cart when she went shopping last week.

"It doesn't start until August, but I'm not sure when I'll have to be there to practice and all," she responded to her father.

"Oh. Well, hopefully you'll be able to make it," he said. She could feel her father's disappointment through the phone and her eyes watered. "I'll do my best, Dad. I promise."

"I know, baby girl." He sighed. "Well, I'm going to go get your mom at the spa. We have a brunch date."

Nyah wanted to say so much more to her father but what could she say? This dual identity thing was getting tricky and out of hand. "Give her my love," Nyah said.

"I will. Love you."

"Love you, too." She ended the call. She tapped her cellphone against her palm, lost in her thoughts about the importance of family. Her father was being honored and she was fucking around with his joy. *I'm such a coward.*

"Good morning," Tommy's voice broke through her thoughts. "How'd you sleep?"

"I have a slight pain in my neck and when I woke up, I had one noodle-numb arm, but it was okay. You make a great pillow." She blushed.

"Yeah, my arm cramped and my shirt was sweaty, but I liked it. It was nice." He smiled. "Thanks for the coffee. I didn't know you liked oat milk."

Her face flared fever hot. "I don't. It's how you take your coffee, right?"

"Wait, so you're saying you got it for me?" He toddled over to her.

"It was no big deal," she mumbled.

"You made space for me in your fridge. I think that's a pretty big deal," he teased.

"Okay, whatever." She quickly changed the subject. "About last night—"

"I'm sorry, Nyah. If something like that ever comes up again, I'll text you and email and call you, even if I'm on my way to where you are. You should have known regardless of whether or not there was a huge showing at Rebel."

She was glad that he had remorse over what happened, but she also had a clearer, Hennessy-free, head also. "I also overreacted. You should have let me know, but it wasn't entirely your fault. I should have been taking care of my press responses and maybe I would have seen it and asked."

"But I'm your agent."

"Yeah, but you're not infallible. You messed up. Lesson learned, right?" she asked.

He nodded. "I still feel shitty about it."

"Good." She nudged him on her way to fix her own cup of coffee.

He strolled into the kitchen and planted himself behind her, pressing his body against hers. The smell of stale cologne and coffee filled her senses. "So, what's for breakfast?" he asked.

"What are you making me?"

"I wasn't talking about food."

"I was." She slipped out of his grip. "You owe me, sir."

He chuckled but the bulge in his pants couldn't have been pleased with her. "I see how it is."

"Yup." She leaned against the counter. "I like my eggs over easy and my toast medium. You're in luck." She raised her coffee mug. "I did some of the work for you."

"Aight," he said, and got to work on breakfast. "So now that you've had a little distance from last night, how do you feel your performance went?" he asked. "Frying pan?"

"Underneath the counter," she answered. Last night she'd been thrown into such a heightened situation. She'd been on survival mode the whole time. "Despite the craziness, I performed well. People still wanted to hear me play even when I got offstage. I think that once I started playing, I let the rest fall away."

"Do you think your fear was because you didn't know that the crowd had grown that big or because you weren't good enough?"

She side-eyed him. "Are you trying to psychoanalyze me or what?"

"No." He pulled a carton of eggs out of the fridge. "I just want to know where the breakdown in your performance process happened."

"I don't want to sound conceited but I can play. I just didn't want to be paralyzed by fear from suddenly being thrown into this massive attendance. My first thought, which was, *what the fuck are all these people were doing here?* My second thought was, *I don't want to disappoint them.*"

Tommy coated the hot pan with nonstick spray and then cracked two eggs inside. They sizzled. "Interesting. You have the talent, Nyah. I honestly don't think that it's the crowd itself. I think that not knowing the size of the crowd is what bugs you."

"How do you figure?"

"You performed on Oh Ship and I know for certain that the amount of people you played to on the cruise was more than what attended Rebel last night."

"No way."

"No lie." He pushed his fine ass toward her. "Check my phone. Oscar sent me stats and the media also got confirmed the numbers."

Nyah faced the phone toward him so he could enter his passcode, and the stats he must have read when he woke up this morning were on the screen. The attendance for her pool deck performance was double what it'd been at Rebel last night. "Oh shit. Really?"

"Really. I think that once you know what you're getting into, you adjust. It's the not knowing that brings up those old fears. It's just a thought. I'm not gaslighting you. It's just something to think about. It might be why you're so good at helping Trinket with her stage fright."

"I never thought about it like that. Maybe."

He continued preparing their breakfast. "By the way, I know the timing may not be great but you got an invitation from Herman."

"An invitation to what?"

"To play at the Sunburst Festival. I know you don't want to play the big festivals but this one is for up-and-coming artists. It's well attended and fairly selective. I am just relaying the invitation. Do you want me to tell him no?"

She liked that he asked even though she'd explicitly told him that presenting something to her like that would just be a waste of their time. Now, with their recent discussion and the conversation with her father this morning about attending his ceremony, she wasn't sure that no was her answer.

"I don't know."

Tommy put the spatula down and faced her. "Do my ears deceive me? I remember when we first discussed me agenting you that you were adamant about not playing the big festivals."

"This one isn't *that* big. It's medium. Plus my dad is being honored there and I really should make all my best efforts to go. Even if I might be in London to play with the symphony."

"So you're going to go if you get it?" he asked.

"Yeah." She knew she'd be leaving her friends and family but it was only a month. "It's something I really want to do."

"I support you. It'll just be strange not having you in New York," he said.

For a year she'd had two objectives. Play at Artistique and get into the BME symphony. Goals change but these were still hers. Then why did her heart pinch at Tommy's statement? She yanked herself from her thoughts. "Anyway, I guess I'll need to think about Sunburst."

"So it's not a no?"

"Right."

"Okay, but the clock is ticking on this one so let me know."

"I will but right now I'm focused on Artistique. I can't believe that it's only three weeks away." She beamed.

"Hey, can you do me a favor and tell Trinket that we're good. She's ride or die and hates me. That is, until she gets the word from you that we're good."

"I love her. I will." Nyah laughed. "Speaking about Trinket. You really need to see her perform already. This is ridiculous."

"Does she even want an agent?" he asked and she saw through his deflection techniques.

"She thinks it's a pipe dream because of her stage fright but we've talked about it and she would love an agent. To have you as her agent would be ah-mazing."

Tommy rolled his eyes.

"Did you just roll your eyes at me?"

"No," he lied.

"I see you, Mills." She squinted her eyes and pointed at him. "I'm trying to do you a solid."

He laughed. "I promised after Artistique. I'll even make a special trip to New York. I'll bring Yaz, who might be a better fit for her."

"You haven't even seen her play and you're ready to pass her on to another agent. Boo," Nyah said.

"That's not what I meant. I just think two agents are better than one." He salted and peppered the eggs before flipping them and readying a plate.

"Whatever. Don't patronize me."

"I wouldn't think of it." He turned the fire off and put two slices of whole grain bread in the toaster. "Do you want butter on your toast?"

"Yes, and strawberry preserves, please."

He found the items and put them on the small kitchen table along with a few utensils. She liked how easy he moved in the kitchen. Had his mom taught him how to cook, or perhaps his aunt, Carmen? So she asked.

"My mom was always in the kitchen. I remember her and Tia Carmen always making enough food to feed armies. There was always enough in the pot to feed us several times over."

"What was your favorite thing to eat?"

"My aunt's rice and beans. I don't know what this woman did to those beans but they were so flavorful. I could eat a ton of it." He laughed and she joined him. "I guess both my aunt and my mom taught me. Plus when Oscar and I came home from school and everyone was still at work, I fed us."

She thought of him younger and her heart warmed. "They did well. You're great in the kitchen."

"Thank you." He slid her eggs onto a plate after the toaster popped and placed the bread on the plate as well. "Your majesty."

"I like that." She took the plate from him and sat down at the table. He joined her with his own breakfast.

"More coffee?" He pointed to her cup.

"Yes, please." He refilled her mug and fixed it how she'd done earlier and returned with the hot coffee.

"Thank you."

"Your wish is my command."

"Come through, genie." She forked a bite of warm eggs and sopped up the runny yolk with her toast. "Heaven." She covered her mouth and mumbled through a mouthful of food. "You know I'm going to fuck you after I eat this, don't you?"

He belly-laughed. "Damn right you are."

"You earned it." She didn't want to assume what was happening between them because if they were going to dive into the deep end, then they better know what expectations they had. "What about what we talked about on the cruise. About just enjoying each other while we were in international waters?"

"I can't stop thinking about you, Nyah. I'm willing to revisit that promise we made, because this feels different. Doesn't it?" He reached for her hand and the pleasure of his caress traveled up her arm.

"Yes. It does." She intertwined her fingers with his. "You're not just saying that because you want to fuck, right? Because I'm still going to fuck you."

He choked on his food and coughed. "No one makes me laugh like you."

"No one makes me blush like you." Her chest filled with air. "So we're doing this? Whatever this is?"

His thumb caressed hers. "Yeah."

And just like that she was booed up.

Nyah's phone rang and she excused herself to pick it up when she saw Gladys's name on her caller ID.

"I got in. Did your letter come?" Gladys's loud and excited voice nearly deafened her to the point where Tommy's eyes widened. He pointed to his ears and mouthed, "Wow."

"What are you talking about?"

"The symphony. The letters came and I got in," Gladys yelled.

"Oh my gosh. Congratulations, girl! I'm so happy for you," Nyah shouted.

"Did you check the mail?" Gladys asked. "Your letter should be in the same batch as mine since CeCe personally asked you to play for her when she was here."

Nyah hadn't because she'd been too busy performing at both the concert hall with Gladys and overcoming huge milestones at Rebel. Not to mention her handsome Dominican agent in her kitchen. "Not yet. Yesterday was busy at DGH and all—"

"Go check your mail!" Gladys yelled.

"Okay, okay." Nyah put Gladys on mute and gave Tommy a quick explanation before heading down to the lobby to check her mailbox. She lost Gladys when the elevator doors closed but called her back when she got out. "I'm here. Give me a minute to check." A bunch of unnecessary junk mail spilled out, along with a few bills she flipped through, and then there it was, like a golden ticket sparkling, her letter from London.

"Well?" Gladys asked.

"I got it." Nyah took a deep breath. "I'm opening it."

"Wait." Gladys stopped her. "No matter what the letter says, you did an amazing audition for CeCe when she visited, and our applications were iron-clad."

"Thanks, Gladys," Nyah said, then tore open the envelope. She unfolded the letter and read:

Dear Nyah:

It is with great pleasure that The Black and Minority Ethnicity Symphony in London invites you to...

"I got in!" Nyah jumped and all the other mail fell to the floor. "I got in too, Gladys."

"I knew it! Congratulations." Gladys clapped and screamed. "We're going to London!"

Nyah hadn't realized how much she wanted London until the possibility of being rejected was a real thing. She hugged her letter and her eyes watered. "I'm so happy."

"We have to celebrate. I think that Martin knows. He'll probably make an announcement tomorrow," Gladys rambled. "Okay, I have to go tell everyone."

"Me too. We'll talk later."

They hung up and Nyah collected her trash mail and tossed it on her way up to her apartment. She entered her apartment and Tommy stood waiting for her.

"Well?" he asked.

"I got in!" She waved the letter.

Tommy scooped her in his arms and spun her. "Congratulations, angel. They'd have been crazy not to accept you."

"Thank you." She stared into the pride for her in his eyes and her heart thumped in her chest.

"So you know what this means, don't you?" he asked.

"What?"

"We have a lot of celebratory smashing to do," he whispered against her ear.

She laughed. "Please, do lead the way."

Chapter Twenty-Four

Artistique finally arrived and Nyah's excitement to play there for the first time both as a classical musician and as Queen Roe bubbled inside her. She welcomed the less mainstream crowd of Oh Ship, as well as her underground residency crowd at Rebel. She couldn't believe that those thoughts floated through her cranium. Rebel's underground environment had shifted since she performed on Oh Ship, and now, she had to face the consequences of not only agreeing to going on that cruise, but for also giving one of her best performances. The contradiction still didn't sit right with her and it was no one else's problem to figure out but her own.

The other highlight was playing the classical fusion improvisational piece with Trinidad. He had sent her an email with some of the logistics and they had texted to connect when she arrived in Michigan. With Tommy's help she had made it here. Since that wild night at Rebel, she'd gotten more comfortable with the bump in her celebrity because Tommy handled all the requests and now that she knew what to expect, she was prepared. Lastly, though Rebel's sizable walls could fit many bodies, it couldn't fit everyone. With the extra security presence and her backstage swillin' fest with Trinket and Oscar, she acclimated to the new normal.

She stayed in one of the lakeside cabanas on Artist Row. She had to remember that she walked around as herself. She was only there for the weekend but without her responsibilities to the philharmonic she could devote herself to Artistique. She also had to send her acceptance for the London Symphony, which started in mid-June. Everything would be covered for them, including hotel and airfare, and she had only a week left to accept. "What the hell are you waiting for, girl?" An image of Gladys and her parents, Trinket and Oscar popped up, but Tommy's image lingered.

"Hey you."

Speak of the devil. Tommy approached her with dangerous magnetic charisma. Her surrender to his charms inserted him into her planning and she needed to fight her way out of his spell if she truly wanted to be in charge of her own decisions. However, thoughts of his loving embrace and his emotional stories made her care about him more than she'd expected or had control over.

"Hey." Her accusatory tone didn't help quiet the case her heart made to let him in.

"What's that about?" Tommy's humor-filled frown was even more adorable to her than his face in any other expression. "Everything good?"

"Yeah." She forced a smile. "I just thought of something."

"I hope nothing too unpleasant. If there's anything I can do—"

"No, everything's okay. Thanks for asking."

He eyed her and she couldn't help but laugh at his sleuth-raised brow. "Everything is fine."

"It's not that. I don't think I've walked around with you as Nyah since our first business meeting at Lincoln Center," he said. "It's weird."

"I have to remember that. Maybe we shouldn't hang out too much like this. It'll be too easy for people to make the connection. It's bad enough I'm performing as both."

"Your evening performance as Queen Roe and the location at the other side of the festival will help."

"Where did you say you were staying again?" She blurted her question, hoping it sounded more light and curious than guided by the pangs her vajayjay made every time he was near. She loved sex with him. The problem was that her heart opened and it would only be a matter of time before it demanded the same.

"I didn't say." His teasing came with that thing he did with his mouth when he wanted to kiss her, and she tripped over a slightly raised rock on the trail toward the festival grounds. "You sure you're not coming down with anything? You look like you're going to be sick." Tommy lifted a hand to her forehead and checked her temperature.

"Maybe it's the heat. I could probably use some electrolytes and some water." She was in deep shit if she needed hydration from the mere thought of developing feelings for Tommy.

"I checked out the scene and there's a water station coming up. They're handing out festival water bottles to keep the kids hydrated."

"Cool. I'll grab one."

"To answer your question, I'm staying at the cabana on the opposite side of Artist Row, where some other industry folks are. I planned on getting a hotel but I figured being on the grounds was better than trying to take the shuttle," he explained. "Is that okay? I know this is probably the one event where you don't really need me but I figured it would be good for me to soak this in for the future."

Was he talking about their future together or with other clients? "Hey, I'm going to meet up with Trinidad to just connect for our classical improv performance tomorrow. I'm sure you have other things to do."

She needed space from him or she'd miss this moment here at the festival.

"Not really. I mean, I'm here for you."

"For Queen Roe. Remember?"

"Right." He idled. "It might be a good idea for me to just meet him to get a sense of things and how they can flow with your performance tomorrow."

"What?" None of his last sentence made any sense.

"I saw him online and he's pretty good."

He wouldn't meet her eye and she wondered if Trinidad being dark, toned, and handsome had anything do with his insisting on meeting him.

Tommy's creamy skin stained red at the tops of his cheeks. "What?"

"Nothing." She bit back a smile.

After she got the festival water bottle and filled it, she and Tommy hiked what felt like a mile to the location Trinidad texted her to meet him. The notes of classical piano floated through the tent and she recognized Trinidad's sound. Those notes he stressed that created surprise emotions. Since she'd heard him play for a special concert at Lincoln Center, she'd loved his sound. Now, she had a chance to play with him.

Trinidad's playing ceased as soon as Nyah and Tommy entered.

"Nyah." Trinidad's face beamed with warm tidings.

She waved like a bit of a fan, but Trinidad rectified that by hurrying to her and squeezing her in a hug. His shoulders reached her chest and she bent to return the friendly hug.

Tommy cleared his throat and Nyah turned to him. "Oh, Trinidad. This is my friend Tommy. He's a friend of my dad's," she said.

Tommy stuck his hand out. "Tommy Mills."

"Nice to meet you," Trinidad greeted him. "Are you a musician or here to enjoy the festival?"

"Actually, I'm here with one of my clients," Tommy corrected.

"EDM," she stated.

"Oh." Trinidad's classical snobbery reared its head, which was exactly what she needed. The farther someone she knew stayed away from her Queen Roe performance, the better.

"You don't like dance music?" Tommy asked.

"It has its place. I'm sure there are many here who are looking forward to enjoying that music."

Tommy's widened eyes met hers and she pressed her lips together to keep her smile from taking over her face.

"I'm sure my husband will make his way over to take in those performances and relive his club days." Trinidad waved the air as if a fly annoyed him.

Understanding softened the harsh evaluation Tommy had been giving Trinidad since they walked in, which confirmed her suspicions. Tommy "Boombox" Mills had a little jealous streak.

"Where is Pierce, anyway?"

"He is checking out the landscape and no doubt getting into trouble." Trinidad pretended to be annoyed but the love in his eyes for his husband shined through.

"I hope I get to say hello to him at some point," she said.

"He'll be at the performance tomorrow," Trinidad stated, and then shifted gears. "My hope was that we'd play around and see what we come up with. I like the freedom to do whatever we want for this so…"

"Sounds good. Do you mind if we have a mini audience while we practice?" Nyah tilted her head toward Tommy. "That is, if you still want to stay."

"Actually, I should probably head out and find my artist," Tommy said.

"You're sure?" She winked at him.

"Yeah." He dipped his head, took off his glasses and cleaned them with the microfiber cloth he kept in his pocket.

"Okay. See you around, Tommy."

"Will someone help you get your bass back?" Tommy asked.

"We'll get one of the festival staff to give her a ride back," Trinidad assured him as he sat back at the piano.

"Great." Tommy backed out of the tent. "Have a good session."

"Oh, by the way, Tommy, tomorrow evening I'll also

be participating in a live art installation featuring Curtis Sterling. I'm hoping to get Nyah to participate."

Nyah stiffened. Queen Roe performed tomorrow night. She hadn't expected Trinidad to invite her to another performance.

Tommy noticed her lack of verbal skills and filled in the dead air. "I'll try to make it but my artist is performing during that time."

"Shame. The artist is really existential. Very Dali." Trinidad painted his hands as if recreating one the Spanish artist's creations.

"Nyah? Didn't you say you had some friends coming in who wanted to check out the other artists and musicians tomorrow evening?" Tommy asked.

Her acting skill kicked into high gear. "Yeah. I think they'll be here for my performance and then wanted to do the festival thing."

"Try to convince them to come and stop by for a bit," Trinidad persisted. His influence in the classical world was high and she wanted to leave a sweet taste in his mouth, especially since he'd given her the opportunity to play with him.

"I'll try, but no promises." If she was any more noncommittal, she would have just said, "No, sorry."

"Pleasure to meet you, man," Tommy interjected. "Nyah. I'll catch up with you another time."

Tommy headed back to his cabana on foot so he could meet up with a few industry people. There weren't many that he needed to see but he never missed an opportunity to network with new colleagues. On his way from one informal chat with a producer, his feet screeched to a halt when he saw the banner and setup for *Trendzy Magazine*.

Tommy's emotions were conflicted when he saw her dirty blond, perfectly coifed hair and the close-fitting royal blue romper she wore. Isabelle Fisher was still sexy as hell but his attraction to her was dampened by the handful of hurt she'd left him with.

"Izzy?" He moved toward her as if through a room full of soapsuds from an overpour of detergent in a washing machine.

She focused on him, flipping her hair. "Tommy. Wow, you are the last person I expected to see here. What are you doing here, love?" Her cheeks flushed a bit.

"My sentiments exactly. A client of mine plays tomorrow night," he responded as her arms stretched and they embraced in an awkward hug, mostly on his side. "I didn't think this was your scene."

"I wanted to branch out to some of the smaller festivals but nothing really suited my fancy until Artistique." Her British accent was a light, refreshing and new sound. "The art installations and music are missing one thing. Fashion. I'm trying to test out a modest launch here to see how it goes."

"Sound investment of your time."

She agreed. "And your client?"

"A new artist I started with this year. Queen Roe."

Izzy's eyes lit up. "Not the same one who has been trending the past few weeks."

"The very same." He could always rely on his success to keep him relevant.

"You really do have a golden touch. She is hotter

than shit these days. I'd love an interview with her," Izzy inquired.

"I see you are still a mastermind at asking without asking."

She pouted her lips. "You remember."

"I'll present it to her and see what she says. She's pretty low-key." Tommy again found himself with a great opportunity for Nyah, yet he still had no idea how she'd respond. *Trendzy Magazine* could be a springboard for Nyah, like it had been over a year ago for his other client Luke. Nyah would likely see it as something adding to the celebrity she didn't want. He both resented and respected her clarity.

"How on earth is a DJ low-key? I thought they all wanted fame and fortune." Izzy crossed her arms.

"Queen Roe is different."

"Ahh." Izzy stroked her chin and curiosity gleamed in her eyes.

Tommy half frowned, half smiled. "What's that 'ahh' for?"

"You light up a bit, just there—" her fingers fanned over her eyes like a mask "—when you say her name."

He scoffed. "No, I don't." He was sure he did.

"Are you staying at one of the cabanas?" Her gaze shifted from business to pleasure.

"Yeah, why did you ask?"

"Because I'm hoping we can catch up." The open-ended statement left room for a lot of various scenarios he could fill in.

"You haven't changed a bit." He smirked.

"What? Can't a girl have her bit of fun? We had fun, didn't we?"

"We did." He put an end cap on it and left their escapades where he needed them to stay—in the past.

"But really, it's been a long time and the way things ended was, well, harsh. I want us to be friends."

He believed her and for the sake of his friendship with her best friend, he did, too. "We are."

"I see." She pouted again, but her flirtations were put on hold when one of her assistants called her over. "I'm terribly busy at the moment, love, but let's catch up. How 'bout a drink later? I'm in cabana number 2-10. I'll text you. That is, if your number is still the same."

"It is," he said.

"So we're on, then?"

"I'm busy here, too. No promises."

She scooted off, giving him a lot of ass in her strut. He shook his head and remembered when that was all it took to get him into her bed. Like her, he'd moved on even if it took him longer, but unlike her, he had no business in rekindling what they had.

Nyah's sarcastic grin popped into his head and he smiled. The sun started to get low and he wondered if she had eaten. She'd likely finished with Trinidad and now that the evening events were on the upswing, he wanted to spend time with her and maybe take in some of the performances.

He sent her a text.

Boombox: Dinner?

Nyah: Eating with Trinidad and a few classical musicians. Want to join?

His fingers typed yes but then he erased it. As much as he wanted to spend time with her, she was in her element and he wanted to avoid crowding her.

Boombox: Maybe another time. Have fun. Meet up later?

Nyah: Can't wait.

She included an eggplant emoji and he laughed out loud.

Boombox: LOL!! Me too.

The exclamation marks were a bit much but he wanted her to have fun as much as he wanted her with him. She'd waited for Artistique for months and he wouldn't be able to enjoy a lot of it with her, even though they had somewhat agreed to date. He still didn't know what to call it and really, he didn't give a shit if they were just dating or boyfriend and girlfriend. The woman consumed him and he wanted to be with her.

He went back to his cabana to change and got a call from Herman. Tommy debated whether or not to pick up the phone. Herman had needed an answer from him two weeks ago about whether or not Queen Roe would be performing at Sunburst. Nyah told him the few times he'd asked her that she needed to focus on her performances at Artistique. When Herman didn't ask, Tommy didn't reach out. His behavior itself was noteworthy. Having an artist play at Sunburst meant so much to him, but his feelings for Nyah rivaled his ambitions.

He picked up. "Boombox."

"You avoiding me again?"

"Nah, man. It's just been busy." Tommy used his regular excuse with his friend. "In fact I'm at Artistique."

"I like that fest. It's quaint," Herman said. "I hear Queen Roe's playing. She's gaining momentum."

"Yeah." *For better or worse.*

"So am I booking her for Sunburst or what?"

"Can you give us a little more time? She wants to see how Artistique goes and—"

"I gave you two additional weeks. I need to know now. My cursor is blinking on the lineup page."

"C'mon, man. You can't even give me a day?" Tommy asked, already certain of Herman's answer.

"I can't continue to hold this spot, man. I need this shit up on the website and solidify the logistics. You're cramping my style. Can she do it or not?"

Fuck! He thought back to Oh Ship and Rebel. Nyah had successfully made it through both of those larger events. He thought they'd had an epiphany the morning he'd fixed her breakfast. She seemed more curious about the possibility of performing at festivals. When he brought up Sunburst, she didn't shut him down and that shocked him most of all. Maybe, just maybe, she'd say yes to Sunburst if he spun it for her like Oh Ship or helped her work through her fear at Rebel, and they could both win.

"Book her," he said to Herman. The decision made him uneasy but he pushed it down and convinced himself that after they discussed it, she'd agree to play. She may not want to play with her father but she had solidified her spot as one of the hottest DJs playing the underground.

"Great. Celebrate, man. You finally got your wish after all these years. You got one of your artists playing at Sunburst. Not only that, but this year we're honoring Pete Monroe. The festival will be great for her. I feel like she would be a nice complement to the Monroe ceremony. What do you think? Maybe I can adjust the lineup."

"I don't know about that, Herman. Like I said, she likes to do things her way. I'm not sure how she'd feel about that." Tommy knew exactly how Nyah felt about that. Unless Nyah decided to DJ with her father, he didn't think she'd want to play anywhere around him, for fear of being found out.

"Who wouldn't want to play opposite an icon? What the fuck, man? This girl want to be famous or what?"

Tommy sighed, buttoning his shirt. "Just keep her off the main stage."

"Okay. Whatever, man," Herman grumbled. "I got a few more calls to make. Let me know if you have any questions."

They hung up and Tommy sat on the edge of the bed. "This is a good thing. This is good for her." The words, however, did little to relax his tense shoulders. He dressed casually with no place to go. He decided to get a ride into town for a sit down dinner when he got a text.

Izzy: Still on for drinks later

Boombox: Don't think so...heading into town for dinner

Izzy: Starving. Can I crash?

He should decline but he needed company and didn't want to talk business. Plus the only person he really wanted to spend time with was enjoying an evening with her fellow musicians.

Boombox: Sure

As Tommy left his cabana, he couldn't shake the feeling that in saying yes to Izzy, he'd only added to a host of bad decisions he'd made in the last hour.

Chapter Twenty-Five

Artist row came into view as Nyah hightailed it back to her cabana at close to one in the morning. She'd had a great time with Trinidad and some of the other artists and musicians who were playing the next afternoon. On her way back, excitement prickled her skin at the thought of spending the night with Tommy. Each time in bed with him felt better than the last, and even during a fun night with her fellow musicians, she'd wanted his arms and to watch him sleep after they made love. She didn't cower at the thought of loving him like she had in the beginning of their re-acquaintance. He was still a pain in the ass, but his intentions toward her were always good. How could she not love that?

Her steps sped up the closer she got to the cabanas. However, nothing had prepared her for the sight of Tommy releasing a statuesque woman with dirty blond hair from his embrace.

"I'm really glad we did this," Tommy said to the woman. "It was long overdue."

"Right. No more hiding from me, love." The British accent was unexpected.

"I wasn't hiding, I just needed space and…" Tommy trailed and the two of them turned at Nyah's presence.

"Nyah?" Mercifully, Tommy spoke first because her brain still processed the images and the inferences while she stood in shock.

"I…umm." *Breathe.* She commanded herself. She inhaled a hearty breath.

"I-I didn't expect to see you here at Artistique," he stuttered. His eyes pleaded with hers. "How have you been?" He squeezed her stiff body and her arms barely tapped his sides.

Nyah plastered a wide smile on her face that she hoped didn't look as plastic as it felt. *You are not Queen Roe. You are not Queen Roe.* "I'm great! I'm playing a classical piece at the modern art tent tomorrow. It's a great festival, isn't it?" She shook her head. "I-I'm just so surprised to see you. What are you doing here?" *With this woman at one in the fucking morning?*

"I'm here with a client who's performing tomorrow night." Tommy rushed on, "What a small world."

Nyah stared at the woman Tommy was with and recognition finally made it through to her memory. "You're Isabelle Fisher."

"The very one. Hello." Izzy served Nyah all her sleek hair with one flowy flip, and a pretty fragrance followed.

"It's really nice to meet you." Nyah's mask of pleasantries started to crack. She had come face to face with fashion magazine's darling, and Tommy's ex. Nyah was both honored and horrified. She'd happened upon Izzy and Tommy during the witching hours, and her mind only created what else she might have interrupted.

"Nyah is a classical musician. Are you playing bass here at the festival?" Tommy urged.

She had to hand it to him. His acting skills could win him Emmys and Oscars. She had maybe a few minutes left before her façade completely crumbled. She swallowed through the tightness in her throat as the shock thawed to expose the hurt beneath.

"How do you two know each other?" Izzy asked, and her eyes ping-ponged between Nyah and Tommy with intrigue.

"We met…what? Six years ago at a party in Miami, right?" Tommy said.

"Yeah, about that," Nyah said. "Were you guys taking in the events tonight or…?"

"We had dinner at a cozy little place in town and drinks. If you get a chance I highly recommend Smithy's," Izzy offered. "Their salmon was divine."

"Oh. Are you two…together?" Nyah couldn't help but ask.

"Just old friends catching up." Izzy smiled.

"How do you two know each other?" Nyah asked Izzy and could feel Tommy's eyes on her.

"My best friend Leona is dating his client and best friend, Luke Anderson. If you follow dance music you might know him. Both of them, actually," Izzy said casually.

"Oh yeah. The Musical Prophet? I know of him." And his whole catalog. "Wow, Tommy. You've really done well for yourself." Nyah pulled the compliment from her mouth in the hopes it sounded natural.

"Thanks. You, too," Tommy said.

Nyah nodded, all her attention focused on centering

her emotions to complete the ruse. "I should get going. My performance is early afternoon and I don't want to have a sloppy bow." She gestured with her hand and arms. "It was great meeting you, Izzy." She turned to Tommy and waved like a swarm of bees attacked her. "Good to see you again, Tommy."

"Take care."

Nyah's anger boiled. How stupid she must be to believe that Tommy only wanted her. Back on the cruise he'd expressed that he was the one getting hurt. Well, he tagged her first.

In her cabana, she body-slammed her suitcase onto the bed and yanked out a set of clothes for her performances. She cursed Tommy as she pulled off her shirt and kicked her skirt clear across the room. She showered and tugged on a nightshirt and underwear. That's when a knock sounded on her cabana door.

"Nyah?" Tommy called her name softly.

She was too angry to give him the benefit of the doubt. Right now, his ass was guilty as fuck and she didn't want to talk. She pulled the covers over her head. Tomorrow was performance day, something she'd looked forward to for so long. She didn't care what it took, she wasn't going to let Tommy, Izzy or anyone steal her joy. She would reckon with Tommy like she did everything else. On her own terms and in her own fucking time.

Nyah rolled her bass to the door of her cabana. She called for a pickup to meet Trinidad at the modern art tent. Her morning had been rough at best. She'd woken up grumpy and it took her at least an hour to sweep her feelings about last night aside to enjoy this moment.

She opened the door to wait for her ride and Tommy paced back and forth. "Shit," she mumbled. So much for the dust settling over her heart.

"I didn't think you'd let me in." He approached her like she was a biohazard. With a lot of caution. "Can we talk?"

She kept her response brief. "I'm waiting for my ride."

"Nyah, just give me a minute to explain."

"I'm getting ready to perform. Something I've been looking forward to. Don't you dare ruin this for me."

"I'm not trying to stress you but I can't let you go, believing that something happened when it didn't. You've got this all wrong."

"What do I have wrong? You went out with your ex last night, right?"

"Yes, for dinner and drinks."

"So I've got it right," she said and her ride pulled up in a similar golf cart to the one she'd taken to meet up with Trinidad yesterday.

The driver hopped out. "Nyah Monroe?"

"Present." She offered him a weak smile.

"Let me help you," Tommy said.

The driver also tried to assist as he warily regarded the situation.

"I got it." She dragged her bass, lifted it, and gently placed it into the back of the cart. "I do it all the time in the city. I don't need your help."

"Izzy is my ex, yes, but she's also friends with those close to me. We never dated."

"I know. You just fucked?"

"Do you two need a minute?" the driver asked.

"No. I'm on a schedule," she explained and slid into the back seat.

"We were supposed to meet up for drinks after I had dinner with you but when that plan changed." He blew out a chest full of air. "We just talked to put some closure to it all."

"So you want me to believe that you were just giving her a friendly hug when I stumbled upon you two?"

"Izzy's a big flirt, but for my part, yes," he stressed. "Where's the trust? I know you're mad but think about it for a second. I came to Artistique for you, not to hook up with my ex. If I wanted to hide from you, then why would I be saying goodbye to Izzy close to your cabana? I thought you were back. I was coming to see you because you are who I wanted to be with last night." He dropped his tone and peeked at the driver, who focused on dodging pedestrians who walked the same road to the festival grounds.

Tommy had shared so much with her but seeing him with Izzy had struck a nerve and all her trust issues rose to the surface like they had the night at Rebel. He may have done something extremely stupid but deep down she didn't think that anything had happened between him and Izzy.

"Nyah, look at me," he pleaded. "I would never disrespect you like that."

She shook her head.

"Look at me, angel."

She did.

"If me and you are going to do this, I need you to trust me."

"I do, Tommy, but the optics? Do you have any idea how that made me feel?"

He touched her arm. "Extremely incriminating. Guilty, Fuckboy-ish. I can go on, but I promise you, there is nothing between Izzy and me. That page turned a long time ago. I needed to close the book so that things wouldn't continue to be awkward when we got around each other."

"Nice literature analogy."

"You're really picking this moment to bust my balls again?"

She shrugged.

He took his hand in hers. "We okay?"

She intertwined her fingers with his. "Yeah, we're okay."

"We did pretty good last night, didn't we?" he teased.

"I gotta admit you saved me and yourself, because I was coming in pretty hot."

"I don't know what I think about your jealous side yet, angel."

"I'm not jealous."

He scoffed. "Yeah. Okay."

"You're one to talk. Mike from The Boiler. Ring a bell? How about Trinidad…and he's gay and happily married."

"Point taken." Tommy leaned back and rested their meshed hands on his lap. "Maybe we both need to work on trust.

"Maybe we do." In the past Nyah hadn't had a problem with jealousy, but no one had ever made her feel the way Tommy did. Her reaction to Izzy just confirmed how much she cared about him and with that came the fear of possibly losing him. Her mind started down a doomsday path.

"Are you ready for this?" Tommy asked, interrupting the deep thoughts and reminding her of why today was destined to be great.

"So ready."

"You look beautiful, by the way," he said softly and she turned into a gooey mess. The linen white headband she'd wrapped around her large Afro matched her maxi dress. The brown wood of her bass would complement her outfit and her skin to create its own art piece.

"Thank you." She blushed.

"Can I kiss you? You know…for good luck and shit?" he whispered.

"Yes." She offered him her lightly glossed lips. Tommy pressed his mouth against hers, his tongue quickly seeking to play. His teasing caresses apologized as much as they aroused a forgiving song in her heart and warmed her center.

"Tommy," she moaned.

"You should have let me in last night," he said, and his low and husky tone made her hotter than the humid festival grounds. "The things I wanted to do to you." He unraveled his fingers from hers and his hand gathered her dress upward until he slipped underneath and stroked her thighs. Her legs opened on autopilot and her back arched in anticipation of his touch.

"You mean…the things I would have done to you." She meant her words to have more power but under his pleasing hand they were weak with desire. The scent of grass, as the golf cart wheels ran over the already flattened blades, filled her nose as she inhaled.

The golf cart came to an abrupt stop and as Tommy's hand withdrew from its upward trajectory, her skin called for his return as if it had a voice.

"That was beautiful," the driver said to them. "It's the Artistique magic."

"Umm…thanks." Nyah smoothed her black and white angle-striped maxi dress while Tommy chuckled like a high schooler.

Tommy smirked as he handled her bass. This time she let him help her.

"Complimentary pomegranate, mango and lemon smoothie?" a young woman from one of the nearby vendor stands asked.

"Of course." Nyah plucked one of the containers from the travel tray and sucked on the straw. "Mmm." She offered some to Tommy, then halted. "There's no dairy in this, right?"

"One hundred percent vegan." The woman smiled.

She pushed the straw at Tommy's mouth and he sucked in a mouthful.

"It's good." His hand found her ass and lingered there for long, delicious seconds. "Thanks for making sure I don't get the dairy shits."

She choked on her drink and covered her mouth to keep her smoothie from spewing all over him or her white and black outfit as she laughed.

They progressed toward the open tent, where Nyah saw Trinidad by the stage with his husband Pierce in front of the gathering crowd.

"Nyah." A female voice that she recognized immediately called to her. She almost dropped her smoothie when her eyes tracked down two people she never thought she'd see at Artistique.

"Hey girl, hey." Gladys greeted her with a hug and Evan trailed behind her.

"Heeeeeeeyyy!" Nyah said. She patted Gladys's back like a grandmother. "What are you two doing here?"

"We thought we'd surprise you. I know you were keeping the thing with Trinidad on the down low, but I knew you'd love the surprise. Someone has to be here to support you." Gladys smiled over at Tommy. "Though it looks like you're covered."

"This is definitely a surprise," Nyah agreed.

"Hi, Gladys." Tommy greeted her friend with a friendly hug. "Nice to see you, too, Evan."

"You too." Evan's face was splotched with rosacea from the heat. "When I heard you were playing with Trinidad, I had to see it to believe it."

"I see the location hasn't changed your musical snobbery."

"Nope," Evan said. "But I know you'll represent the philharmonic well."

Nyah gasped at the compliment, as well as the shock of having both Evan and Gladys here.

"I'm going to bring your bass inside," Tommy said. "See you guys in there."

"Thanks," Nyah said and Tommy's soothing smile relaxed her just a bit.

"I'll go find us a spot." Evan followed Tommy.

Gladys linked arms with her. "I'm so glad I get to see you do this. You're happy I came, right? This isn't freaking you out, is it?"

Of course it is! "Not at all. I'm happy to see you. Where are you guys staying?"

"At an Airbnb in town. The shuttle is so convenient. We can go back and forth quite easily. Are you staying at one of those pretty cabanas?" Gladys winked. "With Tommy?"

Nyah was about to cultivate a beaut of an answer that wasn't quite a lie but not the direct truth either when Tommy came running out to her.

"Gladys, can you excuse us for a second?" Tommy didn't wait for Gladys's permission and pulled Nyah away by the elbow.

"What's up?"

"I'm going to need you to take a deep breath. I promise you that everything will be okay." His voice dropped to that deep, serious, slightly horrifying tone.

"Tommy?"

The next words he uttered sent her into full-on panic mode. "Your parents are here."

Chapter Twenty-Six

Nyah played on autopilot for the first half of her performance with Trinidad as her parents' and Gladys's beaming faces were up front and center. She managed to relax into her instrument after she surrendered to the fact that her parents, her philharmonic musicians, and Tommy had collided in one place. Her parents would want to have dinner when she'd need to play for the Artistique stage. How would she explain Tommy's presence to her father? Would Gladys and Evan pick up on her being way off? How would she extricate herself from Trinidad's invitation to play again later when, technically, she should be free and the "friends" she'd said she had to do the festival thing with were actually here?

Tight shoulders equals a tight bow. If she didn't soften her muscles, she'd seize up and play sour notes. She relaxed into her instrument. Present. *Be present. It's only you and Big D up here with Trinidad.* No one could help her now but herself. She regarded the art their music represented and the notes flowed through her.

She looked at Trinidad and their improvisation swirled together like the art around her. *There it is.* She'd still have to contend with everyone when their performance ended but right now, she and her musical companion created a special moment for the guests.

After their performance she and Trinidad bowed to the applause and as she stared into the faces of her peoples her mind tried to create exit strategies.

She hugged her parents. "I didn't know you were coming. I wasn't supposed to see you both until I went to Florida."

"Your dad is doing a fundraiser in Columbus, so we thought we'd just change our ticket to get here to see you," her mother said excitedly.

"I hope we didn't freak you out, baby girl. When you told us you were playing with Trinidad, we wanted to be here." Her father hugged her shoulders.

"No. Not at all. I was just a little surprised. I'm so happy to see you both." Nyah was happy to see her parents but how was she going to manage all these people?

"I wasn't expecting to see this guy. How're you doing, Tommy?"

"Great to see you, Pete." Tommy shook her father's hand.

"What brings you to Artistique? I didn't think this was your scene."

"I have an artist playing here and ran into Nyah and decided to stay for her performance," Tommy said. It was kind of the truth but Nyah hated that either one of them was put into this position to work the angles of the truth.

"Cool. Anyone I know?" her father asked.

Internally, Nyah cringed.

Gladys and Evan bounced over after a quick hello

to Trinidad. "That was such an inspiring performance, Nyah," Gladys interrupted and hugged her.

"Do you really think so?" Nyah asked honestly, given her tense start.

"I often bust your chops, but the improvisation was remarkable," Evan said.

"Someone gimme a phone so I can record this. Evan just gave me a compliment," Nyah said.

"Yeah, yeah." Evan blushed and Nyah started to see a better side to him. Perhaps Gladys's positive impact had sunk in.

"He's right. You did great," Tommy said.

"Thanks," Nyah said, and she couldn't avoid her mother's evaluation of her and Tommy.

"Nice to see you again, Mr. Monroe, Mrs. Monroe," Gladys said and hugged them.

"You too, Gladys. We didn't think we'd see you until the fall session when we come for our annual trip to New York to spend the holidays with Nyah," her mother said.

"Yes. I look forward to those visits, but it's a treat to get to see you sooner."

Nyah had to admit that, despite her stress, it was nice to see her people together like this. "Should we all get lunch?" Nyah asked.

"That sounds delightful, since me and mom are flying out this evening for Ohio," her father said.

One down. Nyah relaxed. Now all she had to do was figure out how to part ways with Gladys and Evan. Does she use Trinidad? Tommy?

"Yeah. Evan and I want to check out the rest of the festival so lunch would be great. Plus I'm sure you want to hang out with—"

"Great, let's go into town." Nyah grabbed Gladys and interlocked arms with her. "My folks don't know about me and Tommy, so let's keep that under wraps, okay?"

"Oh. A secret. I got you covered." Gladys nodded.

Lunch had gone off without a hitch and Nyah and Tommy found their way back to her cabana, where she breathed a sigh of relief.

"You okay?" Tommy asked.

"I guess," she replied. "I mean, that could have all gone so much worse. That my parents aren't even staying and Gladys had Evan to romp the grounds with are what's saving me right now."

"You handled that all very well." He sat next to her and she snuggled into him. "Don't get too comfortable. You have a performance in a bit and I have to go make sure everything's set up. So don't get any ideas," he teased.

"Me? You're the one who pulled me into your arms."

"Yeah, whatever." He stroked her arm. "Really, though. I know you got a lot of surprises today."

Living these two lives is starting to catch up with me. Over lunch, the guilt of her lies had surrounded her at a round table, with each smiling and excited face looking back at her. "I promised myself to tell Gladys about Queen Roe when I got back to New York. Seeing her here, so supportive… It makes me question if I'm doing all this the right way."

"Hmm," he offered. "And your parents. Any plans on telling them?"

She tensed and he massaged her shoulder. "One reveal at a time."

"So I guess that answer is no?"

"For now, yeah." She nuzzled her nose into his chest and inhaled his cologne. Her arm reached over to embrace his middle and he kissed her forehead.

"Thanks for not bailing. You could have easily left and let me handle that on my own."

"That never even crossed my mind. We're in this together."

She looked up into his face and his warm eyes met hers. "Teamwork makes the dream work."

He kissed her lips a few times, then got up. "I gotta go change and get to your performance site. Your pickup will be here in just over two hours. Just enough time for you to go over your set and get dressed."

"And have a quickie." She licked her lips.

Tommy thought about it and looked at his watch, then inched toward the door and looked at his watch again. "I should get going."

"Okay." She smiled.

He left her cabana. She valued his commitment to his duties but she would have liked to sink onto his dick after such a triggering afternoon. A few minutes later a knock sounded on her cabana door. She opened and Tommy strode in.

"Okay, really quick." He picked her up and led her to the bed.

She crooned in excitement, kissing his neck. "I knew you wouldn't let me down."

Nyah and Tommy rode to the Artistique main stage. The moment she'd waited months for had finally arrived. The embers of dusk still lingered a bit but the bright stars dominated, just like she planned to do with her set tonight. Her parents had texted her when they were on their way to the airport and would send her another one when they landed safely. She couldn't believe her luck that she'd gotten out of all the complications that had presented themselves earlier, and she felt like the Universe was on her side.

She had about thirty minutes to showtime, but already the crowd formed. A group of fans lined the way toward the backstage area and called her name. She waved and signed a few autographs for people who wanted one and was relieved when they were finally inside.

An attendant approached them. "We have a few fans who won a raffle to meet the artists on the main stage tonight. Right this way."

Tommy had gone to do his final checks and network. "I'm going to do a final check. You got this?"

"Yup," she said.

"I'll see you in a few." He gave her a pat on the shoulder and was gone. Her meet and greet was going great and she met fans, took photos and signed a few autographs. On autopilot, she greeted the next group. "Hi. How are you doing tonight?"

"Nyah?" Gladys leaned in.

Nyah looked up into Gladys's face and knew she'd been found out. *Fuck!* "H-hey, um…"

"What are you doing dressed up like this?"

"Queen Roe. It's an honor," Evan said, oblivious to anything Gladys questioned.

Nyah shook his hand, but her eyes behind her glasses stayed on Gladys. "Nice to meet a fan."

"Can I get a picture?" he asked.

Nyah nodded but animated her movements and smiled. Evan took a selfie and the attendant moved them along. "Wait." Nyah stopped Gladys. Evan had been herded with the rest of the folks from backstage.

The attendant who'd been shadowing her touched her arm. "Queen? We have to get you to the stage."

"Please just give me a minute." Nyah grabbed Gladys, pulling her friend to a restricted area section by the stage. Nyah's head swirled with what to say to Gladys. What could she say? She'd been found out in the worst way with no warning for either of them.

Gladys must have been in a little bit of initial shock, but it wore off pretty quick.

"I can't believe you didn't tell me about all this," Gladys accused. "I thought we were friends."

"We are friends." The doubt in Gladys's eyes punched Nyah in the stomach.

"I thought you were pursuing music."

"I am. I'm focused on classical and I'm focused on my DJ career." Even under the disaster of the situation, Nyah defended both of her loves.

"Look at all this. You honestly believe that you'll be able to give CeCe and the symphony your all and leave your DJ career in New York for the summer?"

"No." Nyah straightened. "I'll be taking both my careers to London. There's a great dance music scene in the UK."

"Nyah? Are you serious?"

Fuck yeah, I'm serious. "Wow…the judgment," Nyah said. "This is exactly what I wanted to avoid. I'm doing what I love in both genres and I have to justify it?"

Gladys's face clouded over. "Don't act like it's my fault. You kept a secret from me. A really big one."

"Queen." Tommy's voice. "They're about to announce you. What's the holdup?" Just as Tommy came into her peripheral vision, he screeched to a stop.

"Give me a second," she said to Tommy, whose head slid back and forth between her and Gladys.

"Him too. Is he even your boyfriend?"

Nyah's shoulders sagged even lower. "He's my agent, but—" She tried to hurry her words but Gladys flapped her arms.

"I don't even know who you are right now." Gladys stomped away and Nyah chased her down.

"I know how bad this looks and I want to explain further—"

"Explain what? That you've lied to me about everything?" Gladys crossed her arms.

"Not everything…just a few things," Nyah tried but Gladys wasn't buying it. "Look, I have to perform. Stay or don't stay, but as much as I love you, Gladys, I can't do this right now. I have a really big crowd waiting for me and I'm kind of freaking out," Nyah admitted. "All I can say is I'm so sorry. If you want, we can talk after or when I get back to New York. I'm here."

She and Gladys were at a stalemate until Nyah heard them start a longwinded announcement for her. She felt Tommy's hands on her shoulder. "We have to go, angel," he said in her ear.

"The stage is calling you," Gladys threw at her and stomped away.

As Nyah rushed toward the stage, she was sure that shit felt better than her. This wasn't how she'd seen herself approaching the Artistique stage that evening. She'd avoided her parents finding her out but she'd hurt one of her closest friends. Now she had to give the fans positive energy?

Fear started to tighten her up from her neck to her thighs. She bounced from side to side to the beats of the current DJ in an attempt to loosen up. She'd prepared this set for months and she couldn't let the fans down, or herself. There was only so much she could control. The larger crowd, a result from her recent fame, taught her that.

Fine time to realize that shit.

"Hey." Tommy rubbed her shoulders. "I'll be up there cheering you on. No matter what, this is your moment." The words spread through her like liquid ink on a white shirt and colored her the same way.

She took the stage and gulped several deep breaths. What she could control was her reaction to this entire fiasco. The people in front of her had shown up to appreciate her skills and talent as a DJ, and as she played, she remembered that and pressed the mute button on her troubles for this one-hour set.

She looked out into the sea of faces as the melody to her song played and she lost herself in the surrounding bass. She picked up the microphone. "I've waited a long time to be here at Artistique with you and, boy, do you guys look amazing."

The crowd cheered.

"You ready to shake the place?"

More cheers.

"Let's go," she said as the separated melodies, bass and effects melded together and bloomed into a song that elated the fans and they jumped and danced with her. When she lifted them up with her music, they took her higher with their energy and the exchange continued for their entire set. She'd have to deal with her friends and her family when she got back to New York but here at Artistique, she lived in the moment.

Chapter Twenty-Seven

Nyah's struggles with her duality had wiped her out. Performance-wise, she'd been a downright hit at Artistique. She'd even handled the larger crowd without freaking out too much. But personally, she'd failed. Gladys hated her and she'd lied to her parents. Her apartment had never felt safer than the moment she and Tommy set foot back inside together. If it hadn't been for him, she might not have been able to juggle her Nyah Monroe and Queen Roe quagmire.

She plopped down on the couch, ready to crash.

"I'm going to get a shower," Tommy said. "Join me?"

The invitation energized her despite her vegetative state. She pulled herself out of the sinking cushions on her couch and sashayed to Tommy. She'd almost reached him when her intercom rang.

She groaned at the interruption and pressed the button.

"You have a delivery, Miss Monroe. I can bring it up if you like."

"Yes, please. Thank you," she responded, and then turned to Tommy. "I'll meet you there. Let me just get this."

"Okay. I'll keep it hot for you." He did an awkward gesture with his pelvis and she laughed at his silliness. Even when he behaved like a jester for her, he still made her weak and, dare she say, happy.

A few minutes later, Nyah opened the door and a large yellow basket, as bright as the sun and wrapped in iridescent cellophane, filled her doorway.

"Your delivery, miss."

"Thank you," she said and received the gift basket before closing the door. She set it down on the coffee table in her living room. "Who sent this?" She smiled.

She found a card, plucked it from the ribbon, and read:

Queen Roe:

The Sunburst Festival is excited to have you on our lineup. As a thank-you, please accept this gift. We look forward to seeing you rock the stage.—Herman Elliot

Confusion surfaced first, followed by overwhelming dread. She didn't want to believe it. He wouldn't have done this to her. Would he? She had no idea how long she'd sat there, staring at the basket, when Tommy came out of the shower.

"Hey, did you forget to join me or what?" Tommy walked barefoot in a towel into the living room. "Nyah?" he asked when she neither answered nor moved.

"Tell me you didn't do this."

"Do what?"

She handed him the card and waited as he read. He didn't answer and the realization on his face told her all she needed to know.

"How could you book me for Sunburst without my permission?" Her heart beat like it wanted out of her chest.

"It wasn't supposed to be official but I had to give Herman an answer. Things got crazy at Artistique and I didn't want to hound you about it—"

"So you told them I'd do it?"

"It would be a great opportunity for you." He moved toward her.

"You don't get to make that decision for me. We had a deal. If an opportunity comes up, you present it to me, and I either agree to it or I don't. I didn't agree to do this," she said.

"You won't even consider it after all the progress you've made from playing a smaller club like Rebel to larger crowds than you expected on your last few outings?"

"You took the choice away from me." She jolted to her feet. "I won't even play Sunburst for my father and he's an icon being ceremoniously honored."

"That's why I think you should do it. Think about what a great moment it would be if you go on that stage with your father and play." She saw only glossy imagination in his eyes instead of remorse about the line he'd crossed.

"I can't believe this." She rubbed her face. "Here's what going to happen. You're going to call Herman and undo this. I'm not playing Sunburst."

"It's not that easy. Taking you off the lineup causes a lot of problems."

"I don't give a shit. I didn't agree to that gig and I want out. Now."

"Do you have any idea what pulling out will do to my

reputation? I'll never get another artist to play that festival, and though it may not be a big deal to you, it is to me."

"Are you even hearing yourself? You used me for your own ambition against my will and you're worried about your legacy?"

"Yes. Your career isn't the only one that's important. I have mine to consider, too." He lowered his volume. "I believe in you and your growth as an artist. You can't keep trying to put a lid on your talent, Nyah. That's not how it works. Fame doesn't come with a dial that you can manipulate at your will. I thought you were starting to understand that."

"If you'd been honest with me from the beginning, we could have worked something out. It would have been my decision. Maybe I would have done it, because I…" She choked on sorrow from the harsh betrayal. Didn't he know her? They'd become so close and her feelings had torn off their leash and now there was no way to corral them.

"Because…" he urged. When she didn't answer, he again prodded her. "What, Nyah?"

"Because I love you." She swallowed.

He moved toward her. "Angel—"

"Don't." She stopped his approach, her heart broken into heavy pieces. "You know what? I'll do it."

"What?"

"I'll play Sunburst," She heard him sigh in relief. "But you and me? We're done."

Tommy stared at the plate of food his mother had made. He didn't know how he'd even ended up here when he should be in Singapore. Three sets of eyes were on him:

his mother from the kitchen sink, his father from the entryway and Oscar from the pantry.

What the fuck have I done?

"I've never seen him like this," Tommy's father said, as he went over to his wife by the kitchen sink.

"I have."

"*Di algo, mi amor?* Why are you so quiet?" his mother said to him and then fanned her hand at his cousin. "*Mijo*, make him talk. *El no ha comido nada.* He always eats my food, and he's not eating."

"I'm okay, Mami," Tommy said, even if it was far from the truth. "I'll eat later." He replayed the events with Nyah over and over, pressing pause on the hurt and betrayal on her face when she realized what he'd done.

Oscar dropped in the seat before him. "You're freaking Tia Judy out. What's up, bro? The last time you were like this was in high school when Zulay broke up with you."

When he didn't answer right away, Oscar prodded.

"Come on, man. Whatever it is, you need to get it off your chest."

"I fucked up with Nyah," he sighed out.

"What else is new?"

Tommy sat more erect in his seat. "Wait, you know?"

"Trinket," was Oscar's one-word response. "All I know is you did something that upset her and now she's in Florida."

He felt slightly better knowing that Nyah was with her family, but he wished she was with him. "I betrayed her trust and I don't know if she'll ever forgive me."

"Ay!" His mother smacked his arm. "She will forgive you."

"You don't even know her, Mami," Tommy snapped.

"Yes, she does," Oscar said simply. "They both do."

"What?"

"Yeah, Nyah has been over here a bunch of times with Trinket." Oscar then described Nyah to his mother.

"Ah. *¿La negra bonita y alta? Si... Ella es bien trabajadora,*" his mother confirmed. "I like her."

Tommy looked up in surprise, because his mother saying that someone had hustle was the highest compliment she could give.

"How did I not know any of this?"

"You never asked, and you know Nyah is good at keeping things stealth," Oscar said.

Tommy had to agree.

"You really like this girl, Tommy?" his father, a man of few words, asked.

When she'd cut him off, the shock that his fear of losing her became real had him rolling over without a fight, even after she'd told him her feelings. She loved him and that was worth more than gold. "I love her."

"What?" His mother gasped as if he'd told her they were already married with a baby on the way. "Oh my God."

"You got all the signs," his father added. "Then you have to do whatever it takes to win her back."

"She's done with me." Tommy sank further into despair remembering Nyah's chilling words. "When she makes a decision, she's pretty good at sticking to it."

"So you're just going to take it lying down? Where's all that Boombox swag?" his father said. "You messed up."

Tommy rubbed his face, unable to get the pain on Nyah's face out of his head. "I hurt her, betrayed her trust." His chest ached knowing that he'd done that to her.

"I can see it's tearing you up, son. That's not an easy thing to win back, but just because something is difficult doesn't mean you give up on it. That's never stopped you before. Now, when it's most important, you going to fold? Fix it!"

"Listen to your father," his mother said. "You can't give up now. You need to make this right, Tommy.

"Yeah, stop whining and go get your girl," Oscar said. "Or Trinket will never forgive you and you know how loyal she is," he teased.

They were right. He needed to bandage his skinned knees because he was about to take some more hits in order to make up for what he'd done. It would all be worth it knowing he'd done right by Nyah. A sliver of hope twinkled in his chest.

"I know I was supposed to go to the club tonight, but I have to find Nyah," Tommy said to Oscar. "If she won't answer my calls, then maybe I just have to show up."

"Don't worry, bro. Take care of your business," Oscar said.

His mother clapped.

"There you go," his father said.

Oscar slapped hands with him. "That's what I'm talking about."

Tommy pulled himself out of his misery and jumped into action. How could he live with himself knowing he'd let Nyah down? She meant more to him than all his success, and no matter what it cost him, he'd fix this.

Chapter Twenty-Eight

The Miami sun warmed Nyah's skin as she lay out in her white bikini on the white patio chair by the pool. The picturesque landscape and space of her parents' estate did little to erase the soreness in her heart, but at least she could get a good tan out of it, and a little doting from her parents.

When she'd arrived, her sore eyes and disheveled look were enough for her parents to give her two days to be miserable without the third degree. Now that she'd had her mother's Jollof rice, heard her father spinning music in his man cave, and received long tearful hugs from both of them, she felt like she might be ready to enter the confessional.

A figure blocked the sunrays. "Hey," Nyah complained.

"Okay, baby girl. You can't hide here forever," her father said. Had she spoken her thoughts out loud?

"I'm not hiding." She squinted up at him and the doubt wrinkling the age lines on his face. "Okay. Maybe I'm hiding."

"You look like you've been through the wringer," her

father said. "You said you were having a tough time, but I guess I didn't expect you to actually look like it."

"Thanks for that."

Her father always had a little difficulty navigating his way to a nurturing center when she was visibly upset, but he eventually got there. Nyah didn't know how long she'd be able to hold it together before she completely unraveled and bawled her eyes out some more over losing someone she'd finally loved hard enough to make her this discombobulated.

"Where's Mom?"

"She cleans the kitchen at the homeless shelter downtown today. Remember? She'll be home soon."

"It's Thursday, already?

Her father nodded solemnly.

"I lost track of the days."

He offered her his hand. "You want me to make you some tea, like Mom makes, and we can talk about it?"

"You're going to have to give me something more hardcore than tea, Dad." She grasped his hand and eased off the lounge chair.

"That bad, huh?" her father asked as he pulled her up by the hand, then they headed to the bar.

"You have no idea. It's a shit show," she mumbled.

"Sounds like a job for…" He evaluated her for a moment. "Cognac?"

She smiled. "Double."

Her father raised his eyebrows at her.

She told him everything from start to finish. He hugged her shaking shoulders when she sobbed and choked on her alcohol and handed her a napkin when her runny nose dripped to her chin.

"You and Tommy do a piss-poor job at hiding your love for one another. Mom and I got a kick out of how you both were running around like headless chickens trying to look all professional when we showed up. We've been around the block," he said. "A couple times."

"Dad, I hid my whole DJ career from you and that's what you focus on?"

"Baby girl, you grew up in a house with a DJ. I heard you spin music night and day when we lived in New York, as well as when we moved here. When you wanted to get on the scene, I knew your mixed tapes back and forth because you were following in my footsteps. Do you really think that when buzz about Queen Roe started floating in the underground that your dear ol' dad didn't recognize our sound? I knew, Nyah. I've always known, but you needed to do this your way and if that meant breaking ties from me to do it, then that's what you needed to do."

"What?" Nyah yelled as tears streamed down her face. "Dad…" She squeezed him so tight she felt his bones. She felt so small, like his little girl, and found comfort and protection in his arms. "I'm sorry. You must hate me for denying you."

"Hate you? Nyah, you're my one and only baby girl. You had to do this your way. I mean it when I say I'm proud of you. You're really good, sweetheart, so innovative. I know you want to keep a low profile and still pursue your love of classical music, and that's okay, too. This is your life. You have to live it on your own terms."

She sniffled in his shoulder and nodded.

"The bigger question is, what are you going to do

about Tommy? He betrayed you and if I didn't know him and his character, I'd say good riddance."

"Are you taking his side?"

"Not really. I'm thinking of you both. I'm not going to sugarcoat this, baby girl. Relationships are hard and a ton of work. If you really love him, you owe it to both of you to at least talk again with cooler heads. He's an ambitious guy, but a decent one who made a mistake. Do you think you have another chance for him somewhere inside you? If not, call it quits and move on, but if a little part of you thinks that you both can save this with some elbow grease, then don't hesitate to try again."

She clutched her chest. "I want to, Dad. I just… He hurt me, but I hurt him, too. I walked away and that's a big deal for him. We messed it all up."

Her father sipped his drink. "The good thing about a mess is that you can always break out the supplies and clean it all up, one spot at a time."

Nyah had been running from the shadow of her phenomenal dad for so long that she'd forgotten just how awesome he was. "What would I do without you, Dad?"

"You'd have figured it out without me, sweetheart. It just might have taken you a little longer."

"I want to play with you," she blurted.

Her father shook his head. "You don't have to. You're upset and emotionally drained."

"No, Dad. I do. I want to play at Sunburst with you. Before, when that whole thing happened when I performed, and Carlo… I know he handled your career great but he really dropped the ball with me, Dad. I didn't want to tell you."

"I know. You were really trying to carve out your

own space, but I found out and I let him have it for that. I know he wanted to make things right…tried to, but it was too late."

"I'd bailed by then." She wiped her nose. "I've always been really proud of you, Dad. You're my role model and I love you."

"I love you too, Queen." They hugged again.

Nyah wiped her face. "Okay, give me the details."

Her mother came in shortly after and collected Nyah in her arms. The combination of ammonia and kitchen grease emanated from Eva Monroe's clothes. "Your eyes are red. What happened? Did you two have a fight?" Her mother frowned.

"No, baby. Quite the opposite," her father assured her mother.

Her mother slapped down her bag on the bar. "Okay, you two. Fill me in on everything, right now."

Carlo Hutton stopped by her parents' home for drinks with her father. Nyah'd had plans to reach out to Carlo by phone but when she saw his dark hair and matching linen top and bottoms with loafers she'd realized how much she'd grown and how much he appeared to have not. It was like she was a teenager again but instead of looking at Carlo as the one to make her great, she pitied him for missing out on a really talented artist.

"Hey, Carlo," she greeted him as she poured herself a margarita from a sweating pitcher.

"Hey, kiddo." He leapt to his feet and kissed her cheek. "It's nice to see you. How are things going in New York?"

Nyah glanced at her father. "Does he know?" she asked. She air drew makeup on her face.

Her father shook his head.

"I'll give you two a minute," her father said and disappeared.

Carlo took a sip of his drink, a clear liquid with ice. "It's been a few years."

"Yeah, it has been. How have you been?" She forced the formalities like one did with a relative they weren't close to anymore but had blood ties with. She didn't have blood ties with Carlo but he was family.

"Dad told me about Sunburst."

"Yeah. They're doing a tribute to your father. I know you love your dad and appreciate his contributions to the music industry. His influence has trickled down to you. I know you're focused on classical."

"Oh?"

"Yeah, Pete still keeps me up to date and is excited about your acceptance to the London Symphony. Congratulations."

"Thank you." She smiled at how tight she held her cards. Was this what it felt like to truly have the upper hand?

Carlo scratched the day-old hair on his chin. "Though you rest in the classical space, it would be great to have you there, Nyah. Pete wants you to play but I know that's a long shot."

She kept silent and took a long slow drink of her margarita.

"I think I had a hand in that," Carlo confessed, and she nearly choked on the liquid in her throat.

"Wow." She coughed in a fisted hand to clear her throat. "It was a long time ago."

"Maybe, but I didn't do right by you. I watched you grow up and there may have been a great opportunity to develop you as an artist but I'd been only focused on your dad and making him great. I thought you'd take that Mills kid as your agent and, well, when you didn't… You just weren't in my cards, kiddo, and I should have just told you instead of doing such a piss-poor job for you."

She stared at Carlo. Had she expected an apology she might not have been so shocked. At best she'd wanted to clear the air enough to communicate to Carlo what she wanted to do for her father. What she experienced now was way more than a resolution; this was therapeutic.

She blinked her blurry eyes. She hadn't made it all up. She'd been right and him voicing it lifted an anvil off her chest that had been pressing her down, and she finally breathed away the past. "Thanks for saying all that, Carlo," she said simply.

He nodded. "I owe you," he said. "Anyway, like I was saying, even if you don't want to try to put a DJ set together and perform, it would be a really nice moment if you introduced him."

She hadn't come out as Queen Roe and now that she had a better understanding of who she was and why she wanted the things she did, she didn't feel like she was competing with her dad anymore. Part of her conversation with Tommy, when they'd had dinner together on the cruise, popped into her head.

"I don't know how revealing Queen Roe will impact my classical career and that is still very important to

*me. I also don't know if I can manage both if I got too
big. I'd lose control over, well, everything,"*

"*You can't know unless you put yourself out there,
Queen.*"

She was no longer hiding from her legacy as Pete
Monroe's daughter. She'd claimed her own personal
throne as Queen Roe with the help of Nyah Monroe,
and in this moment the two merged together and she
embraced who she was with open arms.

"Actually, Carlo, I have my own ideas about how I
want to participate in Dad's ceremony if you're willing
to listen to a little story."

Carlo gave her a thick brow that barely arched. "Am
I going to like this story?"

"I ten out of ten recommend."

"Okay, kiddo. Shoot."

Chapter Twenty-Nine

Tommy's footsteps were heavy as he walked a plank right into the sea of career sabotage. He hated having to do this but the guilt tore through him like a flesh-eating disease, ugly and painful. As much as he hated having to have this meeting with Herman, he still had integrity. Integrity he should have had with Nyah.

We're done. Nyah's words echoed through him. What a fool he had been. This wasn't who he was. And having finally found someone he cared for more than himself was evidence enough that he loved her. Yet, he'd gone against her will for his own benefit.

He pulled his slumping shoulders back enough to be presentable to his longtime associate.

"You look fucking ghastly, man," Herman said when he saw him. "You all right?"

Tommy ignored Herman's evaluation and jumped into the deep end of a broken glass-filled pool, from which he would likely come out battered and bruised. "I got some bad news for you, Herman. Queen Roe won't be performing at Sunburst this year, or any year for that matter."

"Today is bad joke day, or what?" Herman asked.

"I'm serious. I'm pulling her," Tommy said.

"We've been promoting her as one of our key artists that fans are dying to see. A lot of marketing dollars have been directed toward advertising her," Herman complained.

"Both you and I know that what has been done can be redirected. You want me to front money? I will, but she's out."

"What the fuck, Tommy? I finally accept one of your clients, because our shit finally lined up, and this is the thanks I get."

"Look, I did my client a disservice by even agreeing to put her on the bill. She never wanted this. I did. Now I've lost her as a client and…" He rubbed his face. "She's not performing."

"You know that we've got some new investors and even though we still have some creative control, the organizers are looking at who they can count on. I told them you could deliver. You have a rep, man. You gonna jeopardize that?"

"I'm well aware that what I'm doing could tarnish the name I worked hard to make for myself. When people heard Boombox, they knew they could count on me to present talented artists, make sound business deals, and make decisions based on expansive industry knowledge. If pulling out one of my artists from Sunburst ruins me, then my career was never shit to begin with." Tommy leaned against the wall.

Herman rubbed his sweaty forehead. "It's gonna be impossible for us to book someone at this late date."

"You're talking to someone who knows how this works. You'll have to pull her picture and name from the lineup like she never existed. She's not your head-liner so you'll get a few cranky tweets and the kids'll move on. They have a whole festival to see."

"Cranky tweets? Her profile's still trending, man."

"I get it, Herman." Tommy's raised tone was more from frustration with his own idiotic behavior than anything Herman said or did. "And… I'm sorry. I screwed you, but it's done."

"Okay, man. Chill, I'll handle it." Herman started to pound on his computer keys. "I hope she's worth it."

"More than you know."

Back in New York and repaired in a way that only being home with her parents could accomplish, Nyah embodied Nancy the Manager and called Herman. She'd agreed to play Sunburst as Queen Roe for Tommy so that she didn't spend the rest of her life feeling responsible for any damage to his career. He'd hurt her and betrayed their trust, but that didn't stop her from loving him. She clutched her chest. They shared so many memories and she missed him—his raunchy jokes, the laughs they shared, and the closeness between them. Regardless of her feelings, she still had to do what was right for her sanity and her heart.

"Hello?"

"Herman? It's Queen Roe."

"Oh. Hello."

Nyah wondered if he answered all the artists on his lineup with such a dry reception.

"Did I catch you at a bad time?" she asked.

"No. I just don't know why you're calling."

She stared at the phone for a second and bit back the urge to call him a dick.

"Well, I'm calling because as an artist on your lineup

I wanted to connect with you directly to get the details about my performance."

"Is this some kind of joke, because I'm not amused."

"Joke? No, I'm handling my own details this time, without Tommy. If you need to transfer me, that's fine." She clenched her teeth because Herman was working her last nerve.

"Boombox pulled you out," Herman said. "Apparently there must be some kind of communication breakdown, because this happened a hot second ago."

"He did what?" Her voice climbed an octave or two. *Tommy pulled me from the lineup?* She'd ignored all his calls, left his texts on *Read* with no response, and archived his emails. When she said she was done, she meant it, but being pulled out of Sunburst might have been some pertinent information. "But I thought he couldn't do that."

"Well, he did, and at the detriment to his stellar rep, I should add. The investors are pissed and new festival management will definitely blacklist him from submitting future artists."

"Why'd he do that?"

"You'll have to ask him, but I have my suspicions," Herman said. "Pulling you out left us with a gaping fucking hole in the part of my lineup that's supposed to be savage and—"

"I can help," Nyah blurted. She shirked the training bra and straightened into her big girl brassiere. She'd written Tommy off but he'd risked the reputation he cherished to do right by her and honor her wishes. She made a note to try to retrieve the deleted messages and check the archived emails he'd sent her. Her heart raced but she

cooled her jets. Trust had been tested and lost and she
wasn't so sure if letting him back in was the right choice.

"How? You're going to perform?" Herman interrupted her reflections.

"Better than that."

"You've got my attention," Herman said.

"Well, you're going to have to expand your span until
I get back to you."

"You're asking a lot and not telling me much."

"And I'm sorry about that but can you give me until
tomorrow?"

"How do I know I can trust you?"

"You can't, but I'm asking you to give me until tomorrow." She prayed he'd say yes because if what she had
planned worked out it could help everyone she loved.

Herman chewed on her statement for a bit. "Okay.
You got 'til tomorrow. Noon. No later. I'm only doing
this because Tommy's a friend."

"Thanks, Herman. I appreciate it."

She hung up and paced for several minutes until she
developed her plans and sorted through the kinks and all
the things that could possibly go wrong. She sat down
and closed her eyes to rest her firing brain. Was this
what it was like to be an agent? She rolled her phone in
her hands a couple of time and finally sent her first text.

Queen: Emergency situation. I need to see you.

All clubs lost their allure in the daytime when the flat-
tering light gave way to the sun that revealed dirty
floor, old, overstressed, shellacked wood bars, and
dingy walls. Rebel was no different. Nyah had never
walked into the club without her cloak, her makeup, or

her dagger—her music. Now she called upon her two worlds and hoped that she wasn't about to make another big mistake.

She saw Oscar first, and he gave her that I know you but I don't know you look. Even though he knew who she was, she never showed up to the club or at any crew event as Nyah.

He hugged her. "I heard you're having a time."

"No doubt." She neglected to add, *from Tommy*. "She here yet?"

He nodded. "In the back, plus one."

A glimmer of hope flipped her stomach. Nyah resolved that whatever happened, she had given all of this one hell of a shot. "Thanks," she said to Oscar and made her way backstage.

As Nyah got closer, she heard laughter and high-spirited conversation. She crept inside to see Trinket and Gladys by the backstage lockers talking about music.

"I'm surprised you know so much about Brahms," Gladys chirped.

"Or that you're such a huge fan of Louis the Child. Does Nyah know?" Trinket asked.

"No." Gladys hung her head. "I wish she had trusted me like she trusts you."

Nyah thought she'd already cried her tears at her parents' home, but apparently, she had more to shed. This is what she'd always wanted but she had been too afraid to meld her two worlds. That Gladys and Trinket chatted like buddies confirmed Nyah's suspicions that they'd make fast friends.

Her sniffles got their attention and they quieted their discussion.

"I do trust you, Gladys." Nyah went in for the hug.

Even if Gladys rejected her, Nyah didn't care. She missed her friend. "It's why I asked you to come today and it means so much to me that you're here."

"It wasn't easy," Gladys said, hugging her back, to Nyah's relief. "I'm still really mad at you. To find out that way…that hurt, Nyah."

"I know and I'm really sorry. I was scared and didn't want to be judged for doing what I love."

"And that's exactly what I did, isn't it?" Gladys asked rhetorically. "Believe me, I've had some time to think about it, and, well, I am… I'm a classical snob. I did judge you when I found out, but you're my friend and I'm trying to understand."

"That's all I can ask."

"This is beautiful," Trinket interrupted, clapping her heavily braceleted hands.

"Come here, you." Nyah pulled Trinket into a hug.

"Okay, okay," Trinket said and pulled away. "We heeded the call, girl. We're here for you. So we're going to need you to reveal."

"Yeah. What's the emergency you sent in the group text?" Gladys asked.

With all the practice she'd had recently, she told Trinket and Gladys another story, this one about her and Tommy and Sunburst.

"He's trash," Trinket said when Nyah explained how Tommy had betrayed her.

"Is there more to the story?" Gladys asked.

"Lots more," Nyah said and looked at Trinket.

"G'head," Trinket said, playing with the curling edge of one of the stickers plastering the lockers, and Nyah continued the rest of the tale, up until the moment when she'd sent the emergency text.

"Wow," Gladys said.

"He's not so bad, after all." Trinket tapped her chin as if still considering it.

"Which leads me to you, Trinket."

"Me? How does all this lead to me?"

"I've always told you that you're the best DJ I know so…" Nyah waited for Trinket to fill in the blanks.

Trinket turned gray, shook her head and backed up into the lockers. Her reaction was better than Nyah expected.

"I think you should take my place at Sunburst." Nyah ripped the bandage all the way off.

"I can't do it," was Trinket's spacy statement.

"Yes, you can," Nyah encouraged.

"What am I missing?" Gladys asked.

"Trinket suffers from stage fright." Nyah clued her friend in. "But we've been working on it. She has done house parties and played in the park."

"She also played Rebel when you were in Florida." Oscar appeared backstage. "Just thought I'd check in in case shit went south."

"What?" Nyah yelped. "Why didn't you tell me?"

"I told her you'd be pissed," Oscar chimed in and Trinket gave him the stink eye.

"I'm not pissed. I'm just sorry I missed your inaugural performance, especially as your coach. I bet you were fucking great." Nyah hugged her again.

"She was fucking awesome." Oscar doused his girl with all the pride.

"I wanted to tell you, but you were going through it and I didn't wanted bug you…" Trinket trailed off.

"Somebody had better gotten that shit on video," Nyah said.

"Facts. It's up on the Tube," Oscar said.

"So, what do you think, T? If you play Sunburst, I'll be there with you the whole time."

"It's just such a popular fest. The people who've played there… I don't know." Trinket paced so fast Nyah was getting dizzy watching her.

Oscar stopped her and held her by the shoulders. "It's time you show 'em your stuff, babe. You got this. We all got your back."

Trinket didn't speak for a long time until she finally broke her silence. "Can I think about it?"

"Of course." Nyah chewed her lip. "But you only have until noon tomorrow to make your decision."

"Noon?" Everyone, even Gladys yelled.

"Well, really I have to know before that so that I can let my contact know by noon." Nyah cheesed, in hopes it would relax her audience.

"Way to put on the pressure, Nyah. At least we had a few days when CeCe sprung the impromptu auditions on us," Gladys said.

"It's not ideal but I think we can rise to this occasion," Nyah said.

"We?" Trinket groaned.

"I know." Nyah remembered how she'd felt when Tommy asked her to play Oh Ship and Sunburst. She knew Trinket's fear and the doubts that floated through her mind. She went to Trinket's side. "Listen. No matter what you decide, I love you, sis. This is a great opportunity, so fuck all the pressure and what we all think. You decide for you."

"Queen?" Oscar said.

"I've been there and I would be a shitty coach if I said otherwise. If you say yes, this train is going to jet out of the station and you with it. You decided to play Rebel on your own. I'm a bit salty that I missed it but so proud of you. As for this? You make the call and let me know. Okay?" Nyah asked.

Trinket nodded.

"Either way I'm inviting you both to Sunburst for my father's ceremony," she said to Trinket and Gladys. "You too, Oz. I know you have the club but it'd be great if you were there."

"I need a drink," Trinket said.

"We all do," Gladys said.

They made their way to the bar, but Nyah held Trinket behind. "Before you make your decision, I wanted to tell you something."

Nyah leaned into her ear and whispered the only secret she had left.

When she looked at Trinket's face, Nyah knew she'd made the right choice for herself and for Trinket with the admission.

"Okay?" Nyah asked.

Trinket squeezed her hand. "Okay."

Later that night as Nyah readied for her performance at the concert hall she got a text.

Trinket: I'm in

Nyah squealed in excitement and did a little dance in her living room. More than anything she was happy for this opportunity for Trinket. She wasted no time reaching out to Herman to tell him about his new booking.

"What's her name?"

"Layla Jones, goes by Trinket." Nyah waited for Herman to speak and thought maybe their connection got warped. "Herman?"

"You're fucking with me, right?"

"Not at all." Herman's response fluttered her intrigue. "Why do you think I'm fucking with you?"

"Her name has been buzzing around the festival circuit after one of her house party sets went up on YouTube. It wasn't viral but over about a month she's gotten over a million likes."

"What?" Nyah'd had no idea. Did Trinket or anyone in their circuit know? "Tommy can get her." She tightened up her card game. "Well, Tommy has her on his client list," Nyah said. "So your people have to accept him back into the fold if you want her."

Herman tried to play the "Let me talk to a couple people" game but his excitement transcended his words, and he caved.

"You got a deal," Herman said. "By the way. I hope there are no hard feelings with Tommy. He asked me to put you in tentatively until he got your final say on playing Sunburst, but I pressured him for an answer. I figured you'd get my basket and get excited to play my fest."

Herman's admission hit her tender heart. "Thanks, Herman." Tommy should have never agreed to put her on the lineup at all but she was glad that he hadn't completely disregarded her wishes.

"No problem," Herman said.

They ended the call and Nyah immediately set the next phase of her plan in motion.

Chapter Thirty

What the fuck is happening? Tommy got a call that he needed to complete the paperwork for his client Trinket to play at Sunburst Festival. He tried to call Herman but for the first time in the history of their friendship, he couldn't get through.

"Yaz?"

"Yes?" Yaz poked her head into his office in every-day fashion.

"Can you see if you can call around and find Herman? I'm being asked to submit a rider and other paperwork for a Layla Jones but she's not my client." Tommy started another text to Herman. He had stopped in LA to repack and was heading to Florida to find Nyah.

"Yes, she is," Yaz answered.

Tommy slowly put the phone down. "Come again?"

"Layla 'Trinket' Jones is your client," Yaz confirmed. Tommy had been so deep in his own world that it took him a minute to retrieve Oscar's girlfriend's real name.

"What?" he asked, his brain striving for clarity.

Yaz cleared her throat but gave him her chin. "Queen

Roe and I worked with Herman to get Trinket squared away to play in place of her at Sunburst."

"What?" Apparently, he only had one word accessible in his vocabulary at the moment. Tommy shot to his feet at the sound of Nyah's name.

"Yeah. It's not official, until you sign…right…here." Yaz placed a document in front of him. "Trinket already signed. I set up a little meet and greet for you both to talk. It's on your calendar. You probably won't be able to go over everything before Sunburst but I thought a little 'welcome to the team' would be nice."

"So you've spoken to her?"

"To who? Trinket?"

"No, Queen Roe?"

"Yes."

"How is she?" he asked before he could stop himself. "I mean, how's she doing in Florida?"

"She's not in Florida. She's in New York."

Tommy paced behind his desk. "Are you sure?"

"Pretty sure," Yaz said. "I mean… Like us, she's probably getting ready to head here for Sunburst Summer Festival."

He didn't know what to say. "I… I haven't even seen her play."

"Who? Queen Roe?" Yaz looked confused.

"No, Trinket."

"I know. I'm just kidding. You look like you need a good laugh." Yaz chuckled then abruptly turned serious. "And shame on you for not signing her sooner. She's a perfect client for you. I should know. Have you seen her performance at Rebel?"

"She performed at Rebel? But she has stage fright."

Tommy thought back to his discussions with Nyah. He'd promised to see Trinket play but he'd never gotten around to it. He did, however, know that part of why it had been hard to see her play was because Trinket was petrified of the stage. He quietly celebrated Trinket's milestone.

"Well, I have and she's really good. She's also got quite the buzz going on. Herman and team were really happy to get her."

Tommy palmed his spinning head. For all his expertise as an agent, what Nyah and Yaz had pulled off was nothing short of genius. "It seems the student is schooling her teacher."

"We've got one of our artists at Sunburst." Yaz cheered. "You should really call Queen Roe and thank her. It was her idea," Yaz said.

Tommy wanted to do more than just thank Nyah. He needed her, and if she'd helped him at all then maybe there was a slim chance that he hadn't completely ruined any chance of having her in his life.

"Yeah." He nodded vacantly. Then he shook himself back to LA. "Okay, Yaz. Tell me everything."

The California sun showed up for the Sunburst Summer Festival and Nyah had one job: with the help of Oscar and Gladys, keep tabs on Trinket and calm her down in the event she turned into a runner.

"We'll be right here, babe," Oscar said, holding Trinket's hand.

"This is your stage, sis. Tear up those tracks." Nyah tried not to hover in case all Trinket needed was space to puke or faint.

"You got this, Trinket," Glady patted her arm.

Nyah's nerves for Trinket were worse than if she were going on the Sunburst stage herself. She was in the middle of another pep talk when she saw Yaz and Tommy.

Nyah's stomach flipped when she saw him walking toward them, looking sharper than a razor. *Damn, can't he just look bad sometimes?*

Yaz greeted her. "Hey, Nyah. It's good to see you... well, as yourself."

Nyah smiled. "Yeah, it's a little weird in this setting, but good." Nyah then introduced everyone Yaz didn't know.

Tommy inched closer to her. "Hi," he said and she'd never seen him make such a tentative move.

"Hi." Her response might have been brief but her heart raced a mile a minute.

"We were checking to make sure everything is all set up for Trinket. She's on in thirty," Yaz announced.

Trinket rubbed her stomach and groaned when she heard the words. Her jerky movements were concerning. "I don't know if I'm going to make it up there."

"How are you, Trinket? You ready to light this place up?" Tommy asked as he approached her.

"Being this nervous is completely normal," Yaz said.

"What can I get you that will help? Maybe a little ginger ale? Gatorade? A puke pail? You name it and it's yours, just tell me. Nothing's off limits." Tommy sought backup from Yaz, who nodded in agreement.

"All those things. I don't think I have anything left inside but don't quote me on that. Maybe a ginger ale?"

Trinket's face was as gray as the day Nyah had proposed she play Sunburst.

"I'm on it," Yaz said and left to assist Tommy in making Trinket comfortable.

"It's going to be okay. They're going to love you. You see all these people backstage? They're here to make sure you have a flawless show." He pointed to the attendants and techs. "Most of all, your friends are here. So you give a great show and we will celebrate like crazy later."

Nyah loved the way Tommy doted on Trinket, a festival newbie in need of a professional hand. Nyah's nervous adjacent energy made her stomach do summersaults, too.

"He's good," Gladys said and nudged her. "Have you two spoken yet?"

Nyah shook her head.

"Well, you're both here now." Gladys grinned.

Oscar took over comfort duties with Trinket and Yaz returned with a ginger ale.

Tommy came over and though Trinket borderlined on being in crisis, Nyah couldn't help but appreciate this man who, in the end, risked something so important to him for her. "How are you doing?" he asked her.

"I've been okay," Nyah said.

"I heard you were in Florida for a bit," he said.

"Yeah," she said. "I guess I needed a little time away."

"I tried to find you but you've been kind of a moving target these past few weeks." Tommy peered down at his shoes for a brief moment. "Why didn't you return my texts or emails?"

"I think I just needed some time. Then things got

really crazy and busy with the philharmonic ending for the season, and accepting the London position and getting organized for that. Then this thing with Trinket," she babbled. "But I thought about you, Tommy."

"Can we talk somewhere? I promise I won't take you too far from Trinket," he said. "Will you come with me?"

"Yeah. Okay." She followed him, as did the eyes of their friends and colleagues.

They found a less loud spot.

"You really saved my ass," he said. "Why?"

"I told you that I would perform. Why did you pull me out?" she asked him.

"Because it wasn't right. I'd rather ruin my career than lose you, Nyah." The intensity in his words shot to the center of her soul. "I'm sorry I did that to you, angel, and I need you to know that you're the most important thing to me."

"I thought you just wanted to check another goal box and it brought up so many bad memories of when Carlo handled my career badly. I didn't know if you wanted this." She studied the emotion in those gorgeous brown eyes.

He enveloped her hands in his. "Of course I want this. Nyah, I love you. You occupy my thoughts from the time I rise to the moment sleep finally takes me. I want you more than breath. I know how much I hurt you, but please tell me you'll give this a second chance."

She hooked her arms around his neck. "You know there's nothing I want more, Tommy." She joined her mouth with his and she gladly greeted his seeking tongue.

"I missed you, baby," he mumbled against her lips

and she felt the urgency in his kiss. "I missed you," he repeated and she opened he mouth, her body and soul to him.

"Oh, Tommy." She pressed her body against his and made out with him as if it was their first time alone and touching. His hand went to her ass and pressed her even closer, which she hadn't thought was possible.

"Tommy? Nyah?" Yaz called their names. They pulled apart and though Tommy held her hand, Nyah's body ached for him.

"Coming, Yaz," he called to her, even though neither one of them saw the young agent.

"To be continued?" Nyah asked.

"Definitely." Tommy stared at her for a long time. "Interesting," he said.

"What's interesting?" she asked.

"Kissing you in this setting as Nyah," he confessed.

"Funny...to me, it feels just right." She smiled and kissed his lips once more.

"I want to stay like this with you forever," he said against her lips. "But I have a client who's about to pass out from stage fright," he teased.

She laughed and tugged him toward the rest of their crew. When they arrived, they found Trinket guzzling her drink with a death grip on Oscar's hand.

Trinket saw her and Tommy together. "Everything cool with you guys?"

"Yeah." Nyah's face went hot.

Trinket smiled and hugged her. "I'm still scared as shit but I'm so happy for you. Both of you."

"Thanks," Nyah said. "It's showtime. Take these." Nyah handed over her rose-colored glasses. "Even if you don't wear them, keep them nearby and remember I'm right out there with you."

"Queen."

Gladys came over. "Have fun out there, Trinket."

Trinket was announced and one of the festival handlers walked her to the stage. Trinket climbed the stairs with legs that Nyah could see wobble from afar.

"Oh boy." Nyah worried her lip like a nervous mother.

"Some nerves are good," Gladys and Tommy said simultaneously.

"I know but this is such a big moment for her," Nyah said and Tommy embraced her shoulders. "She'll be fine," he said.

She squeezed his middle. "Come on, guys. Let's get out front so she can see us and the crowd."

Trinket played the first electronic chords of her set and Nyah lost it. "Go, Trinket." Nyah's scream cracked with emotion as she thought back on how hard Trinket had worked to get here. From the first drunk night they met, to their mutual support for one another. They all cheered for her and when Trinket saw them, her eyes locked on them like a focal point for a pregnant woman in Lamaze class.

Song after song, more of the Trinket that Nyah knew and loved emerged onstage and the crowd rewarded her with cheers and bouncing energy.

"Holy shit. She's phenomenal," Tommy said.

"Yeah, she is." Nyah slapped hands with Yaz. She looked over at Gladys, who for all her classical snobbery shouted just as loud for Trinket as the rest of them.

After Trinket's performance they all tumbled into the backstage area to greet Trinket.

"That was crazy," Trinket yelled, jumping up and down. "I did it. I fucking did it."

They joined her in a group hug, bouncing together like they were on a trampoline.

Oscar kissed Trinket, hard and wild. "You were fantastic, babe. I love you so much."

Nyah couldn't keep still. "You want more, right?" Nyah asked Trinket.

"Hell yes."

"Safe to say we've created a monster," Gladys said.

"Most definitely,"

"You heard your client, Boombox. Make it happen." Nyah patted his ass. "Especially since I'll no longer be yours."

"What?" Tommy stopped in his tracks and Nyah giggled.

"Come on. We have some celebrating to do before we have to honor her father."

Pete Monroe always looked larger than life and today was no different. As Carlo ceremoniously announced his long-term client, Nyah watched the jumbotron with images of her father creating, performing and even some images of his home life. The crowd reacted to each one with laughter, cheers and sentimental sighs, and Nyah joined them, her chest filling with pride. Pete Monroe wasn't just an innovator and an icon. This was her dad who she loved with her whole heart. This was such a big moment for him and when he came to the stage, she thanked all the stars in Heaven that she was here for this.

"This is a great honor and I thank you guys for coming out and making this old man feel young again. The music is still living, still thriving, and thanks to many of the artists here at Sunburst, the music continues to evolve," her father said and the crowd cheered.

"But for me this moment is even more special because I get to introduce you to someone very special. Someone whose sound couldn't be contained in the underground, someone whose knowledge and love of music is as bright and vast as mine. I know, because I raised her. You know her. You love her. And you have become a part of her royal court. Raise your hands, party people, for the one, the only, her majesty and my daughter. Queen Roe! Get up here, baby girl."

Nyah stood onstage with her Afro puffs and sunglasses. The fans screamed her name and her father gathered her into a hug. There was no other place she wanted to be than onstage, honoring her father with the mass of people who showed up and showed out for him. She got on the dials with him and claimed her legacy as his daughter. The reveal thrilled the crowds, the media and the press. She spotted Gladys and Evan with Trinket and Oscar and her world finally felt like her own. *Damn it feels good to stop hiding.* She found Tommy with a dropped jaw, shaking his head in awe at how she'd kept such a priceless moment from him, and seeing his face made it all the more worth it. She laughed and shrugged at him. When she blew him a kiss, he caught it and pressed it to his heart. The cheesy move made her feel gooier than Mallomars in summer.

The old fears threatened but Tommy had helped by exposing her to larger and larger crowds and knowing what she was getting into helped her remember to keep moving forward. She jumped and danced as she played and her father grooved with her. He laughed at her energy and she bowed to the King.

As they came off stage, they were greeted with praise. "That was legendary," someone said as she wiped sweat off her father's face with a towel. All the while photos snapped of her with him. This time Nyah didn't hide or throw her hoodie over her head. She stood proud with him.

Her mother kept a healthy distance like she always did, to give her husband his time to shine.

"Eva? Come." Her father signaled her mother to him and slipped his arm around her waist.

Her mother kissed his lips, her cheeks wet with tears. "You both were so amazing. I'm so happy to see you two onstage together."

"Aww, mom." Nyah squeezed them both in a group hug.

From the corner of her eye she saw Trinket, Oscar, Gladys, Yaz, and Tommy. Once the initial energy of them coming off stage settled a bit, they approached.

"That was great." Yaz clapped excitedly.

"Thank you, young lady," her father said to Yaz.

Tommy scooped Nyah up in his arms and spun her. "You're remarkable." He kissed her cheeks and mouth and it took her a second to remember the audience around them. When he put her down she pointed to her father.

"Pete?" Tommy shook her father's hand. "What can I say? Greatest performance I've seen in a long time. It was great to see you on the stage again. I'm sure that you've influenced a whole new generation."

"I appreciate that," her father said as someone handed her father a bottled water.

"Mrs. Monroe." Tommy gave her mother a quick peck on the cheek.

"I always get the Mrs.," Nyah's mother complained. "Good to see you again. It's been a long time." Her mother gave him a heavy study.

"This is my colleague Yasmin Rosa," Tommy introduced her.

"It's an honor, Mr. Monroe." Yaz almost shook her father's hand off.

Nyah looked on with admiration as Tommy interacted with her parents. She couldn't have dreamed of making this moment better. That was, until Gladys, Trinket, and Oscar hugged her.

"That was the best." Gladys gave her a sweaty hug. "I danced the whole time."

"Queen?" Trinket bowed. "You guys smashed that stage. Especially you, Mr. Monroe."

"Call me Pete." Her father always suggested that. He once told her it made him feel old when people addressed him so formally.

"Yeah, that'll never happen," Trinket said respectfully. "My mama didn't raise no fool."

"It's an honor, Mr. Monroe. Mrs. Monroe," Oscar said.

If Nyah got any happier she'd float. Through all the challenges she had everyone she loved in one place and she didn't have to hide any part of her anymore.

Tommy's hand grazed hers. "Can I steal you for a quick minute?"

"If all you want is a quick minute then you've got bigger problems," her father interjected.

Tommy stuttered for a response.

"Dad," Nyah scolded.

"I'm just kidding, man," her father said. "Take your time."

When her father was out of sight and earshot, Tommy moved closer to her. "That was one of the best surprises I've ever seen pulled off."

"I know how to put on a good show," she said and pointed to her father. "I learned from the best."

"That you did." He smoothed a wayward hair behind her ear. "So what's this about me not having you any-more?" Tommy asked.

"Well, you're a great agent, baby, but let's face it, we have different goals, so…"

"So?"

She went easy on him. "I'm going to have to let you go."

"You're firing me?" He stepped back and checked her seriousness.

"Yes, but the good news is I'm hiring Yaz." Nyah cheesed so hard her teeth started to get cold in the air conditioning backstage.

"Not only are you firing me, but you're replacing me with my own employee?"

"Don't think of this as a failure." She hooked her arm in his. "When I worked with Yaz for Trinket, we realized that we complement each other really nicely."

"Wow." Tommy hugged her waist. "I'm heartbro-ken, angel."

"We'll still make beautiful music together." She winked at him and he laughed. He might be disappointed but deep down she knew that he thought the decision was right.

"Yes. I plan on making lots of beautiful music with you," he said and pressed his pelvis against her. "Tonight." He kissed her neck. "Tomorrow." He nibbled her chin. "And every day after that." He finally kissed her lips.

"We have some catching up to do," she said.

"When do you leave for London?" he asked.

"In two weeks."

"Do you have room for one more?"

"You're coming?" she asked.

"I'll still have to do some traveling and work, but yeah."

She jumped on him, her arms and legs wrapping him like spider legs. She clamped him tight and he embraced her. She didn't have to worry about being without him for her time in the UK. He had no idea how much him coming with her meant. "Tommy! I didn't want to ask because I know you're so busy."

"You happy?" he laughed.

"I'm more than happy." She kissed his face.

"Me too, baby."

The situation was unconventional but she finally felt like they were in harmony and off to a great new start, one where they both were able to be the best they could be to one another.

* * * * *

Acknowledgments

A huge thank-you goes to my amazing agent, Sarah E. Younger, and to my editor, Alissa Davis, for working with me during the many surprises 2020 had to offer. I accomplished much more than I thought I could because of you both. Special thanks to Stephanie Doig for all your help and support. Thank you to the entire team at Carina Press and Harlequin for helping me grow as an author as well as reach more readers with each book.

To my family and friends, I love you. You're the absolute best fans I could ever wish for.

Finally, to the readers and fans, thank you for reading, reviewing, and sharing my stories. See you on our next adventure.

Author Bio

JN Welsh is an award-winning author and native New Yorker. She writes entertaining, often humorous, and provocative tales about strong, career-driven, multicultural heroines of color who are looking for love. Her punchy, flowing dialogue, and mostly big city stories are heartwarming and stick to your ribs.

When she's not writing she can be found dancing, wine-ing, rooting for her favorite baseball team, and/or indulging in countless guilty pleasures.

Superstar or Supernova? Asha "Velvet" Kendall is this close to achieving her dream of headlining the legendary Temptation Festival as half of the DJ duo Bedazzled Beats. Will a chance encounter with sexy-as-sin industry icon Isaak "Zazzle" Van Sandt be the cherry on top? Or the beginning of the end...

Keep reading for an excerpt from
In Rhythm *by JN Welsh.*

Chapter One

"Where there is no Temptation there is no victory." Asha "Velvet" Kendall repeated the Italian proverb to herself as she climbed the stairs to the Temptation Festival's minor stage. She scanned the crowd, undulating like a loose-stitched quilt to the electric sounds of Bedazzled Beats. Their sound played through the speakers at one of the Temptation Festival's small stages. The sun beat down on Velvet's brown skin, but this was par for the course. She and her bestie Bonnie "Candy" Fairchild powered through, playing their music with smiles and energy that rivaled Ritalin for every attendee.

Velvet rotated a dial on the controller, layering an echo effect on the song. As the music approached its crescendo, the crowd thickened until the dense group popped like beans on a beating drum. This was what happened when they played. The participants swayed and waved, frantically waiting for the beat to drop. With her hand on her bedazzled headphones, Velvet continued to tease the crowd, and all the while the melody of Candy's song haunted in the background. Just as the anticipation became almost painful, Velvet picked up the mic.

"You ready, LA? Let's go!"

Both she and Candy released their faders and graced the place with bass. When the heavy beat trembled and the bass covered the crowd, the fans went wild.

Velvet loved these moments. Seeing people enjoy her music encouraged her to grind harder toward her goals. She wouldn't be satisfied until Bedazzled Beats played the main stage as headliners at this festival. The fans had voted them here, like they'd done for every other act. She would do whatever she had to do to get them to vote her and Candy to one of the most coveted spots in their industry.

"Thanks, guys, you've been awesome! We'll see you soon." Velvet whirled and bopped around on the stage, pointing at individual attendees, shooting out hand-formed hearts and mouthing to them. *I see you.*

Candy closed out their set with a remix version of "Be You," their hottest song. The excited cries of the fans echoed through the festival. The words were easy, positive and catchy, and the crowd sang along. If there was anyone there who didn't know who Bedazzled Beats were? They did now.

Velvet gyrated over to Candy, who was entranced by her own set. Velvet draped her arm around her friend's shoulders and couldn't think of a better person to DJ with. Their music styles complemented each other and they both wanted to be the best for the Temptation crowd.

Both she and Candy repeated their farewells into their mics before they unplugged their computers and hurried down the stairs.

Bernard "LED" Royal clapped his hands and pumped his fists. "You were fantastic, babe." He reached for Candy, and puckered for a kiss.

LED turned to Velvet. "Killed it."

Someone handed her and Candy towels and bottled water. "Thanks."

"The crowd was amazing." Backstage, Velvet weaved through festival staff, and passed artists on their way to or decompressing from the stage, and their entourages who hung around.

"Hell, yeah," LED said.

"This chick was fire. I love you, girl." Candy raised her hand and Velvet slapped her high five.

"The way you closed out was epic. I had to hug you to make sure you were real." Velvet laughed.

"The Candy and Velvet love fest is in full swing," LED said and others around them laughed.

"Don't be jelly." Velvet pretended to kiss and make out with Candy.

"You guys are cray." LED had been witness to her and Candy's foolery since they'd been introduced two years ago.

"You know it." Candy patted LED's chest.

Velvet listened as the crowd cheered for the next performer. "I want the main stage. Headlining here would be everything."

"Tall order, but I can see it happening one day. One stage at a time." LED had always been supportive of her and Candy, but Velvet glimpsed a tinge of doubt. She'd gotten versions of that same line every time she announced her aspirations. Though LED's version lacked the level of flat-out amusement and condescending notes as others, it still bugged her.

Velvet didn't have much time to think about it before they glided down the conveyor belt of the festival assembly line. Hired handlers helped them secure their equipment. They stopped for photographers and videographers who snapped photos of their every move. Most of the cameras angled at Candy whose pixie appeal matched the festival standard. They were ushered to press for comments where she and Candy posed for additional pictures as well as ones in their signature face-to-face pose.

"How was your first Temptation experience?" a reporter asked.

"Absolutely awesome," Candy exclaimed. "The crowd gave us pure love."

"We hope the fans vote us back next year. We'd love to play the main stage." Velvet made her campaign for next year official.

"Those are coveted spots. Do you think you have a chance with the famous DJ lineups out there?"

Velvet smiled over her gnashing teeth. "The power is in the hands of the fans. Anything is possible." She raised her hands to the sky and jumped up, her showmanship unwavering. If no one had faith in Bedazzled Beats making it to the main stage, she'd just have to carry the mother lode until they did.

Another reporter jumped in with his question and almost blocked her. "You ladies have been a rocket on the rise. What's next for Bedazzled Beats?"

"Velveteen?" Candy lobbed it over to her.

From the beginning of their career many of the media folks had defaulted to Candy. Her friend's uncontested beauty, posh style and fair-skinned currency gave them what they needed. Access. They played the game when it was in session. Candy lined it up and Velvet hit it out the park. As women they still hit ceilings and walls but since the day they decided to pursue their music career there was no stopping them.

"We'll be doing more festivals and clubs and hope to get started on our album soon," Velvet spoke into the microphone.

"Yeah. We have a lot of great music coming for our fans so stay tuned." Candy pointed into the lens the reporter's camera guy had fixed on them.

"Very cool. If your album is anything like your performance tonight the entire scene will be after your tracks. Any label announcements?"

The reporter highlighted yet another gaping hole in her and Candy's plans. Tommy Boombox, their agent, had lined up a few label meetings but Bedazzled Beats were still label-less.

Candy deferred to her to answer. "We'll have news on that soon so make sure to connect with us on social."

"And sign up to our fan club via our website for Bedazzled Beats merch," Candy added.

They answered more questions and posed for more pictures until the press found another DJ to cover.

They really needed to find a manager and soon. Boombox had gotten them some really great gigs since they'd opened for Luke "The Musical Prophet" Anderson in Los Angeles almost a year ago. They couldn't have dreamed up that type of exposure. Her and Candy's hustle had paid off and now Tommy hustled for them, too. However, with their sights set on the Temptation Festival main stage, they were going to need a lot more help.

They reconnected with LED, and as they made their way backstage to the artist lounge, a member of the press stopped LED.

"I'd love to cover your Egyptian performance tomorrow. Any official press welcomed?"

"I'm sure my manager would love to help you out." LED communicated his manager's name, all while being a one-man bodyguard clearing the path for her and Candy.

Velvet fanned post-performance heat from her neck, in addition to the bit of envy hovering over her. She and Candy handled the aspects of their career not handled by Boombox and Velvet wished the manager volley that LED had just pulled was part of her repertoire. She reminded herself of the moving train she rode, and that eventually more things would fall into place for her and Candy. *You'll get there.*

"You're going to bring the house down tomorrow at the Egyptian." Velvet nudged LED.

Both Bedazzled Beats and LED were playing the nightclub after the festival closed tomorrow night. Velvet's fingers itched to play again and she had just finished her set with Candy.

"By the way, I have a special guest that's going to blow the roof clear off the spot." LED wrapped his arm around Candy's waist, despite the oval sweat mark on her lower back.

"Yeah? Who?" The cool breeze from the air-conditioning backstage blew against Velvet's scalp of her half Mohawk.

LED pressed his index finger against his lips. "He's going to come through after he does a little press."

"Oh. A secret DJ? Is he performing tonight?" Velvet inquired.

"He performs tomorrow night and then will do the Egyptian with us," LED responded.

"Main stage?"

"Yup."

"Closing out the festival? Wow. Those are all big guns on the main stage. That can only be Tekko, The Musical Prophet or Tres Armadas."

"I'm excited to see all those guys," Candy cheered.

Joe "Tekko" Kim and Luke were their friends and wouldn't be in town until tomorrow. Velvet looked forward to seeing them play. She hadn't officially met the members of Tres Armadas but she had seen them perform a few years ago. Back then, Velvet played underground clubs spinning vinyl and she and Candy attended festivals as fans researching their future career.

"Guess we'll just have to see who shows up." Velvet strode toward the snack bar, gulped an energy drink, and fed her face with a granola and fruit yogurt cup. Candy participated, as well.

"If you ladies want something more just let them know, but the festival food is tight. Performers eat free," LED informed them.

"We know," Candy mumbled through a cheek full of chips.

"Post-performance hunger is no joke." LED laughed at them as they finished up their snacks. "Well, our performances are done for the day. Now it's all about networking and enjoying the festival."

Music from the ongoing performances played in the club-lit lounge backstage. Neon bars and signs provided shelter from the sun as well as an evening feel. Candy danced around her, yanking Velvet back to the moment. Velvet marched in place and in time to the music. *Damn, I love music.* "I Love Music," by the O'Jays played in her head, engulfed in one of Candy's sexy, groovy house beats. She grabbed Candy's hand, twirling her bestie.

Velvet shared her O'Jays remix and Candy lit up at the idea to add to their future DJ set. "Let's do it with some underground groove house."

"Now you're talkin'." Velvet's familiarity with those lifted brows and dimpled cheeks spanned back to nights, after college classes, and weekends under the "turn-ta-blism" tutelage of their mentor DJ Reynard "FeNom" West. They later became never-ending students of dance music history and culture. The bittersweet memory of their time with the DJ made her pulse flare and Velvet tried to shake it off. They owed it to themselves and their teacher to blow the scene up.

"That's my cue to get you ladies some drinks."

"Thanks, Bernard," Velvet said. She was glad Candy had chosen a less possessive and more fun boyfriend than the last nightmare she'd gone out with. Though pansexual, Candy settled into LED like she'd finally found her emotional and romantic match. LED treated Velvet like a sister and she liked it when they all hung out together.

"Stop calling out my government name, *Asha.* There's beauty in anonymity."

"All right, all right." Velvet pulled a Charms Blow Pop out of a clip she used to attach it to her hair. She unwrapped the lollipop. "Let me just grab Nuts so we can take her with us."

"You and that scooter are inseparable," LED ragged on her.

"You're just upset because you don't have your own wheels to push." Velvet popped the lollipop in her mouth. She enjoyed riding her through the festivals ever since she was an attendee, whether festival policy allowed it or not. Nuts and Blow Pops, her must-haves, went with her wherever she traveled. She left to reclaim her scooter. "Don't do shots without me."

Velvet walked a fair distance to a secure area to retrieve Nuts from one of the attendants backstage. She glided back to her friends and navigated through makeshift corridors, false partitions and moving bodies.

"Great show, Velvet," someone called to her, and she returned the greeting with a wave.

When she returned her eyes forward, she found herself a split second from crashing into some dude walking ahead. His neon rainbow tie-dyed shirt and black and yellow hat blared like a stop sign on a city street. She swerved Nuts to a halt and tapped the ass of her victim with one of her handlebars.

"Ow." He regarded her and her scooter over his shoulder.

"Oh, man. My bad, I wasn't looking." She hopped off and walked Nuts past the wayward fan. The smell of cherries, maybe almonds, or both awakened her senses. She glanced at the shadowed face and more words followed.

"What?" The tone of his question rested between bass and baritone.

Velvet sounded perfectly clear in her head, but forgot she had a big, red ball of hard candy in her mouth. She pulled at the white stick and stepped back. "Sorry. That was negligent driving on my part. You all right?"

"Yes." His response carried an accent she couldn't

quite place due to his economy of words. But as far as accents went, he definitely had one.

"Cool." Her shoulders sagged back down to a normal level.

"Be careful with that." Many of her fellow DJs hailed from the Netherlands and based on the *d* pronunciation of *th* he used, Velvet identified him as Dutch.

She shrugged. "Okay, byeeee." She didn't need a lecture on scooter safety. She pushed off her strong leg, balanced on Nuts and glided to LED and Candy, who were gathered around a high table glowing with blue light. A centerpiece tray of too many shots decorated the middle. Velvet braked and rested Nuts against a chair.

"What is it?" Velvet asked over the thudding music.

"Fireball," LED said and clinked shot glasses with them.

"Blessed be." Candy readied the glass to her lips.

"Ah! He's here. Come here, man. Have this shot with us," LED called to someone behind her and Candy.

Velvet aimed her attention in the direction of LED's head movements. A man emerged from the shadows in a rainbow tie-dyed shirt. He took off his black and yellow hat and raked his fingers through his hair. Velvet's heart stilled. Isaak "Zazzle" Van Sandt of Tres Armadas, the most famous DJ trio in dance music, headed to their table.

Don't miss In Rhythm *by JN Welsh, available now wherever Carina Press books are sold.*
www.CarinaPress.com